D0324306

PRIZE STORIES 1978
The O. Henry Awards

PRIZE STORIES 1978
The O. Henry Awards

EDITED AND
WITH AN INTRODUCTION
BY WILLIAM ABRAHAMS

DOUBLEDAY & COMPANY, INC.
GARDEN CITY, NEW YORK
1978

THE LIBRARY OF CONGRESS CATALOGED THIS SERIAL AS FOLLOWS: PRIZE
STORIES. THE O. HENRY AWARDS. 1919– GARDEN CITY, N.Y.,
DOUBLEDAY [ETC.] V. 21 CM. TITLE VARIES: 1919–46, O. HENRY
MEMORIAL AWARD PRIZE STORIES. STORIES FOR 1919–27 WERE "CHOSEN
BY THE SOCIETY OF ARTS AND SCIENCES." EDITORS: 1919–32, B. C.
WILLIAMS.—1933–40, HARRY HANSEN.—1941– HERSCHEL BRICKELL
(WITH MURIEL FULLER, 19 –46). 1. SHORT STORIES. I. WILLIAMS,
BLANCHE COLTON, 1879–1944, ED. II. HANSEN, HARRY, 1884– ED.
III. BRICKELL, HERSCHEL, 1889– ED. IV. SOCIETY OF ARTS AND
SCIENCES, NEW YORK. PZ1.O11 813.5082 21–9372 REV 3*

ISBN: 0-385-12847-9
Library of Congress Catalog Card Number 21–9372

Copyright © 1978 by Doubleday & Company, Inc.
All rights reserved
Printed in the United States of America
First Edition

8/3.5
p93
1978

PS
648
.55
O34
1978

CONTENTS

PUBLISHER'S NOTE

This volume is the fifty-eighth in the O. Henry Memorial Award series.

In 1918, the Society of Arts and Sciences met to vote upon a monument to the master of the short story, O. Henry. They decided that this memorial should be in the form of two prizes for the best short stories published by American authors in American magazines during the year 1919. From this beginning, the memorial developed into an annual anthology of outstanding short stories by American authors, published, with the exception of the years 1952 and 1953, by Doubleday & Company, Inc.

Blanche Colton Williams, one of the founders of the awards, was editor from 1919 to 1932; Harry Hansen from 1933 to 1940; Herschel Brickell from 1941 to 1951. The annual collection did not appear in 1952 and 1953, when the continuity of the series was interrupted by the death of Herschel Brickell. Paul Engle was editor from 1954 to 1959 with Hanson Martin coeditor in the years 1954 to 1960; Mary Stegner in 1960; Richard Poirier from 1961 to 1966, with assistance from and coeditorship with William Abrahams from 1964 to 1966. William Abrahams became editor of the series in 1967.

Doubleday also publishes *First-Prize Stories from the O. Henry Memorial Awards* in editions that are brought up to date at intervals. In 1970 Doubleday also published under Mr. Abrahams' editorship *Fifty Years of the American Short Story*, a collection of stories selected from the series.

The stories chosen for this volume were published in the period from the summer of 1976 to the summer of 1977. A list of the magazines consulted appears at the back of the book. The choice of stories and the selection of prize winners are exclusively the responsibility of the editor. Biographical material is based on information provided by the contributors and obtained from standard works of reference.

INTRODUCTION

No doubt, an assiduous student or a meticulously programmed computer could document the precise moment when naturalism and the modern short story were indissolubly joined. But such documentation would only confirm, not alter, one's impression of how things are. Anyone who has read, for example, the successive volumes in this series, going back to its inception in 1919, will know that, even so early, naturalism and the story were in a mutually dependent relation. Whichever came first, the naturalistic chicken or the fictional egg, hardly matters. The implicit assumptions and the explicit consequences have been unmistakable. The characteristic stories of the past fifty years, the stories that have been most admired and regularly taught, and hence most frequently imitated—however idiosyncratic the individual style and voice—aim to reproduce, to invoke, to suggest, some aspect of life as it is or was or might be, without going outside the bounds of credibility. Lifelikeness is all.

I have no wish to engage in polemics, to deplore or celebrate—I am merely describing an innovative situation, hardening into a dominating tradition, that has prevailed for most of this century and that has, as even its detractors will acknowledge, inspired a succession of authentic works of art: what might be fairly summed up as "the modern story." But a dominating tradition has its less admirable aspect: it tends to exclude what it has no need for. And with lifelikeness (or truth to life) as the essential criterion of the modern story, it has allowed scant place in the canon for certain older forms of the story—myths, legends, fables, parables, folk tales, fairy tales, tales of magic and the supernatural, dreams and fantasies—that have no declared interest in reproducing life as it is but seek out truth elsewhere in oblique and imaginative ways. Such older forms required a power of imagination from their authors that has been only rarely evident in our own time, if only because it has not been wanted. A story about a man turning into a beetle or a woman turning into a monkey, when told by Franz Kafka or Isak Dinesen, may achieve "classic" stature yet never comfortably fit into the tradition. The "life" in these stories has a truth that has very little to do with lifelikeness: it begins in imagination rather than observation.

The sense of opportunities missed, of possibilities waiting to be explored or rediscovered; a willingness to admit that the "modern story" is by no means the whole story; the recognition that in the quest for lifelikeness a good deal of life may be lost sight of—here are reasons enough to account for the tremors that, like the wavering line of a seismograph, indicate the discontent with naturalism and its aims that has become noticeable in recent years and that, I suspect, will prove more enriching to the story as it evolves in the future than the picto-, typo-, audiographic experiments that fancy themselves now as the "revolutionary alternative" to the conventional story.

Consider, for example, the theme or subject of the middle-class, discontented male or female seeking escape from the boredom of his or her marriage in a grand romantic passion. It has fascinated naturalistic writers ever since, shall we say, Flaubert; and certainly, in recent years, American writers have dealt with the theme in virtually all possible ramifications and postures. Here, one might be justified in thinking, was a subject imprisoned in its stereotype, "used and reused to the mystical moment of dullness." Yet, extricating it from the naturalistic convention and drawing exuberantly upon the older conventions—magical properties, illusionism, time traveling as uninhibited as anything in the *Arabian Nights*—that once would have been thought inappropriate, not serious enough, for such a subject, Woody Allen, in "The Kugelmass Episode," has instilled the theme with an energy and an inventiveness that restore it to hilarious new life.

Mr. Allen, as we might have anticipated from his films, proves to be a fantasist with a quixotic disdain for the logic of time and space, and a realist with an unillusioned eye for the foibles and absurdities of contemporary life. As we follow wistful, lustful Professor Kugelmass from his analyst's couch in Manhattan to the magic box in Brooklyn of that shoddy necromancer The Great Persky, and from thence—as swiftly as Helen was conjured up for Faustus—to the fields of Normandy and the arms of Emma Bovary, we are aware, though poor Kugelmass is not, that he might properly echo the reputed words of Emma's creator and say, "*Madame Bovary, c'est moi.*" For this fatuous professorial type, yearning to swing, flipping happily out of his own century into Flaubert's, where the "life" he lusts after will be all romantic transports, is merely a latter-day version of Emma herself, that most celebrated incarnation of bourgeois dissatisfaction, yearning for transports of her own. And it is perhaps Mr. Allen's most imaginative comic invention that he should transport Emma (in The Great Persky's box) for a weekend with Kugelmass in New York—at the Plaza, where, as one might have foreseen, she is very much in her element. One feels that, were it not for the demands of Flaubert's *Madame Bovary*, awaiting the return of its heroine to its pages, Mr. Allen's Emma would become a permanent resident in our century, speaking with its accent, expressing its discontent, as much at home in Manhattan as in her native Yonville.

What "The Kugelmass Episode" does, of course, is to turn the naturalistic story of discontent and marital infidelity on its head: its quintessential elements are transmitted to us through the lens of the fantastic, and they turn out to be no less "truthful" in this new guise than in the old. But I think it unfair to burden the story with significances its author almost certainly did not intend. It seems as unlikely that the time-traveling Emma Bovary is meant to symbolize the heroine of the new anti-naturalism as that Mr. Allen has cast himself in the role of literary revolutionary. Nonetheless the story exists, and its distinction lies in its particular imaginative difference. Admittedly, generalization is a useful device for editors and anthologists (and sometimes even for their reviewers), but along with "The Kugelmass Episode" there are a number of stories in this year's collection—Robert Henson's "The Upper and the Lower Millstone," Max Apple's "Paddycake, Paddycake . . . A Memoir," James Schevill's "A Hero in the Highway," Mark Helprin's "The Schreuderspitze," Susan Fromberg Schaeffer's "The Exact Nature of Plot"—that ally themselves with older forms and neglected traditions, giving free play to the imagination, and as such have prompted the generalizations with which I began this Introduction. Taken together, they allow one to suggest that a countertradition is coming into being.

A cautionary word would seem in order here, as much for the benefit of the editor as for his readers. Eighteen stories have been chosen for the present collection from among the more than a thousand that were published during the past year in large and little magazines. The eighteen were chosen for their individual excellence, not to prove a thesis or exemplify a *tendency*. (It is disheartening in that context to discover how often an innovative story may be of interest for what it exemplifies but otherwise be of no interest whatever, innovation and excellence being too often strangers to each other.) A tremor is not an earthquake; discontent doesn't signal the fall of the Bastille. Of the eighteen stories I have chosen, the greater number belong to the naturalistic tradition, and they are written with intelligence, great technical skill, and a fine responsiveness to one or another aspect of life as it is: the encroachments of age (as in Josephine Jacobsen's "Jack Frost"), the uncertainties of youth (Edith Pearlman's "Hanging Fire"), the attritions of middle age (Alice Adams's "Beautiful Girl"). Stories of impressive quality, some by unknown young authors starting out on their careers, others by authors of long experience and established reputation—notably the late Mark Schorer, whose sensitive, enigmatic "A Lamp" is the last of his stories to be published in his lifetime—they remind us how much the tradition has still to offer, and will continue to offer even should a countertradition come into being. There are ways and ways of telling a story; that is its challenge, its fascination, its continuing appeal, for writers and for readers alike.

WILLIAM ABRAHAMS

PRIZE STORIES 1978
The O. Henry Awards

THE KUGELMASS EPISODE

WOODY ALLEN

Woody Allen was born in Brooklyn, New York on December 1, 1935. He is a comedian, writer, actor, and film
director. His essays have appeared primarily in *The
New Yorker* and *The New Republic* as well as in two
volumes published by Random House.

Kugelmass, a professor of humanities at City College, was unhap-
pily married for the second time. Daphne Kugelmass was an oaf.
He also had two dull sons by his first wife, Flo, and was up to his
neck in alimony and child support.

"Did I know it would turn out so badly?" Kugelmass whined to
his analyst one day. "Daphne had promise. Who suspected she'd
let herself go and swell up like a beach ball? Plus she had a few
bucks, which is not in itself a healthy reason to marry a person,
but it doesn't hurt, with the kind of operating nut I have. You see
my point?"

Kugelmass was bald and as hairy as a bear, but he had soul.

"I need to meet a new woman," he went on. "I need to have an
affair. I may not look the part, but I'm a man who needs romance.
I need softness, I need flirtation. I'm not getting younger, so before it's too late I want to make love in Venice, trade quips at
'21,' and exchange coy glances over red wine and candlelight. You
see what I'm saying?"

Dr. Mandel shifted in his chair and said, "An affair will solve
nothing. You're so unrealistic. Your problems run much deeper."

"And also this affair must be discreet," Kugelmass continued.
"I can't afford a second divorce. Daphne would really sock it to
me."

"Mr. Kugelmass—"

"But it can't be anyone at City College, because Daphne also

Copyright © 1977 by The New Yorker Magazine, Inc. First appeared in *The
New Yorker*.

works there. Not that anyone on the faculty at C.C.N.Y. is any great shakes, but some of those coeds . . ."

"Mr. Kugelmass—"

"Help me. I had a dream last night. I was skipping through a meadow holding a picnic basket and the basket was marked 'Options.' And then I saw there was a hole in the basket."

"Mr. Kugelmass, the worst thing you could do is act out. You must simply express your feelings here, and together we'll analyze them. You have been in treatment long enough to know there is no overnight cure. After all, I'm an analyst, not a magician."

"Then perhaps what I need is a magician," Kugelmass said, rising from his chair. And with that he terminated his therapy.

A couple of weeks later, while Kugelmass and Daphne were moping around in their apartment one night like two pieces of old furniture, the phone rang.

"I'll get it," Kugelmass said. "Hello."

"Kugelmass?" a voice said. "Kugelmass, this is Persky."

"Who?"

"Persky. Or should I say The Great Persky?"

"Pardon me?"

"I hear you're looking all over town for a magician to bring a little exotica into your life? Yes or no?"

"Sh-h-h," Kugelmass whispered. "Don't hang up. Where are you calling from, Persky?"

Early the following afternoon, Kugelmass climbed three flights of stairs in a broken-down apartment house in the Bushwick section of Brooklyn. Peering through the darkness of the hall, he found the door he was looking for and pressed the bell. I'm going to regret this, he thought to himself.

Seconds later, he was greeted by a short, thin, waxy-looking man.

"You're Persky the Great?" Kugelmass said.

"The Great Persky. You want a tea?"

"No, I want romance. I want music. I want love and beauty."

"But not tea, eh? Amazing. O.K., sit down."

Persky went to the back room, and Kugelmass heard the sounds of boxes and furniture being moved around. Persky reappeared, pushing before him a large object on squeaky roller-skate wheels. He removed some old silk handkerchiefs that were lying on its top

and blew away a bit of dust. It was a cheap-looking Chinese cabinet, badly lacquered.

"Persky," Kugelmass said, "what's your scam?"

"Pay attention," Persky said. "This is some beautiful effect. I
developed it for a Knights of Pythias date last year, but the book-
ing fell through. Get into the cabinet."

"Why, so you can stick it full of swords or something?"

"You see any swords?"

Kugelmass made a face and, grunting, climbed into the cabinet.
He couldn't help noticing a couple of ugly rhinestones glued onto
the raw plywood just in front of his face. "If this is a joke," he
said.

"Some joke. Now, here's the point. If I throw any novel into
this cabinet with you, shut the doors, and tap it three times, you
will find yourself projected into that book."

Kugelmass made a grimace of disbelief.

"It's the emess," Persky said. "My hand to God. Not just a
novel, either. A short story, a play, a poem. You can meet any of
the women created by the world's best writers. Whoever you
dreamed of. You could carry on all you like with a real winner.
Then when you've had enough you give a yell, and I'll see you're
back here in a split second."

"Persky, are you some kind of outpatient?"

"I'm telling you it's on the level," Persky said.

Kugelmass remained skeptical. "What are you telling me—that
this cheesy homemade box can take me on a ride like you're
describing?"

"For a double sawbuck."

Kugelmass reached for his wallet. "I'll believe this when I see
it," he said.

Persky tucked the bills in his pants pocket and turned toward
his bookcase. "So who do you want to meet? Sister Carrie? Hester
Prynne? Ophelia? Maybe someone by Saul Bellow? Hey, what
about Temple Drake? Although for a man your age she'd be a
workout."

"French. I want to have an affair with a French lover."

"Nana?"

"I don't want to have to pay for it."

"What about Natasha in 'War and Peace'?"

"I said French. I know! What about Emma Bovary? That sounds to me perfect."

"You got it, Kugelmass. Give me a holler when you've had enough." Persky tossed in a paperback copy of Flaubert's novel.

"You sure this is safe?" Kugelmass asked as Persky began shutting the cabinet doors.

"Safe. Is anything safe in this crazy world?" Persky rapped three times on the cabinet and then flung open the doors.

Kugelmass was gone. At the same moment, he appeared in the bedroom of Charles and Emma Bovary's house at Yonville. Before him was a beautiful woman, standing alone with her back turned to him as she folded some linen. I can't believe this, thought Kugelmass, staring at the doctor's ravishing wife. This is uncanny. I'm here. It's her.

Emma turned in surprise. "Goodness, you startled me," she said. "Who are you?" She spoke in the same fine English translation as the paperback.

It's simply devastating, he thought. Then, realizing that it was he whom she had addressed, he said, "Excuse me. I'm Sidney Kugelmass. I'm from City College. A professor of humanities. C.C.N.Y.? Uptown. I—oh, boy!"

Emma Bovary smiled flirtatiously and said, "Would you like a drink? A glass of wine, perhaps?"

She is beautiful, Kugelmass thought. What a contrast with the troglodyte who shared his bed! He felt a sudden impulse to take this vision into his arms and tell her she was the kind of woman he had dreamed of all his life.

"Yes, some wine," he said hoarsely. "White. No, red. No, white. Make it white."

"Charles is out for the day," Emma said, her voice full of playful implication.

After the wine, they went for a stroll in the lovely French countryside. "I've always dreamed that some mysterious stranger would appear and rescue me from the monotony of this crass rural existence," Emma said, clasping his hand. They passed a small church. "I love what you have on," she murmured. "I've never seen anything like it around here. It's so . . . so modern."

"It's called a leisure suit," he said romantically. "It was marked down." Suddenly he kissed her. For the next hour they reclined under a tree and whispered together and told each other deeply meaningful things with their eyes. Then Kugelmass sat up. He had just remembered he had to meet Daphne at Bloomingdale's. "I must go," he told her. "But don't worry, I'll be back."

"I hope so," Emma said.

He embraced her passionately, and the two walked back to the house. He held Emma's face cupped in his palms, kissed her again, and yelled, "O.K., Persky! I got to be at Bloomingdale's by three-thirty."

There was an audible pop, and Kugelmass was back in Brooklyn.

"So? Did I lie?" Persky asked triumphantly.

"Look, Persky, I'm right now late to meet the ball and chain at Lexington Avenue, but when can I go again? Tomorrow?"

"My pleasure. Just bring a twenty. And don't mention this to anybody."

"Yeah. I'm going to call Rupert Murdoch."

Kugelmass hailed a cab and sped off to the city. His heart danced on point. I am in love, he thought, I am the possessor of a wonderful secret. What he didn't realize was that at this very moment students in various classrooms across the country were saying to their teachers, "Who is this character on page 100? A bald Jew is kissing Madame Bovary?" A teacher in Sioux Falls, South Dakota, sighed and thought, Jesus, these kids, with their pot and acid. What goes through their minds!

Daphne Kugelmass was in the bathroom-accessories department at Bloomingdale's when Kugelmass arrived breathlessly. "Where've you been?" she snapped. "It's four-thirty."

"I got held up in traffic," Kugelmass said.

Kugelmass visited Persky the next day, and in a few minutes was again passed magically to Yonville. Emma couldn't hide her excitement at seeing him. The two spent hours together, laughing and talking about their different backgrounds. Before Kugelmass left, they made love. "My God, I'm doing it with Madame Bovary!" Kugelmass whispered to himself. "Me, who failed freshman English."

As the months passed, Kugelmass saw Persky many times and developed a close and passionate relationship with Emma Bovary. "Make sure and always get me into the book before page 120,"

Kugelmass said to the magician one day. "I always have to meet her before she hooks up with this Rodolphe character."

"Why?" Persky asked. "You can't beat his time?"

"Beat his time. He's landed gentry. Those guys have nothing better to do than flirt and ride horses. To me, he's one of those faces you see in the pages of *Women's Wear Daily*. With the Helmut Berger hairdo. But to her he's hot stuff."

"And her husband suspects nothing?"

"He's out of his depth. He's a lacklustre little paramedic who's thrown in his lot with a jitterbug. He's ready to go to sleep by ten, and she's putting on her dancing shoes. Oh, well . . . See you later."

And once again Kugelmass entered the cabinet and passed instantly to the Bovary estate at Yonville. "How you doing, cupcake?" he said to Emma.

"Oh, Kugelmass," Emma sighed. "What I have to put up with. Last night at dinner, Mr. Personality dropped off to sleep in the middle of the dessert course. I'm pouring my heart out about Maxim's and the ballet, and out of the blue I hear snoring."

"It's O.K., darling. I'm here now," Kugelmass said, embracing her. I've earned this, he thought, smelling Emma's French perfume and burying his nose in her hair. I've suffered enough. I've paid enough analysts. I've searched till I'm weary. She's young and nubile, and I'm here a few pages after Léon and just before Rodolphe. By showing up during the correct chapters, I've got the situation knocked.

Emma, to be sure, was just as happy as Kugelmass. She had been starved for excitement, and his tales of Broadway night life, of fast cars and Hollywood and TV stars, enthralled the young French beauty.

"Tell me again about O.J. Simpson," she implored that evening, as she and Kugelmass strolled past Abbé Bournisien's church.

"What can I say? The man is great. He sets all kinds of rushing records. Such moves. They can't touch him."

"And the Academy Awards?" Emma said wistfully. "I'd give anything to win one."

"First you've got to be nominated."

"I know. You explained it. But I'm convinced I can act. Of

course, I'd want to take a class or two. With Strasberg maybe.
Then, if I had the right agent—"

"We'll see, we'll see. I'll speak to Persky."

That night, safely returned to Persky's flat, Kugelmass brought
up the idea of having Emma visit him in the big city.

"Let me think about it," Persky said. "Maybe I could work it.
Stranger things have happened." Of course, neither of them could
think of one.

"Where the hell do you go all the time?" Daphne Kugelmass
barked at her husband as he returned home late that evening.
"You got a chippie stashed somewhere?"

"Yeah, sure, I'm just the type," Kugelmass said wearily. "I was
with Leonard Popkin. We were discussing Socialist agriculture in
Poland. You know Popkin. He's a freak on the subject."

"Well, you've been very odd lately," Daphne said. "Distant.
Just don't forget about my father's birthday. On Saturday?"

"Oh, sure, sure," Kugelmass said, heading for the bathroom.

"My whole family will be there. We can see the twins. And
Cousin Hamish. You should be more polite to Cousin Hamish—
he likes you."

"Right, the twins," Kugelmass said, closing the bathroom door
and shutting out the sound of his wife's voice. He leaned against
it and took a deep breath. In a few hours, he told himself, he
would be back in Yonville again, back with his beloved. And this
time, if all went well, he would bring Emma back with him.

At three-fifteen the following afternoon, Persky worked his wiz-
ardry again. Kugelmass appeared before Emma, smiling and
eager. The two spent a few hours at Yonville with Binet and then
remounted the Bovary carriage. Following Persky's instructions,
they held each other tightly, closed their eyes, and counted to ten.
When they opened them, the carriage was just drawing up at the
side door of the Plaza Hotel, where Kugelmass had optimistically
reserved a suite earlier in the day.

"I love it! It's everything I dreamed it would be," Emma said as
she swirled joyously around the bedroom, surveying the city from
their window. "There's F.A.O. Schwarz. And there's Central Park,
and the Sherry is which one? Oh, there—I see. It's too divine."

On the bed there were boxes from Halston and Saint Laurent.

Emma unwrapped a package and held up a pair of black velvet pants against her perfect body.

"The slacks suit is by Ralph Lauren," Kugelmass said. "You'll look like a million bucks in it. Come on, sugar, give us a kiss."

"I've never been so happy!" Emma squealed as she stood before the mirror. "Let's go out on the town. I want to see 'Chorus Line' and the Guggenheim and this Jack Nicholson character you always talk about. Are any of his flicks showing?"

"I cannot get my mind around this," a Stanford professor said. "First a strange character named Kugelmass, and now she's gone from the book. Well, I guess the mark of a classic is that you can reread it a thousand times and always find something new."

The lovers passed a blissful weekend. Kugelmass had told Daphne he would be away at a symposium in Boston and would return Monday. Savoring each moment, he and Emma went to the movies, had dinner in Chinatown, passed two hours at a discothèque, and went to bed with a TV movie. They slept till noon on Sunday, visited SoHo, and ogled celebrities at Elaine's. They had caviar and champagne in their suite on Sunday night and talked until dawn. That morning, in the cab taking them to Persky's apartment, Kugelmass thought, It was hectic, but worth it. I can't bring her here too often, but now and then it will be a charming contrast with Yonville.

At Persky's, Emma climbed into the cabinet, arranged her new boxes of clothes neatly around her, and kissed Kugelmass fondly. "My place next time," she said with a wink. Persky rapped three times on the cabinet. Nothing happened.

"Hmm," Persky said, scratching his head. He rapped again, but still no magic. "Something must be wrong," he mumbled.

"Persky, you're joking!" Kugelmass cried. "How can it not work?"

"Relax, relax. Are you still in the box, Emma?"

"Yes."

Persky rapped again—harder this time.

"I'm still here, Persky."

"I know, darling. Sit tight."

"Persky, we *have* to get her back," Kugelmass whispered. "I'm a married man, and I have a class in three hours. I'm not prepared for anything more than a cautious affair at this point."

"I can't understand it," Persky muttered. "It's such a reliable little trick."

But he could do nothing. "It's going to take a little while," he said to Kugelmass. "I'm going to have to strip it down. I'll call you later."

Kugelmass bundled Emma into a cab and took her back to the Plaza. He barely made it to his class on time. He was on the phone all day, to Persky and to his mistress. The magician told him it might be several days before he got to the bottom of the trouble.

"How was the symposium?" Daphne asked him that night.

"Fine, fine," he said, lighting the filter end of a cigarette.

"What's wrong? You're as tense as a cat."

"Me? Ha, that's a laugh. I'm as calm as a summer night. I'm just going to take a walk." He eased out the door, hailed a cab, and flew to the Plaza.

"This is no good," Emma said. "Charles will miss me."

"Bear with me, sugar," Kugelmass said. He was pale and sweaty. He kissed her again, raced to the elevators, yelled at Persky over a pay phone in the Plaza lobby, and just made it home before midnight.

"According to Popkin, barley prices in Kraków have not been this stable since 1971," he said to Daphne, and smiled wanly as he climbed into bed.

The whole week went by like that. On Friday night, Kugelmass told Daphne there was another symposium he had to catch, this one in Syracuse. He hurried back to the Plaza, but the second weekend there was nothing like the first. "Get me back into the novel or marry me," Emma told Kugelmass. "Meanwhile, I want to get a job or go to class, because watching TV all day is the pits."

"Fine. We can use the money," Kugelmass said. "You consume twice your weight in room service."

"I met an Off Broadway producer in Central Park yesterday, and he said I might be right for a project he's doing," Emma said.

"Who is this clown?" Kugelmass asked.

"He's not a clown. He's sensitive and kind and cute. His name's Jeff Something-or-Other, and he's up for a Tony."

Later that afternoon, Kugelmass showed up at Persky's drunk.

"Relax," Persky told him. "You'll get a coronary."

"Relax. The man says relax. I've got a fictional character stashed in a hotel room, and I think my wife is having me tailed by a private shamus."

"O.K., O.K. We know there's a problem." Persky crawled under the cabinet and started banging on something with a large wrench.

"I'm like a wild animal," Kugelmass went on. "I'm sneaking around town, and Emma and I have had it up to here with each other. Not to mention a hotel tab that reads like the defense budget."

"So what should I do? This is the world of magic," Persky said. "It's all nuance."

"Nuance, my foot. I'm pouring Dom Pérignon and black eggs into this little mouse, plus her wardrobe, plus she's enrolled at the Neighborhood Playhouse and suddenly needs professional photos. Also, Persky, Professor Fivish Kopkind, who teaches Comp Lit and who has always been jealous of me, has identified me as the sporadically appearing character in the Flaubert book. He's threatened to go to Daphne. I see ruin and alimony jail. For adultery with Madame Bovary, my wife will reduce me to beggary."

"What do you want me to say? I'm working on it night and day. As far as your personal anxiety goes, that I can't help you with. I'm a magician, not an analyst."

By Sunday afternoon, Emma had locked herself in the bathroom and refused to respond to Kugelmass's entreaties. Kugelmass stared out the window at the Wollman Rink and contemplated suicide. Too bad this is a low floor, he thought, or I'd do it right now. Maybe if I ran away to Europe and started life over . . . Maybe I could sell the *International Herald Tribune*, like those young girls used to.

The phone rang. Kugelmass lifted it to his ear mechanically.

"Bring her over," Persky said. "I think I got the bugs out of it."

Kugelmass's heart leaped. "You're serious?" he said. "You got it licked?"

"It was something in the transmission. Go figure."

"Persky, you're a genius. We'll be there in a minute. Less than a minute."

Again the lovers hurried to the magician's apartment, and again Emma Bovary climbed into the cabinet with her boxes. This time there was no kiss. Persky shut the doors, took a deep breath, and tapped the box three times. There was the reassuring popping noise, and when Persky peered inside, the box was empty. Madame Bovary was back in her novel. Kugelmass heaved a great sigh of relief and pumped the magician's hand.

"It's over," he said. "I learned my lesson. I'll never cheat again, I swear it." He pumped Persky's hand again and made a mental note to send him a necktie.

Three weeks later, at the end of a beautiful spring afternoon, Persky answered his doorbell. It was Kugelmass, with a sheepish expression on his face.

"O.K., Kugelmass," the magician said. "Where to this time?"

"It's just this once," Kugelmass said. "The weather is so lovely, and I'm not getting any younger. Listen, you've read 'Portnoy's Complaint'? Remember The Monkey?"

"The price is now twenty-five dollars, because the cost of living is up, but I'll start you off with one freebie, due to all the trouble I caused you."

"You're good people," Kugelmass said, combing his few remaining hairs as he climbed into the cabinet again. "This'll work all right?"

"I hope. But I haven't tried it much since all that unpleasantness."

"Sex and romance," Kugelmass said from inside the box. "What we go through for a pretty face."

Persky tossed in a copy of "Portnoy's Complaint" and rapped three times on the box. This time, instead of a popping noise there was a dull explosion, followed by a series of crackling noises and a shower of sparks. Persky leaped back, was seized by a heart attack, and dropped dead. The cabinet burst into flames, and eventually the entire house burned down.

Kugelmass, unaware of this catastrophe, had his own problems. He had not been thrust into "Portnoy's Complaint," or into any other novel, for that matter. He had been projected into an old textbook, "Remedial Spanish," and was running for his life over a barren, rocky terrain as the word *"tener"* ("to have")—a large and hairy irregular verb—raced after him on its spindly legs.

A LAMP

MARK SCHORER

Mark Schorer, who died August 11, 1977, was born in Sauk City, Wisconsin, in 1908 and educated at the University of Wisconsin and at Harvard. He was for many years a teacher at the University of California at Berkeley. A novelist, critic, biographer, and short-story writer, his most recent book is *Pieces of Life,* published by Farrar, Straus & Giroux.

An Italian lamp can be an object of extraordinary ugliness. This is an order of ugliness that is not to be found in nature but must result from deliberate, perversely original human invention and contrivance, as if each time he put himself to the task, the designer had said to himself, "Now get with it, Signor, and see if you can come up with a *real* horror!"

Franklin Green had had such thoughts before. He had them again as he contemplated with a certain intensity of gaze—almost a glare—such a lamp. It stood on the edge of the *salone* of a Roman apartment where, on one side of the unlighted hearth, he sat holding an empty cocktail glass in a large chair covered with yellow satin and framed in carved, gilded wood. With what was almost a physical tug, he pulled his eyes away from the lamp to his glass and then to the table in front of his chair where he busied himself with ice, vodka, vermouth, and a saucer of lemon peel.

Flora, his wife, who sat on the other side of the hearth in an identical chair, thought in a vein similar to his as she too stared at the lamp. Such an object, she was thinking, is no accident. Behind it might lie a lifetime of mistaken effort, and the motive of that effort might be malice or spleen or even some kind of abstract vengeance. There was something absolutely cruel about it. En-

Copyright © 1976 by The Atlantic Monthly Company, Boston, Mass. Reprinted by permission.

grossed, she did not look down at once at the replenished cocktail glass her husband put before her. He had continued across the room to stand at one of the open pairs of French doors that gave onto a generous terrace and to stare out over tiled Roman roofs. In the deepening summer twilight, swifts incessantly wheeled and cried.

Franklin Green was a tall man, but the lamp behind him stood taller than he—nearly seven feet. It was made of painted wrought iron and pretended to be a gigantic stalk of lilies. It was the pretense of imitating nature that made it so alarmingly unnatural. The spindly stem, not much more than a half-inch in thickness, was pea green, and at six regular intervals sprouted sets of two narrow, dangerously pointed leaves. Then, about five feet from the floor, the thing burst into a horror of iron blossoms. There were five five-petaled, full-blown lilies, each about eight inches across, painted white, their veined petals arching back, and in the center of each, three metal prongs with a yellow knob at the end of each —pistils or stamens, which? There was also one absurd, aspiring bud, just opening. Above all this was the single twenty-five-watt bulb, only partially concealed by a pleated silk shade, disproportionately small and narrow, perched there like some half-hearted, grudging afterthought.

The first time one of the Greens had turned on the lamp, it had spluttered and blown out the main fuse in the apartment. Since then, the cord with its disconnected plug was looped over the set of leaves nearest the spindly-legged tripod that formed the base.

The lamp was all the more remarkable in that there was nothing else in this apartment, which was otherwise quite smartly furnished, that seemed to be related to it. It existed in grotesque isolation. The other lamps, smaller objects on tables and chests, were not beautiful, but they were unobtrusive and even gave a rather decent light when one remembered that they were, after all, Italian. There were many other things on which the eye could rest with comfort: three fine Piranesi prints hung in a row; decent vases; a gilt screen with tapestry panels; the large, arched, truly elegant mirror over the fireplace. But it was the lamp that always commanded the Greens' attention. Franklin Green had turned and, glass in hand, was staring at it again.

"Let's move it out," Flora had said early in their stay after it had proved at once to be as useless as it was horrid. For a day or

two indeed they had it in their bedroom, since there seemed to be
no other place, no storage closet or cupboard where it could be
put out of sight, and they could hardly add it to the clutter of the
maid's tiny room off the kitchen. But in their bedroom it made
Flora positively uneasy, and after those two days, Franklin moved
it again into its corner of the living room. And so, whenever they
were in that room, they found themselves staring at it, thinking
similar thoughts about it, laughing at it, jeering at it as *la lampada*
and *il lampadone*—the great big lamp—but also beginning faintly
and unaccountably to brood.

The apartment was in the Via Giulia and the Greens had
signed a six-month lease for it, half of a strange year in their lives.
They had been in Europe a number of times before, together and
separately, but never for such an extended stay and never so insep-
arably.

Franklin Green was a successful attorney in his middle fifties,
Flora was five years younger. They had been married for over
twenty-five years and their two daughters were married in turn,
each now beginning her own family, one in Connecticut, the
other in California. When the younger girl married almost immediately after the older one, the Greens felt themselves free but, in
a rather uncomfortable way, unnecessary. More than that, Franklin had been suffering from a depletion of energy that he had
never experienced before. For three years he had worked hard on a
complicated corporation tax case that had him in Washington
nearly as much of the time as he was in New York, and his doctor
had suggested that a long vacation was in order. With the successful conclusion of the case at last, his partners agreed to a year's
leave when the Greens had decided that now, before they were
even one year older, was the time really to *do* Europe. After all,
why not?

Their marriage had been uneventful and unusually com-
panionable. Most of their friends had been divorced at least once
and remarried, often in a glitter of scandal, but the idea of separa-
tion had never entered the mind of either Franklin or Flora
Green, not even as an impossibility. There was something inevitable about their union, and there had been from the start.

Flora had been a friend and classmate of Franklin's younger
sister at Vassar. He met her one summer when she came for a

week as a guest in his parents' house at Quogue. She was a tall, athletic girl, good at tennis and golf, in the surf and on a horse, with fine long legs and a handsome face—high cheekbones, amused brown eyes, loosely combed chestnut hair. Their interests, like their height, suited them to one another and they found themselves together all that week. Not long out of law school and a junior member of his Wall Street firm, Franklin saw a good deal of her in the following autumn and winter. In the spring, her last at Poughkeepsie, she began to spend her weekends with him in his bachelor apartment on East End Avenue. On Sunday noons she would make quite a thing of "brunch," scrambling eggs for him in a special way and serving them with a green salad, and then they'd have a long leisurely afternoon in a museum or at the movies. They had gay and easy times together and she enjoyed fussing over him—organizing his possessions, cataloguing his records, straightening out his books, replacing missing buttons. Marriage was hardly discussed; it was simply assumed, as if decreed, and it took place promptly after her graduation in June.

They had leased a slightly larger apartment in his old building and it was as if hardly anything had been changed. Then, all during the war years, he occupied a Navy desk in Washington, and there the children were born. Then New York again, a senior partnership, the new and much larger apartment on Fifth Avenue between 88th and 89th streets, the career, the bringing up of the little girls, then the big girls, the death of parents, the house at Quogue theirs, the career, the girls young women, married, gone. Now it all seemed remote, even rather characterless, and sometimes, here in the Roman apartment with the grotesque, inescapable lamp, Flora could hardly remember what that other apartment in New York, all sheeted and shaded in their absence, was like. And her past, all those years, where was it, *what* was it, she would vaguely wonder as she stared at the lamp.

Well, they had been serene years, and she and Franklin were friends, and the idea of a year together in Europe seemed splendid. After all, why not? Simply lock up the place and go, seize their freedom now that they had it! With a whole year, it would not be the usual hectic scrambling of American tourists abroad. They would take their time, do only what they wanted to do, it would be a long vacation, a ball.

Half the year, they had decided, was to be spent in Italy and
most of that in a single city—Rome, it had developed, after they
discovered what a clutter Florence had become. In the first half of
the year, they would go briefly to other places, and perhaps that
had been their error. They became the victims of some self-im-
posed acceleration they could not hold back, almost as if at first
they were made restless and uneasy by being alone together and
had to keep moving to occupy themselves. Those first six months
had deteriorated into just the kind of packing-unpacking, hotel-
heaped-upon-hotel jumble that they had meant to avoid. In five
months they had been in eight countries—fifty cities, sixty, a hundred? they could hardly say—and in the sixth month, as if now
they were wound up by the first five and could not come to a halt,
in nearly all the northern cities of Italy with a few resort towns
thrown in for good measure—Genoa, Portofino, Cernobbio,
Milan, Garda, Vicenza, Venice, Padua, Verona, Mantua, Ferrara,
Ravenna, Bologna, Pisa, Florence—but Florence even more briefly
than most of the others. Fifteen years before, when the ruins of
the war still lay tumbled along the Arno, they had spent nearly a
month there and loved it, and so they had thought of settling
there now for their half year. But the contrast with the Florence
of their more youthful visit was too painful. You couldn't *walk* in
Florence anymore! Rome, noisy and crowded and impersonal as it
was, was much better; they were living at last in a leisurely, pleasant way, adjusted to one another as even they had never been, sitting here now, for example, having their quiet cocktails, the birds
crying outside as they careened through the twilight, and inside,
the room all softened and charming . . . except for the *lampada!*

But then what of all that had come before Italy, or, for that
matter, before Rome? It was, they frequently confessed to one another, a mad confusion, as if they were drowning in a kaleidoscope
of their own shattered impressions. Castles, cathedrals, gardens,
galleries, pictures, stairways, statues, spires, towers, domes, ruins—
all pieces, shifting, circling, jiggling in and out of the mind, jumbled together.

Their last excursion in Germany, just before flying into Italy,
had been to Schloss Nymphenburg on the edge of Munich. They
had seen the film *Last Year at Marienbad,* and like everyone they
knew had been interested, irritated, and confused by it; they
wanted to see the place where it had been filmed. Now, as Frank-

lin gave Flora her third cocktail, a little tipsy in a gently melancholy way, she said, "You know, it's curious. Out of the entire jumble what remains most clearly with me is Nymphenburg—a kind of elegant jumble itself."

"Yes. It does for me, too." He was looking serious, his heavy, graying eyebrows pulled together as if he were working out some vexing problem. "The hunting lodge especially. Those tidy little cubicles for dogs in the first room. Imagine keeping dogs inside a place like that! With that silver ballroom. Or concert room, was it? It's clear as anything. Then finally the kitchen."

"Just before you enter the ballroom, or concert room—I can't remember the function either, but it's the great, beautiful round room, all mirrors and silver—just before you enter, there's that other room, all yellow gold and silver, with a kind of bed built into a tall niche in the wall, remember?"

"Yes. A place for the princess, returned from the hunt, to rest. The only place, apparently. It's hard to imagine the daily life, isn't it?"

"Remember how we searched for the statue that was so prominent in the movie—of the man and woman? And which was leading which? And not finding it?"

"Something added, we decided. A necessary prop. It had to be added for the sake of the story."

"Story?"

He laughed, and so did she, but then her still rather noble face became sober at once as she pushed her fingers through her abundant hair, held back by a black velvet band, and went on to say, "I feel every now and then that I'm *in* that film."

"I think I know what you mean."

"It's as if I'm that camera, registering all that splendor, but only registering it. Stairs, walls, corridors, plaster, gardens. . . . Remember how the voice intoned those catalogues? That's me."

"I know what you mean," he said. Suddenly he found himself looking at her. Something in her distracted tone had drawn his eyes to her, and he was *looking* at her. This was a shock because with it he knew that he had not really looked at her for years. He had always seen her, of course, but in a way he had not been seeing *her*. Her eyes were settled on the lamp, and he wondered if she saw it, they looked so vacant, so empty of everything except a vague, remote bewilderment. In her neck were lines that he had never noticed, a little tuck of skin under her chin, lines of laughter beside her mouth, some white in the reddish brown hair, and in her earlobes, pearl clips that were new to him. But she may have had them for a decade! He had become like the camera, too, apparently—registering, but merely registering, and not Europe alone. In his mild shock, this most familiar figure in his life seemed suddenly strange to him, a stranger.

She started a little and so did he. Then both, as with an agreed resolve, swallowed the rest of the cocktails, and as they put down their glasses, they said in unison, "Shouldn't we go?" They laughed again.

"My God!" exclaimed Franklin, and "Yes!" Flora answered, with another laugh, and they glanced at their watches. "Past eight-thirty," they agreed as they started from the room, but not without a last look at the lamp, as if they needed its consent to go out for dinner.

When they reached the street, it was dark and the swifts were gone. But it was dark with a difference. Almost at once the Greens saw that the great streetlamps, jutting out at regular intervals on scrolled iron arms fixed in palazzo walls, were not lit. Here and there a shop window leaked out a faint blur of light on the paving stones, but above, the heavy Renaissance buildings loomed black as the night itself, and the street had never seemed so narrow.

"Power failure?" Franklin speculated as they paused outside their enormous arched entry. Flora took his arm and they began a careful walk up the street on its uneven, treacherous stones. They were going to the restaurant, very near them, which they most often frequented—good food and service, quiet, discreet music, no wandering minstrels or flower vendors offering single roses for a hundred lire but hoping for five, or grown men selling silly balloons. In one month, the restaurant had become a kind of habit with them. It was restful, almost a retreat. Busy, jostling, daytime Rome disappeared there. They felt at home, comfortable. It was a habit now.

Abruptly they came to a halt. They were outside an antique shop that they had passed many times without particularly noticing, but tonight, with the street in darkness, the brilliance of its interior illumination through the single very large window stopped them. It was like a stage in a darkened theater, but a stage with its lights turned on at full blaze. Every item of furniture and decoration—a black armoire appliqued with elaborate scrolls of mother-of-pearl, a commode with ormolu mounts, two long case clocks with intricate marquetry, a torchère in the window that held an ormolu clock in the shape of an urn, its pendulum swinging swiftly, and from the ceiling, a veritable crystal arbor of glittering lusters—each of these and other objects stood out sharp and clear, and each as if it had its own illumination. One item did: a Canova-like bust of a woman, set in a concave circular niche above a door at the back of the room, a niche with concealed lighting that gave the marble a cold white glitter, a special dead brilliance within the general blaze.

"Like a stage," Flora murmured. "And there seems to be a play going on, too."

There were two characters, apparently the proprietors. At the back of the room and to one side was a mahogany secretary not very different from two others in the shop except that it was used, with paper on its dropped front and papers in its pigeonholes. At the desk sat a very beautiful young woman with ink-black hair and a magnolia-white face, her right elbow on the edge of the desk, her pen in her hand in midair, as if she had just been interrupted in the act of writing, her head turned, lips parted, her black, heavily shadowed eyes looking up with intense concentration. She was looking at a young man who stood in a doorway beside the desk, leaning indolently against the frame. He was as casual as she was intent. He was elegantly dressed in a moderately sporting way, and his careful hair, his trim brown moustache and short beard, even the polished nails on his extended hand suggested that he had just left his barber. Or the makeup man. In that brilliant interior, they both looked as though they were made up, the individual features highlighted, defined.

Whatever he was saying had galvanized her attention. He seemed to be speaking slowly, with the suggestion of a smile, his hand hardly moving. This was not one of those passionate, profuse verbal exchanges in which Italians seemed forever to be explaining something to someone else. On his part, it was like a meditation; on hers, an offering to receive. Now she put down the pen without taking her eyes from his face and stood up. The top of her head came to about his shoulders, so that, standing close to him, she had still to lift her head to look at him, and he to bend his. Now she was speaking, having seized his extended hand in both hers. His smile broadened; she began to smile. Then both, for a moment, were silent and they simply stood there, completely engrossed, engaged.

That was it! it came to the Greens as they watched in the dark street. The drama was in the intense involvement, the absorption of one in the other, each so strikingly distinct in the bright glare, each so handsomely individual, and yet with a relatedness that presented itself to the Greens as a nearly physical thing in the air between the two, visible vibrations like heat waves.

"I feel that we're intruders," Flora whispered, and they began to walk again.

"Something extraordinary was going on there," said Franklin, who felt suddenly sad, as if he had lost something that he treasured.

"I feel sad," said Flora.

An hour and a half later, after a dinner of many courses and with nearly a liter of fine Frascati, as they waited for the man to bring Franklin's change, they were both yawning. That day they had made one of their usual planned excursions: to the National Gallery, then up to Borromini's church with one of the Four Fountains built into its corner, on to Bernini's circular church in the Via del Quirinale, and ending in the Piazza del Quirinale (where, they learned, they had seen what was perhaps the finest façade of one Ferdinando Fuga)—all very close together, but still tiring. Even a short Roman walk, with its almost inevitable little climb, was tiring, and they were weary. "Rome eats up heels," Flora's nice cobbler had said to her one day. *Roma consuma i tacchi!*

All the shops on the Via Giulia, including the cobbler's, were closed as they went down it, the shutters pulled and locked, but the street lights were on now. As the Greens walked its length, their feet seemed to thrust their long, thin shadows ahead of them until they were so long and thin that they vanished in the stones, but then, rhythmically, they appeared immediately again beside them, thick and dark, only to grow attenuated once more. When they passed the antique shop, they did not mention the vivid scene that they had observed there earlier, but each of them thought about it. In their apartment, after a perfunctory look around, Franklin fixed the terrace shutters for the night and the Greens were ready for bed.

They had not been in their beds more than five minutes when they were both nearly asleep, but then Flora began drowsily to murmur.

"Our name is Green . . . ," she murmured.

He started from his doze. "What?"

"Now I know why they called me Flora."

"I don't get you." He leaned up on his elbow, wide awake.

But more sleepily than ever, as if she were not talking to him at all, she said, "The lamp. Flora Green. It means something, the lamp . . ."

"You've lost me."

"Green and flowers. Flora Green . . ."

"Oh, come!" Softly.

"And Franklin Green . . ."

She was asleep, but he was now wide awake, and staring into the darkness over her head, he saw a vivid image of the *lampada*, as clear in its every detail as any of those antique objects in the shop, as if it were really there, and even when he closed his eyes hard he was still scrutinizing it, as if indeed it were.

Some odd things had happened to the Greens. Flora, for example, often felt curiously adrift, as if the more crowded her mind and senses were with new impressions of old things, the more empty she became of herself, and not only of herself, but of her past, which in itself came to seem nearly empty, and certainly very far away. It was as if the great ponderous past in which they were living was robbing her of her shorter, thinner past.

Franklin, for his part, was experiencing inertia, curious in a man who for so many years had kept himself busy in his profession and active in his physical life. When they first projected their year abroad, he was afraid that he would chafe when he found himself cut off from these habitual activities for so long a time. But not at all. Whether it had to do with his age—was that the time for men, the middle fifties?—or with his recent rundown state, or whether the two were related, he did not know, but the fact was that he was quite content to substitute for his old routines these new activities of galleries, monuments, museums, restaurants, ruins. When it was occasionally necessary for him to communicate with his office, in response to an inquiry from someone there, he rather impatiently dictated a nearly perfunctory reply to a public stenographer (he had found an able one in a Via Veneto hotel) and let it go at that. Without his files and his library, it was difficult to be really helpful; furthermore, he could not take these inquiries very seriously. His habitual life, somewhat like Flora's, seemed also to have slid away into the distance, paled out.

In this condition they were completely comfortable with one another and content to seek no further company. At first, in London and Paris, they had hunted up New York connections, but as they progressed on their journey, they did this less and less. Now they were almost always together and almost always alone. They had been in Rome for a month, and at least half a dozen acquaintances of theirs were there in residence, and they had letters to a dozen more, but they had done nothing about either possibility. "After all," Flora sighed on occasion, when a name was mentioned, "we didn't come to Europe to be with a lot of Americans." But they were not, of course, being with Europeans either.

If they were not making the acquaintance of many Romans, they were making a nearly systematic acquaintance of Rome itself. As soon as they had found and settled into their apartment, one of them had said to the other, "From here on, we've got to do things more deliberately, more self-consciously, or we're going to end up with nothing at all."

"Agreed!"

And Franklin said, "I think I'll get a notebook and start keeping a record."

"A diary?"

"No, just a record. Notes on what interests me. Just writing these things down may help me to remember them and keep them separate in my mind."

"Splendid."

He bought his notebook and almost every day found him making his faithful notations. He enjoyed this effort and he decided that it was helping him to see more and to see more closely than he had before. He knew a little about architecture, and most of his notes were about buildings—churches, palaces, temples—and the remains of buildings. What he put down was descriptive, matter-of-fact, and it contained little that he did not find in his guidebook. Often he echoed the guidebook, but he wrote only after he himself had observed the details to which it directed him, and the fact that it was his own writing was important. He studied closely a reconstruction of the Forum and the ground plans in his guidebook, and then, wandering endlessly back and forth in the Forum for an entire day, made his own plan of it on a double page of his notebook while Flora sat placidly watching him from various fallen stones.

Flora took to buying postcards of everything that she particularly liked, chiefly paintings, and she began to write on the back of them. "I have no vocabulary for art," she said, "but if I can just put down my own impression, maybe I can keep these things separate too, as you do the churches and so on."

"Good," said he.

"What I must remember is that every great work is an individual creation, a unique thing, like nothing else."

"Yes."

"It's true, isn't it, that every living work has its own special quality, its own character? And if it doesn't have it, it's dead, not art but an artifact?"

"I suppose so."

"And Franklin—that's what's so awful about the *lampada* there. It's an extreme case. A dull imitation of something real, of something that is lovely in nature, and that's why it's so dead, so grotesquely artificial."

"Perhaps," he said uneasily.

"But to pinpoint the special quality in a given painting, I'd be helped by a real vocabulary. Some of the things I write sound just silly."

"I doubt it," he said.

"Schoolgirlish."

"Now don't get self-conscious in that way."

"And sometimes, even when I get a real charge from a picture or a statue, I have nothing to say, or I can't say what I feel. Like the enormous Pompey in the Spada."

"Just put down the approximate measurements then, or some other simple physical facts," Franklin said. "Anything to help remember it clearly. Don't try to describe the expression."

"Pictures are easier," she said.

"Some are."

She looked through her growing stack of cards as he turned his attention to his notebook. Every now and then she would draw one out of the pile and silently read what she had written.

"Caravaggio. *Narcissus*. The young man absolutely sick with yearning for himself. The painting of the sleeve—the texture. The bright spot of blue in the deep shadow above the pool. Codpiece?" She had since studied a large reproduction, and now, flushing, she crossed out the last word and wrote, "No. The other knee. One knee is bare. This one clothed." And then she added, "I've learned that this is probably not Caravaggio at all. C. didn't like blue."

Franklin glanced up at her. He was troubled. It was the day after she had fallen asleep murmuring about their names and the lamp—he glanced over her head to the lamp, angrily—and he had said nothing about the matter. Nor had she, even just now, when she had been talking about the thing. He wondered if she knew.

She was reading her words on another card. "Borghese *Leda*. Unknown painter. Probably after Leonardo. The swan absolutely domesticated. A family man, the pompous husband, and that naked girl's complete servant. The twin boys in the grass. Helen's egg still unhatched, behind them, as if forgotten. Other birds standing around. A very comic picture. It gives joy and laughter."

When he closed his notebook she put her cards away. "Do we pursue Zucchi today?"

"There's only one left. In a church called San Giovanni Decollato. *John the Beheaded*."

"Shall we?"

"Why not?"

This was one of their systematic projects—to hunt out all the work of a given artist. They had seen every Caravaggio in Rome and he was now their favorite painter. A few days before they had found themselves amused in the Borghese Gallery by two extravagant allegorical paintings by someone they had never heard of, a presumably minor Florentine named Zucchi, and now they were pursuing the Zucchis, of which there were not nearly so many as there were Caravaggios, and they did not expect this fantastic fellow to replace him in their affections. About Caravaggio they felt positively possessive, but only tolerant of this other one, entertaining as he was.

It was in the cab on the way to the Piazza Bocca della Verità,

which was as close to the obscure street of San Giovanni Decollato as they could direct the driver, that Flora suddenly asked,
"What was that dream again?"

"What dream?"

"You told me this morning. About the antique shop."

"What about it?"

"You said you had this dream in which you could hear what
those people were saying."

"Flora, you're crazy. I said nothing of the kind. I didn't have a
dream."

"But I thought . . ."

"It must have been your dream. What *did* they say?"

"I don't know . . . Did I dream it?"

"You must have. I didn't."

"I think you did. I think you've forgotten. I'm sure you told me
about it just as we were waking up."

He laughed abruptly. "That'll be the day!"

"What?"

"When we start having each other's dreams."

The cab pulled to a stop beside a fountain. Paying and getting
out, they dropped the matter.

"Let's have another look at the Truth Mouth since we're here,"
Franklin said, and they walked over to study the curious object
through the grille that protected it. The flat round face with its
staring eyes and open lips made Flora shudder. "I have the most
awful feeling that it's going to start telling me something!"

"It does look as though it could talk. What would it say?"

"Yes, what?"

Silence, while they looked. He broke it with, "You were doing
some strange talking last night."

"I? When?"

"When you were falling asleep. Or perhaps you were asleep.
You don't remember?"

"No. What was I saying?"

"Something about a connection between your name—our
names—and the *lampada*."

"What?"

"I don't know quite. 'Flora Green,' you were saying and 'The
lamp, it means something.' You don't remember?"

She looked puzzled. "Yes . . . yes . . . vaguely. I must have been on the very edge of sleep."

"Well?"

"I've thought it before, but not quite like that."

"Thought what?"

"The lamp wouldn't bother us so much if it didn't have some meaning."

"But what meaning? It's just a frightful lamp."

"Yes, it's that for sure."

Suddenly she turned from the wall with the head and looked directly and hard and freshly into his eyes. In dismay she said, "Franklin, you're tired!"

"Not particularly," he replied. "Let's go."

The curious thing that he had half-jokingly suggested in the cab did in fact happen to them at some time during that night. When they were at breakfast next morning, Flora said, "Well, last night I did dream it."

"The antique shop," he said at once.

"Yes."

"Only we were the characters, not those others."

She looked at him in alarm. "Yes."

"Only we weren't talking, were we? We were sitting among all that furniture, all the glitter and the polish, the little gold clock with its pendulum swinging, the white bust smiling, everything there—we were sitting . . ."

"With our backs to each other," she finished for him.

"Yes," he said. "And . . . ?"

"Under the *lampada.*"

They stared at one another and neither of them laughed. Either one of them might have made the next remark, since both were thinking it. It happened to be Flora who said, "We've been in too many countries." Each was aware that the observation was hardly adequate to the situation as they looked away from one another and waited for the next remark, which again might have been made by either of them: We should leave here now, adjust this lease, change our reservations, go back. Then each of them would hear the final word echo into a question: Back?

And neither would ask it aloud.

THE UPPER AND THE LOWER
MILLSTONE

ROBERT HENSON

Robert Henson was born in Oklahoma and is now on the
faculty of Upsala College in New Jersey. This is the second time his work has appeared in PRIZE STORIES.

The king of Jericho lived in a state of rising hysteria. His soldiers
combed the streets looking for spies, and arrested people for
throwing rubbish over the wall—though this had been done for
so many years that the dry moat was filled and the rampart half
covered before anyone ever heard of the people of Israel. Instead
of having the rampart cleared, or the wall repaired where it was
cracked and eroded, he ordered the earthquake intervals filled—as
if they were flaws!—so that there was no longer any way to isolate
collapses—the whole wall would fall down flat!

The other kings of Canaan shunned treaties of mutual defense
with him—they seemed to regard the fall of Jericho as inevitable,
perhaps unimportant. Deadliest of all, rumors circulated that the
Egyptian garrison would soon be withdrawn, Pharaoh having succumbed to the view that his real interests lay farther north.

Blind! Deaf! Were the rumors true? The captain of the garrison
would say neither yea or nay but took refuge in maddening Egyptian non-answers—"All would be as Pharaoh wished . . ." The
king stamped his feet, ground his teeth and behaved ever more ir-
rationally, as on the day when he summoned Rahab to a private
audience and demanded information from *her*.

"What information could I have that you have not?" she cried
indignantly.

"You—the captain's harlot—what information!"

"I've heard the rumors everyone has heard, nothing more."

Copyright © 1975 by Orion Press. First published in *Eureka Review*. Reprinted
by permission.

"Your protector hasn't set a date, then? Hasn't said goodbye?"

"No."

"Then there's still time for you to prevent it."

"I? Pharaoh moves the garrison, not I!"

"But you move the captain. Your witchcraft is well-known. Redouble it. Bind him so fast he'll persuade Pharaoh that remaining here is a military necessity—as it is," he raged, "though I won't try to explain that to you—much less appeal to a non-existent loyalty. For you I have just this one word of warning: Jericho's fate is your fate. If Egypt pulls out don't imagine that you'll be going along. If their terror—" he pointed east across the Jordan—"falls on Jericho you'll be here to suffer it. Beware! They have a god fiercer than Reshef or Mekel—he made the waters stand up on either side and crash down like a wall on Pharaoh's horsemen and chariots. What they did to Heshbon in the land of the Amorites you know. Never again will the Amorites boast in song, 'Fire went forth from Heshbon, flame from the city of Sihon.' Furthermore, mistress harlot, they abominate the flesh—there are none of your profession among their women. So be moved—be moved by practical considerations, if not by the plight of Mother Jericho!"

Rahab went home with an angry smile. Mother Jericho! From a brigand who collected taxes two years in advance! And while the Hebrews were swarming up from the south like locusts, razed houses and shops to make room for more royal stables, larger palace gardens! Nor was she pleased at being called harlot. In that, as in his demand that she serve Jericho, she heard the groan of a long-suppressed passion. When he first set eyes on her she already belonged to the captain. Was that her fault? Where in *any* of this was she to blame? What justice in threatening her?

Nevertheless she made special preparations for the captain's visit that evening. Because the king's passion had never been satisfied he could not conceive that the captain's might be dulled —that he might be more friend than lover these days, likelier in fact to go apart with one of her little sisters than with herself. But so it was. Witchcraft indeed would be needed to make things otherwise. She hung an amulet of Astarte around her neck, one of Asherah around her waist, bound another of Anath to her arm. Whether they were one goddess or three she had never known. She prayed to the first while she scented her body, to the second as she painted her eyes, to the last as she thickened her hair with dyed rope. Then she poured a single libation to all-in-one.

The captain came bringing a gift—an amethyst ring set in gold. Exquisite. It should have been a good omen, but was it? "They don't make things like this anymore," she murmured. She didn't mean that he'd probably got it from a grave robber but that he could hardly have got it anywhere else in these times of cheap ivory plaques and fake scarabs set in copper.

He followed her thought with his customary Egyptian ease. "On the other hand, where but in Jericho could one find these extraordinary tables?"

She smiled—with a chill in her heat. Jericho's furniture was a long-standing joke between them—he pretending to be unable to get used to tables with two legs at one end and only one at the other, she exclaiming (as she did now): "Why, surely wherever the ground is uneven they have such tables?"

"Practical Jericho!" he said. "I assure you that in other places they stupidly level their floors."

"I wonder Pharaoh can abandon us when we have so much to offer. Why does Egypt prove faithless?"

He studied her with his long eyes. "I know about your audience with the king."

She flung herself at his feet. "I wouldn't stop you if I could! I don't care where you're going, or when, or why—only take me with you!"

"You shouldn't let tales of the Red Sea frighten you."

"It's not the Hebrews I want to flee, but this dunghill Jericho!"

"The same story will soon be trotted out again," he said, just as if she hadn't spoken. "When they come to the Jordan they'll turn upstream—to Adamah, perhaps, or some other place where they can tumble a cliff into the river and dam it for a while. Then they'll cross dry-shod and swear their god parted the waters. They produce these miracles especially for Canaanites. Pharaoh isn't moved by signs and wonders but by practical considerations. Jericho is no longer vital to his interests. The trade route to Syria is."

"Speak more plainly. Will you take me with you?"

"What about your family—your father and mother—the sisters?"

"What about them?" she asked startled.

"Suppose the king sends after you and I refuse to give you up?
He'll take revenge on them."

"He won't send after me, he won't do anything! Your inform-
ants took his rantings too seriously."

He saw things differently. "The moment a departure date is announced he'll issue a decree: no one from Jericho to accompany
us in our 'flight'—not a saddlemaker, not a baker, not a wife or
child. He'll dress up this childish spite as pride—'Mother Jericho'
—but he'll be in deadly earnest. You, my Rahab, would become a
traitor, not"—he again surveyed her with his long eyes, "a loving
mistress."

"I'll hide in a basket—among the provisions—you needn't even
know where!"

"And your family?"

"Bastard! Son of a hippopotamus! When have I ever shown
this family feeling you're suddenly hiding behind? My loyalty for
seven years has been to you—to Pharaoh. Am I not called 'the
Egyptian woman'? Take me with you!"

Even as she raved and pleaded she knew she was wasting her
breath. There was goodbye in the amethyst ring—in the familiar
joke—in the disparagement of the Hebrews—but most of all in the
appeal to practicality, that thing which those having the upper
hand called down like a curse on everyone else. What she pro-
posed was not "practical." Pharaoh wanted him to leave with as
little incident as possible. She wanted to involve him in an act of
rebellion. He advised her to be patient. Seven years, after all,
though muting desire, had not left him entirely without a sense of
obligation. He would find some less provocative way to achieve
what they both wanted . . .

And so he passed out of her life, or withdrew from it. When
the king's soldiers found her—in a hamper of raisins slung on one
side of an ass—he didn't even turn back from the head of the column to investigate the commotion.

She was not, to be sure, the only deserter rooted out that day.
But whereas the others were strangled and thrown over the wall,
she was offered a way out, and did not scruple to take it. Yet she
fell on evil days, for there was so much muttering against the
king's mercy that he scarcely had time to enjoy it before he was
forced to withdraw it. Torn between Baal-tyranny and Anath-lust

—or rather, twisting in the single grip of the brother-sister, king-and-consort pair—he spared her life, saying privately that the criticism would soon die down while blustering publicly that disgrace would serve justice better than death. He denied any other motive for letting her live, and to enforce belief turned her out of the house the captain had given her, seized all her movables except some jewelry, and drove her back where she came from—back down among the rout and rabble who lived against the wall. At the same time he privately ordered her to reenter the house of her parents, where he would set a secret guard over her to keep her safe until he could again put his left hand under her head and embrace her body with his right. Until then (he half groaned, half snarled) he would sleep with a waking heart; and she—she must keep herself as a garden that is enclosed, or a spring shut up, or a fountain sealed . . .

Rahab's heart burned in her breast. Seven years earlier, with the light of Astarte just beginning to gleam in her eyes, she had stood in the door of her father's wineshop and turned the captain roundabout in his tracks. But who was the more dazzled? Egypt seemed to promise an escape from the anarchy of Jericho. She gave herself willingly, not because it pleased and profited her father. She was proud to be called the Egyptian woman. Yet what *was* Egypt finally? Repository of strength, order, beauty? Yes, as the grave is! Truly the Land of the Dead—her people empty vessels, her promises a scroll that is rolled up! Strange and bitter that Rahab—who, above all women, craved, above all things, principle and consistency—should find only caprice and disorder wherever she looked. Chaos had returned, as it always did in Jericho. Now she must go backward in time and place, must—ultimate anarchy! —be born again to her father and mother.

They wailed and beat their hands together over their heads. What had she ever done for them these seven years, except take her sisters off their hands? Now even that was undone! Her mother climbed the ladder to their house on the wall and would not come down. She had borne two sons in Rahab's absence. The younger, still in swaddling clothes, she kept as well hidden as if he were not. There was talk these days of reviving the old custom of infant sacrifice to the War God, and she was filled with dread that Rahab would bring this fate upon him. The father, blind with cataracts, crouched in the door of the shop and implored passers-by not to ruin him because of his daughter's transgressions. He could hear hissing in the streets, and vows—made or extorted —never to cross the Egyptian whore's threshold.

Notwithstanding, her disgrace was short-lived. Besides the fact that the wineshop was near the East Gate, where traders and farmers came and went, there was that exceeding beauty, not to be hid among jars and bushels in the storeroom over the shop. Like the Mistress-Virgin's own (who bore the lily in one hand, the serpent in the other) it fascinated and disarmed. Business revived—improved—needed only to be put on its true basis to flourish as never before.

To that end Rahab looped her braid forward, like the tail of a scorpion ready to strike, and paid her mother a visit. "The little sisters and I are no longer content to sleep on mats in the storeroom," she said, gazing all about but letting her eyes rest especially on the lolling misshapen head of her younger brother. He had been conceived too near the upper limit of child-bearing; he would never—even if such a danger existed—make a suitable offering to the War God. His mother, however, gathered him up as if he were some precious possession; and, muttering charms and scattering signs, moved into the storeroom that very day. Rahab and the sisters took possession of the house on the wall.

This was no more than a one-room mud-brick hut—there were several near the East Gate, where the oldest and thickest part of the wall stood. Some were larger than anything below—in places the wall was thirteen feet thick; and most had windows with refreshing outward views—Rahab could look down on emerald fields near the city, a stretch of pale desert beyond, and in the distance, the Jordan flowing among dark-green tamarisk groves. But houses were not built on the wall because of any such advantages. Actually they were extruded by the crowding below. The advantages were accidental and revocable. A window looking out of the city meant a house set between the king and his enemies. Any dwelling below was preferable. Now, however, Rahab saw an advantage she hadn't seen before; and she proceeded to make use of it.

The wineshop and storeroom were connected by a ladder that rose from the street, but the house on the wall had its own ladder at the end of a short alley alongside the shop. Patrons inflamed by wine and Rahab's beauty could be sent discreetly outside, around the corner, up to the sisters—who sat waiting, each in her own newly-curtained-off alcove. Not that the sisters were treated like women who crouched by the side of the road wrapped in the veil of a harlot—they had Rahab for their sign and shrouding garment —she was discriminating on their behalf. Some patrons grumbled because she herself did no consorting. Most felt, mysteriously, that she did not and yet did; and that they had possessed her even when they had not, as goers-in to temple prostitutes might feel both embraced and not embraced by the Goddess.

She prospered, and could expect to prosper more as harvest time approached—but, like someone in exile, uncertain of deliverance, she was restless and dissatisfied. For a time she vented her feelings on her father: "What! Fallen silent? No more whining at the door? You bleated like a goat when I tried to save myself by leaving Jericho. Now that I'm abandoned—and *all* your daughters whores!—you smack your lips and count feet crossing the threshold. This is a father indeed! Pimp! Jackal!"—and so on until he would gladly have joined his wife in the storeroom had not the clink of coins and shuffle of feet somewhat drawn the sting from her contempt.

Then she fell to mocking Jericho; and though this was especially ill-advised now that the people of Israel were rumored to be hastening toward Shittim, just across the Jordan, still she compulsively paraded the little store of knowledge she had from the captain. If someone said thankfully that the Jordan was beginning to overflow its banks as it always did at harvest time, she would say that the god of the Hebrews made a specialty of heaping up waters. But if someone babbled fearfully about the Red Sea, she would say that no miracles would be needed at the Jordan—only common sense on one side and negligence on the other. The Hebrews had no battering-rams? No weapons except curved swords and old-fashioned square shields? No chariots? Well, but they had legs, hadn't they, to carry them up ramparts littered with footholds? Arms to hurl torches over the wall onto thatched roofs and wooden beams? The wineshop buzzed at her audacity. Did she know more about these things than the king? Undoubtedly he had some plan to prevent the wall from being turned into a fiery furnace. "Oh, undoubtedly," she would reply with a fine smile. "After all, he has only to look down from the palace to see what the problem is."

The king's men, knowing his obsession, had been reluctant to accuse Rahab of harlotry—especially when, in a technical sense, they might be wrong. They were doubly quick therefore to report signs of her other disloyalty. They repeated all her sayings, and reminded the king that the wineshop was in a location bound to attract spies and saboteurs. They did not, of course, accuse her of aiding Jericho's enemies directly (though she had commandeered a room with a window on the Jordan and was not scrupulous about giving a warning to outsiders when the city gates were about to close for the night). But at the very least she was encouraging defeatism and panic.

The king sent for her in secret; no sooner saw her again than he began to writhe in the double-grip.

"Why do you prolong your exile?"

"How do I prolong it?"

"By drawing attention to yourself—arousing suspicion."

"Of what?"

"Of . . . unfaithfulness to the king," he said ambiguously.

She had come prepared to defend herself against a charge of harlotry and said promptly, "I am no harlot but an honest innkeeper."

"No harlot?" he echoed.

She saw that she had made a mistake and, as if it had been deliberate, asked mournfully: "What else could I be accused of that would so distress my lord?"

He gazed into her eyes, deep as the deep spring that had drawn men to Jericho time out of mind: "Take care, Rahab! I would lead thee and bring thee out of exile—let there be no spot in thee! Take care whom you speak to with your lovely mouth—whom you see with those eyes like doves' eyes—what you say with those lips like a scarlet thread. Oh thou absolutely fair! I would bring thee and lead thee—my left hand here—my right hand there—and yet I do not love thee absolutely—beware!"

He refused to be—perhaps could not be—more coherent. Next day, however, soldiers came to block up her window, and she noticed that a political informant had taken the place of one of her guards. She felt no fear, only disgust. While the Hebrews licked up the land across the Jordan the way an ox licks up grass, the king of Jericho took measures—against Rahab! Not for harlotry, which would have made some sense, but for hand-me-down criticism!

She waited three days, then knocked the bricks out of the window. The sisters were appalled and refused to obey her any longer. They crowded into the storeroom with the mother—who unaccountably made them welcome. Rahab shrugged. She would replace them with daughters bought from poor farmers. Meanwhile she put the room to a use which had tempted her before. She began to harbor outsiders who didn't have a permit to stay in the city overnight. Since the penalty for this was high, so was her price. Then she ceased to be, even technically, a garden that is enclosed, or a fountain sealed. If an after-dark supplicant could pay the price she asked for the room, he could very likely pay an added sum as well. Seldom, at any rate, did a lodger refuse to empty his purse when Rahab came gliding through the curtain—wily as a serpent, yes, but beautiful as a garden of lilies glimmering in the dark.

Because it went somewhat against her grain to enter upon the sisters' work she trafficked only with these profitable few. She seldom took in more than one; some nights, none. If a search party broke in she could claim she had been lied to. Or perhaps would not. Her defiance had reached fever pitch and cried out to be heard.

As it was, for now the Hebrews appeared on the opposite bank of the Jordan. They had arrived speedily at Shittim and encamped there. Advance parties were already scouting fords and crossings of the river, as if no amount of flooding would stop them. Panic spread through the countryside. Farmers deserted their fields and tried to move inside the walls. The king drove them back, saying that fruits and grains must be gotten into silos; sheep and cattle into pens. Typically he didn't look to prices. Uncontrolled they shot up uncontrollably, with the result that only palace and patrician granaries were filled—public ones remained empty; sheep and cattle clogged the narrow streets—on their way to the palace and patrician dwellings, where ground-floor rooms were being converted into pens. The turmoil at the East Gate each dawn and dusk threatened to overwhelm the guards. To importunate farmers were added refugees from across the Jordan and all manner of other unidentifiable outsiders. Permits to enter the city, permits to remain were ignored, evaded, falsified, gotten by brib-

ery, theft, even murder. Dwellers inside the wall began to clamor
for the gates to be shut up. The king replied that the harvest was
not half in. They pleaded for more haste in filling public silos, lest
the Hebrews prevent it altogether. He sent word that the Jordan
would detain the Hebrews—the real enemy was within; and multiplied the patrols which scoured streets, shops and houses. When
cries arose that these were not efficient but only capricious and
brutal, he multiplied them again.

Rahab's personal overseers disappeared. The wineshop was
harassed like any other—or rather, more than any other, in line
with its reputation as a meeting-place for conspirators. Business
was not affected. A raid might empty the place for a while, but
customers soon jammed in again. People were not opposing the
king, they had simply ceased to support him. They were waiting
for a miracle, and whether it saved or destroyed them seemed not
to matter. A kind of madness for oblivion had seized them—even
if the sisters had not retired, they would have wanted only wine,
more wine.

Rahab rarely went down. The passivity and defeatism repelled
her. Even her own rebellion was faltering. Though she now stood
ready to hide lawbreakers who could pay little or nothing, there
were fewer, suddenly, coming to her door. Paradoxically these few
never lacked for money. Several times search parties invaded the
house—but only by day. She might have seen the signs but didn't.
She supposed it was only a matter of time before a patrol would
burst in after dark. In this she was correct. One night she was
arrested, next morning taken before the king. Their meeting was
not private this time but well attended by courtiers and soldiers.
She did not expect to return from it. In that, she was wrong.

He began a little distance away from the arrest—with the daytime search parties. "You are accused of saying that your window
was unsealed by my personal order."

"Yes."

"In case the room should be needed for military purposes."

"A plausible lie. Was it believed? I told it more than once."

"So plausible it will soon become truth." He looked around the
court for approbation and got it, but misunderstood Rahab's
expression—she was shrinking from the thought that she might be
forced to move in with her mother and sisters. "Not that you'll be
compelled to practice your profession by the side of the road," he

said. "At least not right away. Until I need the house for my purposes, my soldiers will use it for theirs."

She spat.

The king smiled and combed his beard with his fingers. "You scorn my soldiers? Look around. Don't you see even one you've already entertained? You there, take off your helmet—plead for an overnight hiding place. Do it in a low voice."

Rahab saw with disgust that the grinning soldier was the man she'd been arrested with.

"I see you do recognize him. There have been others too."

"Yes—and still others *not* sent by you!"

"No doubt. It's reported, though, that you never ask your visitors any questions."

She was silent.

"Except about money, of course." He looked around with a broad smile. "Well, that was wise, Rahab. For if you'd asked these men how they happened to get trapped by the shutting of the gates—whether it was by accident or design—and if you'd hidden only the ones who answered, 'By design,' then I would have to charge you with treason. But it appears that your house—and your person—have been open to anyone, not reserved exclusively for the enemies of Jericho. So it was only whoredom after all. Some few may have been spies and saboteurs, but how many more weren't even violating the curfew! I don't mean the ones sent by me, but those others you boast of. Did you expect your generosity not to attract men who would swear falsely that they were fugitives?"

"I wouldn't expect anything else—in Jericho."

"Oh, Jericho—Jericho knows the difference between rebellion and harlotry. It is Rahab who dresses up one as the other."

Rahab, swaying like a lily on its stalk or a serpent on its tail, raked the court with terrible eyes: "I'm glad these the king's dependents have had so reassuring a demonstration of the king's good government. He has proved Rahab a whore! Can anyone then doubt he'll prove a bulwark against Israel? Ah, what Heshbon could have done with such a king!—the Amorites who will never again boast in song, 'Fire went forth from Heshbon, flame from the city of Sihon.'"

The king did not look around for fear of seeing only downcast eyes. The mockery that he alone understood angered him more than the rebuke that everyone understood. But it was exactly his purpose to discredit damaging notions about their intimacy, and he did not allow his condescending manner to be shaken:

"Rahab has already shown that government, like gratitude, is beyond her comprehension. She does so again. A careful king concerns himself with everything that might affect the welfare of his subjects. Though his vigilance consume and exhaust him, he cannot prejudge whether a matter will be great or small. Luckily, this of Rahab proved small, unimportant—mere whoredom, as I have said. I would have been remiss not to look into the other possibility, but now I say in justice: Go home, Rahab. You are free to resume your trade—bound only to practice it honestly. It will be the only livelihood open to you, but the one you know best. If you're tempted to play any other role you must find a better way to unmask those who will be role-playing with *you*. My advice is, stay in your own depth. You will not suffer by being honestly what you are. My soldiers will see to it that your house becomes as well known by day as it was by night. However, you can hardly succeed if you go back to fobbing your sisters off onto those who thirst for *you*. It is my express wish that you and you alone—"

Long before he finished (the court egging him on, as if in these convolutions they saw a proof of strength) Rahab had stopped listening. She scarcely heard the jeers that followed her out of the palace. At the wall she saw without seeing that the wineshop had been boarded up. Her father came to the foot of her ladder, wailing and clutching the air. She did not answer but stood at her window staring eastward. It might be as the captain said, that the Hebrews didn't prevail by miracles but by foresight, planning, discipline—yet she was ready to believe now, as the wineshop did, that they also had some Power which went before them and prepared the way. Until today she had wanted Jericho to remedy its follies, at worst had only wanted to leave it. Now she craved to see it lying in the dust—a heap of ruins forever!

Late in the afternoon she heard the sisters sniffling at the door. She faced them venomously. "Well?"

"The wineshop—closed—the king's orders—"

"Well?"

They fell to their knees and knocked their heads on the floor, weeping. "The father said you wanted to see us."

She felt a twinge of pity mixed with irritation. "I bought some flax, simpletons—I need you to help me carry it to the roof."

They looked mistrustful but hastened to lug the bundles through the trapdoor. She did not help them. A moment or two later she went up. "So—I must do it all alone," she said with a crafty smile. "You don't want to help me . . ."

They began to weep again. "It is not our fault—"

"What is not?"

"We are afraid—"

"Afraid—to spread flax out to dry?" They rolled their eyes at her. "What did you think I meant? Untie the bundles!"

She noticed the trembling of their fingers—felt another twinge of pity—then, suddenly, anger so overwhelming that she fell to screaming like one possessed: "You cannot do even this thing right! The stalks must be laid in order—tops this way, roots that way—not scattered about like straw and dung! In rows and ranks —thick here, thin there—else how shall we ever turn and dry them evenly? Cannot even such sluts as you comprehend rot? Oh thou befuddled—unteachable—malicious!"

She seized a thick stalk and began beating them. She could see herself, hear herself; but as if she were divided she seemed to be shouting something that set the walls to swaying. The sisters teetered on the brink of the trapdoor—she saw them drop from sight as the walls collapsed outward, slowly, as in a dream, and so compactly that they girdled Jericho with a broad pathway leading to destruction, and every man came straight ahead of him into the city—

"Greetings to Rahab!"

Her outer vision cleared. Two young men stood in the alley below—one already had his foot on the ladder. She moved back from the edge of the roof. Out in the street a party of soldiers grinned at her, gestured obscenely, then moved on through the gathering crowd toward the gate. In either direction the wall stretched away intact.

The young men were waiting nervously outside her door. She seated herself on a mat and spread her skirts out all around her; she was perspiring, disheveled, bits of flax clung to her skin and garments. They stared doubtfully when they came in. "Rahab the innkeeper?"

"Rahab the harlot!" she said with harsh emphasis. "But the soldiers mocked you. They know well that the custom of women is upon me. I am unclean."

They seemed to bow a little. "Our Rachel," they murmured. "So said she when Laban pursued Jacob. Hide us from our pursuers, as Rachel hid the teraphim from hers!"

"Ah—you are pursued! Why? The gates are still open. If you came in without a pass, you can surely go out the same way—"

"Our life for yours!" they interrupted fiercely.

"Do you intend to murder me? Very well, but don't plan to stay here afterward. This is the first place the king will look—if indeed he *is* looking and hasn't sent you to entrap me."

"The king is hunting us—now! His men are watching for us at the gate—now!"

Her inner vision began to confuse her again. She fought to stay clear-headed. "Why? Who are you?"

"Deal faithfully and kindly with us now and we will deal kindly and faithfully with you when the Lord God delivers the city into our hands!"

The walls fell outward with a rush and roar, paving and preparing the way. Amid the din she had one clear thought: the soldiers hadn't *sent* these visitors but *had* seen them. Time was short. She couldn't wait till dark. She must hide them now.

She went up into the deceptive twilight and resumed spreading the flax. At her signal they wriggled through the trapdoor and onto the roof, flat on their bellies as snakes. When she touched them with one hand, they ceased and lay motionless. She began to cover them with the flax she held in the other hand.

"I know your god has given you the land," she whispered in their ears. "Fear of you has fallen upon us, we have heard that you do not prevail by miracles but by planning, discipline, cooperation for the common good—"

They rustled under the flax like adders trod upon. "Have you not heard how the Lord dried up the Red Sea when we came out of Egypt? and how—"

"Yes, yes," she said hastily. "I only meant that no such wonders will be needed here. Your report will show it: the condition of the walls, the faintheartedness of the people. This business of yours will prepare the way . . ."

They were covered to the chin, visible only in profile; for a moment she did not understand the smiles they exchanged. "So be it.

Do not tell this business of ours and we will spare not only you but also your father and mother, brothers and sisters. Them too we will save alive!"

"Them too?" she echoed inadvertently. Then understood: they thought she was bargaining! This was not some of the captain's trickery—they expected it, approved of it.

"We have sworn . . ."

"Well, I will keep my part," she said, and covered their faces.

Just as she expected, the king's men arrived before the closing of the gate. She had changed into a soft white robe that left one shoulder dazzlingly bare, and was braiding her hair with scarlet yarn when they burst in.

"True, two men were here," she shrugged, "but who they were or where they came from, I don't know. I'm no traitor but an honest harlot, as the king commanded. Two men, that's all. True, they delayed until a short time ago, then jumped up and ran, as if they'd suddenly remembered the gate would close at dark. If they did leave the city they can't have gotten far. Go after them now and you can overtake them. Or," she said indifferently, "if you don't believe me, you may use your time searching the house . . ."

When total darkness fell she called the men down. "As soon as your pursuers rode out, the gate was shut. They'll be back when they can't find you. There'll be no hiding place in the city, and especially not here."

"You have heard what we did to the kings of the Amorites," they began, "to Sihon and Og—"

She was searching through a chest for a rope, and cut them off impatiently. "Go into the hills behind the city—hide there. They'll be watching the fords of the river."

"With respect to the oath you made us swear," they said as they secured and tested the rope, "we will be guiltless. Gather your family into the house when we come before the walls. If anyone goes into the street we cannot be responsible, but all who stay in will be delivered from death."

She wasn't bargaining—the rope was already dangling out the window—but: "This house? when the city is under siege? Give me some token—some sure sign."

They turned to gaze at her admiringly. "Our wise Rachel! That
scarlet cord—bind it in the window on that day."

"This?" she said incredulously, touching her braided hair.

"The Lord will pass through to smite the Egyptians but when
He sees the blood on the lintel and side posts, He will pass over
the door and will not suffer the Destroyer to enter and smite
you . . ."

Words dark as the darkness at the bottom of the rope. She was
disappointed at their riddling way of speaking, as if plainness were
not enough. Nevertheless she coiled the rope and laid it in the
chest, coiled the scarlet yarn and laid it inside the rope. Against
the day. Words aside, she had seen the fate of Jericho.

Now the city was straitly shut up. None went out and none
came in—except Rumor with her thousand tongues: the Hebrews
had crossed the Jordan and had not; had come through dry-shod
or half drowned; were turning back at Gilgal or regrouping there.
People heard sappers at work under the wall—felt quakes and
tremors—saw pillars of fire in the shape of a drawn sword, or
raised trumpet, or uplifted arm. One morning the entire city
suffered what seemed to be a mass delusion. Out of the desert
came a great host of armed men, perhaps forty-thousand in all,
moving in perfect silence and order. Half preceded a band of nine
priests, half came after. Two of the priests bore a golden chest
slung from poles, seven carried trumpets made of rams' horns. As
the advance host reached the corner of the city, the seven raised
their trumpets and shattered the very air. Roundabout the city the
eerie procession marched, and still the forty-thousand uttered no
sound, but the trumpets blew continuously. One circuit only—
then gone again into the desert.

On the second day they did the same, and every day thereafter
for six days—by which time they were no longer delusion but waking nightmare. At the first blast of the harsh unceasing trumpets
people went into convulsions, beat their foreheads on the ground,
stormed the gate crying for release into the hills. Afterward they
wandered up and down the streets with vacant eyes and twitching
mouths. The king, as if a spell had been woven round him, withdrew into silence and seclusion. His commanders fought for pre-
eminence. Soldiers received contradictory orders, manned the wall
haphazardly, their morale melted away.

Rahab's house was forgotten. She stayed in it undisturbed. During the first march around the city she went down to the storeroom to gather up her family. If the Hebrews valued filial piety, she would display it! But her father and mother rebuffed her soundly, even reproached her for unseemly exultation. "Stay here then and be slaughtered with the rest!"

She was not inclined to see black magic in the silent marching and brazen trumpets. She admired the controlled and channeled energy, but as she might admire it in a troupe of acrobats; she awaited the issue. By the sixth day nonetheless she felt a kind of panic. Suppose she alone were saved? she alone taken to dwell among strangers? Her father and mother, after all, had never mistreated her out of ill will, only poverty and fear—and she and the sisters had been close . . . On the seventh day the marchers did not stop with one circle but wove another, and another, and another . . . She hung the scarlet yarn out her window and hastened down to the storeroom.

The sisters were lying in a corner with pillows over their heads. The brothers were squalling horridly. "Today is surely the day!" she said wildly. "There is no time to explain or beg! Destruction is at hand!"

The father and mother shook their heads, but their refusal was not so categorical this time—they seemed, in fact, ashamed. The sisters sprang to their feet. Without waiting for permission they fled. "Leave us," murmured her mother. "See, your sisters have gone—return after them . . ."

"Entreat me not to leave you! Where I go, you will go, and where I lodge, you will lodge. Today our lives will be delivered from death. Afterward, where you die, there too will I be buried!"

She found herself shouting in a sudden overpowering silence. The incessant blare of the trumpets had stopped. Her father put out his hand—whether to find hers or to steady himself was all one: in that moment the house shuddered profoundly—a wooden box pitched out of its niche in the wall, scattering the sisters' little supply of combs and shoulder pins—the older brother sat down flat, his legs stiff with surprise—a row of wine jars skittered out of line. "*Now!*" said Rahab, seizing her father's hand. Just where he would have touched the wall, a crack opened up from floor to ceiling.

"No!" her mother said sharply, "your brothers!"

Rahab obeyed; carried one, dragged the other through the stampeding crowd. The attackers had broken their silence; the air throbbed with their high-pitched ululating battle-cry—it seemed to pierce and dissolve the very bricks and mortar that would keep them out. At the top of her ladder Rahab handed the boys to the sisters, then turned to look for her parents. They were just struggling into the alley, the mother leading the father by the hand— urgently but carefully so that they would not be torn apart in the chaos . . .

Touching, yes—but oh, to have been at the window or on the roof instead of waiting at the door! By the time she gathered her parents in, the wall had been breached, the Hebrews were in the city. They were scrupulous about their oath—and prompt. The East Gate, outflanked and under attack from within, was quickly abandoned. Almost at once two men—the same two men—came to hurry the family down the long ramp leading from the Gate to the plain. As they set their faces toward Gilgal they were sternly warned not to look back lest they be turned into pillars of salt. Rahab supposed this meant become transfixed by tears, and did not hesitate to disobey, though surreptitiously. Armed men were still scrambling up the littered rampart, but not every man could go straight ahead of him into the city. The ways were few and narrow, some had to be bloodily forced. She could see one place only where the wall had fallen outward as in her vision, one section carrying another down with it. Other gaps were isolated, as if the earthquake intervals had done their work in spite of the king's tampering. Stretches of the wall that remained standing, however, were being fired with brushwood debris. The very bricks turned red, and bursts of smoke and flame rose on the other side.

By nightfall Jericho was no more. Word raced to Gilgal of the solemn curse Joshua had laid on any man who should ever try to rebuild it. "A heap of ruins forever!" exulted Rahab. She only regretted that she hadn't seen every step in that great downfall.

For a while she was a heroine. Joshua summoned her in order to look upon her and thank her for saving his spies. Marriages were arranged for the sisters—they accounted for their lost maidenhood, little hypocrites, by way of husbands who had refused to flee the wrath to come. The father and mother were treated as blessed among parents—a role they played with laughable seriousness. Rahab, at least, had to smile when she heard them praise her for her modesty, her piety, her many devoted services—a daughter if ever there was one!

No doubt they sensed that she would soon become a problem. Nothing, unfortunately, could prevent it. She could not remain unmarried when every man who saw her lusted for her in his heart. But who among the married men would risk domestic upheaval by taking her as a second or third wife? or who among the young men would want her for his first? Even at the height of her popularity she was secretly called "the Canaanite *zonah*"—a word that might mean "innkeeper" only but also "keeper of a house" in a worse sense. Who would give his mother such a daughter-in-law?

Rahab helped in her swift fall from grace. She was disappointed to find idolatry flourishing in dark corners—images, charms, potions, spells for warding off or curing sickness, divining the future, resolving matters of the heart. In the last she might have earned gratitude, since women were inclined to regard her as possessing both natural and supernatural powers in love. But when they came to her secretly, she rebuked them, saying they were no better than Canaanites; she marvelled at their disrespect for their own Law, not to mention their lack of fear of Joshua. Had they not seen the same thing she had seen after the sack of Jericho? The man named Achan had hidden a bar of gold and two hundred shekels of silver under his tent instead of putting them in the common treasury. Joshua made every tribe pass before him; chose one and made every family in it pass by; chose one family; then one household; then finally, infallibly, confronted the hidden faithless individual.

Rahab had been impressed equally by his intuition and by the swift incorruptible justice that followed. "As for me," she said passionately, "I would strive rather to be worthy of such a man than go about to deceive him!"

Nor did she approve of the version of the fall of Jericho that began to take shape when the women sat in a circle clapping their hands and making up verses. For a while she held her peace, then not: "I saw! I was there!" Joshua had cunningly demoralized the city—devised stratagems to nullify a river and wall—taken quick advantage of an unexpected stroke of luck. They disparaged him when they substituted mere wonders for hard work and foresight: heaped-up waters! walls struck flat! an angel taking charge the

night before! Ah, if the people of Israel could live just one day
under the leadership of the king of Jericho!

"More Israelite than the Israelites!" they said behind her back.

They also detected something they thought was more in line
with her real character than a desire for righteousness. Joshua was
a handsome vigorous man in his middle years. He was not, however, married—a condition the women had never regarded as anything but temporary, celibacy being as inconceivable to them as
profligacy was abhorrent. The mere possibility that *Rahab* would
breach that wall—the great probability that she would try—the
utter certainty that she would like to—sealed their antagonism toward her.

She might have told them that from the moment she met
Joshua she knew he was wed only to his mission. She had seen
celibates before. He called her "my child" and was remote as a
monument. She would have been disappointed to find him any
other way. But their spitefulness so angered her that she deliberately put out a flickering tongue, musing aloud upon that other
leader whom everyone seemed to value so much more highly than
Joshua. Moses had married an Ethiopian, had he not? And when
the woman Miriam spoke against it, behold, she was made lep-
rous, white as snow. Was this not true?

"We are weary of our lives because of the Canaanite *zonah!*"
the women said to their husbands. "If he marries such a woman
why should we go on living?"

The men had been away at the siege of Ai and the rout of five
kings at Gibeon. They were not surprised to hear that Rahab
often thought of Joshua, and ordinarily would not have been
alarmed if he sometimes thought of her. But there was an element
in their wives' complaints that went beyond female envy, something touching their very enterprise. Soon they too were saying,
"If he is beguiled by a woman such as this, what good will *our*
lives be?" The question was, how to set the matter before him
with the proper emphasis? They had no wish to be misunderstood. However else he fell short of Moses, it was not in wrath
and denunciation.

While they debated, Joshua looked around and saw for himself
that Rahab was shunned. It seemed ominous that she was trou-
bling Israel just when he was preparing to move against Lachish,
Libnah and cities of the south, to do to them what he had done

to Jericho. He demanded that his advisers tell him what she had said or done, and to hide nothing from him. Then he sent for her.

She had been expecting a summons and took care to answer it with unenhanced beauty. But though she suppressed her lily side, when she stood before him in the presence of witnesses she succumbed to the other and gave an angry twisting reply: "I've done nothing, said nothing except to give credit where it is due. You must ask those who complain of it why Joshua makes them weary of their lives, or arouses evil imaginings—why they whore after magic and miracles—why they set Moses' heel on Joshua's neck—"

He cut her off with a gesture, set aside his remote manner and said with terrible directness: "Why will you be a stumbling-block to me, beguiling me with words and tempting me to vaingloriousness? Why will you be a thorn in the side of the people? Soon all Israel moves south to lay hold on the Promise. What meaning will their lives have if their victories glorify *me*? One man of them puts to flight a thousand because the Lord God fights for them. They keep me from pride when they say, 'There has not arisen again in Israel a leader like Moses, who saw the Lord face to face, none like him for signs and wonders, and for great and terrible deeds.' They do not exalt me further than I exalt them, for I also remind them and say to them, 'You are mighty men of valor because you obey the Lord.'

"The night before Jericho," he said after a pause in which he resumed his cloaked and withdrawn air, "behold, a man appeared to me with a drawn sword in his hand. I said, 'Are you for us or against us?' He said, 'I have come as commander of the army of the Lord.' I fell on my face and worshipped: 'What does my lord bid his servant do?' For He alone had the whole circumference of the wall in view, to strike it flat or leave it standing, in whole or in part, all at once or in good time. What He did, He did. Give glory and thanks to Him, as those do whom you slander saying, 'I saw, I was there.' All who were there saw through a chink. They are not the ones who whore after magic and abominations, but you—who credit Joshua with deeds no man could do, the Lord not commanding!"

Rahab bowed herself to the ground. It was a moment when she could have wished the walls of Jericho would rise again. Between that tyranny and this demagoguery, what was there to choose?

Like a grain of wheat fallen between two millstones she waited to be ground up.

The silence, profound as that silence when the trumpets ceased to blow, was broken by a voice she did not recognize: "The woman has behaved foolishly out of ignorance, being a foreigner. She deserves this rebuke but now remember what she did for Israel, under whose wing she took refuge. Remember also, Joshua, that Moses was called 'very mild, more than any man on the face of the earth.'"

Rahab did not dare look up. And indeed, almost before she herself could find out who had spoken, the whole camp knew that it was the honored young man Salomon. He had turned Joshua's wrath aside, so that she was not cut off from Israel, nor even put outside the camp for seven days like Miriam, but only told to go and make ritual atonement of the easy kind allowed to foreigners, and afterward to dwell in peace in Israel.

Even if this mildness had displeased the people, there would have been no arguing with Joshua. Salomon stood too high in his esteem. He had just returned from Shechem with the good news that the king there was friendly to Israel and would allow a cadre of officers and advisers to be planted in his city. Joshua, planning to lay hold first on the cities of the south, then the north, needed an ally betwixt and between; he had dispatched Salomon to get one for him soon after the crossing of the Jordan. The victories at Jericho, Ai and Gibeon helped persuade Shechem, of course, but no one—least of all Joshua—underestimated the influence of Salomon's agreeable manners and worldly temperament. He was just such a man as could make the Promise seem desirable and not merely inevitable.

The people were not displeased with his intervention on Rahab's behalf. They seemed, rather, to be greatly entertained by it.

> She tied a red string to Joshua's hand,
> But Salomon made the breach!

they sang, muddling the facts a little but getting at the truth. A few days after her atonement Rahab went to draw water, and Salomon in sight of everyone followed her to the well.

She tried to be gracious but was sore at heart. Her atonement had been a form and a lie. She thanked him for judging her kindly and made a move to leave. When he begged her to stay she said somberly, "Look around you—all Israel is watching—they're laughing at you with their hands over their mouths."

"I see them," he said easily. "I even know what they're saying: 'The tribe of Judah—naturally!' or 'what else?' I don't mind. Anyway it's the truth. We *are* self-willed, passion prone. A scarlet thread runs through all our history."

"Is that why you take notice of me—a foreigner?"

"Exactly my point," he said with a smile that acknowledged *her* point. "Perhaps you've heard of Tamar?"

"No."

"She was a foreigner too."

"Then she was to be pitied."

"Not at all. She triumphed exceedingly."

"I should like exceedingly to hear about her—some time."

He was not so easily put off. He told her the story then and there, resting his arm on her water jar so that she could not lift it to her shoulder and be gone. He had a way of speaking that surprised her—both serious and self-mocking—she hadn't heard the like since Jericho. It should have refreshed her—instead it made her uneasy. And the tale! The woman Tamar, twice widowed and childless, wrapped herself in the veil of a harlot and enticed her father-in-law to lie with her. When she conceived and was brought up on charges of harlotry, she produced certain tokens he had given her, and forced him to acknowledge his part. Was there ever a sorrier, more confused history? It seemed to Rahab to defame the Canaanite woman and made Judah her victim. Where was her triumph except in low trickery?

"Why, in justice," Salomon said good-naturedly. "Judah himself admitted that she was more righteous than he. She'd been married to his first two sons. When they died she was entitled by law to marry the third. Judah promised but procrastinated. He was fearful for his third son's life—though Tamar had nothing to do with the death of the other two—they were struck down from their own wickedness. Why should she, a young woman, be cut off and remain a childless widow all her days?"

"But she conceived by the father, not the son—"

"He was the one who'd reneged."

"—and played the harlot to do it!"

"Truly—'played.' Judah, though, was *not* playing. His sin was like scarlet. Of course," Salomon added, "he atoned."

"And his tribe has many such tales?" Rahab asked in a neutral tone.

"Oh, many! Perhaps you've heard of Pharez and Zarah? No? Well, when the time of Tamar's delivery came, there were twins in her womb. During labor one of them put out a hand and the midwife tied a red string to it to show that he'd arrived first. But suddenly the hand was pulled back—maybe voluntarily, maybe not. His brother came out instead. The midwife named him Pharez—Breach—because, she said, 'I tied a red cord to the other one's hand but this one made the breach.' Pharez was the founder of my clan."

"So I supposed," Rahab murmured.

"Sitting in the door of Joshua's tent on the second day of my return," he said in his half-eloquent, half-humorous way, "I raised my eyes and saw a young woman pass by with a water jar on her shoulder. Whether she was foreign or a daughter of Israel I couldn't tell—only that my soul fainted within me. I was saying something about Shechem to Joshua—the thread snapped, like that! I demanded to know who she was—and learned that this was Rahab, whom I alone had not set eyes upon."

"And when he told you that this same Rahab was making Israel weary of its life?"

"My soul fainted a second time—from jealousy! 'She praises Joshua?' I said, or stammered. 'Why should that offend Israel?' Then he told me he had sent for you—I could hear and judge for myself."

"So that was the way of it," she said, half to herself. "You weren't there by accident. . . ."

"How could I be?"

She stared at him with eyes that no longer saw him: she was again in Joshua's tent—bowed down in profound silence—hearing the eloquent plea—and Joshua's abrupt response—one following the other so closely they might have been twins. "You judged kindly—you turned away his wrath," she said, but it was more of a question.

"Did I? Well, if you like . . . though really he only sent for you to remind you that no man is good, none righteous. A useful thing to remember, especially in leaders and governors."

"So that was it!" she burst out. "I suspected it! He denounced *me* in order to flatter *them!*"

"Don't you think it cost him something to refuse that flattering worship of yours?"

"No, nothing—he gained by it."

"Or I did," Salomon said gracefully.

"It wasn't worship," she brooded. "It was admiration for a mortal man."

"You're still free to admire him."

"Luckily I'm forbidden to praise him. I'd be at a loss unless I should compliment his adroitness in demagoguery."

"Joshua—a demagogue? You're too categorical."

"What is a man who denies vainglory in one breath and receives angels in the next?"

"Well, these are less heroic times than formerly," Salomon said with an enigmatic smile. "The Jordan isn't the Red Sea. The conquest of Canaan won't rank with bringing the Commandments down from the mountain. That's the burden he bears. Still—he has to lead. Must he proceed entirely by rule, law, statute, ordinance, covenant? Can we do entirely without inspiration? At least he's clear on the point that he doesn't talk to the Lord face to face, as Moses did. . . ."

She knew he meant to put a hand under her foot when she was in danger of sinking, but the comfort was less than it should have been and did not increase in the days that followed, when he came to her father's tent. He reminded her obscurely of the captain. He was partly soldier but mostly diplomat, emissary, negotiator; therefore somewhat lacking in sense of outrage. He expected flaws and failures—they were embedded in some larger scheme of things which required patience to unfold—any other attitude, he said, was impractical.

The captain!—to have come all this way only to find herself back at the beginning!

There was, however, this difference: when Salomon departed for Shechem with the cadre she was not left behind, she went with him as his wife. Or was that only a seeming difference? Once again she was helpless to oppose what was happening to her. Salomon passionately desired it. Joshua, with an air of dignified relief, gave it his blessing. Her father literally died of joy: sealed the contract, then fell on his back, staring upward as if blinded by a miracle. The sisters, now more Israelite than the Israelites, were, like Joshua, content to see her go, but they must remain with their husbands. They pressed the mother to stay too, but she elected to hold Rahab to a former promise. Shechem, she had reason to believe, was not unlike Jericho, for which she increasingly had secret fits of nostalgia. " 'Where you die, there will I be buried'—you have said it."

"Yes," answered Rahab. "I have said much in my time."

She'd been given one vision of the future but was not vouchsafed another. She joined her nature to Salomon's willy-nilly, so to speak, and bore him a son named Boaz—the same who comforted Ruth when she was a stranger in the land. His son's name was Obed; his, Jesse; Jesse's, David; and so on in that half-practical half-passionate direction. In time Jericho rose again. People went back and rebuilt it, not knowing or not caring that Joshua had cursed it "forever." The spring there was very deep, the waters living. The story does not record, however, that any of Rahab's line ever looked back. It is not there that she dwells "to this day."

BEAUTIFUL GIRL

ALICE ADAMS

Alice Adams grew up in Chapel Hill, North Carolina, and graduated from Radcliffe; since then she has lived mostly in San Francisco. Her third novel, *Listening to Billie*, was published by Knopf in January 1978; a collection of stories (of which "Beautiful Girl" is the title story) will appear in September 1978. This is her eighth O. Henry inclusion.

Ardis Bascombe, the tobacco heiress, who twenty years ago was a North Carolina beauty queen, is now sitting in the kitchen of her San Francisco house, getting drunk. Four-thirty, an October afternoon, and Ardis, with a glass full of vodka and melted ice, a long cigarette going and another smoldering in an almost full ashtray, is actually doing several things at once: drinking and smoking, of course, killing herself, her older daughter, Linda, has said (Ardis is no longer speaking to Linda, who owns and runs a health-food store), and watching the news on her small color Sony TV. She is waiting for her younger daughter, Carrie, who goes to Stanford but lives at home and usually shows up about now. And she is waiting also for a guest, a man she knew way back when, who called this morning, whose name she is having trouble with. Black? White? Green? It is a color name; she is sure of that.

Twenty years ago Ardis was a small and slender black-haired girl, with amazing wide, thickly lashed dark-azure eyes and smooth, pale, almost translucent skin—a classic Southern beauty, except for the sexily curled, contemptuous mouth. And brilliant, too: straight A's at Chapel Hill. An infinitely promising, rarely lovely girl: everyone thought so. A large portrait of her then hangs framed on the kitchen wall: bare-shouldered, in something gauzy, light—she is dressed for a formal dance, the Winter Germans or

Copyright © 1977 by The New Yorker Magazine, Inc. First appeared in *The New Yorker*.

the May Frolics. The portrait is flyspecked and streaked with grime from the kitchen fumes. Ardis despises cleaning up, and hates having maids around; periodically she calls a janitorial service, and sometimes she has various rooms repainted, covering the grime. Nevertheless, the picture shows the face of a beautiful young girl. Also hanging there, gilt-framed and similarly grimed, are several family portraits: elegant and upright ancestors, attesting to family substance—although in Ardis's messy kitchen they have a slightly comic look of inappropriateness.

Ardis's daughter Carrie, who in a couple of years will inherit several of those tobacco millions, is now driving up from the peninsula, toward home, in her jaunty brown felt hat and patched faded jeans, in her dirty battered Ford pickup truck. She is trying to concentrate on Thomas Jefferson (History I) or the view: blond subdivided hills and groves of rattling dusty eucalyptus trees that smell like cat pee. She is listening to the conversations on her CB radio, but a vision of her mother, at that table, with her emptying glass and heavy blue aura of smoke, fills Carrie's mind; she is pervaded by the prospect of her mother and filled with guilt, apprehension, sympathy. Her mother, who used to be so much fun, now looks as swollen and dead-eyed, as thick-skinned, as a frog.

Hoping for change, Carrie has continued to live at home, seldom admitting why. Her older sister, Linda, of the health-food store, is more severe, or simply fatalistic. "If she wants to drink herself to death she will," says Linda. "Your being there won't help, or change a thing." Of course she's right, but Carrie sticks around.

Neither Linda nor Carrie is as lovely as their mother was. They are pretty girls—especially Linda, who is snub-nosed and curly-haired. Carrie has straight dark hair and a nose like that of her father: Clayton Bascombe, former Carolina Deke, former tennis star, former husband of Ardis. His was a nice straight nose—Clayton was an exceptionally handsome boy—but it is too long now for Carrie's small tender face.

Clayton, too, had a look of innocence; perhaps it was his innocent look that originally attracted Ardis's strong instinct for destruction. In any case, after four years of marriage, two daughters, Ardis decided that Clayton was "impossible," and threw him out —out of the house that her parents had given them, in Winston-Salem. Now Clayton is in real estate in Wilmington, N.C., having ended up where he began, before college and the adventure of marriage to Ardis.

Ardis has never remarried. For many years, in Winston-Salem, as a young divorcée, she was giddily popular, off to as many parties and weekends out of town as when she was a Carolina coed. Then, after the end of an especially violent love affair, she announced that she was tired of all that and bored with all her friends. With the two girls, Ardis moved to San Francisco, bought the big house on Vallejo Street, had it fashionably decorated, and began another round of parties with new people—a hectic pace that gradually slowed to fewer parties, invitations, friends. People became "boring" or "impossible," as the neglected house decayed. Ardis spent more and more time alone. More time drunk.

The girls, who from childhood had been used to their mother's lovers (suitors, beaux) and who by now had some of their own, were at first quite puzzled by their absence: Ardis, without men around? Then Linda said to Carrie, "Well, *Lord,* who'd want her now? Look at that face. Besides, I think she'd rather drink."

In some ways Ardis has been a wonderful mother, though: Carrie sometimes says that to herself. Always there were terrific birthday parties, presents, clothes. And there was the time in Winston-Salem when the real-estate woman came to the door with a petition about Negroes—keeping them out, land values, something like that. Of course Ardis refused to sign, and then she went on: "And in answer to your next question, I sincerely hope that both my daughters marry them. I understand those guys are really great. *Not,* unfortunately, from personal experience." *Well.* What other mother, especially in Winston-Salem, would ever talk like that?

Ardis dislikes paying bills—especially small ones; for instance, from the garbage collectors, although she loves their name: Sunset Scavenger Company. Thus the parking area is lined with full garbage cans, spilling over among all the expensively imported and dying rhododendrons and magnolia trees, the already dead azaleas in their rusted cans. Seeing none of this, Carrie parks her truck. She gets out and slams the door.

Five o'clock. Ardis will have had enough drinks to make her want to talk a lot, although she will be just beginning to not make sense.

Carrie opens the front door and goes in, and she hears her
mother's familiar raucous laugh coming from the kitchen. Good,
she is not alone. Carrie walks in that direction, as Ardis's deep,
hoarse voice explains to someone, "That must be my daughter
Carrie. You won't believe—"

Carrie goes into the kitchen and is introduced to a tall, thin, almost bald, large-nosed man. He is about her mother's age but in
much better shape: rich, successful. (Having inherited some of
her mother's social antennae, Carrie has taken all this in without
really thinking.) In Ardis's dignified slur, his name sounds like
Wopple Grin.

"Actually," Ardis tells Carrie later on, "Walpole Greene is
very important in Washington, on the Hill." This has been said
in the heavily nasal accent with which Ardis imitates extreme
snobs; like many good mimics, she is aping an unacknowledged
part of herself. Ardis is more truly snobbish than anyone, caring
deeply about money, family, and position. "Although he certainly
wasn't much at Carolina," she goes on, in the same tone.

Tonight, Ardis looks a little better than usual, her daughter
observes. She did a very good job with her makeup; somehow her
eyes look O.K.—not as popped out as they sometimes do. And a
gauzy scarf around her throat has made it look less swollen.

Walpole Greene, who is indeed important in Washington, although, as the head of a news bureau, not exactly in Ardis's sense
"on the Hill," thinks how odd it is that Ardis should have such a
funny-looking kid.

Carrie, reading some of that in his face, thinks, What a creep.
She excuses herself to go upstairs. She smiles privately as she
leaves, repeating, silently, "Wopple Grin."

In Chapel Hill, all those years ago, in the days when Walpole
Greene was certainly not much—he was too young, too skinny
and tall; with his big nose he looked like a bird—he was always
acutely and enragedly aware of Ardis. So small and bright, so admired, so universally lusted after, so often photographed in the
Daily Tarheel and *Carolina Magazine*, with her half-inviting, half-
disdainful smile; she was everywhere. One summer, during a session of summer school, Walpole felt that he saw Ardis every time
he left his dorm: Ardis saying "Hey, Walpole" (Wopple? was she

teasing him?) in the same voice in which she said "Hey" to every-one.

He saw her dancing in front of the Y, between classes, in the morning—smiling, mocking the dance. He glimpsed her through the windows of Harry's, drinking beer, in the late afternoon. She was dressed always in immaculate pale clothes: flowered cottons, cashmere cardigans. And at night he would see her anywhere at all: coming out of the show, at record concerts in Kenan Stadium ("Music Under the Stars"), emerging from the Arboretum, with some guy. Usually she was laughing, which made even then a sur-prisingly loud noise from such a small thin girl. Her laugh and her walk were out of scale; she *strode*, like someone very tall and im-portant.

Keeping track of her, Walpole, who had an orderly mind, began to observe a curious pattern in the escorts of Ardis: midmornings at the Y, evenings at the show, or at Harry's, she was apt to be with Gifford Gwathmey, a well-known S.A.E., a handsome blond Southern boy. But if he saw her in some more dubious place, like the Arboretum, late at night, she would be with Henry Mallory, a Delta Psi from Philadelphia.

Ardis always looked as if she were at a party, having a very good time but at the same time observing carefully and feeling just slightly superior to it all. And since his sense of himself and of his presence at Carolina was precisely opposite to that, Walpole sometimes dreamed of doing violence to Ardis. He hated her al-most as much as he hated the dean of men, who in a conference had suggested that Walpole should "get out more," should "try to mix in."

It was a melancholy time for Walpole, all around.

One August night, in a stronger than usual mood of self-pity, Walpole determined to do what he had all summer considered doing: he would stay up all night and then go out to Gimghoul Castle (the Gimghouls were an undergraduate secret society) and watch the dawn from the lookout bench there. He did just that, drinking coffee and reading from "The Federalist Papers," and then riding on his bike, past the Arboretum and Battle Park, to the Castle. The lookout bench was some distance from the main building, and as he approached it Walpole noted that a group of people, probably Gimghouls and their dates, were out there drink-ing *still*, on one of the terraces.

He settled on the hard stone circular bench, in the dewy pre-
dawn air, and focussed his attention on the eastern horizon. And
then suddenly, soundlessly—and drunkenly: she was plastered—
Ardis appeared. Weaving toward him, she sat down on the bench
beside him, though not too near.

"You came out here to look at the sunrise?" she slurred, conver-
sationally. "God, Wopple, that's wonderful." Wunnerful.

Tears of hatred sprang to Walpole's eyes—fortunately invisible.
He choked; in a minute he would hit her, very hard.

Unaware that she was in danger, Ardis got stiffly to her feet; she
bent awkwardly toward him and placed a cool bourbon-tasting
kiss on Walpole's mouth. "I love you, Wopple," Ardis said. "I
truly and purely do." The sun came up.

He didn't hate her anymore—of course he would not hit her.
How could he hit a girl who had kissed him and spoken of love?
And although after that night nothing between them changed
overtly, he now watched her as a lover would. With love.

"Lord, you're lucky I didn't rape you there and then," says Ardis
now, having heard this romantic story. She is exaggerating the slur
of her speech, imitating someone even drunker than she is.

Walpole, who believes that in a way he has loved her all his
life, laughs sadly, and he wonders if at any point in her life Ardis
could have been—he backs off from "saved" and settles on "retrieved." Such a waste: such beauty gone, and brains and wit.
Walpole himself has just married again, for the fourth time: a
young woman who, he has already begun to recognize, is not very
nice, or bright. He has little luck with love. It is not necessarily
true that Ardis would have been better off with him.

She is clearly in no shape to go out to dinner, and Walpole
wonders if he shouldn't cook something for the two of them to
eat. Scrambled eggs? He looks around the impossibly disordered
kitchen, at stacks of dishes, piled-up newspapers, a smelly cat box
in one corner, although he has seen no cat.

He reaches and pours some more vodka into his own glass, then
glances over at Ardis, whose eyes have begun to close.

By way of testing her, he asks, "Something I always wondered.
That summer, I used to see you around with Gifford Gwathmey,
and then later you'd be with Henry Mallory. Weren't you pinned
to Gifford?"

Ardis abruptly comes awake, and emits her laugh. "Of course I was pinned to Giff," she chortles. "But he and all those S.A.E.s were almost as boring as Dekes, although he did come from one of the oldest and *richest* families in Charleston." (This last in her nasal snob-imitating voice.) "So I used to late-date on him all the time, mainly with Henry, who didn't have a dime. But the Delta Psis were *fun*—a lot of boys from New York and Philadelphia." She laughs again. "Between dates, I'd rush back to the House and brush my teeth—talk about your basic fastidious coed. Henry teased me about always tasting of Pepsodent." For a moment Ardis looks extremely happy, and almost young; then she falls slowly forward until her head rests on the table in front of her, and she begins to snore.

Carrie, who has recently discovered jazz, is upstairs listening to old Louis Armstrong records, smoking a joint. "Pale moon shining on the fields below . . ."

She is thinking, as she often does, of how much she would like to get out of this house for a while. She would like to drop out of school for a term or two, maybe next spring, and just get into her truck with a few clothes and some money, and maybe a dog, and drive around the country. There is a huge circular route that she has often imagined: up to Seattle, maybe Canada, Vancouver, down into Wyoming, across the northern plains to Chicago—she knows someone there—New England, New York, and down the coast to her father, in Wilmington, N.C.; Charleston, New Orleans, Texas, Mexico, the Southwest, L.A.; then home, by way of Big Sur. Months of driving, with the dog and the CB radio for company.

In the meantime, halfway through her second joint, she sighs deeply and realizes that she is extremely hungry, ravenous. She carefully stubs out the joint and goes downstairs.

Walpole Greene, whose presence she had forgotten, is standing in the pantry, looking lost. Ardis has passed out. Having also forgotten that she thought he was a creep, Carrie experiences a rush of sympathy for the poor guy. "Don't worry," she tells him. "She'll be O.K."

"She sure as hell doesn't look O.K.," says Walpole Greene. "She's not O.K. No one who drinks that much—"

"Oh, well, in the long run you're right," says Carrie, as airily as though she had never worried about her mother's health. "But I mean for now she's O.K."

"Well. I'd meant to take her out to dinner."

"Why bother? She doesn't eat. But aren't you hungry? I'm starved."

"Well, sort of." Walpole looks dubiously around the kitchen. He watches Carrie as she goes over to the mammoth refrigerator and extracts a small covered saucepan from its incredibly crowded, murky interior.

"She likes to make soup," says Carrie. "Lately she's been on some Southern kick. Nostalgia, I guess. This is white beans and pork. Just made yesterday, so it ought to be all right."

The soup, which Carrie has heated and ladled into bowls, is good but too spicy for Walpole's ulcer; the next day he will feel really terrible. Now he and Carrie whisper to each other, like conspirators, above the sound of Ardis's heavy breathing.

"Does she do this often?" asks Walpole.

"Pretty often. Well—like, every day."

"That's not good."

"No."

Having drunk quite a bit more than he usually does, Walpole feels that his perceptions are enlarged. Looking at Carrie, he has a sudden and certain vision of her future: in ten or so years, in her late twenties, early thirties, she will be more beautiful than even Ardis ever was. She will be an exceptional beauty, a beautiful woman, whereas Ardis was just a beautiful girl. Should he tell Carrie that? He decides not to; she wouldn't believe him, although he is absolutely sure of his perception. Besides, even a little drunk he is too shy.

Instead, in an inspired burst, he says, "Listen, she's got to go somewhere. You know, dry out. There's a place in Connecticut. Senators' wives—"

Carrie's bright young eyes shine, beautifully. "That would be neat," she says.

"You'd be O.K. by yourself for a while?"

"I really would. I'm thinking about getting a dog—our cat just disappeared. And there's this trip. But how would you get her there?"

"Leave that to me," says Walpole, with somewhat dizzy confidence.

Carrie clears the table—without, Walpole notices, washing any dishes.

Carrie goes back upstairs, her heart high and light.

She considers calling her sister, Linda, saying that Walpole Greene is taking their mother to Connecticut. But Linda would say something negative, unpleasant.

Instead, she puts on another record, and hears the rich pure liquid sound of Louis's horn, and then his voice. Beale Street Blues, Muskrat Ramble. A Son of the South. She listens, blows more joints.

Downstairs, seated at the table, Walpole is talking softly and persuasively, he hopes, to Ardis's ear (her small pink ears are still pretty, he has noticed), although she is "asleep."

"This lovely place in Connecticut," he is saying. "A wonderful place. You'll like it. You'll rest, and eat good food, and you'll feel better than you've felt for years. You'll see. I want you to be my beautiful girl again—"

Suddenly aroused, Ardis raises her head and stares at Walpole. "I am a beautiful girl," she rasps out, furiously.

PADDYCAKE, PADDYCAKE . . .
A MEMOIR

MAX APPLE

Max Apple was born in Grand Rapids, Michigan. He is
married, with two children, and teaches at Rice University in Houston, Texas. He is the author of *The Oranging
of America and Other Stories* (Viking 1976); his *Zip: a
Novel of the Left at the Right* will be published in the
spring of 1978.

When he took walks, G.R. hummed cruising down the river. Now
and then he munched on red pistachio nuts and spit the shells
over the curb. I had to trot to keep up with his long steps. Once
we got to the bakery, he'd go donut wild. Cream puffs, eclairs,
even the cherryfilled danish were nothing to him. He headed for
the plain brown donuts, what my father called fry cakes. He ate
each one in two bites, coming down exactly in the middle of the
hole every time. Daddy would give him a couple dozen like nothing. Everybody on Franklin Street gave things to G.R. There
wasn't a housewife who didn't feel proud to fry him a few donuts
herself. And why the hell not. He raked their leaves, carried groceries, opened doors, and smiled at the old folks. He was an Eagle
Scout. I was just his nigger sidekick but people liked me for being
that. Much later I got good jobs, loans, even my own business because of being his sidekick. But when we started, it was G.R. that
needed me. He used to think my old man gave him the donuts because he was my buddy. He didn't know for a long time how
much people liked him.

"Christ," I used to tell him, "Daddy would give you fry cakes
even if you stomped me once a week. He likes you, G.R. You're
his neighbor."

Originally appeared in *The Ohio Review*, Spring/Summer 1976. Reprinted
in *The Oranging of America*, by Max Apple. Copyright © 1976 by Max
Apple. Reprinted by permission of Grossman Publishers.

In fact we were sort of double neighbors. Our houses were on the same block and his father's paint store was just down the street from the American Bakery where my dad was the donut and cake man.

G.R. and I hung around the Bridge Street branch of the public library. He read the sports books and I did the science fiction. Then we'd go to the bakery and he'd start to wolf down the fry cakes. He ate all he could, then stuffed his pockets. My old man just used to laugh and throw in a few more. A dozen was a light snack to him. After football games, he always had his twelve fresh ones waiting in the locker room. He never shared although he was generous with everything else. He ate them with his cleats and helmet still on and sometimes mud all over his face.

When my father died, G.R. and I were in college. He came over to the Alpha Kappa Psi house, hugged me and said, "Sonny, you know how he did it, you've got to take over." And like a dumb ass, I did. I made them at night in the big Alpha Kappa Psi deep fryer. But G.R. always paid for the ingredients.

You've got to remember that this was 1937 and he was the social chairman of the DU's, the best of the white houses, and a big football player, and I was still his nigger sidekick from home to everyone except the brothers of Alpha Kappa Psi where I was the house treasurer.

It only took about an hour once a week or so and he liked them so much that I just couldn't stop. It would have been like weaning a baby. I didn't want to put up with all his moping. G.R. wasn't unhappy much, but when he was, the whole DU house could burn up and he wouldn't leave his room. I was the only one he let in. He'd sit and stare at a 12x5 of his father and mother in front of the paint store. He'd say things like, "Sonny, they did a lot for me and no goddamn girl is going to ruin it." Or if it wasn't a girl, it was a goddamn professor, or sometimes a goddamn coach.

After a mope, he'd be good for two dozen and a half gallon of milk. The brothers used to call me his mammy. "The big old ball-player needs Mammy's shortnin bread," they used to say when they'd see me starting up the deep fryer after an emergency call from someone at DU. That's why half the house called me Mammy even though my actual nickname was Sonny. In the Michigan *Ensign* for 1938, there I am in the group picture of the

only black frat house in Ann Arbor. "Sonny 'Mammy' Williams"
it says, "Treasurer." G.R. is all over the book with the DU's, the
football team, the Audubon Society, the Student Union, the In-
terfraternity Honor Council. I counted him eight times and who
knows how many I missed.

I think the only reason I ever went to Ann Arbor instead of JC
like my sisters was that he was going and he got me a piece of his
scholarship somehow. But when he went to law school, I said,
"No dice, ace, I'm not hauling my ass up to Harvard." And I got
a job back in Grand Rapids working for Rasberry Heating. Law
school was the first time he got by without the fry cakes and he
said he was a grump all three years.

"I lost seventeen pounds and almost married a girl I didn't
love," he told me when he came back. "I lost a lot of my judgment and some of my quickness. Harvard and Yale may have
class, Sonny, but when you come down to it, there's no place like
home." He came back from Harvard as patriotic as the soldiers
shipping back from Guam a few years later. I met him at the
Market Street station with a sign that said, "Welcome back,
Counselor," and a dozen hot fry cakes. His ma and dad were there
too and his brother Phil. He hugged us all, ate the donuts and
said, "If you seek a beautiful peninsula, look around you." Then
he said it in Latin and we thought it was lawyer's talk and we
looked the train station over real good. Then he told us it was the
motto of the State of Michigan which was founded in 1837 and
was the first state west of Pennsylvania to have its own printing
press. He said he wasn't leaving Michigan for a good long time,
and if it wasn't for the war a few months later, I don't believe he
would have.

The war started in December and he came back from Harvard
in the June before that. The first thing he did was make me take
my two weeks from Rasberry and head up to the Upper Peninsula with him, "To the thumb, Sonny, to the tip of Michigan
where three great lakes sparkle and iron and copper dot the landscape."

I still couldn't say no to the guy so I went along even though I
knew the Upper Peninsula was for Indians and not for Negroes.

We drove two days in my '35 Chevy, up through Cadillac,
Reed City, Petoskey, Cheboygan. The roads were bad. When we
had a flat near the Iron River, it took an hour for another car to

come by so we could borrow a jack. I wished all the time that we were on our way to Chicago or Cleveland or Indianapolis or someplace where you could do something when you got there. But old G.R. was on a nature kick then. I believe Harvard and no fry cakes had about driven him nuts. While I flagged down the jack, he stood beside the car and did deep knee bends and Marine push-ups. He took off his shirt and beat his chest. "Smell the air, Sonny, that's Michigan for you," he said. People were suspicious enough about stopping for a nigger trying to flag them down without this bouncing Tarzan to scare 'em worse.

When we finally got the ferry boat to take us to Mackinac Island, I knew it was a mistake. The only Negroes besides me were the shoeshine boys on the boat and here I was in a linen suit and big straw hat alongside Mr. Michigan who was taking in the Lake Superior spray and still beating his chest now and then and telling everyone what a treat it was to live in the Thumb State. Everybody thought I was his valet, so when I caught some real bad staring I just went over and brushed his jacket or something and the folks smiled at me very nicely. I didn't want trouble then and I don't now. I've been a Negro all my life and no matter how hard I try I can't call myself a black.

Another thing I tell people and they can hardly believe is that I don't think G.R. ever once said anything about my color. I don't believe he ever noticed it or thought about it or considered that it made a bit of difference. I guess that's another reason why I didn't mind baking his donuts.

But Mackinac Island was a mistake for both of us. I was bored stiff by talking about how good the food was in the hotel and taking little rides in horse-drawn carriages. G.R. seemed to like it, so I didn't say much.

One morning he says, "Sonny, let's get clipped," and I go with him to the hotel barbershop without giving it a thought. After being there a week, I must have lost my sense too, to just go along like that. He sits down in one vacant chair and motions me to the other. There are a couple of thin barbers who look like their scissors. I'm just getting my socks adjusted and looking down at "Theo A. Kochs" written on the bottom of the barber chair when my thin man says almost in a whisper, "I'm sorry, sir, but we don't do negro hair." G.R. hasn't heard this because his barber has snapped the striped sheet loudly around him and is already combing those straight blond strands.

I step out of the chair. "No hard feelings," he says.

"None," I say, "I didn't need a haircut anyway. I'll just wait for my friend here."

"Fine," he says and sits down in his chair to have a smoke while he waits for another customer.

When G.R. gets turned around and sees this little barber lighting up, he says, "Sonny, c'mon, I thought we're both getting clipped this morning."

"I'll wait, G.R.," I say hoping he'll let it go.

"No waiting," he says, "it's sharp country up here, we've got to look sharp for it, right boys?" He looks at my little barber who blows some smoke and says, "I'm sorry, but we don't cut colored hair here. In fact, I don't think there's a spot on the island that does. We just don't get that much in colored trade."

"What do you mean, you don't cut colored hair?" G.R. says.

"Just what I said," the barber is a little nervous. He stands up and starts to wash some combs, but G.R. is out of his chair now and facing him against a row of mirrors.

"What do you mean by colored," he asks the barber.

My barber looks at his partner. I am getting pissed at G.R. for making something out of this. I should have known better. At home I wouldn't just walk into the Pantlind or the Rowe Hotel and expect to get a haircut.

"It's okay, G.R.," I say, "sit down and let's get going. We've got lots to see yet, Indian villages and copper mines and remnants of old beaver trappers' lodges."

"I want to know what this man means by colored," he says crowding the little barber against a display of Wildroot Cream Oil. The other barber, G.R.'s, says, "Look, mister, why don't the both of you just take your business someplace else." G.R. is a very big man and both barbers together don't weigh two-fifty. He says it again. "I want to know what this man means by colored." He is trailing them in the white cover sheet with black stripes and a little paper dicky around his neck. He looks like Lou Gehrig in a Yankee nightshirt. My barber is afraid to say anything but the other one says, "Well, look at your friend's teeth, real white, see, and the palms of his hands are brownish pink, and his hair is real wooly. I couldn't pull that comb I just used on you through that wooly hair now, could I?" G.R. looks surprised.

"And when you've got white teeth and pinky brown palms and wooly hair and your skin is either black or brown, then most people call you colored. You understand now?"

"But what's that got to do with haircuts?" G.R. asks. Nobody knows what to say now. The barbers don't understand him, so I step up and say, "They need special instruments to cut my hair, G.R. It's like he says, those puny little combs don't go through this, see. I got to go to my own kind of barber so he'll know how to handle me."

G.R. was edgy all through his haircut and he didn't leave a tip, but once we left the barbershop I believe he forgot the whole thing.

But the way he was with those barbers, that's how he operated with girls too. What I mean is, he didn't understand what they were getting at. And this was a shame because he really attracted the ladies. They didn't all come at him like ducks to popcorn, but if he stayed at a school dance for an hour or so the prettiest girl there would be over talking to him and joking and maybe even dancing with him. He never did anything but talk and joke them. He'd walk home with me. I'd say, "G.R., that Peggy Blanton was giving you the eye. Why'd you pass up something like that?"

"Training," he'd say, or "hell, Sonny, I came to the dance with you and I'm leaving with you." If there'd ever been a good looking colored girl there I sure wouldn't have left with him. Don't get me wrong, G.R. was a regular man, nothing the matter with his glands, he just wasn't as interested in girls as most of us were. One weekend in college he drove to Chicago with me and some of the brothers of Alpha Kappa Psi. The brothers wanted some of that good jazz from down around Jackson Avenue and G.R. wanted to see the White Sox play baseball. He took a bus to Comiskey Park for a doubleheader and met us about eight at the Blue Box where those great colored jazz groups used to be in those days. G.R. stood out like a lightbulb. We'd been there all afternoon just mellow and strung out on the music. G.R. came in and wanted to talk baseball. Don't forget that in those days the White Sox really were white and the brothers couldn't have cared less what a group of whites were doing that afternoon up on Lake Shore Drive.

"You should have seen Luke Appling," he was saying, "there's not a man in either league who can play that kind of shortstop." Nobody paid any attention to G.R. He didn't drink and the music was just noise to him. He had taken a book along and was trying to read in the candlelight at The Blue Box. You had to feel sorry for him. It was so dark in there you couldn't see your fingers at arm's length. The atmosphere was heavy with music, liquor, women. I mean the place was cool, relaxed, nobody doing more than tapping a glass, and he sits there squinting over a big blue book, underlining things and scratching his head like he's in the library. He was alone at a table so he could concentrate but I kept my eye on him just in case anything came up. Pretty soon two really smooth numbers come over to his table. Now you'd call them "foxes." They were in evening gowns and very loose, maybe even drunk. He was the only white man in the place and they kind of giggled at him and sat down. I couldn't hear a word they said but I watched every move. I could see because they'd started using a spotlight for the small stage and G.R. was a little to one side of it.

One of the girls starts rubbing the spine of the blue book. The other one takes his finger and puts it on the page. She uses his hand like a big pointer. Maybe she's asking him what some of those big words mean. They're both real close. I start to get a little jealous. I've been there all day with nothing like that kind of action. But, it's like I said, he had a way with the girls. They seem to be talking a lot. The girls are real dreamy on him, one under each arm. It looks like he's reading out loud to them because one of them is holding the book up for him to read from. Whatever he's reading is really breaking the girls up. One of them is kind of tickling his belly with a fingernail between the buttons of his shirt. Sam Conquest and his combo were doing a set then that really had us going. I mean, as much as I was keeping an eye out for G.R., I was into the music too and couldn't really be sure about what my buddy was getting himself into. All I know is that I slipped into the music for just a couple of minutes and when I looked back he was gone. So were the girls and his book. "What the hell," I thought, "anyone else would, why not G.R. too?"

It wasn't until we got back to Ann Arbor and were alone together in his room that G.R. told me what really happened with those two girls.

"I was robbed," he said. "They got about four dollars, but it was all I had. I think Shirlene did it." He showed me his finger with a band-aid on it. "I cut myself on the sequins of her dress. She was giving me kind of a chest rub and my arm was around her. I thought she really liked me, Sonny. I cut my finger real deep on one of those sequins. Doris went to the drug store for a band-aid. While she was gone I think Shirlene got her hand into my trousers and took the four bucks. I was telling them about World War I. They were interested in Woodrow Wilson and the League of Nations. I don't know why they robbed me. If she would have asked me, I'd have given her the four dollars, you know I would have, don't you, Sonny?"

"G.R.," I said, smiling but real sad about him, "you good looking DU social chairman, you football captain and White Sox fan, what the hell is ever going to happen to you in the real world. You can't tell robbery from love, you don't have the ear for music or the eye for color. You can eat donuts and tackle people, you're a good citizen. Get tough, get mean, drink whiskey, swear, slap some chicks around, fuck a few, stop saying yes ma'am, turn in your homework late, cut football practice, cheat on exams, wear dirty socks. . . . I mean, Jesus Christ, be like everybody else." I broke down then. I liked him so much the way he was that it killed me to say these things but I did it for his sake. Somebody had to warn him.

He put his arm around me while I sobbed. "Sonny," he said, "I'll try."

When he ran for Congress he laid off the fry cakes. By then, with his help in getting me a loan, guess who owned the American Bakery? He was making good money as a lawyer. I thought he was crazy to run for the Congress. When I heard it on the radio, I brought a dozen fry cakes fresh from the oven right up to his office in the Federal Square Building. He had a little refrigerator where he kept his milk and his lunch. I hadn't even taken off my white baker's outfit. Some court photographer happened to be in the building and snapped a picture of me in whites carrying the donuts and looking mad as hell. Right after he became the President, the New York *Times* printed that picture and I started getting flooded with requests from T.V. That's when the President's baker thing got started. I sold the American Bakery in '58 and have hardly dipped a fry cake since then, but once a story gets on

T.V. you're stuck with it. Never mind that I'm in auto leasing and sporting goods now, the "President's baker" is what I'm destined to remain.

But the day of that picture was an important one, it was the last day of our real friendship. I slipped past a secretary and gave him the dozen. His desk was full of papers. "Later," he said. "Right now," I told him and I stood there waiting. He was always more sensible after donuts and milk. I went right to his refrigerator and brought out the bottle of Sealtest. I stood there until he was done. "G.R.," I said, "why the hell are you doing this? Aren't you the man who told me you'd never leave Michigan? You've got your friends here and your family, what's all this about going to Washington, D.C.? If you want politics, what about being mayor?"

"Sonny, there's a big country out there and most of it is full of democrats. And there's untold Communists around the world just waiting to get their fingers on your bakery and my law office and everything else we've been working for."

"G.R.," I said, "if you leave this town you're making the mistake of your life."

He looked up at me from his desk. "Sonny, if you're not for me you're against me."

"Get your fry cakes in D.C.," I told him, "and your friends too." I walked out. I voted against him that time and in every other election, and as far as I know he never again tasted one of my donuts. He moved to D.C. that January. Every year I get a Christmas card and a district newsletter but until he became President, that was it. Not even a phone call when he was in town. "What the hell," I thought to myself, "he turned his back on his old friends but I guess it's what he really wanted." He spent twenty-five years in D.C. without me and without those donuts and he didn't seem to miss Michigan all that much either. I, who was his nigger sidekick and his college 'mammy,' never saw his wife nor his kids. When his dad died, I went to the funeral but the crowd was so big I didn't even get into the chapel. At the cemetery, it was private. I thought I saw G.R. in one of the limousines while they were loading the casket in, but you can't run up and talk to a man at a time like that. Yessir, G.R. and I were through, cold turkey, until that night last August when Nixon resigned.

To tell you truth, until the minute it happened none of us believed Nixon would ever be out of there until '76. When they interrupted the Tiger game with the news you could have knocked me over with a feather. People all over town started walking around the streets like they were drunk. The JCCs painted a big Home of the President poster and had it up at the northern city limits within an hour. My mother, who's in a home now, called up to remind me that she taught the President how to tie his shoes. He was fast, Mama remembered, and double knotted every time. And the truth is, although I had resented him being a Congressman all those years, I spent a few minutes just saying out loud, "G.R., Mr. President." I said it over and over. I was still saying it when I got a phoned-in telegram from his press secretary. "Sonny—Emergency. Air Force One will pick you up midnight Grand Rapids airport." It was signed "G.R." A White House operator read it to me at ten o'clock while I was watching the newsmen do a wrap-up on Nixon. He wasn't officially President until the next day but already he could send Air Force One out to do his errands.

I knew what this meant. I packed a blue suit and my own deep fryer, and it's a good thing I did. With all the stuff in that White House kitchen, there isn't a single deep fryer. I heard one of the cooks grumbling that Jackie Kennedy had it thrown away and Johnson used to eat all his fries on the ranch. Nixon only cared for pan fried. The cooks were mighty suspicious. Here was the new President who they didn't even know sending over his own old boy with a personal deep fryer.

I was met at the airport by a nice young fellow. He took my grocery order. The Presidential limousine waited outside the all night Safeway while we shopped. I overbought, made twelve dozen because for all I knew he wanted to treat the whole cabinet. By seven a.m., on the morning of the day he was to become the President, G.R. had his fry cakes, crisp on the outside, soft on the inside. I was a little nervous in case I'd lost my touch but this was one sweet batch. An FBI man delivered all twelve dozen. The White House cooks treated me very uppity. They were all tears about Nixon, wondering whether he could stomach bacon and eggs for his last breakfast, and here I was whipping out twelve dozen donuts for the new boy. They didn't know if they could keep up with an appetite like that.

I hung around the kitchen because I didn't know where else to go. You wouldn't believe the chaos. Nixon sent back the coffee, bacon, and eggs. He was going to be on T.V. at ten. They sent up cream of wheat, rye toast, coffee, and vegetable juice. It came back too. The juice glass was empty but there were lipstick stains on it.

"The poor man hasn't moved his bowels yet," the cook said when he saw Nixon giving his last speech. "Without morning coffee, he is cement. He hasn't slept either. Oh God, what's going to happen to all of us." He looked at me and then spit into the sink. We were crowded together watching a twelve-inch Sony color set.

I had a late breakfast with the kitchen staff and hung around the T.V. for G.R.'s swearing in and his speech. I played some gin rummy with a few maids. Limousines kept pulling up outside but the whole place was quiet as a white funeral parlor. Just before noon that same young man who met my plane came into the kitchen and gave me an envelope. There was a regular Central Air Lines ticket in it but for first class, a hundred-dollar bill, and a note. The note said, "Just like old times. Thanks, G.R."

I watched him on T.V. with Nixon's kitchen help. They were all zombies by noon. One of them said he dreamed that Nixon changed his mind in the air and was going to phone in at eleven fifty-nine to say hold off that swearing in. I was the only one blindly excited and proud. And I don't have to tell you that my man was cool as a cucumber and straight as an arrow. There were some snickers in the kitchen when the camera showed General Haig brushing some crumbs off the new President's lapel. I saw them in color, the yellow crumbs I knew. "Here fellas," I said, tossing the hundred in the air, "have a drink on your new boss."

I was home by nightfall and haven't heard from him since. I guess that he's trying to make a go of it with that bunch of cooks he inherited. Still, who knows G.R. like I do? When it gets really tough in that oval office he'll start to smell the fry cakes. When that happens, watch out Kissinger and the Joint Chiefs. Mr. Donut and Dixie Cream won't be enough. His lips will start to twitch and his teeth will bite the air. He'll remember the glorious peninsula and the three Great Lakes of the Thumb. His mouth will water for the real thing. And when that happens, in the pinch, the President knows old Sonny won't let him down.

PASTORALE

SUSAN ENGBERG

Susan Engberg was born in Dubuque, Iowa, and educated at Lawrence College in Wisconsin. She is married, with two daughters. Her stories have appeared in the *Kenyon Review*, the *Massachusetts Review*, *Ascent*, the *Sewanee Review*, and the O. Henry volumes for 1969, 1977, and 1978. Stories are forthcoming in the *Southern Review*, the *Prairie Schooner*, and *Epoch*.

There was a woman who for a time loved a younger man. Her name was Catherine, and she had lost a child. Her daughter had been in a coma one week, two weeks, and then one morning in October her expression had changed slightly and she had died. Hanna. She had had honey-colored hair and pale eyes with an outer rim of darker blue to the irises. Until the brain tumor she had been healthy enough and lively and competent. She had bought two goats with her own money, raised them up, rode with John to have them bred, and when they freshened, milked them herself, morning and night, and with part of the milk made yogurt for the family. Catherine took over the milking. The boys should be doing that, John said, but she wanted it for herself; the goats, at any rate, were almost dry.

She was forty; Hanna had been ten. Sometimes the rounded numbers rose up in her mind as a meaningless chant—ten, twenty, thirty, forty—and then she would look backward and forward and see nothing but inexpressive decades. Her own face, resting against the goat's fur above the stream of milk, felt used up, like a landscape of dry runnels. She cleaned the stall methodically, accepting everything—the smells of urine and dung, the impatience of the goats, the cold in her hands as she fetched the water—as she had begun to accept the death itself.

Copyright © 1976 by The University of the South. First published in the *Sewanee Review*. Reprinted by permission of the editor and the author.

But beneath this methodical impassive continuance of life, she could feel her grief changing into something less bearable than the immediate anguish; it was a sense of absolute physical loss, of strange yearning: she wanted to touch the child again. There had been no chance to be alone with her, dead. At night Catherine would lie in the dark and think that she might be all right if only she could cradle the child's actual corpse one more time.

But of course that was impossible. Months were passing. The adolescent energy of their two boys continued on a course of its own, as if it had been a stream of water passing through the house and out again, seldom anything to hold on to, and she had the feeling that wherever they were going, they were already on their way. Childhood had never seemed to her so brief.

She and John were the maintainers. In the past they had occasionally joked to each other, companionably, about how they were merely the keepers of an establishment. A door would slam somewhere, there would be a thumping on the stairs, a call from the barnyard, and when they looked at each other, what was between them had to do with seventeen years of marriage and the pleasure they could still take in each other and the way these people who were their children had invaded their house, but only for a time. Now between them Catherine sensed a self-consciousness that it seemed discussing would only aggravate, and although they might be alone, she no longer felt the same privacy. She would lie in bed, watching him undress, and the sight of his bare back, twisting to pick up a shoe in the half-light, or of his hair and beard— how grizzled he had become!—made her want to cry out to break through this theatrical intimacy, but the sound remained voiceless. He seemed to have become gentler with her, sometimes distant. They talked, of course, and they had wept together and with Tom and Drew, and they both had their work, which was a blessing.

John had been having good success with his pottery; he would be showing at two large invitationals that early summer in addition to the usual regional exhibits, and he was working steadily now, seldom sleeping late in the morning, seldom coming in early from the shop to read or tinker with an odd repair. She herself was finishing up one commission from the nursing school, the illustrations for a handbook for expectant mothers, and on the strength of this had been given another by a biology professor, an essay on reproduction intended for high-school and college students. The coincidence between these subjects and Hanna's death she endured, because of her desire for work; she was practical and energetic by nature, and she had always handled periods of unclarity or doubt simply by applying herself to what was at hand. Several times a month she drove in to the university with her sketches, had quiet conferences in one office or another, ate lunch in one of the cafeterias around the science and medical complex, shopped a bit perhaps, or saw a friend, and then drove home.

Once she had felt drawn up to the fourth floor of the hospital past the room where Hanna had died; another child lay in the bed, and another mother sat in the green vinyl chair by the window. A shout of laughter came down the hall from the nursing station; a metal cart was clattering along a hallway out of sight. She didn't go back again.

She looked at children on the street, blond children, and at mothers who didn't seem to understand the full value of what was theirs. Once in the checkout line of a supermarket, she had rushed away in confusion, leaving behind the basket of groceries, because of her overwhelming desire to pick up the child in front of her and hold her close, perhaps even to run away with her and to keep running until she could find a quiet place to talk.

She tried to tell herself that it was natural her sorrow should be taking these different forms, and that she must simply wait and accept its evolving transformations.

One late afternoon as she drove into their lane, a thick wet February snow was beginning to fall, windless, very still, like a false oblivion, and two crows were screaming over the catalpa skeletons at the bottom of the pasture. Her body was worn down by the last stages of the flu. John too had been ill, and she found him in bed, muffled in a shawl, reading, smoking his pipe. His clay-splotched trousers hung from a chair.

"You look ravishing and curative," he said as he stretched and threw aside his book. His stiff hair was raked up and the creases beneath his eyes looked personal and contemplative.

"I'm frazzled and sick," she said. "You're just playing the lascivious old man again; none of it is genuine." But she went to him and sat down close, laying a hand on his chest.

"Spending an afternoon in bed has had certain effects," he said.

"You've improved your mind and the state of your health, I hope."

"My mind has been rotting away with carnal lust. For you, of course, my dear," he added.

"You sound venereal," she said as she rested her weight against him. The play of their bantering went on by itself, remote. Outside the window the snow continued, thicker now and bluish. "Where are the boys?" she asked.

"I told them to go out and do the goats for you."

"That was nice." It was all distant, even the sadness, even the dried mask that was pretending to be her face.

They were snowed in the next day, and on the following noon Louie came with the tractor to clear the lane. He brought in the mail, standing huge and good-natured in the mudroom in his layers of sweat shirts and coveralls, talking about the snow.

"That was some snow," he said.

Catherine watched him trudge out to the corncrib. Once in the army in Alaska Louie's legs had gotten frozen from the knees down. Watching him work made her think of life as being a matter of putting one stolid foot in front of another, endlessly.

"Well, he's coming," said John, holding out a letter, "Laurits Jorgensen—that fellow I told you about. He's taken the apprenticeship and has agreed to twenty hours of work per week in exchange. How does that sound?"

"For how long?" asked Catherine. She read hurriedly down the paragraphs.

"Six months or so—we'll see how it goes." He sat in his ragged down vest, nursing his pipe and coffee and slowly working himself up to go out to the shop. It was a familiar sight. He had been up until four that morning with a firing.

"This is going to be good for you, isn't it?" said Catherine. "You might actually get the new kiln finished."

"He does say he's good with tools. He's a find, I'd say."

"You'll take him sight unseen?"

"I trust Merton—he wouldn't send a slouch."

"He'll get a room in town, I suppose?" asked Catherine, returning to her dish of fruit and yogurt. She had been up at seven with the boys and for most of the morning, while John had slept with the covers over his head, had been at her drawing board in their sunny bedroom.

"He could do that," said John.

Later in the afternoon he came in for a sandwich and brought it up to the bedroom. He squeezed the back of her neck, kissed her ear, and then sat down in the old wing chair. She heard him biting through lettuce and sucking from his can of beer.

"I've been thinking," he said as he set aside his empty plate and leaned back with the beer can balancing on his chest, "that fellow Laurits could take Hanna's room, if you'd agree. It seems a waste of time for him to go back and forth to town every day when he could just as well stay right here."

Catherine turned her pencil around and around in the sharpener. She squinted at the network of mammary ducts on her paper.

"We'd have to do something about the curtains," she said at last.

"That's simple enough, isn't it? It just seems to me that it's time now to start using the room; I mean, love, we've got to do it some day."

She heard the school bus on the road and looked out to the lane where Tom and Drew were jumping down from its steps.

"All right," she said slowly, turning back to her husband. "I think we could manage that."

II

"You must be Catherine," says the voice in the barn door. She turns from the fresh straw she is forking down and sees his shape against the light. It is April.

She goes over and sees him better. He has blond hair that is parted in the middle, and it hangs straight on either side of his face. His eyebrows are black.

"Then you're Laurits."

"The master there sent me out to meet you." He tosses his head slightly toward the shop.

She smiles as he smiles. It is one of the first warm days.

"This is quite a place; it's really beautiful. What else do you have besides goats?"

"Nothing, except a hundred or so cats."

"You own it all?" He is leaning against the old timbers of the doorway and looking out towards the undulating Iowa fields.

"Just the house and the barn and the shop. Louie has the land.

You'll meet Louie before long." The pregnant goats are outside the door drinking from a trough. She has filled a large pan with grain. Now she heaves up a basket of old straw and droppings.

"I'll take that," says Laurits. "Where to?"

"That dung heap over there."

"This is fantastic," he says as he jauntily brings back the basket. He tosses the hair from his eyes.

They walk together toward the shop where they find John sponging smooth the rim of a large tureen. The reddish clay glistens like a moistened lower lip. Catherine has seen John take a finished piece like this, to her eyes perfect, and slice it relentlessly apart to reveal a slight inconsistency in the thickness of the form. There are other days when he is unable to work at all; then he might lie hour after hour in the darkened bedroom, harshly humorous against himself and the world. She has understood for a long time that her strength is different from his.

"Well," he says to Catherine, screwing his face above the pipe smoke, "the slave has arrived. Have you shown him to his miserable quarters?"

"Not yet," says Catherine, "he's been helping."

"That's good, lad. I'm glad to hear you haven't wasted these precious minutes cavorting aimlessly in the barnyard. It's work we want around here. Work! do you hear?" He makes his eyes look fierce and insane.

"Yes, sir," drawls Laurits. He has propped an arm along a drying rack and seems as much absorbed in the tureen as in either of them. Catherine wonders where he has gotten his confidence.

John seems invigorated, boyish himself. He stops the wheel and draws a taut string under the base of the tureen. "That's it," he says; "let's go talk about the future."

They are very gay. Catherine sees that it is a good combination of personalities. When the boys come home, they hang on the railings beside the porch swing, fascinated. Laughter gushes out over the lawn and the beds of spring flowers and the freshly tilled garden. They are talking about the new kiln for salt glazing, about the distances to the surrounding towns, about the farm girls in the neighborhood. John allows himself a leer. "They grow up fast around here," he says.

A meadowlark is singing from the walnut tree by the lane, a piercing, slurred call that seems to contain the entire moment.

Clouds are rapidly riding out of the west, fanning out into an expanse of sky and disappearing over the house. Catherine feels herself breathless at the spaciousness these approaching masses make visible. She is sitting on the steps with her coat collar up, hugging her knees. Tonight she will make a large salad with fresh mushrooms and chopped cress. Her mind is planning. She looks at her sons, and it seems weeks since she has noticed them. They are growing quickly. Their heads of identical brown curly hair are like lively, irrepressible masses of energy.

Later, in the night, she wakes and feels the house full of sleepers. Catherine turns her face into her pillow and smells her own hair. Her body is radiating heat, her cheeks feel smooth. Sometime during the night the first of the goat kids is born.

Laurits makes competent pottery, mostly smaller pieces like bowls and mugs and casseroles. He does not seem apologetic about what he has to learn. He listens carefully, and he is keeping a chart of glazing mixtures. When he sits at the kitchen table for tea, he turns the mug thoughtfully, sometimes holding it by the handle and sometimes cupping both hands around its belly.

Today he has come back from town with the onion sets Catherine has ordered. When he has made the tea, he calls up the stairs to her. He seems to like the kitchen. He talks to Catherine about an idea he has for building some shelves over the stove; getting up, he shows her how they would span, from here to here, with hooks underneath for pans and open space above for pottery. He has started to grow a blond mustache, and now when Catherine looks at his face she notices even more the darkness of his brows. She has stopped being surprised at how comfortable Laurits seems talking about these everyday household matters. He makes himself useful, but he doesn't seem to need their praise.

When they finish their tea, they go down the side yard together to the garden. They take turns making trenches with the hoe and placing the onion sets. Catherine has already planted radishes, beets, and carrots. Laurits says that when the time comes he will make some circular supports for the tomatoes from some old fencing he saw in the corncrib loft. He follows along beside her, pushing dirt onto the onions with the flat of his hoe. Catherine can feel the heat of the sun through her jacket, and she thinks that there are only seven weeks until the summer solstice. She has stopped being surprised at how comfortable she is working with Laurits; it is almost as peaceful as working alone, and yet even the simplest of motions seems to be enhanced. She is crumbling compost into the bottom of a trench, and her hands seem to be understanding exactly the nature of its richness. When she was a girl Catherine used to sketch her own hands, with wonderment, and now, remembering that, she seems to be reminded of the richness of her own nature. She straightens up to see Laurits at the edge of the garden, aiming walnuts up into the tree at the last few nuts still clinging to the branches in their green casings.

Laurits is reading in the rocking chair by the dining-room window. After lunch he always takes this rest; Catherine has told him he reminds her of her grandfather, and he has told her that he reminds himself of his own grandfather. She has come up the lane with the mail, and she taps on his window as she passes on her way to the shop. In a few minutes she returns to the house.

"You have two letters today, Laurits," she says. "I think your lovely lady must be missing you." The postmarks are from California. Laurits has said that her name is Leah and that she is studying marine biology. She is twenty years old; Laurits is twenty-three.

Laurits puts down his magazine and takes the letters. A Swedish ivy plant is hanging in the window above the library table; Laurits begins to read his letters beneath this cascade of scalloped leaves. Outside the window green maple-blossom discs drift in the sun. Catherine sees Louie in the south field beyond the garden making a sweeping turn at the end of a row with the corn planter lifted from the ground; he drives with one hand as he twists in the tractor seat to gauge the beginning of the new row. Her own hands feel empty.

She pours herself a cup of coffee in the kitchen and goes upstairs to her drawing board. The bed is unmade, and the air is warm and still, almost like a summer afternoon. She is working on a schematic frontal section of the female reproductive organs, using books and charts loaned by Maxine, the biology professor. The new women's center has inquired about the publication date of this booklet; it will be used as well by high-school family-life classes and will be among the free literature available to incoming college freshmen. Maxine is in her late fifties. One of her daughters ran away from home at the age of seventeen; it was very bad for a while, Maxine has said, but then gradually things worked themselves out. Catherine looks at her drawing and understands that what she is seeing is a section through a moment in evolution.

It is June. The boxes are packed, the van is loaded for John's Chicago fair. Today Tom is fifteen. They are having his party at lunchtime, before Catherine and John must leave, and while Tom assembles his new fishing gear, Catherine cuts down through the cake. John is at the other end of the table, waiting for the coffee to be ready. His effort the last few weeks has been tremendous. Even he has called himself a maniac. The kiln has been fired twice a week. His final project has been a series of huge vases, almost human in their forms, with gentle bellies and flared rims and handles akimbo—his vestal vessels, he has said, giving one of them a pat.

He works at his pipe and squints at Tom; Catherine can see him searching for a humorous attack: no son of his is going to come off easily from a birthday.

"That's pretty sophisticated gear for a young whippersnapper like you," he says.

"Whippersnappers are good at things like this," says Tom as he carefully fits together the sections of the rod. He is barely suppressing his excitement with the gleaming tackle and newly fitted-out box, all chosen by his father, everyone knows. Laurits has promised to take the boys catfishing and camping overnight on the river. Drew watches everything from a calculated slouch.

"So, Laurits," says John, "do you think you can keep these lads in line? No ruckuses on the Mississippi?"

"We kids will not besmirch the family name," says Laurits. "Simply think of us as young gentlemen off on a naturalistic holiday."

"Mind you look to the goats before you leave," says John to the boys.

Catherine pours the coffee in silence. She is disorganized; her bag is scarcely packed. She is remembering the long labor of her first son's birth, her partial disbelief that it was actually happening . . .

"Now there's a well got-up woman," says John to her later in the bedroom. "The brow, the bosom, the lovely thighs—a figure-head for our ship, worthy, if you pardon the expression, of breasting the crest. Together, my dear, we will navigate the evil city and bring back lots and lots of money."

"John, will you please be quiet? You're exhausting me."

"I'm exhausting you?"

"How was I exhausting you?" he asks on the highway.

"Just talk straight now, all right? We're alone, there's no one listening."

"We are alone, aren't we?" he says that night in the hotel, smiling down at her. City sirens pulsate on an eerie stratum of air, disembodied. All night there are voices and shouts, neon-light waves. Catherine does not feel that she is sleeping, but then she wakes, terrified for the safety of her children; in a moment she remembers that one child is already dead. John sleeps curved and dark.

The bathroom is white, white everywhere, but she can only think of the thousands of people who have touched its slickness without leaving a mark. She sees that her period has begun: her skin, their toothbrushes, and the brownish blood are the only colors in the room.

She sleeps again, floating on sound and the sensations of her body. Hanna is calling her on the telephone, a child's voice, difficult to make out. Yes? she says to her. Yes? Speak up! Everything but her own voice is indistinguishable; the telephone cord is slowly disintegrating. She wakes into the morning.

"This hasn't been too bad for a rickety-dinky hotel," says John, pleased with himself.

He is opening the curtains. "Will you come with me to the village square, my love, to peddle our wares?"

She puts on a large straw hat and over her swollen breasts a white blouse, open at the neck.

The week before Laurits had worked bare-chested in the garden, and she had seen that he was smooth and compact, self-contained. He had knotted a red scarf around his brow, and his back had glistened.

"Come on, lass, let's get a move on," says John.

Movement: she must move in spite of herself; she can no longer be in last week's garden, bending over vegetables.

"Are you all right, love?" asks John in the coffee shop.

Outside in the street the light is too bright; there is too much light, everywhere; even beneath the mottled plane trees at the fair she finds only an overexposed confusion of dapple. She hides beneath her hat.

"You're quiet, love," says John after he has made another sale. Year after year many of the same people return to his booth. Catherine looks up to see the face of Dr. Avakian, inviting them to dinner that night. She feels herself nodding. Dr. Avakian has greyed remarkably in the past year. He and his wife live childless in a high apartment near the lake. Catherine knows all about the evening already; she can see the iced wine, the crêpes filled with crab, the fresh strawberries, the strong coffee and pastry in the living room above the reflecting water. Each year Dr. Avakian buys two, perhaps three or four hundred dollars' worth of pottery. It is obvious that he considers himself a patron and that he must search for ways in which to spend the money of his middle age.

Catherine presses her knuckles into her eyes. The innards of her body are heavy and sinking toward the gravity of earth; within and without the world seems constructed of motion and loss. She tries to imagine her sons in a rented boat at the mouth of a Mississippi slough; what she sees is Laurits, selecting bait from a bucket.

As they speed home across Illinois the next afternoon, the landscape for many miles outside the urban fringes seems tentative and barren, as if it had already lost its vigor in the face of the impending lava-creep of the city. It is not really until the Mississippi itself that Catherine begins to relax. Looking down from the bridge, she sees the wide river flowing effortlessly between its banks and feels reassured, as if she herself had caught an easier current. Inland John turns onto back gravel roads and they approach the farm into the sun, beside newly cultivated corn rows that look like giant thin-man legs running with the car. Catherine opens her window and takes a full breath of earthy air; she feels the presence of her heart.

The weather turns very warm. At the end of the month Tom and Drew prepare to take a bus out to camp in Colorado where they will ride horses, backpack, and fish for trout.

"I hope those whippersnappers appreciate this," says John as he closes the van on their gear.

Catherine takes the pipe from his mouth to kiss him. "Take care of yourself in that big-town bus station."

"I plan on being alert," says John. "Not a hussy will pass my notice."

"You sure know how to talk big," she says, feeling his arm around her. The boys are in the shop saying good-bye to Laurits. The yard is still and empty except for scattered dozing cats, and yet Catherine thinks that perhaps she and her husband are being observed. He seems charming and inscrutable, and as she lets him shuffle her through a few dance steps and lower her into an embrace of mock passion, she finds herself looking up with alarm into his grinning face.

"John," she says suddenly. "Maybe I should come along for the afternoon. Do you want company?"

"I thought you wanted some precious solitude."

"I did. I do." She looks at her watch. "There really isn't time to get ready."

"Look," he says, taking her by the shoulders, "I'll take care of our sons, and I'll take care of myself, and you take some time for yourself the way you planned, all right?"

Catherine stands silent in front of him, and for a moment his mannerisms seem to fall away, and what slams against her is his suffering.

The boys come loping across the yard from the shop.

She wants to touch him. Her throat tightens into pain. Hanna! John!

Laurits follows slowly behind the boys, wearing a rubber apron, his forearms and hands reddish.

"The troops are assembled," says John, and the moment has passed.

Catherine kisses her sons, everyone is joking, and then the doors slam and the van pulls away.

"I hope they get some good trout," says Laurits; "there's nothing in the world like mountain trout."

Catherine nods. She goes inside the back door and presses her fist to her mouth. "O, my God," she hears herself whispering, "O, my God," and she feels that her hands are being flung, taut, above her head. And then she picks up a rainjacket from the floor and

puts it back on a hook. In the kitchen she watches her hands
finishing the dishes. When they are done and the plants hanging
above the sink have been watered, she takes down a sketchpad
from the top of the refrigerator and goes out to the side porch.
She draws the walnut tree and in the foreground the trunk of the
wounded maple. Then she goes down to the garden and sits close
to a pepper plant, letting her pencil understand the way the white
blossoms are giving way to tiny green buds of fruit. She is sitting
on a mulch of straw. Not far away a yellow and black spider is zig-
zagging a reinforcement in his web between two tomato plants.
It is almost too hot to stay where she is, but she continues, turning
from the peppers to the fuzzy eggplant leaves, and then to the
squash vines and nasturtiums. For a long time she feels as if only
the motions of her hands are keeping back the tears; then gradually she begins to forget about everything but the nature of what
she is observing. At last she takes off her shoes and lies back on the
hot straw.

All around her are the rustlings of insects or of plants growing.
A hawk circles several times overhead and then banks out of sight.
She shields her eyes with a forearm smelling of tomato leaves and
herbs.

She doesn't know if she has slept, but at an indeterminate moment the air has changed; a faint cool dampness has swept the
garden. She sits up. From the south a mass of round white clouds
is approaching rapidly; from the north a front of blackness is bearing down with amazing speed. It is fascinating, she thinks, and
the heat, thank God, will lift; then an instant later she knows the
danger.

"Laur-its, Laur-its," she yells, scrambling into her shoes and running to the shop. She throws the sketchpad inside the screen door,
shouting, "Laurits, a storm is coming," and without stopping further heads for the small goat-pasture behind the barn. "Here
babes, here babes," she calls to the already frightened animals.
She has to lift the kids over the stone sill of the barn. One door
after another she runs to secure; the cloud masses converge as she
is struggling with the huge double doors of the barn's central pas-
sageway. Laurits appears beside her. By the time they are running
for the house, a whipping rain has begun. A trash can sails across
the yard, then a tree branch.

They tend to doors and windows. The house is moaning, the

windows rattling, the metal weather stripping whining above even
the high-pitched fury of the storm. Outside the air is greenish
through the almost horizontal slant of the rain. A bolt of lightning to the west appears to stab a nearby field; thunder shakes the
house. Laurits thuds down the stairs with a blanket around his
neck. He takes her by the arm—"Upstairs is all right, let's get
down"—and they descend into the basement fruit cellar where the
hundred-year-old lime foundation stones are damp and motionless. Laurits sinks down underneath a workbench and opens his
blanketed arm like a wing for her to enter.

They are in one of Hanna's old forgotten playhouses, one of the
many hideouts that she had fashioned for herself around the farm.
This one consists of a few peach crates beneath the bench, set up
as shelves, and on the floor a mildewed playpen pad. The child
had tied some yarn around one of the crates as a sort of decoration, and inside Catherine finds a canning jar filled with rotting
kernels of corn and one large spider, alive. She puts it down
slowly. The mind of her child seems near enough to touch.

Catherine cannot stop the tears now; she feels that she has
never been so close to her sorrow. Lowering her forehead to
Laurits's knee, she lets herself become a rounded shape of grieving. "Hey," he says, "hey," as he begins to stroke her hair and
back. Her body is wracked by an accumulation of feeling, as if the
sobs are coming out of her bones. "Catherine," says Laurits,
"here, here." He has taken her close to him in the cramped musty
space; from upstairs comes the faint screaming of the wind.
"Catherine, what is it, what is it? There, don't talk. Catherine."
His hands over her ears are muffling all sound. Her brow is being
stroked; he is kissing her eyes. They are underneath a storm, in a
space made by a child. "You're having a bad time," says Laurits,
holding her head against him. She is snuffling now and breathing
more quietly; her brain feels as if a searing connection has been
made between its two sides, leaving behind a warm fluidity.
"That's better now," says Laurits. She feels herself being rocked
slightly; with her eyes closed she has a slight sensation of weight-
lessness. Laurits is cupping her breast with a gentle hand of comfort.

"There now," says Laurits after a time. "Let's go upstairs and
see what's been happening. Do you think it's safe?" He wraps the
blanket around them both and pulls her in close against him as

they start up the stairs. "Catherine," he says, stopping halfway up to kiss her hair. He lowers his forehead to hers, and she lets her hands rest upon his chest.

They go from room to room, window to window. The yard and lane are strewn with tree limbs, and one huge branch has crashed down through the electrical wires to the shop. "Laurits, that's a hot line then, we should call," but when they go to the telephone, those wires are silent. They test random lights and all are dead. In the wake of the lightning and thunder and furious wind is now a heavy turbulent rain, being blown in thick curtains across the fields. The light inside the house is a brownish chiaroscuro.

Laurits sits down in a chair against a kitchen wall. Catherine goes across the room and sits beneath the useless telephone. They are being careful now. "I'm going to guess that for you there has always been only John," Laurits says quietly.

"How do you know that? Do you find it strange?"

"I think I would have expected it."

"It's not that I haven't loved others, but well, yes, there's been only John. We moved from place to place; we went through a lot together. And then, too, I've been a mother for a long time." She draws an uneven breath. "You must understand that has something to do with it."

"You don't have to apologize."

"It's different for you?"

"Literally, yes, but I've told you, Catherine, I'm my own grandfather; I'm not sure where I belong."

"And Leah?"

"Leah? Leah is like water, you could say she follows her own natural laws. She's living with someone else this summer."

"I had no idea," says Catherine. "Is that all right with you?"

"I take large chances," says Laurits. "She's a brilliant girl; she's absolutely set in her scientific interests." In the half-light Catherine watches him shrug. "We'll see," he says.

"And meanwhile, back at the farm?" she asks gently.

"God, Catherine, don't mock me—are you mocking me?" He comes and stands in front of her. "Answer me." He is smiling.

"I'm not mocking you, Laurits. It's just us, here; I'm seeing it all."

He hunkers down in front of her and circles his arms around her hips. "Why were you crying? Can you tell me that?"

She tips back her head against the wall and feels how close the tears still are. Images are welling to the surface: the face of John that noon, the layers and layers of his reality; the countless vibrant expressions of her daughter, her lovely child; her own life, obscure essence, visible movement, change, desire.

Laurits has laid his head in her lap. "Come on," he says, "we can't talk here." He lifts her to her feet. "Come on, follow grandpa." He leads her up the stairs and into Hanna's room, his room, and to the same bed where the child had first wakened in the night with the pain—a headache no mother's hand could touch.

"Laurits—"

"We'll be good. Just talk to me." He covers them both with a light blanket. "Just tell me." He opens her blouse and lays his cheek against her breast; she can feel the steady waves of his warm breath across her nipple. She strokes his hair and begins to talk. She tells him about the hospital, the days and nights that became indistinguishable, the one resurgence of hope when the child's eyelids fluttered and her mouth seemed to be straining to speak; she tells him about the dreams, how she is certain that the child's spirit is present, that the other side of death exists even though it's untouchable; and then she is talking about John, about the days when he cannot work at all and his mockery turns inward and consumes his energy and her own as well, about the way the death has cut through their marriage to reveal a section-view of bewilderment barely concealed by stylized action—not that they aren't tender, not that there isn't pleasure in each other and in life: it's just—how shall she put it—it's perhaps that a reality has been given them that they haven't been able to incorporate yet; it doesn't fit into the old patterns. Does he understand, is she making sense at all? And then she realizes that it is herself she is talking about, grieving for: the inability of her hands to help her child, the weakness of her mind to understand what is now happening, the confusions of her heart. Her voice continues. She doesn't know what is coming next, she simply doesn't know, and she is asking herself, will she be able to live it?

When John returns at dark, they are in the kitchen making supper in candlelight. He is drenched from having run up through the rain from the end of the branch-choked lane. "The survivors!"

he exclaims, coming to the stove and putting an arm around each of them. "Did you know, my children, that you have only narrowly escaped the fate of Louie's great-aunt?"

"We haven't had any radio, John," says Catherine. She has laid her own cheek against his wet one.

"The tornado touched down four miles north of here."

"That close!" whistles Laurits.

"Was anyone hurt, John?" asks Catherine.

"No one reported, but I saw damage to buildings, and lots of trees."

"What's this about Louie's great-aunt?" asks Laurits.

"You mean you haven't heard that story yet?" says John. "Catherine, love, I'll leave you to the telling while I go get dry and then may I suggest a bottle of wine for this murky night?" He shudders dramatically in his clothes.

She lays a hand on his arm. "And how were the boys? Did they seem to feel all right about leaving?"

"They couldn't wait to get away, and that's the honest truth. They said, bye, Dad—that's all, just bye old Dad." John waves his own hand in farewell and soft-shoes himself out of the kitchen.

Catherine begins to set the table.

Laurits is looking at her. "So? the story?"

"Well, once upon a time Louie had a great-aunt. I don't know her name but she lived in the days of high button shoes. Now this great-aunt was caught up in a tornado, picked up bodily; and she was finally found in a field two miles away, unhurt but covered with scratches and bruises, her hair was a mass of brambles, and—here's the crazy thing—the wind had left her absolutely stark naked except for one high button shoe."

"One high button shoe?" repeats Laurits.

"One high button shoe."

"She was lucky. But she must have been mortified."

"So to speak."

They are laughing, and it is a great relief. The thought of Louie's great-aunt being propelled naked through the air with one external item of dignity intact is exactly the image they need for the end of this day, in this world of astounding variety. "What a story," says Laurits, whooping, breathless, and then he says more quietly, "but she must have blacked out, surely the force of the wind must have knocked her out."

"I suppose so," says Catherine, and she pauses above a sliced tomato. "Tell me, Laurits, if you had your choice, would you go
through a tornado like that conscious or unconscious?"

"Good God, Catherine," says Laurits, "I'm going to make you
answer that one yourself."

III

One hot afternoon in September while Laurits and John were
testing the new kiln, Catherine took herself for a walk along the
back roads of the section. There had been no rain for weeks, and
the hushed crops and weeds were coated with a film of dust from
the baked roadbed. Catherine strode along in spite of the heat;
her body was strong from the months of outdoor work, and she
felt vital and continuous to herself beside the stretching fields.
The landscape to some eyes would have seemed monotonous, she
supposed, but she was coming to exult in its apparent plainness;
here her eyes could spread out, rested, and her mind could empty
itself, and she could be seeing nothing but straight road, fields,
fences, and predominant sky until one detail—a changing of light,
the thwacking up of a pheasant from a thicket, or a stream of
water, invisible from a distance, cutting through the surface ferti-
lity—would simultaneously define for her both the plainness and
variety of her surroundings, like the first stroke on a sheet of blank
paper.

Today she was thinking how much this vast swelling land
seemed to have retained its character of primordial ocean floor,
and her own eyes were seeing it: the knowledge of a progression
through millennia to this present moment of late-summer dry
lushness and quiet was passing through her, making her a special
child of the universal elements. She stepped off the road and sat
down in the minimal shade of an Osage orange tree, looking up
with curiosity at the globs of wrinkled greenish fruit. It was true:
she felt almost like a child, and what was more, she was gradually
understanding that her own lost child was being returned to her,
not as she in her suffering had dreamt of the reunion, but simply
as she herself was moving to the embrace.

She rested until she became thirsty, and then she got up and
continued on the last two-mile stretch, lowering her eyes slightly
under the sun, tasting dust on the dryness of her lips; and but for
this chance direction of her gaze, she might have missed the dead

frog: levelled by a car in the dust of the road, it was like the perfect shadow of a leap, yet really there, paper-thin and dried, complete with flattened eye sockets and delicately spread feet. She bent down to study the creature, her own shadow a foreshortened shape beside her on the dust; and toward this desiccated carcass that like a hieroglyph said purely, *frog,* and toward the even more cryptic configuration of herself she felt a quickened outpouring of that which long ago had come to be called love.

ALL RIGHT

BLAIR FULLER

Blair Fuller lives most of the year in San Francisco with
his wife and two children. An older daughter is now in
college. He is part owner of two bookstores in that city.
In 1970, he and Oakley Hall founded the annual Squaw
Valley Community of Writers, and they continue as di-
rectors. This is his second appearance in the O. Henry
collection, and his most recent novel is *Zebina's Mountain*, Harper & Row, 1975. In 1978 he will be teaching for
one quarter at the University of California, Irvine.

My mother's stance as she told us, summoned and seated, that
our father would "have us" for the summer and that this would
be an annual arrangement did not encourage questions. In a week
my mother's cook and a maid would go with us children by overnight train to North Haven, Maine, where he had rented a house.
We had never seen North Haven but neither Sage, who was thirteen, nor I, eleven, nor Jill, seven, expressed much curiosity.

He met us in the city at the Grand Central Station gate. He
looked business-brown in the yellowish light except for a new
straw hat with a bright, polka dotted band, and among com-
muters he looked surprisingly like just another one. His suit was
wrinkled and he carried a briefcase and a roll of architectural,
onion-skin drawings under his arm. He was sweating and seemed
distracted.

Halfway down the platform we said goodbye to the cook and
the maid who were going further forward to the coaches where
they would ride sitting up. Although both had been with us since
before my birth their flowered dresses and little church-going hats
and their cheap, strapped suitcases made them strangers under the
flood lights. Their pale, Irish faces were flushed.

There were four bunks in our compartment and my sisters and

Copyright © 1977 by Risht Press. Reprinted by permission.

I argued over who should have which, where to put the suitcases and what we needed for the night. "Make up your minds, for God's sake," my father said in a familiar tone that made me feel spiritless and sickly cool.

We turned out our lights as the train was clicking uptown through the tunnel. As it came out onto the elevated tracks, I was peering around the shade to see the people in the lighted Harlem windows. We stopped at 125th St. and when we were moving again and had picked up blurring speed I got under the covers. My father's reading light was on and he was lying on his bunk in his undershorts, smoking, with a closed book on his chest. My sisters seemed to be asleep.

There was a loud rap on the door and a shout from the corridor, "Tickets!" My father twitched violently, then ground out his cigarette and swung off the bunk. He yanked open the door, reached out and dragged in the conductor by the lapels with both hands and slammed his back against the wall. "How dare you wake my children!" in a hoarse whisper. The conductor's jowls jiggled as he babbled something. His hat and his goldrimmed glasses had been knocked askew. "How dare you!" My father pulled him away from the wall and marched him backward out into the corridor, then reached back for the tickets in his coat pocket and waited, speaking in a low, dangerous voice, until the conductor had handed in the stubs. He closed the door and sat down on his bunk. His face was glistening with sweat and his hands trembled lighting a cigarette.

Above me Sage asked sleepily, but urgently, "What is it?"

"Never mind," he said. "Go back to sleep."

My father's Royal Blue Packard convertible was parked at the Rockland station. He had driven up to North Haven the weekend before and had returned by train. He put the top down and opened the rumble seat and we crowded into it with our suitcases on our knees and drove to the ferry. It was a startlingly bright day and the clangs and dongs of the bell buoys carried far over the blue-black water, glittering under a light breeze. When we neared North Haven the white wooden houses on the almost treeless hillside were minutely detailed—shadows under the clapboards and spots of shine on brass door knockers and knobs.

Our house was on the far, north side of the island, a fixed up farmhouse reached by rocky roads and surrounded by stonewalled but abandoned hayfields. The barn had been made into a summer living room. A swing had been hung from one of the rafters, a pingpong table had been set up, and my father's phonograph was ready to play. The barn doors slid open onto a long view of Penobscot Bay and the mountains behind Camden, and just outside was a patch of grass which Sage used when she did her dance exercises. Encouraged by my father, she had recently made up her mind to become a dancer and was working hard to catch up with others who had started younger. In a gym suit, totally concentrating, she stretched and split and assumed ballet positions during the long practice periods that she had set for herself, and at every other odd moment. When he talked about our futures my father stressed "professionalism," the necessity of being truly professional at whatever we did.

My father read a great deal, several books at a time. He would drive Sage and me into the yacht club where he had rented a dinghy for us and I would sail it very badly. I rammed other boats at their moorings, capsizing more than once, and in the races came in last or near it. Sometimes Sage would take the tiller, but she did little better. We had had no instruction and, being newcomers, we were not much helped by other children. My father would meet us at the dock, coming in, and we would go home and play records, "Gloomy Sunday" and my father's collection of jaunty French songs, and sleep in the heavy, cold nights.

The township was legally dry although "real" prohibition had ended five years before, and I once went with my father to the bootlegger. His small, badly weathered house was about halfway between ours and the village, set off by itself near a little cove. "Mornin'," he said curtly when he answered my father's knock. He was a wizened old man and wore a watch cap.

"Good morning," my father said, smiling. "I understand from Mr. Felton that you have supplies of something I might be interested in."

The bootlegger did not smile back. "Will ya come in." The walls of his kitchen were covered with pictures of girls cut from Sunday color sections, most of them badly faded, and the place smelled old and sour.

"I'm happy to have found you. Happy to know you're here," my father chuckled.

"Will ya sit down." The bootlegger perched on a crate and stared at us.

"That's a pretty little cove down there," my father said.

"Ya don't mind the boy?"

"No no."

"Ya keep your mouth shut, sonny?" I nodded. "You, too, Mister?"

"Oh, sure," my father said.

We left with a case of beer, the only kind of drink he had just then.

Nothing noticeable happened.

One evening my father led us three children down to the rocky shore nearest our house and we built a fire and steamed clams and lobster in a bed of seaweed over it. He looked tremendously healthy, tanned, with the sleeves of a sweater tied around his neck. As the light dimmed on the bleached rocks and night fell we sang songs and laughed. He was very happy and sang Harvard's "With Crimson in Triumph Flashing" and funny things from his Navy days in World War I. Jill fell asleep and when the fire got to embers he carried her up to the house while Sage and I dragged the blankets after him, still singing.

Three days before we were to go home he told us that he was going to visit a playwright friend whom we knew, who owned a small island off Vinal Haven. He would be back to put Jill and the cook and maid on the ferry. They were taking the train and Sage and I were to drive home with him the day following. He left and, during his absence, Sage and I exchanged not a word about him.

We could not get to town, but we did not mind. We were looked after and for the first time in the summer Sage and I paid attention to Jill. We went walking along the shore skipping rocks and trying to climb the hard places, showing off for her, and at home we played parchesi together. Sage taught her dance steps to record music.

My father returned on schedule—drunk, the Packard skidding to a dusty, scraping stop. From his exuberant expression it seemed he had brought back a supply. "Hi! How is everybody? Everything all right? All ready to go?"

Sage said, "We aren't going till tomorrow are we?"

"Absolutely right! But there's nothing like being forehanded, is there? *God*, those islands are beautiful!"

He took his bag into his bedroom and I heard the snaps click open and a bottle being set down on the dresser. Sage followed him and they spoke in low voices. He said quietly, but distinctly, "I've been good all summer, haven't I? This is the first time all summer." After a silence, he enunciated, "And I'm going to have a drink."

I went over to the barn and played some music and looked around for things I might have forgotten. After a time the maid came out the front door wearing her travelling clothes, hat on her head, and waited restlessly. Her mouth was hard set. Then my father appeared smiling his nothing-to-worry-about, aren't-I-pleasing smile which almost immediately vanished. He looked increasingly angry, but she went on shaking her head. The situation must have been painful for her; she was very sentimental about my father. Then he slammed inside and the cook brought the bags out, and Jill. They waited together in a bit of shade and after a while a taxi drove up, the only island taxi, and I went over to say goodbye. Sage came out, too.

The maid and the cook were silent. The maid did not want to say that she had refused to ride in the car with my father, and Sage and I were silent because we knew she had. Jill looked small and sad, her mouth drawn into a little ball. I envied her so much I felt like crying.

Sage and I had little to do for the remainder of the day. My father was at his desk in his room with a book, but he was drinking. Toward sunset he went for a walk, brief and alone. Sage and I ate something the cook had prepared before leaving and went to bed early.

"All right," my father said. The car was packed and the house closed. He was wearing a fedora hat. His cheeks were sunken in under his cheekbones, his lips were pursed—it was a particular look he had at these times. We reached the ferry without trouble. The sky was overcast and the white hulls of the sailboats moored at North Haven looked wintry on the dark water as we left them behind.

When we landed at Rockland, Sage was given the road map and we headed for Port Clyde down the coast, where we would meet Aunt Clarkie, my father's sister. We rarely saw her since she lived in Wisconsin, but her Christmas presents—ingenious, useful things for unexpected purposes—had made her a nice person in my mind.

Some miles along the highway Sage said, "I have to stop."

"All right." My father glanced at his watch. "It's about lunchtime, we'll stop."

We passed several places that offered food and Sage began to ask why not here?

"I didn't like the look of it. Did you, Blair?"

She said, "I've got to stop, Pa."

"All *right*."

We stopped at a roadhouse and Sage rushed off to find the bathroom.

"Sorry, Mister, we don't have the license."

He reddened. Wouldn't the owner have a supply of his own, perhaps? "I'd certainly be glad to pay for it."

The woman went out to the kitchen and returned to say she was sorry, the proprietor didn't drink, there was nothing. Sage heard the last of this, sitting down beside me. When the woman had gone—could someone be sent out?—Sage leaned across the table and whispered to my father.

He sat back. "That's the situation, is it? Well. Let's see. Which one of us will go and get the Kotex?"

Silence.

"This is a democracy, isn't it? Who shall we elect?" He grinned suddenly. "What is your vote, Sage?"

Silence.

"Blair?"

Silence.

"No votes." Then he said slowly, "Eeny meeny miney mo. Blair will go and get the Kotex. You'll do that for your dear sister, won't you, Blair?"

"No, I won't." At that time women whispered their orders for "napkins" to druggists, and the boxes, kept behind the counter, were wrapped in plain brown paper.

"You won't help out your *sister?*"

"I don't know where a drug store is."

"There are always drug stores, everywhere."

"No, I won't."

Sage leaned close to me, but I wouldn't look at her. She said, "I've got to have some. Couldn't you?"

"But where?"

When our attention went back to my father he stopped smiling and became 'judicious.' "Sage and I have elected you the one to get the Kotex."

"I won't."

It went on, Sage and I becoming angrier at one another. He interrupted by slapping the table so hard it jumped. "All right, *I'll* get it. Wait here." He left, aggrieved.

He was gone for I don't know how long, maybe two hours. Meanwhile the waitress, pitying Sage's tears, had solved the physical emergency. At one moment Sage and I discussed eating to pass the time, but we had no money and did not dare order. We did not speak much and I knew that she truly hated me, at times, not because I had refused to go but because my refusal had sent our father out.

He came back very drunk. *"There,"* he said, chucking the brown box on the table. "Satisfied?" he said to me. "Drug store's just up the road. No distance at all." He sat down, joined his hands on the table in front of him and looked up at us from under the brim of his fedora. He was someone new. "Have you eaten? Had lunch?"

We shook our heads.

"How about . . . *poulet roti normandine,* or, say *scallopini Pisano?* The establishment would be honored by your choice, my children." He shook and coughed with laughter.

"I'm not hungry," I said.

"Then let us go on to Clarkie." He got up, lurched and grabbed the chair's back, then went to the door.

Sage whispered to me, "I won't go with him. Don't you either."

On the porch outside she told him she refused to go. "Of course you will," he said. "Get in the car."

"I won't."

I stood to one side hearing the pitches of their voices, his changes of tactics, her weakenings and firmings. Then I walked down to the car parked on the far side of the street, against the traffic, and got in. I thought that if I could get with him to Aunt Clarkie that she must see and stop it. She was his older sister. Then Sage could be found somehow. I looked around to fix the name of the roadhouse in my memory and saw a red-haired man crossing the street to me. He leaned on the window and said, "That your father on the porch there? He is, ain't he? Your father?"

"Yes."

"Yeh, well. I believe that man's been drinking, ain't he? Been drinking a whole lot, I'd say. My advice is, put him in a hotel and let him sleep it off. Don't drive nowheres. I wouldn't."

I nodded.

"That's the best thing for him, I'd say."

"What hotel?"

"There's one a mile or two back on the highway. Big old place, you couldn't miss it."

"Thank you."

"That's my advice," he said. He went back to the roadhouse, skirting the argument on the porch. My father held out his arms to Sage and beckoned, then punched his fists into his hips. Sage stood still. He turned away, staggered, saying something to her over his shoulder, nearly fell down the steps and came across to the car enraged.

"All right," my father said. "You and I'll do it. Your sister can stay here and think it over."

"What'll she do?"

He raced the motor, ground the gears into first and we jolted forward.

The two lane highway wound sharply along the rocky coast. We would head straight for a telephone pole then jerk past it at the last second and head straight for the sea. Often the median line was visible beside my window—I was looking out it not to look ahead. There was almost no traffic but one car, coming the other way, braked to a stop on the narrow shoulder over the water, honking, and its driver screamed with furious terror while my father, who had braked, too, wheeled around him to the right, laughing. Safely out of earshot, my father's face looked shocked.

We came to a village sign, Port Clyde, and my father stopped the car, turned off the ignition, and breathed deeply. The car ticked with heat in the silence. "I have some directions," he said, his voice quite different, soft and slurry. He fished a paper from his pocket. "Can you read it?"

"Yes."

He turned the mirror to look at himself and smoothed his hair and curled his lip to see his teeth. "You read and I'll follow the directions." We went slowly through the narrow streets. I missed one turn and he had to back up, and he snapped at me, "Do your job, for God's sake."

We stopped beside a grassy yard before a low white house, and Aunt Clarkie appeared through an open barn door toward the rear, dressed as I remembered her in a man's suit with her hair cut short. Behind her was Cousin Alfred. They both were smiling broadly. I sat still while my father hugged Clarkie and shook Alfred's hand. The three of them spoke and laughed at once. My father looked back and waved impatiently for me to join them and I got out and shook hands. The friendly things they said sounded like barking.

As I followed them through the barn door into Alfred's studio my father was being extremely interested in Clarkie and Alfred, surprised and fascinated by what they said. I remembered his doing this before. If he made other people think about themselves they would not see him. "Don't you think so, Clarkie?" I could hear the slur, but she was concentrating on the expression of her opinion and if she heard it too, it only made her more insistent on getting what she had to say across. She repeated herself several times. Clarkie and Alfred had half-full drinks sitting on the coffee table.

A very large, realistic painting of a stormy sea was standing on an easel. My father took a long time looking at it from one angle and then another, close to it and then from the furthest point in the room. "Wonderful, Alfred! Just wonderful. It seems to me you've made great strides since the last time I saw your work. The light there near the horizon . . ." he shook his head admiring it. It was the kind of painting I knew my father despised.

Alfred was glad my father had noticed the light near the horizon and had a lot to say about it. "Won't you have a drink, Chas?"

"Just a light scotch, if you have it."

"Nothing easier."

My father turned away from the painting toward the open doorway and I could see that for some moments he was glassily drunk. Then he shrugged his shoulders, sat down in a dim corner of the couch and asked them about distant relatives. He made them laugh at me, ramming other dinghys at North Haven. His speech slowed down after a while. "Time to go. Don't you think so, Clarkie?"

Clarkie's car was a huge black "touring" Chrysler, crammed inside with bags and household things. She would spend the night with us on the road and then head for Wisconsin. She had her hand on its door when she laughed suddenly and asked, "But where is *Sage?*" He went over to her and spoke in a voice I could not hear. She looked surprised, but nodded.

If I went over to them I could say that I wanted to ride with her to see what it was like, the big Chrysler, and then tell her what had been happening. But, no, I could not. I could not talk to anyone about my father except, sometimes, to Sage.

One Friday afternoon during the winter I had been sent in on the train from Mt. Kisco to spend the weekend with him, and he had not been waiting for me at the Grand Central gate. I had stayed there fifteen or twenty minutes and then had picked up my overnight bag and gone into the newsreel theater, thinking I would spend the night there. I did not want to try to telephone him if he was not able to meet the train.

I had watched the newsreels a number of times and had fallen asleep, but had been woken up and shown the door when the theater had closed at midnight. After some minutes of sleepy lostness I had gone to the waiting room and had again fallen asleep and again been woken up, this time by a janitor. He had told me that if I were lost I should go to the police. I had not liked the mention of police, they would obviously have called one of my parents, and I had left the waiting room and wandered in the station until a lunch counter opened. I had stayed there until I boarded the 8:45 train.

My plan had been to call my mother from the Mt. Kisco station and to say that I had told my father I wanted to go ice skating that day and that he had put me on the train. Would she believe that he had gotten up that early? It had appeared to be thawing, too. Would she notice? But when I did call there had been no point in telling my story. My father had phoned her the night before and they both had been "worried sick." By the time the chauffeur had come for me and got me to the house I had decided that there was no way around telling the truth about my night in Grand Central, but that I would not explain why I had not called. I preferred to be thought stupid or irresponsible. The next time I saw my father he was angry at me. My disappearance had embarrassed him. He had got to the gate just after I had left it, he said.

Now I could see that if I went with Clarkie I would have to answer questions. My father seemed soberer now and perhaps it would not be so dangerous.

In fact, he drove much better. The trip back to the roadhouse was astonishingly short. Clarkie pulled up behind us and she and my father walked across together to find Sage. She came out on the porch and I stood below it while they talked, Clarkie doing most of it. Clarkie treated the situation as a family squabble. Sage had got mad at my father for some obscure reason and he had lost his temper and had left her. Now we were all back together and everything would be all right. Sage was stubbornly silent for a time. Her face gets pinched in anger. Her eyebrows close down and her lips go white. My father stood aside, blandly listening. Clarkie said, "It isn't far. We won't go far tonight." And Sage agreed to come, with Clarkie.

We ate supper at a seafood restaurant on the highway. Clarkie and my father had several drinks to start. It was very hot in the place and the food was slow arriving. I could eat very little and the process was very long.

Afterwards, Sage got silently into the car with my father and me, and we drove further along Route One to "Cabins"—motels did not yet exist. When we pulled safely into the parking lot the stars were out in the warm night. I had never felt so tired.

Sage and I got our shared overnight bag from the floor of the rumble which was open because the phonograph was sitting on the seat. "What shall we do with the record player?" my father asked. I did not understand what he meant. "Shall we leave it out overnight?" Silence. "Might it be stolen? Do you think it might rain?"

Sage and I looked dumbly at one another. He said, "It's up to you," smiling now. "Do you want to leave it or carry it inside?"

I said, "It won't rain."

"But someone might steal it," Sage said.

"Who'd steal it?"

"It's up to you," my father said. "The decision is yours alone." He was smiling more broadly now.

We argued. Since it would take both of us to carry it we must agree. My father stopped us and said he must have our votes. Sage voted to take it into our room and I voted to leave it out. Deadlock. The smile dropped from my father's face. "All right. Since you can't decide, there is just one way to settle this." He reached into the rumble, brought out the phonograph, and stepped backwards from the car. He swung it to one side, "One," swung it back, "Two," and "Three!" threw it high into the air. It seemed to arc very slowly and then it fell and smashed apart on the asphalt. Parts tinkled, rolling away. "Now that's settled."

He walked away toward the cabins and Sage and I went to look at the wreckage. The wooden cabinet had split and collapsed and pieces were spread wide. Sage said, "*Why* wouldn't you carry it?" Her eyes were full of tears.

When we followed him he was standing in a cabin doorway holding a bottle in a paper bag. He pointed to another door and said, "Go to bed now. It's a long time since I've seen Clarkie and we're going to have a few drinks. Good night now."

Sage and I did not speak before we slept.

In the morning he was red-eyed and shaky. He nipped. I could smell the whiskey. We said goodbye to Clarkie in the parking lot. She did not look so well herself and was fussed about all the things in the car and preoccupied with her long trip to Madison.

The day was crisp and sunny and we started for Boston with the top down. Sage sat next to my father. I did not pay attention to what they were saying until, after quite a few miles, he pulled the car over to the shoulder and stopped. "All right," he said angrily to Sage, "you drive, you know so much about it. You're going to drive the car." He got out, slamming the door, and so did I so he could sit beside her.

He told her where the seat adjustment lever was and then about starting, and the clutch and gears, to some of which she said, "I know." When she had started the motor his mood changed. "Off

we go!" he said and laughed. The gears ground and the car bucked
getting onto the highway but he never stopped smiling. Soon I
was smiling, too. She drove for many miles, stopping at the traffic
lights and starting again, staying in her lane correctly, and even
passing other cars when he told her to. "Now, *go!*" She frowned
at the road ahead, gripping the wheel so closely that her back did
not touch the seat, and she did everything right!

He told her to pull to the roadside and stop and she did so, and
although he was smiling broadly, I could see from her face that
she wondered what she'd done wrong. "Now it's Blair's turn," my
father said. "Fair's fair." He laughed tremendously, coughing and
having to wipe his eyes. Since I had not moved, he said, "You
want to, don't you? Drive the car?"

"Sure."

"All right, then, what are you waiting for? Switch places."

The seat had already been moved as far forward as it would go.
Some sweaters and other loose things were piled on the seat for
me to sit on. I listened to the instructions and I started.

I could drive, too! I went at the right speed and stayed on the
right hand side and even passed other cars, which threw my father
into laughing fits. I made no mistakes and when he finally
stopped me at a roadhouse, where he had several beers and we ate,
I felt immensely proud and excited. Sage did not look happy but
that did not damp my feelings.

He took the wheel through Portland and he did again through
other large towns, but most of the day either Sage or I were driving and he was grinning away beside us under his fedora hat. It
was so strange I could not make an accountable experience of it in
my mind. No one would believe the police had not stopped us.

He drove into Boston and to the Ritz Hotel. Our bags were
taken to adjoining rooms—wonderfully quiet rooms with pale curtains, and silky coverlets on the beds. He ordered a bottle on the
phone and told us to take baths, that we were going to dinner at
the house of an old college friend. We were ready on time and he
was wearing fresh clothes and a necktie. He looked over our appearance very critically before we started.

The house was in Brookline and his old friend had a wife and a
son about Sage's age who was told to show us various things like
his room and the ping-pong table in the basement, at which we
took turns playing. We were not good company for him. The old

friend, a heavy, red-faced tweedy man had had the martini shaker in his hand when he opened the door, and we heard it shaken several times.

Mrs. Old Friend called down the stairs that we should come up for dinner and we did, but her husband was pouring when we came into the living room. My father was already drunk. She went to the kitchen to tell the cook to hold dinner and came back to urge the men to drink up. Finally she said, "We've got to go in. It's burning up." She was jittery and wrung her hands.

Her husband said, "Go ahead and we'll be in in a minute. You'll have a dividend, won't you Charlie, with me? Sure you will, you others go ahead."

"You bet," my father said.

We followed her into the dining room and sat where we were told, all three children on one side of the table. Didn't we like the soup? she asked. We said, very much, and a minute later she asked the same question.

When they came in, the host sat at one end of the table opposite his wife, and my father sat across from us. The light cast dark shadows across his face and his smile was strange. He looked at us one by one and then raised a finger and pointed down the line, "Three, grim, faces," he said, and chuckled.

I looked into my plate. I believe that Sage was weeping. When finally we were released from the table she and I managed to get together by ourselves. She said she would not get in the car with my father. She swore it.

"What can we do?" I asked.

"I don't know." We did not know where we were so we could not go out the door and walk.

Sage went to the hostess and told her. "*What?*" she shrieked, as though Sage had insulted her. "What?" She giggled in a hopeless way and called her husband. *What?* He couldn't believe it. Charlie had had a few, no more than himself, and was perfectly all right. Who in hell did we think we were, talking like that about our own father! One of the finest men alive! His loud voice brought my father into the hall, red and angry. But Sage stuck to it. And I said I wouldn't, either.

The old friend said that he had never heard of such a thing. What kind of children were we? This struck an owed-loyalty note

in my father. He looked very sad for us. "You know how children
are," he said, patting his old friend's back.

At last the host said that simply to show how absurd Sage's
fears were he would follow us to the Ritz in his car. Although log-
ically there was nothing to choose between them, Sage rode in
with the host and I went with my father. We hopped a curb at
one point but we got there safely and so did they. When Sage
said good night to the host he shouted to my father, "She'll know
better next time, won't she Charlie? She'll learn some manners.
She'd better!"

We went up to the rooms. While Sage and I were getting into
our pyjamas my father came in through the connecting door. He
had taken off his shirt and was barefoot and had a glass of whiskey in his hand. He said quietly, slurrily, to Sage, "Sweetie, it's
been a bad evening, I know. He was very rude to you, and you
didn't deserve it. Come and sleep with me in my room. Let's
make up."

"No," she said. "I'm going to sleep here."

They began to argue. I did not want to listen and went about
brushing my teeth and washing my face, but the tones of their
voices changed, although both of them kept low key, and I
stopped and went to the bathroom door to see them. His hands
were on her shoulders and her face was cast down.

"Wouldn't you be happier?" he asked. When he was drinking
and wanted something, he wheedled in a sugary way. She shook
her head. "Are you sore at me?" He turned and held her against
him with one arm. "I shouldn't have left you in that roadhouse,
damn it!" He looked down at her and kissed her forehead. His
eyes were glittering, partly still in anger, I thought. Suddenly
memories flashed through my mind of his asking Sage and Jill to
take their clothes off in front of him. He would ask them to turn
this way and that and would admire their figures but would make
comments about the length of their legs or their posture as
though they were statues. Then in a jumbled rush, which parched
my mouth, I saw the pictures that I had found in the night table
beside his bed in his New York apartment one weekend night
when he had gone out and, sleepless and bored, I had opened a
drawer and found an old photograph album. The pictures were
brown with age so that for a moment I thought they were of his
childhood. The people in them wore turn-of-the-century clothes,

when they wore any, and had hairdos and moustaches of that period. They were fucking in strange positions, most of them staring at the camera, or they were alone and showing off their genitals. One very young girl was sitting on a rocky beach with her dress held up to her waist and holding a long stick in her cunt. Among other thoughts, I had wondered why the pictures were antique. Didn't my father like present day women, and sex? Had this something to do with my parents' divorce? When my father had come home he had stumbled in the dark taking off his clothes. I had not budged when he got into the bed we shared—it was the only bed in the apartment. I had never spoken of the pictures to anyone.

Perhaps now I made a sound or moved. I had a momentary, blinding vision of myself hurtling across the room and hitting him like a football player. My father looked up at me, annoyed, and I felt hotly suffocated.

"Sweetie, do come on with me," he said.

"No." She shook her head in a very definite way and he turned his face away from her, toward nothing, and a burst of pain and regret came across it. He blinked slowly and his jaw sagged to one side as he gave up. After a moment he ran his finger under his eyes and then stared into a corner of the room, looking deeply frightened and alone, so much so that I had an impulse to go and touch him, and perhaps I did move again for his eyes closed and he shook his head like a dog shaking off water.

He said, "I'll say good night to you, then." He kissed her forehead and walked unsteadily through his door and shut it behind him.

She fell on the bed and muffled her face in the pillow and cried a very long time. She was, and is, a person of great courage and is not easily cast down. At that moment I scarcely understood her grief.

In the morning we set out again for home. He said to Sage—his voice was broken down now, "All right. If we take the secondary roads you can drive more. You'd like that, wouldn't you?"

She did not reply and I don't believe he noticed it. Just beyond Worcester she took the wheel.

I sat between them. My father had a pint in the glove compartment and took occasional swigs. He was no longer laughing or smiling. His back was braced against the door and he watched the

road from under the pulled down brim of his hat. Around midday
the bottle was empty and he threw it out the window and I heard
it smash at the roadside. After that we stopped several times for
beer.

Sage let me drive a part of the way. I was excited but my eyes
seemed foggy and my back ached, and I was afraid of making a
mistake and being arrested. I was glad to give it back to her.

Near Bedford he told her to stop and he got out and brushed
off his clothes and then looked at himself in the mirror, just as he
had before we had met Clarkie and Alfred. He was driving, and
pretty well, when we began to pass familiar landmarks near home,
the riding stable and Hockley's Garage. It seemed years since I
had seen them.

We turned into the driveway and stopped in front. My father
had designed the house and he paused before walking to the door,
looking at it. It was large and formal, with cream stucco walls and
dark shutters, and a slate, mansard roof, "traditional," although
not of any one style. At its third floor level there was a triangular
frieze in which was mounted a sculpture head of a unicorn, done
by my mother, with a golden horn and a gold sunburst around his
neck. Below it, a rotunda shaded the front door which was of
dark, oiled wood with a large silver knob exactly in its middle.

One Easter, when they had still been married, a party of my
friends had come for an Easter egg hunt. It had rained and indoor
games had been substituted. After my guests had gone home the
rain had stopped, and I had been sent out to collect the hidden
eggs. I had been standing in the drive with a half-full basket, hoping I could pretend there were no more to be found, when my father had come out the door, grinning. He had picked an egg from
the basket, hefted it, and then pitched it at the door knob, and
then another. "Can you hit it?" he asked me, and I tried. Very
quickly hard boiled egg and bits of colored shells had speckled the
door and the terrace around it. My mother's window had gone up
and he had suddenly run off down the drive, laughing and shouting, "Come on!" to me, "Run!" But I had looked at her and him,
and had not followed.

Now my mother walked into the dim hall to meet us, dressed in
immaculate cool clothes, her heels clicking loudly on the floor.
Sage said goodbye to my father and went upstairs "to unpack"

and did not come down before he left. I would have, too, but my mother said, "Come and sit with us."

I followed them into the living room and they sat down on either side of the fireplace with its polished bronze cat andirons, also my mother's work, and me between them, but across the room in the window bay.

"Wouldn't you like something?" my mother asked. "What would be good? Some iced tea or coffee, a drink?"

"What I'd like's a beer," my father said. "I'm easing off."

I knew she knew what that meant, yet she asked no questions. She rang the bell and in a minute the maid came in wearing her summer dress uniform of a black silky material with lace at the neck and cuffs. She nodded grimly both to my father and me, and when she had brought the beer and iced tea she looked over my head out the window, her pale eyes perfectly blank.

My father and mother began to talk in a way that sounded like flirtation. Bits of news of other people and about what each had been doing. Almost natural. A year ago I had been sitting where he sat now and he had told me that my mother was in Reno getting a divorce.

"Why?"

I do not know what he answered. I had been totally surprised.

There had been guests for dinner, perhaps eight of them, and my father had not changed from his tennis clothes. The martini shaker had been crackling for a long time. When the maid announced dinner he had said to me, "Stay a minute here, please. I have something I want to tell you." He had asked the guests to go ahead of him and to start dinner, saying that he wanted to talk to me. The guests had glanced in such a way that I felt very uncomfortable. Then he had filled his glass and told me.

"Why?"

When I could hear him he was saying that people sometimes found it impossible to live together and believed that they would be happier apart. "I'm sure we will be happier apart." He was sitting with his elbows on his knees and his face was beaded with sweat. After a pause he had asked, "Do you have a question? Anything you'd like to know? You'll be living here with your mother, but you'll see me on holidays and weekends."

"Where?"

"You'll come to visit me in New York."

I had been told my mother was visiting a friend in Wyoming. "When is she coming back?"

"In ten days or so. I'll stay in the house until then. Don't you want to cry?"

"No." The suggestion had offended me.

"It might make you feel better."

"No."

"Would you like to be alone a minute?"

"Yes."

"Well, I'll go in now and join the others. You'll be all right?"

"Yes."

I had not wanted to walk into the hall with him. The door could be seen from the dining room. I had waited, hearing their voices and then a hush, and then their voices again, and laughter. The only other way to my room was to go outside and back in through the kitchen where there would be other people. I had remained hidden beside the door until the voices in the dining room seemed busy with each other and then had stepped around the corner and gone upstairs.

Sage had been visiting elsewhere for the night. I later learned that she already knew and had not been surprised. She had guessed where my mother was.

Jill had a governess at that time, a small, pretty woman in her twenties, and she had heard me come into my room. Although I would not tell her what I had been told she guessed and tried to comfort me. I had not been much comforted but I was grateful to her. Several days later she had been fired by my father, and would not tell me why. She blushed and was tight-lipped and angry. When I had asked him the reasons, what he said was clearly false.

Now he finished his beer and said that he must leave. He had to get on to the city. My mother and I got up and walked with him to the front door. She asked me if I wasn't going to thank him for the summer.

"Thank you, Pa," I said.

He leaned down and kissed my cheek. The whiskey smell was very strong.

My mother went back toward the living room and I stood inside the screen door to watch him go. The afternoon sun turned the screen a bright copper-yellow—it was first class, expensive screening, he had once explained to me. I could see him through it very plainly. The Packard started and hummed. It kicked up some gravel when he moved, and he drove fast out the drive, pulling up a dust cloud behind.

One morning, thirty-five years later, I called a doctor and told him that I could not stop drinking. I was drunk, sitting at the desk in my office-studio in San Francisco. I told him I felt I had to leave the city for a time to dry out and get well, that a couple of days in a hospital would not do it. He knew I had had a nearly fatal attack of pancreatitis, alcohol-caused, and should not drink at all. He said that he would make some arrangements and call back.

I poured some vodka into a coffee cup from the bottle which was hidden, usually, in my desk, and phoned my wife. She walked over from her gallery and sat with me. She was shocked, I believe, and frightened. I felt a leaden, vinegary despair.

The doctor arranged that I be picked up at home. I took a taxi there, poured a drink, and put some things in a suitcase. Then I waited what seemed an endless time, occasionally slopping vodka into my glass, until the doorbell rang.

The man who had come for me was sixty or more, meticulously groomed with a pin of some order or fraternity in his buttonhole. I asked him to wait a minute, went back to the bar for a last hefty belt which nearly made me vomit, and then went out with him to his car. When I'd got in he reached across my chest and pushed down the lock button. "There's a half-pint of bourbon in the glove compartment," he said. "In case you feel you need it during the trip." He started the car and we began to rock along.

Early in World War II, four years after the trip down from Maine, four years that had been all descent, my father had gone to a "farm" in Rhode Island for alcoholic treatment. The Navy had refused to reactivate the commission he had held as a pilot in World War I and I think the shame of that refusal had produced his decision. Perhaps, though, he had simply come to a despairing morning like my own. After some weeks he had returned sober to New York and then had gone to sea as an Ordinary Seaman on a merchant ship. He had continued to ship out until he injured his hand in 1944.

The six years following must have been the happiest of his life. He got a Masters degree in City Planning from MIT. He remarried and he and my stepmother bought a house in Stonington, Connecticut, and both found there a new center of work and interest. I saw him often while I was at Harvard and we became untrusting friends.

Then he began to drink again. He was less destructive, less dramatic and irresponsible, but his last ten years were not cheerful for himself or others. His health failed: bad emphysema, then strokes. He retired at fifty-six, spoke of himself as a person whose life had been of some minor historical interest, and died at sixty-one.

Well. Here I was being carried to "Rhode Island," Calistoga, California, in my case, the countryside blurring by me. From twenty on I had been a daily drinker and had lived with a ghostly fear of just this result. I had once told a friend that I did not understand myself. My father had scared me so, and so clearly shown me the risks, why was I drinking? My friend had said, "He scared you but, still, you must have thought there was something in that bottle." Yes, and that something's power affected me as much as him, although where he had acted I mainly fantasized.

We were halfway to Calistoga before I opened the half-pint and took a slug. The bottle was empty before we arrived at "Myrtledale," a converted old resort hotel with palms planted along its driveway and a long, shaded verandah. I stumbled up its steps and went into a dim lobby in which a number of others were sitting. I could not and did not wish to see them very clearly.

I registered and sat withdrawn in a dim corner. After an hour or so an aide, a former patient, gave me my first "hummer," a double shot of bourbon in water given to new arrivals over the first forty-eight hours to prevent the withdrawal dangers of convulsions and DTs. I picked up the glass with two hands to drink. Some of the others could not hold a glass and drank through straws while the aide held it. One could not keep the straw between his lips and the drink was poured into his open mouth.

That night the woman in the new-arrival room next to mine, rooms with no doors and barred windows, had DTs nonetheless. Her cries sounded tortured, in pain and terrified, and then exhausted and pathetic, then terrified again. An ambulance came and took her to a nearby clinic with medical staff. There is a better than ten percent chance of death from DTs. She returned two days later, a tiny Scottish woman with a shining, smiling face.

By then I was feeling tremendously relieved, as though I'd lost half my weight. It had happened at last. All right. No more unacknowledged suspense. Here I was among the alcoholics. I was an alcoholic. Survival must bring better things.

When my father died my mother telephoned me in Rome where I was temporarily living. She suggested that I need not return, that no one would expect me to come from so far. My sisters were on a Caribbean vacation, she said, and she had urged them to stay on there as long as possible.

I flew to New York and did what I could to ease the business of it for my stepmother. After the quite impersonal service at St. James' I took her home. She had had the apartment before they married and it was almost entirely hers in personality. I stood for a time looking at the plain brown urn of his ashes standing on her dresser, hearing an electronic-sounding discord. Not all right. Not the manner (alone from a heart attack while he was hospitalized for rest and drying out), nor the moment of his death, nor his and my relationship when last I'd seen him, or ever, nor my feeling at that moment for his memory, shaded and spattered as it was with awareness of my inadequacy to have made him well, guilt for his recent neglect, and resentment of his past uses and disparagement of me.

During his last drinking years I had been the most faithful of his children. He had hurt Sage at the time of her first marriage by so insulting her husband that her later divorce and remarriage did not change her feeling. Jill avoided him. I had gone to doctors, to an AA meeting, to his friends attempting to find something helpful to him, and I was the last person who should have done so. He was not going to accede to anything serious coming from me. One evening, in other company, he told me I was the least "bright," the least "interesting," in fact the least of his children.

It may be that his appraisal of me had to do with my attempts to help. It may as certainly be that my attempts to help had to do with his appraisal of me.

He had never lost a childlike joy in being "bad," meaning unexpectedly destructive, an applecart upsetter. Drunk, he liked to recount wild insults and dangerous pranks, and when he did so his eyes glittered. But he could not be "bad" without whiskey. My "help" would have ordered his life.

I, on the other hand, wanted others to think of me as "good," a good person, responsible and sensitive. Thus I had to try to get him well. I failed, but even had I succeeded, I could not believe myself to be "good" without whiskey.

Alcoholism is a disease. Perhaps he and I were both alcoholics before we ever had a drink. But alcoholics, like other people when they drink, find the effects they want in it.

Three years have now passed since I left Myrtledale. In that time I have almost never felt the urge to drink and, until now, the urges have quickly passed. It has turned out that, sober, I can like myself. Not too much, I think, just sufficiently. Perhaps the act of giving up the stuff has provided enough feeling of goodness to satisfy that vanity. I have a son, soon to be eleven.

In principle, of course, my father could have been more intentionally, cleverly bad without whiskey, but in fact he was not. He was at least as good as most men, sympathetic, understanding and generous. Without the help of the drug he could scarcely be bad at all. Simply, he could not accept his own goodness (or mine), any more than I could accept my own badness (or his).

So, let me try the phrase in a different tone. All right, Charles Fuller. Finished. All right.

All right.

THE TATTOO

JOYCE CAROL OATES

Joyce Carol Oates was born and raised in the countryside south of Lockport, New York (the somewhat fictionalized setting for "The Tattoo"). At present Ms. Oates is living in Windsor, Ontario, where she teaches English at the University of Windsor. Her most recent book is a collection of short stories, *Night-Side* (Vanguard Press), and her next novel will be *Son of the Morning*.

The first time I saw Gerry Lund my head snapped back with the shock of it—of her: the coarse black hair falling to her waist, the man's undershirt stuck to her damp skin, the soiled blue jeans straining at her wide, strong hips, the filthy bare feet. On her left arm, up near the shoulder where you would expect to see a vaccination mark, there was a tattoo in bright reds and blues: it looked like a bird of some kind. (In fact it was a falcon, its wings stiffly outspread, eyes fierce, feathers garish in the primary, slightly off-key colors of comic strips.) Behind Gerry, on top of the refrigerator, an old radio was blaring country music; her long curved toes kept time with it. I stared at Gerry so intently I had no consciousness of being rude—but of course it would not have mattered, not to Gerry—and anyway, the music was loud, and other people were in the kitchen. I could not believe what I was seeing and so I continued to stare while my friend Jeannette introduced me, pushing me forward with a playful poke of her elbow.

"This is Ellen," Jeannette announced. "She's staying for supper."

One of Jeannette's brothers greeted me, mumbling something I couldn't decipher, on his way out the back door; another brother —I *thought* he must be her brother, he was standing at the sink with both faucets on hard—glanced at me over his shoulder and did no more than nod. Gerry finally looked up, turning from the

Copyright © 1977 by Joyce Carol Oates. Reprinted by permission.

dime-store mirror that was propped against something on the kitchen table; she squinted and grinned and said hello, did I want a Coke, would I like to sit down? Not only did she have a tattoo on her arm, but there was another, a small yellow butterfly smudgily outlined in black, on the back of her left hand, and right now she was working with a sewing needle and several indelible pencils—she was tattooing her eyelids. I must have flinched visibly at the sight because Gerry laughed and said in her quick, brusque voice, still grinning: "Relax, it doesn't hurt. It won't hurt *you*."

Jeannette got us both Cokes and a package of slightly stale Cheez-Bits, and we pulled chairs up to the crowded, rickety table and watched Gerry. She wasn't at all self-conscious; she seemed pleased to have an audience. Though the tatooing was a delicate, dangerous operation, she kept up a steady stream of chatter, firing questions at me, dabbing now and then at her eye with a piece of cotton batting that was already blood-stained. On her left eyelid there was something curly, purplish-green, like a tiny vine with tendrils and heart-shaped leaves; it looked, in a bizarre way, quite attractive. She was working on the right eyelid now, holding it out from the surface of the eye, hunched over the mirror. I stared in fascination. The Coke was tasteless, the Cheez-Bits all salt and grease, even Gerry's conversation floated past me—I was completely absorbed in Gerry Lund and what she was doing. From time to time Jeannette glanced at me, smiling her small, prim, satisfied smile. "Ellen wants you to do her next," she said, leaning over to whisper in her sister's ear. "She wants a big red heart on her arm."

"I do not!" I said, blushing. "I certainly do not."

"You sure?" Gerry said, grinning. She was regarding her handiwork in the mirror; she frowned severely and squinched her face up, as if she were displeased or thinking very hard. Then came the needle again for a quick, light jab, and the cotton batting, and the indelible pencil. "I could do it so you wouldn't feel anything at all."

"It doesn't hurt?" I asked hesitantly.

"Well—a little," Gerry said. "It stings."

"It hurts like hell," Jeannette said with a snort. "She started me once, it was going to be a bluebird on the inside of my shoulder, you know, where people wouldn't see it—except if I wore a bath-

ing suit, you know—but the needle hurt and we had to stop. I
don't like *blood*," she said, shivering.

"The problem was it really tickled, the needle really tickled,"
Gerry said, leaning back to smile at me, one eyelid lower than the
other, "but Jeannette thought that was pain so she got all excited
—she's such a baby."

"I'm not a baby," Jeannette said. "I'm just intelligent."

Gerry laughed and unwrapped a stick of gum. When she
moved an odor of slightly stale clothes or unwashed flesh was
released—or perhaps it was her long, coarse, jet-black hair, which
fell in straggly clumps to her waist. She was twenty-seven years
old, Gerry Lund, and her rough, rather sallow complexion, her
uneven grayish teeth, and the frown lines on her forehead made
her appear at least that old, up close; but I remembered having
seen her once or twice, in town, not knowing she was Jeannette's
sister at the time, and I had supposed she was in her late teens—
boisterous, unfeminine in men's or boy's clothing, good-natured,
with a sharp merry laugh and a loud voice. If her hair had been
straight she would have looked like an Indian, her face was that
sharp, her eyes that dark. She was very ugly. No—she was very
striking. I found myself staring at her, blushing when she happened to look directly at me. She kept up a peppery barrage of
questions: where did I live, what did my father do, which classes
at the high school did I have with Jeannette, was I in love with
What's-his-name, the math teacher, the way Jeannette was—and
here Jeannette got angry and slammed her Coke bottle down so
hard on the table that some of it spilled. "You don't know anything about it," Jeannette cried, "you don't know anything about
me." I laughed, dazed and pleased and bewildered, wanting to
give the right answers so that Jeannette's remarkable sister would
like me (for it was easy to tell, by the grimaces and eye-rollings
that accompanied her comments about certain people, that Gerry
was very critical and didn't like just anyone). I was not aware
until afterward, until the next morning, that she had really been
quizzing me: she found out by way of her casual, seemingly hap-
hazard questions not just the street we lived on in Derby but the
number, the size of the house, what it was made of, and not just
my father's profession but the men he worked with and how long
he'd been working with them, where he had gone to law school,
and how and when and where he'd met my mother; not just the

size of my family but the names of everyone, even my cousins, and how old we all were, and whether we got along. What make was our car? Oh, we had *two*? Did we go anywhere in the summer? Did we like to watch television? What were our favorite dinners? Favorite desserts? At one point she said, in the midst of describing a neighbor of theirs whose son was always fighting with their twelve-year-old brother Bobbie, that if there was one thing she hated it was nosy people—"I just can't *stand* people who are always poking into everybody else's business"—and her manner was so vehement that both Jeannette and I agreed at once. That was the thing about Gerry Lund—you always found yourself agreeing with her.

The man at the kitchen sink was trying to clean a pair of workshoes by scrubbing them with a brush. He appeared to be about thirty years old; he was bare-chested, with a small potbelly; from time to time he glanced over his shoulder at us, or at Gerry, but did not trouble to join the conversation. When Gerry said supper would be franks and sauerkraut and some leftover potato salad and rhubarb pie, he said loudly, "Well, that figures," but I couldn't guess whether he was pleased or displeased, and Gerry did no more than wave at his back, languidly. She asked him to turn the radio down because the announcer's voice had begun to boom, but he didn't hear, and Jeannette turned it down. A few minutes later he left by way of the back door, allowing the screen door to slam after him.

"I didn't think Moody was going to be here," Jeannette said.

"Yes, well," said Gerry.

"I mean, last night—"

"Well—" Gerry shrugged.

"I sort of told you, didn't I, that Ellen would be—"

"*Did* you?" Gerry asked, genuinely curious. She turned to me, blinking. She smiled. Her right eyelid was pink and raw-looking above the delicate, purplish-green vine. The left seemed in better condition. Was the tattoo meant to be a fragment of a grapevine, I wondered—and where had she gotten the idea? I was too shy to ask. (Afterward I learned from Jeannette that her sister got many of her "ideas" from dreams—she thrashed about at night, visited by all sorts of strange people who held things up for her to see, sometimes pictures, sometimes living creatures, sometimes objects that could not be identified. "Not all of her dreams are from this planet, so she *says*," Jeannette laughed, partly embarrassed and partly proud.)

"Ellen," Gerry said, laying a hand on my arm, "you don't mind Moody hanging around, do you? He won't bite."

I shook my head, meaning no, of course not, but Jeannette cut in irritably: "The thing *is*, Gerry, you said. The two of you, you know, *said*. And that business about Mike sending somebody—I mean I know it's crazy and all, and Mike wouldn't *have* any friend that close—"

"That's for damn sure," Gerry laughed shrilly. Then to me: "Mike's my old man, you know? Did Jeannette tell you? Up at Shaheen for three-to-five years, armed robbery it was; the poor bastard got drunk and held up a gas station on the highway—Jeannette didn't tell you? You mean she isn't proud of her big, handsome brother-in-law? Anyway, he's at Shaheen and no worry to us tonight. Poor bastard's lucky to be alive, the gas station manager shot him in the chest. But, you know, he's no worry to us tonight."

Jeannette was crumbling Cheez-Bits and staring at her fingers. I could tell that she was upset.

"Moody is just a friend, in fact he's a friend of Mike's," Gerry said, unwrapping another stick of gum. "These guys all know one another. They ride together, you know? Motorcycles. Except Moody wants to sell his. Dave Arkin's thinking of buying it—did I tell you, Jeannette? Yeah, he's thinking of buying it. The problem is he's broke."

"We're not going to stay, then," Jeannette said flatly.

"What?"

"Ellen and me. We're not going to stay for supper then."

"But why not? There's plenty. Andy isn't going to be here: he's over at the Rapids. Having supper there. And Pa's in town till Saturday."

I looked from Gerry to Jeannette, and back to Gerry again. Her eyes were bright, very black; her eyebrows were thick as a man's; she was grimacing as if deep in thought or annoyed, one side of her face crinkling and seeming to lift. She was ugly, suddenly wizened, like a witch—her coarse-pored skin had broken into a hundred sharp little lines. Then in the next instant she smiled—tried to smile—and said in a voice that was almost hesitant, almost tender: "But I just got to *meet* Ellen. Her and I—her and me—we just got to *meet*. You can't drag her away so soon!"

"But what are the Lunds like?" my mother wanted to know, careful to keep her voice light and pleasant. "I've seen Jeannette; I know she's pretty and she can be sweet, but what is her family like—what is their house like?"

"It's fine," I said. "It's really fine."

"From the outside it seems—"

"It's really nice inside. They keep it up nice."

"Mr. Lund is—? He works at—?"

"Some lumberyard, I think. I don't know."

"Mrs. Lund—?"

"Oh, she's dead. I guess she's been dead a long time."

"She's dead?" my mother said, perplexed. "But when did she die?"

"How would I know?"

"Ellen, don't be smart—please don't be smart."

"I'm not being smart, I'm not being anything. I just meant— how would I know?" I said, raising one shoulder and one side of my face to show baffled, exasperated innocence. "Mother, I don't *know*. Jeannette and I never talk about things like that."

"What do you talk about, then?"

"Oh," I said, blinking, "things—"

My mother considered me, unsmiling. She was a small-bodied woman with a frail, washed-out, once-pretty face; her eyes were a pale, hazy blue that looked as if they might flood with tears at any time. It was said that she had "married well"—for my father was a lawyer and had a real estate company and was one of the mayor's aides, and we lived in one of the big fieldstone houses on Church Street; but it was also said that she had "married beneath her"— for her father had been a prominent businessman in another part of the state, and at one time, in the early part of the century, the family had been extremely wealthy, and there was always vague, fluttery talk among the aunts and uncles of "important" ancestors back in England—how far back I didn't know, but it must have been centuries.

"This Jeannette," my mother said fastidiously, "she has sisters and brothers? What are they like?"

"I don't know. They're fine."

"Yes, but what are they *like?*"

"Her older sister Gerry was there and cooked dinner for us; she was very nice, she was in charge—she was very nice."

"Her older sister?"

"Gerry. Yes."

"She lives at home?"

"Yes. She's in charge there."

My mother drew in her breath slowly, still watching me. "So— someone was there to cook dinner. Was the food good?"

"Mother," I said, laughing, "why are you quizzing me? It was just a dinner. It was just food."

"I wasn't quizzing you, Ellen. Why do you use that expression?"

"It was just food, for God's sake."

I didn't tell her that I found the heated-up franks and sauerkraut delicious and the potato salad, made with vinegar and peppers and onions, better than the kind she made, and that I didn't have to be bullied by Gerry to have a second piece of the soft, sugary rhubarb pie.

"It's just that I can't understand why you like Jeannette so much," my mother said, her voice tremulous. "You have plenty of other—"

I smiled and pretended not to understand and escaped.

A few miles south of town, where the Moran Creek is at its widest and laziest, and where scrappy poplars and willows and beech and softwood bushes of all kinds grow wild along the roadside, the Lund family lived in a sprawling, ramshackle, weathered-gray farmhouse that had the appearance of being a half-dozen tarpaper shanties flung together. Scattered in the bumpy yard around the house were various abandoned things: cardboard boxes, plywood packing cases, bottles, tin cans, boards, sticks, parts of bicycles and children's toys, farm equipment, and cars, a rusted tractor, even the front part of a snowplow turned on its side in the weeds. One of the barns had been made over into a garage; the others had been allowed to fall in upon their crumbling foundations.

The land in that part of the county is beautiful but it isn't much good for farming except in small, odd-shaped patches. Someone in the Lund family *had* farmed at one time or another,

Jeannette told me; a great-uncle, maybe, long dead. No one in the family at the present time had the slightest interest in farming. Mr. Lund had various jobs, always in town; one of Jeannette's brothers drove forty miles to an auto-parts factory in Port Oriskany; her married sister Irene lived in Rockland with her husband, who had a trucking job; and, of course, Jeannette wanted to leave, too—she hoped to be a nurse, or at least a dental assistant. Gerry, who claimed to like the area well enough—"It isn't bad compared to *some* places I've been"—nevertheless had plans to move away soon. She talked of driving out to California with Moody and another friend. She talked of getting to Hawaii somehow. There was the whole world waiting for her, she said—and she was the girl to see it all.

In my room overlooking Church Street and the hill beyond it that dipped to town, and the hazy, green-glimmering foothills in the distance where the Lunds lived, I dreamt of Gerry Lund: I composed conversations between us, I staged passionate scenes. Jeannette was my friend, of course; suddenly she had become my closest friend (perhaps because my other friends, for some reason, had begun to drift away), but it was Gerry I thought about constantly. On the street any black-haired stranger, female or male, had the power to alarm me in the instant before I realized it wasn't Gerry; the sound of raucous, jeering laughter made me whirl about, my eyes darting wildly—but of course it wasn't Gerry. "Why do you make such faces?" my mother asked irritably. "Who are you imitating?" my father asked, winking. "A movie star? Anyone we know?" I blushed, I waved away their questions, I stammered and made excuses and escaped. Alone in my room I shut the door against them—my mother with her perplexed, sorrowful eyes, my quick-witted dapper father who loved me but did not know me at all.

Gerry and I were driving along the highway, north toward Lake Oriskany. It was raining. She offered me one of her cigarettes; I accepted. "Christ, I know what it's like," she said, "living at home like that. All you want is for them to leave you alone, right? But they won't. They can't." When I began to cry, she stroked my head and drew her fingers through my hair as I'd seen her, once, draw her fingers through her brother's hair—or was it Moody's or a friend of theirs lounging against the kitchen table with a beer can in his hand—mocking and sympathetic at the same time.

"How'd you like to move out, Ellen? Just move out? I was thinking of renting an apartment in town, myself—" Then we were walking somewhere, Gerry and Moody and myself and another man, a stranger, and we were talking and laughing together, and the man who was with me had his arm around my shoulders the way Moody's arm was around Gerry's shoulders, and my arm was tight about his waist as Gerry's was around Moody's waist, my fingers locked about his belt. . . . We stopped and kissed. I wasn't afraid: I gripped him tight. He had no face that I could see, no features, yet his mouth was hard and demanding and. . . .

Snarled, ugly, lovely visions.

With a blue ball-point pen I inked my initials on the inside of my left arm, a few inches above the wrist. I outlined them in red ink, then again in green. The ends of my hair brushed against my desk. Tears sprang into my eyes: why? I blinked them clear and saw Gerry sprawled on the Lunds' living room sofa, a Coke in one hand, a cigarette in the other, showing her gums as she laughed. The second time we met she called me Ellie—Ellie!—a name no one had ever thought to call me before. Ellie. I loved it, I loved *her*. "Ellie," she said, "how's things on Church Street? I heard some interesting news about City Hall—*not* the kind reported in the paper—you want to make your daddy listen hard, just mention G. R.—you got that?—the initials G. R. He'll know what you mean; bet his eyes will bulge out of his head." I was flattered by her interest, though, of course, I wouldn't say anything to my father. It had always been the case in our family that my father didn't talk about his work at home, and we never inquired about it, as if—it must have been my mother's doing, I think—his work were both beyond and beneath our interest, something sacred and yet contemptible. (Which was why the bickering about money that went on at the Lunds', in the open, even in front of a guest, astonished me: I hadn't known people could talk about money so frankly. Once Jeannette wanted to borrow two dollars from Gerry for a few days, and Gerry blew up at her. I offered to lend it, but Jeannette ignored me and went for Gerry's purse, an old, battered, fake-leather pouch lying on the stairs, and began pawing through it, and Gerry came running and slapped her, and Jeannette slapped *her*, and Gerry shoved her so hard she fell down, crying— and I stood there frightened and amazed. In the end Gerry tossed a five-dollar bill at Jeannette and muttered something like, "Suck on that, then.")

Invite your friends for dinner, my mother said often. Invite them to stay overnight. That's what the house is for, this big house: your friends are welcome anytime.

She didn't lie but she didn't tell the truth. What was the truth? She wanted me to have friends, the daughters of her friends; or maybe the daughters of women she would have wished to have as friends. When I was thirteen I overheard her talking to someone on the telephone, and the tone of her voice—wheedling, cringing, flattering—was a stranger's, unrecognizable. She was *begging*—but for what? The words were ordinary words having to do with a luncheon, the women's sodality of our church, Mrs. Fleischmann and Mrs. Hendricks and Mrs. Carpenter, a litany of important names, but the tone, the tone—it reminded me of a fat, unpopular girl in my class, trying to bribe us into sitting with her at lunch, promising us brownies or chocolate-chip cookies; it reminded me of the way I'd sounded myself, at times, when I was much younger.

Jeannette came to our house for dinner several times when we were in ninth grade and she stayed overnight once, but she didn't enjoy herself; she thanked me profusely, and even Gerry remarked that Jeannette had had a "great old time there," but it was obvious that she was very uncomfortable all the while. My father tried to be nice at the dinner table, asking Jeannette about school and her plans for nursing and what "her people" thought about the freakish weather we'd been having. (Everyone in Eden Valley believed weather there was exceptional and always worthy of excited conversation: it wasn't until I left home that I came to see that everyone in all of North America feels that way about local weather.) Afterward he remarked that Jeannette was a sweet, quiet girl, certainly very pretty—Was she always so shy?—but his gregariousness intimidated her, and I wanted to shout at him to leave her alone, let her eat dinner in peace. My mother didn't ask so many questions but she was over-solicitous about food, and her strained, insistent smile had the effect of discomforting both Jeannette and me. She was *trying* to like my new friend; couldn't we see that she was *trying* very hard? At the end of our meal I wanted to lean over to poor Jeannette and say, in Gerry's rough, raw, delighted voice: "Let's get the hell out of here!" But of course I didn't, I was capable of nothing like that and I felt, later, that Jeannette liked me less after that first visit to my house and that she saw me always in the context of my family: I was nice, I was funny, but maybe I couldn't exactly be *trusted*.

I wondered if she told Gerry about me. I wondered what Gerry would have said, sitting through that stiff, overlong dinner.

"Jeannette isn't quite as nice as Peggy, is she," my mother said. Or: "Jeannette just doesn't seem quite as *friendly*, does she, as Valerie. . . . What happened to Valerie Donahue? I thought the two of you were so close, and you looked so cute together."

One evening my father said something about the Moran Creek area—"those people"—and he and my mother exchanged a significant look; but I pretended not to understand. Evidently there had been trouble of some kind—a drunken fight at a tavern, maybe, or a smash-up on the highway, or someone's barn burnt under suspicious circumstances. I pretended not to understand, I said nothing. I was too clever to defend the Lunds—"But that has nothing to do with *them!*"—though I could hardly resist a shiver of apprehension. Whatever had happened, Gerry Lund would know all about it—would probably have been at the center of it. "I'm a girl," she said often ruefully and yet with obvious self-satisfaction, "people just can't leave *alone*."

On her sleepy, hooded eyelids those uncanny, delicate little vines; on the muscles of her upper arm a stiff, fierce falcon; on the back of her big-veined hands, a yellow butterfly; on her right thigh, a black panther with a curling tail and scarlet eyes. What strange, unsettling images . . . almost pretty in a cheap, comic-book way and at the same time almost frightening, nightmarish. Gerry "did" a friend of Moody's named Joe Kaiser one warm afternoon in the Lunds' back yard, the radio blaring as usual, the men sitting around drinking beer, talking and laughing coarsely, lazily; she gave him an American eagle on the tough muscle of his right arm. It turned out rather crudely, I thought, but no one else seemed to notice.

I dreamt of eagles, falcons, spidery vines curling across my eyes. I dreamt of barechested men, slick with perspiration, tossing beer cans into a heap. "This is Ellie Proctor," Gerry said gaily, loudly, adding in an undertone that I was only fourteen—and my father was a friend of the sheriff's. The men laughed. They laughed a great deal.

"Oh God," Jeannette said, rolling eyes when she heard one of them—it might have been Joe Kaiser or a friend of Moody's named Gene—"God, Ellen, isn't he something? Isn't he something? He's married and his wife moved back with her family, don't you think she must be *crazy*? If *I* was married to him," she said, giggling, "I certainly wouldn't be living with any *parents*—"

I dreamt of Joe Kaiser and the eagle on his arm; I dreamt of Gene and even of Moody—a homely bad-tempered man with thinning, frizzy hair; I dreamt of a golden butterfly tattooed on my breast. When I awoke I was shivering. Gerry? Did you say something? Are you here—blinking into the darkness of my room? *Gerry?*

She wore blue jeans and men's shirts and sometimes floppy sweaters, and she had a battered sheepskin jacket I coveted—I stared at one that resembled it in the window of Grant's on Main Street, wondering without hope how it would look on me. In warm weather she wore cut-off jeans that showed her pale, mottled thighs and the black panther; she wore halters that made her breasts all the more prominent. Though she could move quickly, she was a large-boned woman, sturdy and tough and possibly thickening at the waist. She might have weighed 150 pounds. But when she slipped her earrings on and looped beads about her neck, put on lipstick and appeared downstairs in a dress that strained against her body, I could feel the men's interest—I could understand it: there was something jarring about her, something very attractive. She wasn't beautiful. Yet she was beautiful. When she was in a group, everyone naturally looked at her, turned to her, was drawn to *her*.

Sometimes the men quarreled in her presence. Was it because of her, I wondered.

Sometimes (so Jeannette said) it wasn't Moody who came home with her but one of the other men.

She had dropped out of school at the age of thirteen, having done poorly all along; by the age of fourteen she was married. Mrs. Lund was still living then—working at Laird's Bakery, in town—and there were five children still at home. So she was anxious to get out, and she was—she said—crazy in love with Mike at that time. (He was twenty-one, a carpenter's assistant who made fairly good money.) So she was married at fourteen and by the age of fifteen she'd had the first of several miscarriages, and by the age of eighteen her relationship with her husband had gone bad. ("It was his drinking," she said sadly. "The poor bastard just can't *drink.*") He had been in and out of trouble with the law for years. Suspended sentences for drunken driving and disturbing the peace and resisting arrest; a six-month jail sentence for aggravated assault in a Marsena tavern. They quarreled and separated. They made up and lived for a while in a trailer just outside the Derby city limits; Gerry had a job downtown as a cleaning woman in the County Building. Mike got work where he could: day-laboring, even picking tomatoes and peaches and apples and cherries alongside migrant workers who were shipped up north in battered school buses, many of them black, a good number jabbering away in languages no one else could understand. They quarreled again and fought, and one of Gerry's ribs was cracked. So they separated. And were again, after a few stormy months, back together. . . . (It was Jeannette who told me all this, reciting her sister's history in a casual, unemphatic manner. The implication throughout was that Gerry could take care of herself, no one could push *her* around. And also, more disturbing, that Gerry brought these troubles onto herself—she deserved them, in fact.) So it went over the years: Gerry and Mike were always fighting, no one took them seriously, they were in love in spite of everything, and if Mike blackened one of Gerry's eyes or Gerry went after him with a hammer, it was just what happened, what often happened between married couples in this part of the world. "But wouldn't she be afraid he might kill her?" I asked, shivering with excitement; and Jeannette shrugged her shoulders and said blandly, "And then what would happen to *him?* He knows what my brother Andy would do."

Moody was an old friend, Jeannette said, unemployed right now though once he'd made good money working with a construction crew. He had injured his back somehow: he received compensation from the county and the state both, and it was enough to live on. He was an old friend of both Mike's and Gerry's and he was always *there* . . . in between other men Gerry got involved with . . . not very jealous, at least not most of the time.

"But isn't she afraid of him—of them?" I whispered.

Jeannette blushed a little. "Whyever for?" she said lightly. "She *likes* them."

(Three years later Jeannette married a man in his mid-thirties who owned a hardware store in Port Oriskany; he'd been married before, I heard indirectly, and even had two children from that marriage in his custody. He was a very nice man, it was said. Kind and considerate and fairly well-off. Devoted to his family. Very nice. Wasn't Jeannette fortunate?)

On my left shoulder there blossomed a tiny pink rose.

It didn't hurt. It stung a little; it tickled.

Gerry opened a bottle of beer for me. "You won't feel a thing," she said. "It's nothing. It's fun."

She pricked with the needle and dabbed the blood off with a tissue while Jeannette hung over us, biting her lip. "Jesus," she said, "if your mother finds out. . . ."

I laughed.

Gerry's hair fell forward in a warm, heavy cascade. It smelled of —of unclean bedclothes, of kitchen odors, of grease, smoke, chewing gum. A rich, rank animal smell. Up close her skin was very coarse; it was grainy; there was something flat and dead about it. But her smile! And her eyes! So quick. So lovely.

She drank one bottle of Coke after another, nervously.

"I told you it wouldn't hurt, right? I never lie."

I twisted my neck to stare at the small blotched flower. "It's perfect," I said. There were tears in my eyes; I didn't know why.

"It isn't bad," Gerry said critically. "But I must admit I've done better."

My parents didn't discover the tattoo until many weeks later, and by then my relationship with Gerry was finished. My friendship with Jeannette was finished.

It came about that I went home with Jeannette on the school bus one Friday in October to spend the night. When we got to the Lunds', however, there were a number of people there, most of them strangers, most of them men. Mr. Lund wasn't home; no one seemed to know where he was. Gerry had been drinking and when she saw me, she grabbed both my hands and pulled me forward to introduce me to her friends. She insisted that I show them the rose tattoo. I tried to pull away. I was very embarrassed, but she wouldn't let me go—her fingers around my wrist left a mark afterward.

"You shouldn't let her bully you," Jeannette said when we were alone. "She likes to show off, pushing people around."

"I didn't mind," I said.

"Oh, that bitch—"

"I didn't mind, really," I said.

Gerry and her friends didn't eat until quite late, and we waited for them, getting hungrier and hungrier. Jeannette was subdued; there didn't seem to be much for us to talk about. We sat on her bed leafing through romance magazines and listening to a Derby radio station. We talked about girls in our class. And boys. And certain of the men downstairs who were better-looking than the rest—who was most attractive. When Gerry and another of the women finally served dinner, the kitchen and living room were both so crowded, and the din so upsetting, that Jeannette and I brought our plates upstairs. I hadn't any appetite—the meatloaf was cold and not very tasty; the fried potatoes were slick with grease. Jeannette ran downstairs to get some Cokes and was gone quite a while, and I lay on her bedspread and stared at the rain-marked ceiling, seeing there ugly, nightmarish designs—a deformed infant, a hand with seven fingers, a bird with an enormous curved beak. *I hate it here,* I thought.

When Jeannette came back she had a can of beer for herself and a Coke for me, and a bag of potato chips; most of the chips were broken. Certain characters were "acting up" downstairs, she said—they were a little crazy, that bunch, a little too loud—she hoped the neighbors wouldn't call the police. Her laughter was high and nervous. She brushed her hair out of her eyes repeatedly, as Gerry did, and avoided looking at me. "Of course, I just hate it when they get drunk," she said. "They're so stupid and gross."

Around midnight the party quieted down; I heard several cars pull out of the driveway. By then Jeannette and I were in bed. I lay awake, not moving, not wanting Jeannette to know I wasn't asleep. What was there to talk about? We'd leafed through the magazines, we'd snickered at the silly photographs and stories; we'd discussed in detail many of our classmates; we'd discussed Gerry's friends. Every time someone downstairs laughed loudly or shouted one of us would say, "Aren't they awful" or "Isn't that person obnoxious" until we couldn't say it again—we'd come to the end of all we could say to each other.

Then I was asleep. And Gerry was sitting on my old swing, her long legs extended, her bare feet slapping at the ground. Someone was pushing her. My father? He was pushing her as he'd once pushed me. She yelled, she giggled, her hair whipped back. I stood to one side, for some reason frightened. Daddy, I said. Gerry. Daddy? Gerry? But they ignored me. They were completely oblivious of me.

I whimpered in my sleep, turning away from them.

But Gerry wouldn't let me go. She began to shake me, scolding me, her hair falling in my face. "Hey. For Christ's sake. Ellie—— Jeannette—wake up, will you? C'mon. Please. Wake *up*."

Someone turned on the light.

"What the hell . . . ?" Jeannette said groggily.

It was Gerry, stumbling against the bed. She appeared to be drunk. Her eyes were wide and black and shiny, like an animal's eyes; she gave off an odor of panic. "Get dressed, you two. Quick. Are you listening? Wake up! Jeannette? Some of the guys downstairs, they're kind of high and fooling around—it's just Joe and Pete and Davy left, Moody's flat out in bed—they've been fooling around—I don't know how serious they are—about coming up here, you know—about you and Ellie—so you'd better leave, you'd better get dressed and get out of here before something happens—"

"What?" Jeannette said blankly.

"You heard me! For Christ's sweet sake," Gerry said.

"But where can we *go*?" I whispered.

"Just get out of the house! Hide in the barn, or go back to town —anywhere! This isn't any picnic," Gerry said. She was throwing our clothes at us. Her face was haggard, her voice low and hoarse and slurred. Jeannette began to cry. "Damn you," Gerry said, "don't make any *noise*." She slapped Jeannette on the side of the head. She turned to me, glaring, and I ducked. My teeth were chattering. Everything was so confused, so cold—I couldn't understand what Gerry was saying.

"Is Mike back? Is Mike back?" Jeannette whispered.

"This has got nothing to do with *him*," Gerry said. "Look, will you get moving? Here, Ellie—these are your shoes, aren't they? Hurry up! For Christ's sake! If they figure out where I've gone, they'll be up here. The bastards are getting mean, the damn dirty loud-mouthed drunken *bastards*—"

Jeannette and I managed to get dressed, whimpering like small children. Then Gerry shoved us out of the room and along the hall to the back stairs. "Just get out of here! I don't care where you go! Get *out* before it's too late!"

"But—"

"Get *out*, I said—do you want me to knock your stupid heads together?"

We hid in the barn, frightened and shivering and silent, until the last of the men drove away a few hours later.

When I came home I went up to my room, lay on the bed and wept for hours. My mother knocked at the door; I told her to go away. I saw Gerry's ugly, contorted face; I felt her fingers closing around my wrist; I heard the drunken laughter; I smelled her hair, her body, her breath. I hated her. I loved her. Twisting my neck I pressed my hot cheek against my shoulder, against the tiny rose tattoo. Gerry? She had been frightened of the men—she hadn't been able to control them after all—she had had no real power over them. I hated her. I hated that image of her—white-faced, drunk, stumbling against Jeannette's bed. She had grabbed me by the shoulders and shaken me, hard. Wake up! Wake up! Get out of here before it's too late!

"You are never to see that girl again," my parents said, afterward. "You are never to stay overnight with anyone unless we know the family—unless they're friends of ours. Do you understand?"

"I don't want to see her again," I said. "Her or any of them. I hate them. I wish they were dead."

"As for that ugly tattoo—"

"I wish they were all dead!"

Once when I was home from college, my second year, I think, I saw Gerry Lund downtown, coming out of Sears, in the same old sheepskin jacket. Her hair was shorter and very messy; she wore mud-splattered cowhide boots and jeans too tight for her big legs and sunglasses with cheap white plastic frames. The sight of her went through me like an electric shock, and I drew back at once, not wanting to be seen. An ugly, strange woman. Was she muttering to herself? She was only in her mid-thirties but she looked a decade older: there were sharp, savage creases on either side of her mouth.

Gerry?

I drew back, my heart hammering.

She strode past without recognizing me, without even glancing at me. She seemed angry about something; she *was* muttering under her breath.

And then again, five or six years later, when my husband and I were visiting my parents, I went with my mother to the new shopping mall east of Derby, and there I saw Gerry Lund again.

Her hair was cropped short as a man's and her body had become thick and unwieldy, almost obese; she wore pink cotton slacks that were soiled and a red pullover sweater that strained against her breasts, giving her a bloated, rather grotesque appearance. She was a woman well into middle age, frankly ugly. She looked gigantic. What was most alarming, however, was the fact that she wore glasses with thick lenses—very thick lenses—and that she was clutching at the arm of a young girl, as if she couldn't see well enough to walk by herself.

"The poor thing, I've seen her out here a few times now," my mother said. "There seems to be something wrong with her."

Gerry's lips were moving in agitation. Perhaps she was complaining to the girl or talking to herself or just chewing gum. Behind the thick lenses her eyes swam darkly, magnified many times.

Gerry?

Gerry Lund?

I saw a smear of color, a drab mustard yellow, on the back of her left hand as we passed one another.

"I know her—I knew her—"

My words were so faint that my mother had to ask me to repeat them, and then she said: "But that woman's too old to have been a classmate of yours."

"I knew her sister."

I felt my face stretch into a bright, terrible expression—I was about to burst into laughter. And then everyone would stare at me as they were staring at the ugly fat woman in the pink slacks. And then. . . .

"I saw her once in Kroger's," my mother was saying, "arguing with one of the cashiers. Evidently she's almost blind, and I don't think she's quite right—quite right in the head. Someone told me she's the woman whose husband beat her so badly, a few years ago. I *think* she's the one, but of course I don't know for certain . . . I don't really know. You say you knew her sister?"

My parents had driven me eighty miles to a doctor who removed the tattoo within several hours. He had been fussy and methodical and very efficient. The procedure hurt, I remember crying helplessly like a small, frightened child, but when he was through, almost nothing remained of the tattoo.

Almost nothing remains. My arm is smooth there, except for the faint scar from a smallpox inoculation, which fades year by year.

Gerry? That woman? *That* . . . ?

My mother asked again about the woman's sister, where had I known her, what was their name, and I heard myself saying, in a calm voice, that I really didn't know: it had slipped my mind.

JACK FROST

JOSEPHINE JACOBSEN

Josephine Jacobsen lives in Baltimore in the winter and Whitefield, New Hampshire, in summer. She served two terms as poetry consultant to the Library of Congress, 1971–73, and is presently honorary consultant in American letters to that library. She has published two books of criticism, and five books of poetry the most recent of which, *The Shade-Seller*, was an N.B.A. nominee. Her first collection of short stories, A *Walk with Raschid & Other Stories*, will be published by The Jackpine Press in 1978. This is Ms. Jacobsen's fifth appearance in the PRIZE STORIES.

Mrs. Travis was drinking a sturdy cup of tea. She sat in the wicker rocker on her back porch, in a circle of sun, after picking Mrs. James' flowers. Exhausted, she thought she felt a little tired, and she rested with satisfaction. Mrs. James' motley bouquet sat by her knee, in one of the flower tins.

Mrs. Travis wore a blue cotton dress, with over it a man's suitcoat, with around that a tie, knotted for a belt. Her legs were bare, but her small feet had on them a pair of child's goloshes, the sort that have spring-buckles. Since several springs were missing, she wore the goloshes open, and sometimes they impeded her.

Half of her back porch, the left-hand side, was clear, and held her wicker rocker with its patches of sprung stiff strands; but the other half was more fruitful, a great pile of possessions which she needed, or had needed, or in certain possible circumstances, might come to need: a tin foot-tub containing rope, twine, and a nest of tin containers from the insides of flowerbaskets; a hatchet; a golosh for the right foot; garden tools; a rubber mat; a bee-keeper's helmet for the black-fly season. Near by, a short length of hose; chunks of wood. The eye flagged before the count.

Originally appeared in *Epoch*. Copyright © 1977 by Cornell University. Reprinted by permission.

There was a small winding path, like the witch's in a fairy-tale, between cosmos so tall they brushed the shoulders. To its right almost immediately, vegetables grew: the feathery tops of carrots, dusty beet-greens, the long runners of beans, a few handsome mottled zucchini. Last year there had still been tomatoes, but the staking-up and coaxing had become too much; she said to herself instead that such finicking had come to bore her. To the left of the cosmos, below a small slope of scratchy lawn, was the garden proper—on this mellow September afternoon a fine chaos of unchosen color, the Mexican shades of zinnias, the paper-cutout heads of dahlias, a few grownover roses, more cosmos, the final spikes of some fine gladioli, phlox running heavily back to magenta, and closer to the cooling ground, the pink and purple of asters. There were even a few pansies, wildly persisting in a tangle of grass and weeds.

Until a few years ago, her younger brother Henry had driven over two hundred miles, up from Connecticut, to help her plant both gardens; but Henry had died at eighty-two. Mrs. Travis herself did not actually know how old she was. She believed herself to be ninety-three; but having several years ago gone suddenly to check the fact of the matter in the faint gray handwriting of her foxed Bible, a cup of strong tea in her hand, she had sloshed the tea as she peered, and then on the puffed, run surface, she could no longer read the final digit. 3? 7? 1883? Just possibly, 1887? For a moment she felt youth pressing on her; if it were, if it possibly were 1887, several years had lifted themselves off. There they were, still to come with all the variety of their days. Turn those to hours, those to minutes, and it was a gigantic fresh extension. But she thought the figure was a 3. It was the last time she looked in the back of the Bible.

Tacked onto the porch wall was a large calendar; each day past was circled in red. Only three such showed; she would circle September 4th when she closed the door for the night.

Now before she could swallow the last of her tea, here came Mrs. James' yellow sweater, borne on a bicycle along the dirt road outside the hedge. Dismounted, Mrs. James wheeled the bicycle up the path and leaned it against the porch post. She was sweaty with effort over the baked ridges of the road, and, half a century younger than her hostess, she radiated summer-visitor energy and cheer.

"Oh Mrs. Travis!" she cried. "You've got them all ready! Aren't they lovely!" She was disappointed, since she had hoped to choose the picking; but she and her summer friends regarded Mrs. Travis' activity as much like that of Dr. Johnson's dog walking on its hind legs.

Mrs. Travis looked with satisfaction at the jumble of phlox, gladioli, dahlias and zinnias which, with all the slow, slow bending and straightening, had cost her an hour.

"Oh it's so *warm*," said Mrs. James with pleasure, sitting down on the step at Mrs. Travis' feet.

Mrs. Travis had so few occasions to speak that it always seemed to take her a minute to call up her voice, which arrived faint with distance.

"Yes," she said, almost inaudibly. "It's a very good day."

"Oh look!" said Mrs. James, pleased. "Look how well the rose begonia's doing!" She had given it to Mrs. Travis early in the summer, it was one of her own bulbs from California, and she could see its full gorgeousness now, blooming erratically beside the path, hanging its huge rosy bloom by the gap-toothed rake and a tiny pile of debris, twigs, dead grass, a few leaves.

Mrs. Travis did not answer, but Mrs. James saw it was because she was looking at the begonia's gross beauty with a powerful smugness. They sat companionably for a moment. Mrs. James seemed to Mrs. Travis like one of the finches, or yellow-headed sparrows, which frequented her for the warmest weeks. Exactly as she thought so, Mrs. James said, suddenly sad, "Do you know the birds are all going, *already?*"

"No, not all," said Mrs. Travis soothingly. "The chickadees won't go." But Mrs. Travis did not really care; it was the flowers she created out of nothing.

"I hate to see them go so soon," said Mrs. James, stubbornly sad.

"But you'll be going, too," said Mrs. Travis faintly and comfortingly. Mrs. James, lifting her chin, looked at Mrs. Travis. "Are you going to stay here all winter, *again?*" she asked.

Mrs. Travis looked at her with stupefaction. Then she said, "Yes." She was afraid Mrs. James was going to repeat what she had said for the past two autumns, about Mrs. Travis moving into the village for the winter; here she was, no phone, no close neighbors; nothing but snow, and ice, and wind, and the grocery boy with his little bag, and the mailman's Pontiac passing without stopping. But Mrs. James said only, "Look, here comes Father O'Rourke."

There was the clap of a car door, and Father O'Rourke appeared between the cosmos, surprisingly wearing his dog-collar, his black coat slung over his white shoulder. Mrs. James stood up, pleased that Mrs. Travis had a visitor. "I've got to get these flowers back," she said. Now came the embarrassing moment. "How— er, they're so lovely; what . . . ?"

"That's three dollars for the pailful," said Mrs. Travis with satisfaction. Mrs. James, whose grandmother, as a little girl, had known Mrs. Travis in Boston, continued to feel, no matter what she paid, that the flowers had come as a gift from Mrs. Travis' conservatory. She laid three dollars inconspicuously on the table by the oil lamp, and Mrs. Travis watched her and Father O'Rourke saying hello, and goodbye for the winter, to each other in the hot slanting sun.

As Mrs. James wheeled her bicycle away, Father O'Rourke replaced her on the step. He did not offer to shake hands, having noticed that such gestures seemed to distract Mrs. Travis, as some sort of clumsy recollected maneuver. He had just come from making the final plans for the Watkins wedding, and fresh from all that youth and detail, he looked at Mrs. Travis, whose pale small blue eyes looked back at him, kindly, but from a long distance. The purpose of Father O'Rourke's visit embarrassed him; he was afraid of Mrs. Travis' iron will.

"What a lot of flowers you've still got," began Father O'Rourke, obliquely.

Mrs. Travis looked out over the ragged rainbow on the slope. The sun, at its western angle, was still a good bit above the smaller of the big dark mountains behind which it would go. "Oh yes," she said, "they'll be here a long time. A couple of weeks, probably." He saw that she meant just that.

"Well," he said, "you know, Mrs. Travis, after five years here, I've found you just don't know. Things may go on almost to October; and then, again, a night in late August will do it."

Mrs. Travis did not reply to this, and Father O'Rourke plunged. "I saw Mrs. Metcalfe at the post-office this morning," he said, looking placatingly at Mrs. Travis' profile. "Did you know that she's finished making that big sitting-room, off her south porch, into that little apartment she's going to rent out?"

Mrs. Travis, who had had enough of this for one day, indeed, for one lifetime, turned her head and looked him straight in his hazel eyes.

"I'm not going anywhere," she said, surprisingly loudly, adding, from some past constraint, "Father O'Rourke."

A final sense of the futility of his effort struck him silent. They sat quietly for a few seconds. What on earth am I trying to do? he thought suddenly. Why *should* she move? Well, so many reasons; he wondered if they were all worthless. He knew that before he was born, Mrs. Travis had enlisted in the army of eccentric hermits, isolates, writing their own terms into some curious treaty. But she was so much older than anyone else that the details became more and more obscure; also, more romanticized. There was even doubt as to a dim and distant husband. A fallen or faithless lover appeared, along with factual but tinted tales of early privilege. But the Miss Haversham motif he tended to discount; it was so widely beloved.

All he knew for certain was that, with Mrs. Travis, he was in the presence of an authenticity of elimination which caused him a curiously mingled horror and envy. At times he thought that her attention, fiercely concentrated, brought out, like a brilliant detail from an immense canvas, a quality of some non-verbal and passionate comprehension. At others, he saw a tremendously old woman, all nuances of the world, her past, and the earth's present, ignored or forgotten; brittle and single, everything rejected but her own tiny circle of motion.

With a fairly complex mind, Father O'Rourke combined a rather simple set of hopes, not many of which were realized. One of these was to enter Mrs. Travis' detail, as some sort of connection with a comfort, or even a lack of finality. The bond between them, actually, was a belief in the physical, a conviction of the open-ended mystery of matter. But since Mrs. Travis had never been a Catholic, that particular avenue wasn't open to him. Her passion was in this scraggy garden, but he distinguished that it was coldly unsentimental, unlike that of most of the lady gardeners he knew. He was not sure just how Mrs. Travis did feel about her flowers. He considered that, in homily and metaphor, the garden-thing, Eden to Gethsemane—had been overdone; nevertheless, in connection with Mrs. Travis, he always thought of it.

He had, on a previous visit last month, brought up some flower passages from the Bible; but the only interest she had shown was by a question as to which type of lily the lilies-of-the-field had been. She had at least five kinds, lifting their slick and sappy stalks above confusion. But when he had said they were most like anemones, she had lost interest, having forgotten after fifty years in the New Hampshire mountains, what anemones looked like.

"I have to go back to the Watkins' tomorrow," said Father O'Rourke. He knew he should have been back at the rectory half an hour ago. Here he sat, mesmerized somehow, by the invisible movement of the sun across the step, by the almost total stillness. It was cooling rapidly, too. He picked up his coat and hunched his arms into it. "Can I bring you something, then?"

"No," she said. She was sorry to see him go. She turned her head to look fully at him. "Do you want any flowers?" she asked.

He hesitated, thinking of Mrs. Metcalfe's pious arrangement, three pink gladioli in a thin-stemmed glass on either side of the altar. "Well," he said, "how about some zinnias for my desk? I'll pick them tomorrow," he added hastily, as he saw her eyes cloud, rallying for action. On the step he lingered, smiling at her. Oppressed. "Well," he said idiotically, "don't let Jack Frost get your flowers."

She watched him attentively down the path. Just as his starter churned, the sun left the porch, and looking up to the mountain, Mrs. Travis saw that it had gone for the day.

She went in at once, forgetting her rake lying in the garden, her empty tea-cup and the three dollars on the table, but carrying a short chunk of wood under each arm. She took at least one each time she went into the house. She never turned on the furnace before October, but there was a small chunk stove in the corner, by the lamp-table, and it warmed the room in a matter of minutes. She decided to have supper right now. She had a chop; and there was still some lettuce. She had picked a fine head this morning, it was right in the colander, earth still clinging to its bottom.

By eight o'clock it had got very cold, outside. But the room was warm. Mrs. Travis went to sleep, in her chair. Sleep often took her now with a ferocious touch, so that every thing just disappeared, and when she woke up, she found that hours had passed. On a warm night, in July, she had slept in her chair all night long, waking up, disoriented, to a watery dawn.

Now she not only slept, she dreamed. An unpleasant dream, something extremely unusual. She was in a dark huge city lit by thin lamps, and she was afraid. She was afraid of a person, who might be coming toward her, or coming up behind her. And yet, more than a person—though she knew it was a man in a cap. She must get into a house before he found her. Or before he found someone else. A strange-looking girl went by her, hurrying, very pale, with a big artificial rose in her hair. She turned suddenly into an opening on the dreamer's right, it was the darkest of alleys, and the dreamer hurried faster than ever. Ahead of her, in the fog, she could see the dimly-lit sign of an inn, but as she hurried faster, a terrible scream, high and short, came out of the alley. It woke Mrs. Travis, her hands locked hard on the arms of the chair.

She sat quite still, looking around the familiar room. Then memory handed her one of the clear messages that now so seldom arrived. The Lodger. That was just it. She had suddenly, after all these years had a dream about Jack the Ripper, as she had had several times when she read of his foggy city streets a very long time ago. But why this dream should have escaped from the past to molest her, she could not think.

The little fire in the stove went out, but the stove itself still ticked and settled with heat. The wall-clock said two minutes to eight. Stiff from sleep, Mrs. Travis reached over and turned the dial of the small discolored radio under the table-lamp, and immediately a loud masculine voice said, ". . . front, all the way from the Great Lakes, throughout northern New England, and into Canada. Frost warnings have been issued for the mountain areas of Vermont and New Hampshire. Tomorrow the unseasonable cold will continue, for a chilly Labor Day; but by Wednesday . . ." Appalled, Mrs. Travis switched off the evil messenger.

Frost. It was not that it was so strange; it was so sudden. She could still feel the heat of the sun, on the porch, on her hands and her ankles. Two weeks, she had thought.

As she sat, staring for a moment straight ahead, a brand new fury started up, deep inside her. Two weeks. It was an eternity of summer. The long nights, the brutal chill, the endless hardness of the earth, they were reasonable enough, in their time. In their time. But this was her time, and they were about to invade it. She began to tremble with anger. She thought of her seeds, and how dry and hard they had been; of her deathlike bulbs, slipping old skin, with everything locked inside them, and she, her body, had turned them into that summer of color and softness and good smells that was out there in the dark garden.

She turned her head, right, and left, looking for an exit for her rage. Then suddenly she sat forward in her chair. An idea had come to her with great force and clarity. It grew in the room, like an enormous plant covered with buds. Mrs. Travis knew exactly what she was going to do. Her intention was not protective, but defiant; her sense was of battle, punitive battle.

She stood up carefully, and went and got the flashlight from the shelf over the woodbox. She went to the porch door and opened it, and then closed it hastily behind her, protecting the room's warmth. There was no sound or light in any direction, but there was a diffused brightness behind the mountain's darker bulk. She tipped over the pail that had held Mrs. James' flowers, so that the leafy water poured down the sloping porch. Then she began fitting the tin flower-holders into it. She could not get them all in, and she took her pail into the house and came back for the last three. She arranged the pail and the tins on the kitchen floor, and then she attached a short length of hose to the cold water spigot, dropped the other end in the pail, and turned on the water. She filled the big tins the same way, and then lifted the small ones into the sink, removing the hose, and filled them. Turning with satisfaction to look through the doorway at the clock, she was disconcerted to see that it said five minutes after nine. She stared at it, skeptical but uncertain. It could *stop*; but surely it couldn't skip *ahead*. Perhaps she had mistaken the earlier time. She began to move more rapidly; though she was so excited, all her faculties had come so strongly into one intention, that it seemed to her that she was already moving at a furious pace.

She went over to the kitchen door and took off its hook a felt hat and an ancient overcoat of Henry's. She put the hat on her head, got carefully into the overcoat and stuffed her flashlight into the pocket. She took down from the top of the refrigerator a cracked papier-mache tray Mrs. James had sent her several Christmases ago; its design of old coins had almost disappeared. At an open drawer, she hesitated over a pair of shears. Lately she had found them hard to open and close, and after standing there for half a minute, she took a thick-handled knife instead. She went to look at the empty sitting room and then moved through the kitchen faster than was possible.

Out on the porch, a square of light came through the window, and looking up, she could make out a cloud over the mountain, its edges stained with brightness.

She lit her flashlight, and went cautiously down the step and along the path, carrying her tray under her arm. Faces of cosmos, purple and pink, loomed at her as she went, but even in her tremendous excitement, she knew she couldn't bring in everything, and she went on, the tops of her goloshes making little flapping noises in the silence. She turned carefully down the slight slope, and here were the zinnias, towered over by the branchy dahlias. She laid her tray on the ground.

But now, breathing more rapidly, she saw that she was in trouble. To cut with her knife, she had to hold the flower's stem, and she had to hold her flashlight to see it, and she had two hands. Fiercely she looked about her for an idea; and at just that moment, a clear thin light streamed over the edge of the cloud and hit her. The moon was full. She might have known; that was when a black frost always came.

Mrs. Travis made an inarticulate sound of fierce pleasure, and dropped the flashlight onto the tray. Then she began to cut the flowers, working as fast as she could, giving little pants of satisfaction as the shapes heaped themselves up below her. Inch by inch she moved along the ragged rows, pushing, with a goloshed toe, the tray along the ground before her. She cut all the gladioli, even the ones which were still mostly flaccid green tips; she cut all the dahlias, even the buds, and every zinnia. She felt light and warm, and drunk with resistant power. Finally the tray was so full that blooms began to tip over and fall into the cold grass.

Very cautiously indeed she got the tray up, but she could not hold it level and manipulate the flashlight. It made no difference. The moon, enormous and fully round, had laid light all over the garden, the house's shadow was as black as though a pale sun were shining.

Teetering a little to hold the tray level, Mrs. Travis went up the path, carefully up the step. She set the tray on the table, knocking over her dirty tea-cup and saucer, and each broke cleanly in two pieces. She stepped over them, opened the door on warmth, and went back for her load.

First she filled the pail; then every tin. There was a handful of zinnias left, and a pile of phlox. Threatened, Mrs. Travis looked about the kitchen, but saw nothing helpful. She could feel her cheeks burning in the room's summer, and with a little noise of triumph, she went through the door to the bedroom, and came back with the big china chamberpot. It had a fine network of fractured veins, and on it was painted a burst of magenta foliage. When she had filled it under the tap, it was too heavy to lift down, so she stuffed in the flowers and left it there. A small chartreuse-colored spider began to run up and down the sink's edge.

Then, just as she was turning to look at all she had done, like a cry from an alley, like a blow between the shoulders, came to her mind's eye the rose-begonia. She could positively see in the air before her its ruffled heavy head, the coral flush of its crowded petals; from its side sprang the bud, color splitting the sheath. The bulb had thrust it up, and there it was, out there.

Though she felt as though she were drunk, she also felt shrewd. Think of the low ones you can't stoop to tonight, she thought, the nasturtiums, the pansies, the bachelor's-buttons. But it made no difference. She knew that unless she took the rose-begonia, she had lost everything. She looked at the clock; it was half-past ten. She would be back in ten minutes; and she decided that then she would sit right down by the stove, and sleep there, deliberately, and not move into the cold bed and take off bit by bit so many clothes.

There were four sticks of wood by the stove, and under the lid the embers were bright. She put in three sticks; then she went empty-handed onto the porch. It was very cold and absolutely still. The moon was even brighter; it was almost halfway up the sky. She found a terra-cotta flowerpot on the porch corner and rooted in the footbath until she found her trowel. Then she went, as fast as she could go, down the path to the halfway point, when she came upon the rose-begonia, paled by the chill of the night. As she bent over, her head roared; so she kneeled, and drove the blunt trowel-edge into the earth.

When the roots came up in a great ball of earth she pressed them into the pot, stuffing more clods of fibrous earth around them. Then she started to get up. But with the pot in one hand and the trowel in the other, it was impossible.

She dropped the trowel. She did not even think that she would get it tomorrow. Suddenly she was cold to her very teeth. She thought just of the room, the hot, colored, waiting room. Holding the pot in her left hand, pushing with her right, she got herself upright; but it made her dizzy, and as she lurched a little to the side, the rake's teeth brought her down in a heavy fall. The pot shot from her hand and disappeared into the shadows and a bright strong pain blasted her. It was her ankle; and she lay with her face close to the cold dirt, feeling the waves of pain hit her.

Mrs. Travis raised her head, to see how far away the porch was. It was perhaps ten or eleven yards. Another country. Things seemed dimmer, too, and wrenching her head sideways and up, she saw that the huge moon had shrunk; it sat high and small, right at the top of the sky.

Mrs. Travis lowered her head gently and began to crawl, pushing with her hands and the knee of her good leg. She went along, inch by inch, foot by foot; she had no fear, since there was an absolute shield between one second and the next.

The porch was so shadowed now that she nearly missed it, the step struck her advancing hand. It took her three tries, but she got up over it, and went on, inch by inch, toward the door. A raw edge of china bit her hand. Bright light came through the keyhole. She reached up and easily turned the doorknob, then like a crab she was across the sill.

She could not, she found, turn; but she pushed out with her left foot, and miraculously the door clicked shut just behind her. She felt no pain at all, but there was something forming under her ribs.

In the room's heat, the foliage of the marigolds gave out a spicy smell, stronger than the fragrance of the phlox. A dozen shapes and colors blazed before her eyes, and a great tearing breath came up inside her like an explosion. Mrs. Travis lifted her head, and the whole wave of summer, advancing obedient and glorious, in a crest of color and warmth and fragrance broke right over her.

SPEAKING OF COURAGE

TIM O'BRIEN

Tim O'Brien is a native of Minnesota. His stories have appeared in *Esquire, Redbook, Shenandoah, Denver Quarterly, Ploughshares*, and other magazines. His new novel, *Going After Cacciato*, was published in February of this year.

The war was over, and there was no place in particular to go. Paul Berlin followed the tar road in its seven-mile loop around the lake, then he started all over again, driving slowly, feeling safe inside his father's big Chevy, now and again looking out onto the lake to watch the boats and waterskiers and scenery. It was Sunday and it was summer, and things seemed pretty much the same. The lake was the same. The houses were the same, all low-slung and split level and modern, porches and picture windows facing the water. The lots were spacious. On the lake-side of the road, the houses were handsome and set deep in, well-kept and painted, with docks jutting out into the lake, and boats moored and covered with canvas, and gardens, and sometimes even gardeners, and stone patios with barbecue spits and grills, and wooden shingles saying who lived where. On the other side of the road, to his left, the houses were also handsome, though less expensive and on a smaller scale and with no docks or boats or wooden shingles. The road was a sort of boundary between the affluent and the almost affluent, and to live on the lake-side of the road was one of the few natural privileges in a town of the prairie—the difference between watching the sun set over cornfields or over the lake.

It was a good-sized lake. In high school he'd driven round and round and round with his friends and pretty girls, talking about urgent matters, worrying eagerly about the existence of God and theories of causation, or wondering whether Sally Hankins,

Reprinted from *The Massachusetts Review*. Copyright © 1976 by The Massachusetts Review, Inc. Reprinted by permission.

who lived on the lake-side of the road, would want to pull into the shelter of Sunset Park. Then, there had not been a war. But there had always been the lake. It had been dug out by the southernmost advance of the Wisconsin glacier. Fed by neither springs nor streams, it was a tepid, algaed lake that depended on fickle prairie rains for replenishment. Still, it was the town's only lake, the only one in twenty-six miles, and at night the moon made a white swath across its waters, and on sunny days it was nice to look at, and that evening it would dazzle with the reflections of fireworks, and it was the center of things from the very start, always there to be driven around, still mesmerizing and quieting and a good audience for silence, a seven-mile flat circumference that could be traveled by slow car in twenty-five minutes. It was not such a good lake for swimming. After college, he'd caught an ear infection that had almost kept him out of the war. And the lake had drowned Max Arnold, keeping him out of the war entirely. Max had been one who liked to talk about the existence of God. "No, I'm not saying *that*," he would say carefully against the drone of the engine. "I'm saying it is possible as an idea, even necessary as an idea, a final cause in the whole structure of causation." Now he knew, perhaps. Before the war, they'd driven around the lake as friends, but now Max was dead and most of the others were living in Des Moines or Sioux City, or going to school somewhere, or holding down jobs. None of the girls was left. Sally Hankins was married. His father would not talk. His father had been in another war, so he knew the truth already, and he would not talk about it, and there was no one left to talk with.

He turned on the radio. The car's big engine fired machinery that blew cold air all over him. Clockwise, like an electron spinning forever around its nucleus, the big Chevy circled the lake, and he had little to do but sit in the air-conditioning, both hands on the wheel, letting the car carry him in orbit. It was a lazy Sunday. The town was small. Out on the lake, a man's motorboat had stalled, and the fellow was bent over the silver motor with a wrench and a frown, and beyond him there were waterskiers and smooth July waters and two mud hens.

The road curved west. The sun was low in front of him, and he figured it was close to five o'clock. Twenty after, he guessed. The war had taught him to figure time. Even without the sun, waking from sleep, he could usually place it within fifteen minutes either way. He wished his father were there beside him, so he could say, "Well, looks about five-twenty," and his father would look at his watch and say, "Hey! How'd you do that?" "One of those things you learn in the war," he would say. "I know exactly what you mean," his father would then say, and the ice would be broken, and then they would be able to talk about it as they circled the lake.

He drove past Slater Park and across the causeway and past Sunset Park. The radio announcer sounded tired. He said it was five-thirty. The temperature in Des Moines was eighty-one degrees, and "All you on the road, drive carefully now, you hear, on this fine Fourth of July." Along the road, kicking stones in front of them, two young boys were hiking with knapsacks and toy rifles and canteens. He honked going by, but neither boy looked up. Already he'd passed them six times, forty-two miles, nearly three hours. He watched the boys recede in his rearview mirror. They turned purply colored, like clotted blood, before finally disappearing.

"How many medals did you win?" his father might have asked.

"Seven," he would have said, "though none of them were for valor."

"That's all right," his father would have answered, knowing full well that many brave men did not win medals for their bravery, and that others won medals for doing nothing. "What are the medals you won?"

And he would have listed them, as a kind of starting place for talking about the war: the Combat Infantryman's Badge, the Air Medal, the Bronze Star (without a V-device for valor), the Army Commendation Medal, the Vietnam Campaign Medal, the Good Conduct Medal, and the Purple Heart, though it wasn't much of a wound, and there was no scar, and it didn't hurt and never had. While none of them was for valor, the decorations still looked good on the uniform in his closet, and if anyone were to ask, he would have explained what each signified, and eventually he would have talked about the medals he did not win, and why he did not win them, and how afraid he had been.

"Well," his father might have said, "that's an impressive list of medals, all right."

"But none were for valor."

"I understand."

And that would have been the time for telling his father that he'd almost won the Silver Star, or maybe even the Medal of Honor.

"I almost won the Silver Star," he would have said.

"How's that?"

"Oh, it's just a war story."

"What's wrong with war stories?" his father would have said.

"Nothing, except I guess nobody wants to hear them."

"Tell me," his father would have said.

And then, circling the lake, he would have started the story by saying what a crazy hot day it had been when Frenchie Tucker crawled like a snake into the clay tunnel and got shot in the neck, going on with the story in great detail, telling how it smelled and what the sounds had been, everything, then going on to say how he'd almost won the Silver Star for valor.

"Well," his father would have said, "that's not a very pretty story."

"I wasn't very brave."

"You have seven medals."

"True, true," he would have said, "but I might have had eight," but even so, seven medals was pretty good, hinting at courage with their bright colors and heavy metals. "But I wasn't brave," he would have admitted.

"You weren't a coward, either," his father would have said.

"I might have been a hero."

"But you weren't a coward," his father would have insisted.

"No," Paul Berlin would have said, holding the wheel slightly right of center to produce the constant clockwise motion, "no, I wasn't a coward, and I wasn't brave, but I had the chance." He would have explained, if anyone were there to listen, that his most precious medal, except for the one he did not win, was the Combat Infantryman's Badge. While not strictly speaking a genuine medal—more an insignia of soldierdom—the CIB meant that he had seen the war as a real soldier, on the ground. It meant he'd had the opportunity to be brave, it meant that. It meant, too, that he'd squatted on his heels to defecate and wiped himself with weeds, seen brave men masturbate in their foxholes while under fire, see Frenchie Tucker crawl into the tunnel so that just his feet were left showing, and heard the sound when he got shot in the neck. With its crossed rifles and silver and blue colors, the

CIB was really not such a bad decoration, not as good as the Silver Star or Medal of Honor, but still evidence that he'd once been there with the chance to be very brave. "I wasn't brave," he would have said, "but I might have been."

The road descended into the outskirts of town, turning northwest past the junior college and tennis courts, then past the city park where tables were spread with sheets of colored plastic as picnickers listened to the high school band, then past the municipal docks where a fat woman stood in pedal-pushers and white socks, fishing for bullheads. There were no other fish in the lake, excepting some perch and a few worthless carp. It was a bad lake for swimming and fishing both.

He was in no great hurry. There was no place in particular to go. The day was very hot, but inside the Chevy the air was cold and oily and secure, and he liked the sound of the big engine and the radio and the air-conditioning. Through the windows, as though seen through one-way glass, the town shined like a stop-motion photograph, or a memory. The town could not talk, and it would not listen, and it was really a very small town anyway. "How'd you like to hear about the time I almost won the Silver Star for valor?" he might have said. The Chevy seemed to know its way around the lake.

It was late afternoon. Along an unused railway spur, four men were erecting steel launchers for the evening fireworks. They were dressed alike in khaki trousers, work shirts, visored caps and black boots. They were sweating. Two of them were unloading crates of explosives from a city truck, stacking the crates near the steel launchers. They were talking. One of them was laughing. "How'd you like to hear about it?" he might have murmured, but the men did not look up. Later they would blow color into the sky. The lake would be like a mirror, and the picnickers would sigh. The colors would open wide. "Well, it was this crazy hot day," he would have said to anyone who asked, "and Frenchie Tucker took off his helmet and pack and crawled into the tunnel with a forty-five and a knife, and the whole platoon stood in a circle around the mouth of the tunnel to watch him go down. 'Don't get blowed away,' said Stink Harris, but Frenchie was already inside and he didn't hear. You could see his feet wiggling, and you could smell the dirt and clay, and then, when he got shot through the neck, you could smell the gunpowder and you could see Frenchie's feet jerk, and that was the day I could have won the Silver Star for valor."

The Chevy rolled smoothly across the old railroad spur. To his right, there was only the open lake. To his left, the lawns were scorched dry like October corn. Hopelessly, round and round, a rotating sprinkler scattered water into Doctor Mason's vegetable garden. In August it would get worse. The lake would turn green, thick with bacteria and decay, and the golf course would dry up, and dragonflies would crack open for lack of good water. The summer seemed permanent.

The big Chevy curled past the A&W and Centennial Beach, and he started his seventh revolution around the lake.

He followed the road past the handsome low-slung houses. Back to Slater Park, across the causeway, around to Sunset Park, as though riding on tracks.

Out on the lake, the man with the stalled motorboat was still fiddling with the engine.

The two boys were still trudging on their hike. They did not look up when he honked.

The pair of mud hens floated like wooden decoys. The water-skiers looked tan and happy, and the spray behind them looked clean.

It was all distant and pretty.

Facing the sun again, he figured it was nearly six o'clock. Not much later the tired announcer in Des Moines confirmed it, his voice seeming to rock itself into a Sunday afternoon snooze.

Too bad, he thought. If Max were there, he would say something meaningful about the announcer's fatigue, and relate it to the sun low and red now over the lake, and the war, and courage. Too bad that all the girls had gone away. And his father, who already knew the difficulties of being brave, and who preferred silence.

Circling the lake, with time to talk, he would have told the truth. He would not have faked it. Starting with the admission that he had not been truly brave, he would have next said he hadn't been a coward, either. "I almost won the Silver Star for valor," he would have said, and, even so, he'd learned many important things in the war. Like telling time without a watch. He had learned to step lightly. He knew, just by the sound, the difference between friendly and enemy mortars, and with time to talk and with an audience, he could explain the difference in great detail. He could tell people that the enemy fired 82 millimeter mortar rounds, while we fired 81's, and that this was a real advantage to the enemy since they could steal our rounds and shoot them from their own weapons. He knew many lies. Simple, unprofound things. He knew it is a lie that only stupid men are brave. He knew that a man can die of fright, literally, because it had happened just that way to Billy Boy Watkins after his foot had been blown off. Billy Boy had been scared to death. Dead of a heart attack caused by fright, according to Doc Peret, who would know. He knew, too, that it is a lie, the old saying that you never hear the shot that gets you, because Frenchie Tucker was shot in the neck, and after they dragged him out of the tunnel he lay there and told everyone his great discovery; he'd heard it coming the whole way, he said excitedly; and then he raised his thumb and bled through his mouth, grinning at the great discovery. So the old saying was surely a lie, or else Frenchie Tucker was lying himself, which under the circumstances was hard to believe. He knew a lot of things. They were not new or profound, but they were true. He knew that he might have won a Silver Star, like Frenchie, if he'd been able to finish what Frenchie started in the foul tunnel. He knew many war stories, a thousand details, smells and the confusion of the senses, but nobody was there to listen, and nobody knew a damn about the war because nobody believed it was really a war at all. It was not a war for war stories, or talk of valor, and nobody asked questions about the details, such as how afraid you can be, or what the particular sounds were, or whether it hurts to be shot, or what you think about and hear and see on ambush, or whether you can really tell in a firefight which way to shoot, which you can't, or how you become brave enough to win the Silver Star, or how it smells of sulfur against your cheek after firing eighteen fast rounds, or how you crawl on hands and knees without knowing direction, and how, after crawling into the red-mouthed tunnel, you close your eyes like a mole and follow the tunnel walls and smell Frenchie's fresh blood and know a bullet cannot miss in there, and how there is nowhere to go but forward or backward, eyes closed, and how you can't go forward, and lose all sense, and are dragged out by the heels, losing the Silver Star. All the details, without profundity, simple and age old, but nobody wants to hear war stories because they are age old and not

new and not profound, and because everyone knows already that
it hadn't been a war like other wars. If Max or his father were ever
to ask, or anybody, he would say, "Well, first off, it was a war the
same as any war," which would not sound profound at all, but
which would be the truth. Then he would explain what he meant
in great detail, explaining that, right or wrong or win or lose, at
root it had been a real war, regardless of corruption in high places
or politics or sociology or the existence of God. His father knew it
already, though. Which was why he didn't ask. And Max could
not ask. It was a small town, but it wasn't the town's fault, either.

He passed the sprawling ranch-style homes. He lit a cigarette.
He had learned to smoke in the war. He opened the window a
crack but kept the air-conditioner going full, and again he circled
the lake. His thoughts were the same. Out on the lake, the man
was frantically yanking the cord to his stalled outboard motor.
Along the causeway, the two boys marched on. The pair of mud
hens sought sludge at the bottom of the lake, heads under water
and tails bobbing.

Six-thirty, he thought. The lake had divided into two halves.
One half still glistened. The other was caught in shadow. Soon it
would be dark. The crew of workers would shoot the sky full of
color, for the war was over, and the town would celebrate independence. He passed Sunset Park once again, and more houses,
and the junior college and tennis courts, and the picnickers and
the high school band, and the municipal docks where the fat
woman patiently waited for fish.

Already, though it wasn't quite dusk, the A&W was awash in
neon lights.

He maneuvered his father's Chevy into one of the parking slots,
let the engine idle, and waited. The place was doing a good holiday business. Mostly kids in their fathers' cars, a few farmers in
for the day, a few faces he thought he remembered, but no
names. He sat still. With the sound of the engine and air-conditioning and radio, he could not hear the kids laughing, or the cars
coming and going and burning rubber. But it didn't matter, it
seemed proper, and he sat patiently and watched while mosquitoes and June bugs swarmed off the lake to attack the orange-
colored lighting. A slim, hipless, deft young blonde delivered trays
of food, passing him by as if the big Chevy were invisible, but he
waited. The tired announcer in Des Moines gave the time, seven

o'clock. He could trace the fall of dusk in the orange lights which grew brighter and sharper. It was a bad war for medals. But the Silver Star would have been nice. Nice to have been brave. The tactile, certain substance of the Silver Star, and how he could have rubbed his fingers over it, remembering the tunnel and the smell of clay in his nose, going forward and not backward in simple bravery. He waited patiently. The mosquitoes were electrocuting themselves against a Pest-Rid machine. The slim young carhop ignored him, chatting with four boys in a Firebird, her legs in nylons even in mid-summer.

He honked once, a little embarrassed, but she did not turn. The four boys were laughing. He could not hear them, or the joke, but he could see their bright eyes and the way their heads moved. She patted the cheek of the driver.

He honked again, twice. He could not hear the sound. The girl did not hear, either.

He honked again, this time leaning on the horn. His ears buzzed. The air-conditioning shot cold air into his lap. The girl turned slowly, as though hearing something very distant, not at all sure. She said something to the boys, and they laughed, then she moved reluctantly toward him. EAT MAMA BURGERS said the orange and brown button on her chest. "How'd you like to hear about the war," he whispered, feeling vengeful. "The time I almost won the Silver Star."

She stood at the window, straight up so he could not see her face, only the button that said, EAT MAMA BURGERS. "Papa Burger, root beer and french fries," he said, but the girl did not move or answer. She rapped on the window.

"Papa Burger, root beer and french fries," he said, rolling it down.

She leaned down. She shook her head dumbly. Her eyes were as lovely and fuzzy as cotton candy.

"Papa Burger, root beer and french fries," he said slowly, pronouncing the words separately and distinctly for her.

She stared at him with her strange eyes. "You blind?" she chirped suddenly. She gestured toward an intercom attached to a steel post. "You blind or something?"

"Papa Burger, root beer and french fries."

"Push the button," she said, "and place your order." Then, first punching the button for him, she returned to her friends in the Firebird.

"Order," commanded a tinny voice.

"Papa Burger, root beer and french fries."

"Roger-dodger," the voice said. "Repeat: one Papa, one beer, one fries. Stand by. That's it?"

"Roger," said Paul Berlin.

"Out," said the voice, and the intercom squeaked and went dead.

"Out," said Paul Berlin.

When the slim carhop brought him his tray, he ate quickly, without looking up, then punched the intercom button.

"Order," said the tinny voice.

"I'm done."

"That's it?"

"Yes, all done."

"Roger-dodger, over n' out," said the voice.

"Out."

On his ninth revolution around the lake he passed the hiking boys for the last time. The man with the stalled motorboat was paddling toward shore. The mud hens were gone. The fat woman was reeling in her line. The sun had left a smudge of watercolor on the horizon, and the bandshell was empty, and Doctor Mason's sprinkler went round and round.

On his tenth revolution, he switched off the air-conditioning, cranked open a window and rested his elbow comfortably on the sill, driving with one hand. He could trace the contours of the tunnel. He could talk about the scrambling sense of being lost, though he could not describe it even in his thoughts. He could talk about the terror, but he could not describe it or even feel it anymore. He could talk about emerging to see sunlight, but he could not feel the warmth, or see the faces of the men who looked away, or talk about his shame. There was no one to talk to, and nothing to say.

On his eleventh revolution, the sky went crazy with color.

He pulled into Sunset Park and stopped in the shadow of a picnic shelter. After a time, he got out and walked down to the beach and stood with his arms folded and watched the fireworks. For a small town, it was a pretty good show.

UNDEVELOPED PHOTOGRAPHS

JESSIE SCHELL

Jessie Schell was born in Greenville, Mississippi, in 1941. She has published one novel, and her stories have appeared in various magazines (including *The Greensboro Review*, *McCall's*, and *The New Orleans Review*). "Undeveloped Photographs" marks her second appearance in the O. Henry collection. She lives with her husband outside Boston.

My father is in love with death. Although he will never admit his feelings of outrage, anger, each time his obedient heart guides him to the rim of destruction, then abandons him there, he is hungry for dying. Six heart attacks, the first at forty-five years old, have chewed up years of present time, ground it down to slow-motion hours in hospital rooms. Here, sweetly drugged, he swims against the hours—backwards, steadily.

"I'm not ready to die," he protests to me today. It is obligatory, the preamble to what his mind, his straining blood aim towards. The blue, striped pajamas have grown two sizes too big; his face is yellowish against the white hospital pillow. He is fifty-eight years old.

"Of course, you're not ready," I tell him. "No reason to be either."

I am settled where he has grown accustomed to having me— my chair pulled close to his bed, my hands busy with needlework. His skin is papery, dry. His fingernails, bitten and jagged. But when I look into his face, smoothed by sedatives, washed clean of pain, I see that he is already gone from me—here, now. Is still working peacefully behind the mask of medicine and rest to be done.

I have brought him the small transistor radio. He waits impatiently through the last bars of Chopin, this airy extravagance is

Copyright © 1977 by The Carolina Quarterly. Reprinted by permission.

not for him. When the Bach variations come on, I see him relax, although it is only a shifting of shoulders as he settles against his pillows. Here is order, intricate and precise, the rhythm of his memory; now, he may begin. For if his life has not turned out at all as he'd anticipated, not at all, still it is his—locked inside the camera of his skull—and he must show me what he can.

He always begins and ends with my grandfather, though his stories spiral off to lasso cousins and distant aunts, most of whom I have never met, most gone before my time. Still I see them all quite clearly. They move like forward shadows in their dance. And they are always disappearing in his recreations. That is the point.

I

My grandfather, orphaned, twelve years old, is taken in by second cousins whose motives are only peripherally charitable. They are childless, they need young hands to help with farm work. The farm is in Poland, the sloping hills desolate through most of the year, blooming with grain only in summer months, when the air buzzes with insects, when the sky stretches round as a blue bowl above.

He sleeps in the kitchen, his pallet near the wood stove, warm, well-fed. He is not often mistreated, but he works for every scrap of comfort, works for Saturday mornings, when he is free to walk the ten miles of dusty road to the village. Here he mails weekly letters to his brother and sister, each with a different cousin. Here he receives their weekly letters in return. Most Saturdays, he windowshops, his few coins rattling in his pocket. After fourteen weeks, he has saved enough to buy a good pair of shoes.

Even now, at twelve, my grandfather is vain. He likes the look and texture of fine things. The shoes he buys are not the sturdy boots he requires, not built for hard use and weather. He buys, instead, with the savings of winter months, a pair of shoes made for city streets in summer: soft leather, a delicate stitched sole. He does not wear them, is saving them for some day he cannot define.

But three weeks later, his cousin finds him heading towards the barn barefoot, his ordinary custom, and because the weeks have been rainy and cold, because he is, himself, for whatever numbered reasons, a part of the harsh weather this day, orders my grandfather to wear his shoes when he slops the pigs. Says shoes are to be worn, "why go barefoot like an orphan, you're not an orphan anymore. You bought them, wear them now."

My grandfather refuses and they argue bitterly. It is a disagreement having nothing to do with shoes. They are fighting over the monotonous, hard days, over the cousin's childlessness, the simple fact of emptiness between them: because necessity, instead of blood, has joined them together. In the end, my grandfather, beaten by his cousin, cuffed round the nose and eyes, gives in. Wears the fine-tooled shoes into the pigpen, where the mud and rinds of food ooze over the leather, up to his ankles.

The next night, silent and warmed by fury, he cleans the shoes as best he can, although they are worthless now, stiff and brittle. Ties his one change of clothes into a pillowcase, which he will steal. Walks off down the ten mile path to town. The mud sucks at his footsteps. By dawn, he has hitched a ride on a wagonful of chickens to the next village. Three days later, riding in a series of wagons carrying produce, animals, milk, he arrives at the edge of Warsaw. Twelve years old.

When he walks down the city streets, his shoes still carry the odor of mud and pig slop in their grain. There is a large hole rotting in one heel, already.

II

My father, five years old, sits at the bottom of the darkened stairs, wearing his nightshirt. He has waited there for hours. Although it is four in the morning, the household is up—his older brother and sister, eight and ten, are making hot chocolate in the kitchen. He hears the pot clang on the black wood stove, can see the finger of light point towards him where he waits alone. Upstairs, in her bedroom, his mother makes a terrible sound, half-cry, half-scream. Her voice has cracked open the night like an eggshell. Pain pours out of the edges.

An endless time ago, the doctor arrived, opening the door for himself without knocking, climbing past my father with no word whatsoever. The crying bloomed wider when the bedroom door opened, curled back for an instant as the doctor closed himself inside. My father's father has been in the room since before the doctor came. In the few quiet moments between his mother's terrible cries, he has heard my grandfather's voice murmuring behind the door. The sound of his voice, wordless but musical, falls down the darkened stairwell and rests in my father's ears like a lullabye. Then the awful rising scream pours over my father's head, washes over him in waves that push against his tender back. He lowers his head to his knees and waits, wrapped in his own thin embrace.

Later, much later, he hears a different sound—the noise of silence, utter quiet. Pink daylight seeps through the rose-colored glass above the front door. His sister and brother, who have tried for hours to move him from his place on the stairs, come out of the kitchen, stand holding the staircase bannister, looking up. In the dreadful quiet, the door opens; closes. The doctor and my grandfather descend the stairs. Their footsteps are cushioned by the velvet runner, but my father feels the weight of their bodies as the stairs shift beneath him.

At the front door, "Jake," the doctor says, and clasps my grandfather's shoulder. "I'll be back within an hour."

My grandfather continues to stand in the rose light for minutes, facing the closed front door, and when he turns and walks to his children, the outline of his body seems, to my father, precious and magical with colored light.

"It's over now," he tells them, looking from face to face. His gaze rests on my father last, lingers there, but my father knows that he is not seen, that my grandfather watches something else invisible to him.

"Your mother's resting, she'll be all right." Still my father's sister and brother wait for news of something more.

"The baby's dead," he tells them, and they seem to move slightly, then, as if his words have loosened them. They shiver and lower their heads.

And now my father's clear voice rises: "I'm glad," he says, still seated on the bottom stairs. The words pop out of his mouth like bullets. "I'm glad," he says again, louder.

In the instant before his father moves, he sees the shocked white faces of his brother and sister, their mouths stretched in twin O's. Then his father's open hand slams across the side of his face, pushing his teeth into the tender, inner flesh of his lip. Blood flows down the corners of his mouth, his father's face fractures before him, multiplies, filling up his sight; his father's outraged face, pulsing towards him; larger and smaller, closer and farther, to match the pounding rhythm in his head.

He waits, quite calmly, in his circle of pain, at the edge of the rose-colored light sidling towards the stairway. Then he is lifted, raised to his father's tight embrace. Pressed so near his father's weight that he feels he will sink into, become that flesh. The tears that did not come when the blow fell, come now, clouding his sight. He does not see the red blood stains he leaves on his father's good, white shirt.

Later, two weeks later, his mother will soak and wash the shirt, scour the stains, but the stains will not leave. "Where did this blood come from?" she asks her husband. "Did you hurt yourself?"

"Yes," his father answers, but will say no more.

Later still, defeated, she will tear the cloth into strips and use them for rags, scrubbing to clear the surfaces of her house from the dust of living.

III

It is the thirteenth summer of cousin India Smith's visits, but this July she is different. She and my father, born within two weeks of each other in June of 1915, have still another bond: they are double first cousins, my grandmother and her sister marrying my grandfather and his brother. My father and cousin India even share physical traits: they are both feline, have lean limber bodies, gold-flecked eyes. Their dark hair curls to ringlets in the moist Alabama heat. They tan to a copper brown in the sun, never burning or freckling as my father's brother and sister do.

Cousin India has driven all the way from Albany, Georgia, two hundred miles, in her parents' car. "We only had four flat tires," she tells my father, who is dutifully impressed. They are swinging on the front porch swing while their parents' voices mingle in the house: his mother and Aunt Molly in an upstairs bedroom, unpacking; his father and Uncle Herman smoking pipes in the dark front parlor.

My father is waiting for India to suggest the first activity. Always, for years, it was India who named the proper progression of events, ordered the yawning days—fishing pond, swimming creek, swinging from the tire on the live oak tree. Today, she sways back and forth, letting him push the swing alone, whistling through her teeth. To every suggestion, she shakes her head, smiles sadly. Swimming? Biking? Picture show? Even Tom Mix holds no interest. At last, she agrees to view the new rabbit, my father's recent birthday present.

"Her name's Hilda," my father says, reaching in to pet the rabbit's quivering skin. "She eats almost anything, she's not particular."

Cousin India bends her head close, studying the rabbit, but her hands are clasped together behind her back; she does not reach for the soft fur. "What are those little rabbits?" she asks then, pointing to three small lumps wriggling under Hilda's stomach.

"Her babies, they're brand new—want to hold one?" My father's hand reaches, but India stops him, circling his wrist.

"Let's go," she whispers, "I'm going," and runs off to the kitchen, where she plants herself on a stool to watch Nancy mixing pone bread. India stays in the kitchen with Nancy until almost supper time. (They have never liked Nancy—Nancy smells of chewing tobacco and has a sharp tongue; has no use for children's appetites and reaching hands inside her kitchen.)

Just as the sunlight fades, India emerges from the kitchen, her pale skin shiny with heat. Comes smiling to my father, who is carving chucks from a piece of wood—the first smile, says, "I'll race you to the creek. Loser owes a nickel."

"It's supper time," he tells her, "too late to swim."

India laughs over her shoulder, already getting a head-start through the pecan grove. She looks different, this old, familiar mirror image. Her lips glisten, her neck seems long and white and she holds her head carefully.

"Where's your swimming suit?" my father calls, but India flees on through the shadowed grove. He has no choice but to follow, her laugh calls him after, though she has never acted this way before. He thrashes after her.

At the creek she is reckless—diving off into the pool they've dammed up over past summers without care for stones, her travelling cotton dress sticking to her skin. Her energy is infectious. He jumps in after her, gasps against the cool sting of water, the weight of water pulling at his shirt and shorts. After a while, India floats on the water's surface, her body buoyed and rippled by the waves he's made. Her hair streams out around her head in tendrils, her waist-length hair uncoiled like sea-grass. She has closed her eyes against last night, her arms stretched out from her sides in an upward arc, fingers entwined in her hair. He watches her body raised against the little tides his kicking makes, then turns away because he feels fear, like a water bubble in his throat, though he cannot say why.

When they walk back to the house, their clothes chilled now in the twilight, they do not speak—only India hums a tuneless song. Met by his mother and Aunt Molly at the back porch door, reprimanded in shocked voices, they are sent to their rooms without supper. After an hour, he hears the porch swing creak, his mother's voice swaying nearer and further with his aunt's. Gathers his pockets full of hidden sweets he's saved against such a night: 2 almond Hersheys, a fistful of stale oatmeal cookies, an apple tucked away just yesterday.

"Already?" his mother's voice asks distinctly below, and Aunt Molly's murmuring reply.

India is already truly in bed, the white sheet pulled up to her chin, her arms lying neatly beside her. In the streetlamp light which illuminates the room, her face looks pale and sickened. He sits, for the first time tentatively, on her coverlet, just the edge of his bottom resting on the bed, and offers his hidden supper.

India smiles thinly, takes one bite of an oatmeal cookie and hands it back politely. My father chews on the Hershey bar and feels the chocolate fill his mouth and chews and chews, quickly, as if to eat is shameful, here, now. India watches him closely.

Finally, "Are you all right?" he asks her, amazed at the sound of his voice against the crisp, white silence of the room. India's cat-eyes gleam back at him, then fill with tears, though they do not fall. The tears fill up her eyes like a cup and glisten there.

"No," she says, looking straight at him. Then, "Things move too fast, everything's going too fast, don't you feel you want the days to slow down like last summer?"

"I can't tell the difference," he tells her.

The silence lies unwrinkled between them for a long while, then India's soft voice says, "You will," and, "I want to go to sleep now."

At the door, he turns to say good night, but India moves her head aside on the pillow.

The next day, and each successive day of the month-long visit, cousin India is more her old self. But always between them, walking to the picture show, fishing for bream at the pond, building a platform in the pecan tree, is a space of silence like a knot in a rope they carry between them—distance they are each too polite and helpless to untangle.

The last day of July, my father watches Uncle Herman pack the car, submits himself to his Aunt Molly's crushing embrace. This year cousin India does not even wave goodbye. But he sees her face pressed tight against the car's back window, as Uncle Herman drives away, watching him. At the last moment, her mouth says "goodbye" and then his name. He can see the words she makes.

And he wishes that cousin India's trip will be marked by at least six flat tires; that the bridge over Casper River will be washed out; that Uncle Herman will suddenly, after years of experience, find himself lost and bewildered by a wrong turn. He wishes for anything at all that will slow down her journey, anchor this day. They are double first cousins, and his time is near.

That night he counts against his bedside clock, checking to see if time has speeded up, but it is as regular and rhythmic as the cricket songs outside his window. Only later, years later, does he recall this summer at all—cousin India's face pressed tight inside its window-frame—and knows it to be the last summer of his life before desire and hunger gnawed and feasted on his heart.

IV

My father's Aunt Gussie descends upon the house each autumn, on her way to winter in Palm Beach. Gussie has married up, her husband will soon be president of a textile company, importers of silks and fine linens now, but one day creators of man-made fabrics—though who could have conceived of such a phrase. Her husband calls her Gertrude, properly, and the breadth of his kindness encompasses Gussie's manic spirit, allows her the freedom of her temperament.

"Poor Sam," my grandmother says of her brother-in-law, "Gussie never stops—she reminds me of Stitches," and my father laughs to think of his pet terrier and Aunt Gussie in conjunction. But the image, as always with my grandmother, is precise. Gussie is ferocious in her opinions, quirks, energies.

For weeks before each yearly visit, my grandmother sweeps and scrubs, irons the best linen, and in the last days preceding Aunt Gussie's arrival, even snaps at the children, her husband—this quiet, private woman who has never, otherwise, given herself over to weakness of any sort.

"Move your feet off the couch," she orders my father, "I've warned you never to read lying down," although she has never told him any such thing. She spends hours ferreting him out of whatever nook he has found—"Go help your sister hang out the laundry," knowing, in her helpless rage, how much this chore unmans him. He is too old to be seen with his sister, gathering lacey underdrawers, his father's dark socks, to pin up on the line strung across the side yard.

The house gleams and shines against Aunt Gussie's advance, the silver and crystal send off shards of light, and my grandmother moves in slow motion now against the waves of her spent effort, hollowed out by work.

She suffers Gussie's pretend-embrace, and when his aunt's thin arms open to summon him, my father experiences what his mother surely felt: fevered pats on the back, the knick of elbows and sharpness gathering him in, the cold prick of jewelry grazing his face. Diamonds pierce her ears, necklaces of pearls, cold as marbles; a sunburst of mixed stones on her pillowy breasts, and the hands and wrists that flash colored light when she talks: green, red, they stop and go.

"Well," Gussie exclaims, and claps her small hands together. She looks at the bodies she has squeezed and feather-patted, nudged close to her own, while my father wishes he were Lawrence, the elder brother mercifully off at college. Gussie talks over her shoulder to Sam, no matter where he happens to be standing at the moment.

"Jacob, you've lost weight," she declares, and "Susannah, where did your color go!" My grandparents smile fondly at her, although my father sees his mother's mouth pinch at the corners, that slight tuck at the ends of her clear lips which means she practices extreme patience.

"And Livvie!" My father's sister blushes, although she has told herself she will break this weak-willed habit. "Why, Livvie, you're actually pretty!" My aunt Olivia's cheeks bruise with flame, and even the comfort of her mother's encircling arm cannot drain the blood that rises up her neck. Olivia has always thought herself pretty, is astonished and shamed to hear she has tricked herself until now. All those years.

"And look, Sam," Gussie says over her shoulder, even though Sam is standing straight across from her, "Matthew's grown two feet, at least. Matthew, you're getting far too tall—how much does this animal eat every day?" My father, at sixteen, self-conscious of his height, which has stretched him painlessly as a rubber band, hunches his shoulders down into his shirt, curves his back to lower his head, shrinking like a tortoise. He will grow to six feet five, and his posture will never improve.

Sherry in the parlor before dinner. Aunt Gussie holds her fresh sherry glass to the light before accepting her brother's offered decanter, checking for spots. Runs her finger over the mantelpiece, then slaps her hands together, as if banishing dust. My father knows not one mote of dust could have possibly survived the last few days. Pronounces the newly upholstered chair, "Sweet." My grandmother leaves the room, presumably to check on dinner.

"Livvie," Gussie insists, "you should marcel your hair, you're too old for long curls." Olivia's cheeks are a dull pink, her eyes glazed over in retreat.

My father slouches out of the room, but not before Gussie, talking over her shoulder at the reading lamp, says, "Jacob, can't you afford to buy that boy a new pair of pants? He looks like a hillbilly with those knobby anklebones."

By supper time, the air's electric with advice, opinions, criticisms. Sam smiles sweetly round the glittering table, while Gussie raises a plate to check the underside. Olivia will sit protected between Sam and her father, buffered on each side. Aunt Gussie is on her brother's right, next to my father. My grandmother faces her husband down the table's length. They stand in the yellow candlelight behind their chairs. The crystal goblets seem to catch and fill with flame, throwing off rainbow colors. The silver is glossy with light. In the center of the table is a bowl full of late-blooming lilies from grandmother's garden, waxy white.

My grandfather clinks his glass with his fingernail. Chimes float over the candlelight, and his family faces him now, waits. He has filled their glasses with wine, as they arranged themselves around the table, and now he lifts his goblet and is joined by a circle of raised glasses, glittering together. The quiet rings them round.

"Joy and health, happiness to you all," his soft voice says. The company repeats his words, clinking the glasses to their right and left, but my grandfather does not drink and so they wait for the rest. Olivia smiles for the first time all day. My grandmother's face blooms pink with color and her brow smooths. Uncle Sam's smile is stretching to a grin, while my father's back straightens—he seems to grow whole inches at his place. Only Gussie is still—not chastened so much as calmed and lulled. She gazes quietly at her wineglass.

"To the girl in the red velvet dress," my grandfather says, and the company echoes his toast, "The girl in the red velvet dress."

Aunt Gussie is silent, her heart-shaped face tilted in the candlelight, staring into her raised glass as if she might find in the fine chablis a vision she has lost. My grandfather drinks; they all drink.

Then the room is full of motion: chairs scraped back, laughter as they turn to each other. Napkins whisked out and shaken in the air. The candlelight flutters. When my grandmother rings the porcelain bell by her plate, Nancy comes in on cue, holding two serving dishes in her hands, her face above the steam daring anyone to question the quality of her cooking. Chatter fills the room, light and easy, voices rising and falling like musical scales. Only Gussie and my grandfather face each other over the conversation, silent and bemused, their fingers almost touching on the crisp white linen tablecloth.

Here is what they see in each other's eyes—a photograph lost long before I was born: Aunt Gussie, my grandfather, Uncle Herman, reunited after a decade, the first week of Gussie's arrival in America, 1895. At last the brothers have saved enough for her ticket. After Ellis Island, after a day of sleep, a bath so hot that her skin turned lobster pink, Gussie is taken in her black wool skirt and blouse to choose any cloth she desires for a dress. A welcoming present from her older brothers. She fingers fine wools, nubby tweeds, then the plush, deep pile of the velvet. "This," she exclaims, "this."

The day the dress is finished, they visit the photographer. Aunt Gussie at seventeen in her red velvet dress (although in the photograph the colors are only sepia): her pale skin shining with light, her brothers sentinels behind her, and in her eyes, a look of hunger almost diminished, almost satisfied.

v

Legs Hornihan and my father, hunched together in the morning light, step off the sidewalk, shortcutting through the Maynards' back yard. They are skipping school today, in the last semester of their senior year. They aim their lowered heads in silence towards the pecan grove. The grove stretches out, one quarter acre of trees and shade, to form an irregular star; one side edges my father's back yard. They will enter from the rear, near the Brantley house, in order to avoid my grandmother's random gaze, as she shakes rugs from her bedroom window, sweeps off the back porch steps. It is ten o'clock in the morning, Economics class buzzing on without them, and spring lies heavily on the air.

Legs and my father are on the senior basketball team, close friends not only for the gangling height they share between them, but for their mutual penchant for silence. When they do speak, their words glance off topics better left in shadow; they talk instead of Gloria Penwood in her new sky-blue sweater, of Bunny Kosinski's latest brawl with his older brother.

"Bunny got locked in the toolshed for hours," Legs says, "Walter was so drunk on moonshine, he kept heaving bricks at the toolhouse door. All night long."

My father scowls against the light, shakes his head in disapproval. The image of slender Bunny, the most gentle of all his acquaintances, pressed tight against the toolhouse door while Walter rampages outside, distracts my father briefly from his own sadness: it is 1932, money is scarcer than diamond nuggets. My grandfather's clothing store, while open, runs on the dry whisper of credit. Mr. Hornihan's drugstore closed its fountain parlor down just last week. Only prescriptions filled now or over-the-counter remedies.

And even though my father and Legs are two of the lucky ones (they have been told this over and over by their mothers, had their good fortune drilled into their heads daily), they are filled with a pained longing. It is the longing which forces them out of school, which presses on them even now in the fragrant spring air. They are not ungrateful for their scholarships—room and board and half-tuition for each year, next year (my father's a University grant in Mathematics, Legs' from the Athletic department), for the miraculous series of summer jobs they have managed to scrape and beg. They know how magical their luck has been. But they are young, they have never expected the world's hard way to touch them—and so soon, now, when the university's freedom is so close. They must banish thoughts of fraternities, of pitching in with two more friends to purchase a worn-out jalopy. Of Saturday night football victory dances, of living out their youth until it slips them by. (My father has dreamed for the past two years of syrupy nights between lush campus trees, of holding some honey-haired girl while the orchestra plays, over and over, his favorite song— *Goodnight, Sweetheart.*)

He thinks now of the summer leaning against him. Next month he will begin: at six a.m., as he's done for the last ten years of his life, he will sweep out his father's store, straighten stock, empty wastebaskets. By seven he will be carrying logs (perhaps with Legs at the other end) for the lumber mill. Already he can feel the weight and splintery resin smell against his cheek. Back and forth, hefting logs from shoulder to shoulder to ease his back, taking logs from the flatbed trucks to a growing pile beside the saw that screams through the moist June air. At noon, he will eat his lunch walking to his afternoon job—digging trenches for Mr. McPhee, the town plumber, narrow trenches in the red Alabama clay, where pipes will be lowered and set, where someday water will flow. At five, he will come home and stand beneath the garden hose for fifteen minutes, soaking himself, drinking from the nozzle. Undress on the back porch, leaving his clothes on a nail, then lie in the bathtub until he falls asleep and the water chills him. Supper with his parents, then he is off to the last job of the day— ticket-seller at the Paramount, the local movie theatre. He is trusted by the owner, Mr. Logan, to make correct change, to total up the evening's earnings at midnight when the last show is almost over, then take the money inside to the vault, where Mr. Logan thanks him, turning his back, even so, as he dials the combination. Then to bed.

He is lucky for all this—and yes, he is grateful too—and yet, it is not at all as he had hoped, he cannot help the taste of gall that rises in his throat; he cannot help feeling cheated. He is young.

"Hey, Matt, are you still growing?" Legs asks. He stops by a flowering quince, pinches off the blossoms.

My father sighs mournfully, "Yes," and Legs nods. (He will deliver the Valedictorian speech, my father, with his best suit riding up above his anklebones; wink at Legs, flashing white shins as he accepts his high school diploma.)

They move on through the ponderous spring morning, flower smells brocaded in the air, then enter the cool dark of the pecan grove from the back. Here proper shadow lies around them, close, dank. Beneath the trees, where light sifts through in shining beams, the smell of old wood, nuts, the damp odor of moss soothes them. It is darkness they want, the sense of fruition decayed, spent. My father breathes in the transformed air and feels the dull ache inside his chest expand, luxuriously. They amble towards the center of the grove, Legs bending now and then, like a crane, to gather stray pecans. His pocket is jumbled with nuts they may presently share for lunch.

"Go left," my father instructs, heading them deeper into trees, away from the back border of his yard.

And then Legs' arm swings out, blocking his way. "Look," Legs whispers, his voice almost inaudible.

My father blinks against the shadow, scanning the trees ahead. "I don't—" he begins, then sees: under a large tree, his handkerchief spread like a picnic cloth beneath him, jacket turned inside out and folded into a pillow against the tree-trunk bark, my grandfather.

He sits in a pool of light, perfectly still, the smoke from his cigarette rising like haze in the sunbeams. His head rests against the tree, the perfect acquiline silhouette of his delicate face turned slightly upwards, eyes closed. He is so still. The creases in his seersucker suit, the frail pressed linen of his shirt, shine in the arc of light in which he seems to be warming himself. Only now and then he raises the cigarette to his lips, breathing deeply, and my father can see the cloud of smoke rising in sunlight. He is so still, he seems, to my father, fragile and sick, as if sunlight sliced through the strength and power he projects each day, revealing naked bone, blue vessels throbbing against all hope.

"What's he doing here?" Legs asks. "Why isn't he at work? Who's managing the store?"

My father shakes his head, makes a motion, finger to lips, for silence. They stand there, as quiet as they can be, my father trying not to breathe, holding his breath, while my grandfather exhales a cloud of smoke, then carefully crushes the cigarette, grinding it over and over into the ground. When he is done, his head arches back to the tree trunk, his eyes close against the sun shedding light on his upturned face.

"Come," my father signals, pointing over his shoulder, and he and his friend turn cautiously, their weight balanced, nimble, sure.

They walk back through the grove as if they are air, on tiptoe, silent as Indians.

Inside my father's chest is a knocking ache now that makes of his own longing something frivolous and light. A weight inside his chest that drags at his heart. What is his father doing? What grief pulls him here—and how often—what magnet of care, so that he abandons the rock of business, the shelter of his duty there? Regret floods color into my father's face; he pushes his fists into frayed pants pockets.

Nothing will ever be said of this day—no questions ever asked or answered. My father will work, digging trenches, carrying logs, as if fierceness nipped at his heels, pushing himself beyond strengths he knew he owned, into a sleep at night heavy, dreamless, and nearly cleansed of shame.

VI

Although it is years past Prohibition, the summer of 1941, my grandfather still keeps his liquor under lock and key in his bedroom—it is his only eccentricity. He has not left his bed in seven months, having suffered then the first of three heart attacks which will take him, finally, within the year.

The room is filled with the sound of the ceiling fan as it stirs thick, summer air, and with my father's voice, answering questions. He has come home to Alabama, having left his pregnant wife with her family, his law office locked and closed, "on a case," he tells my grandfather, although there is no such thing. Carefully, he describes the legal maneuverings involved, the records he must search out in the State Capitol fifty miles away, inventing on the spot details he cannot quote from memory from his old Torts lawbook. It is all fabrication—he has come to visit his father one last time.

"Success," my grandfather toasts from his bed, and they raise their small brandy glasses in the morning light, drink the fruity liquor down.

"So you think you have a chance of winning," my grandfather says, and my father nods, goes on to say why. My grandfather's greatest pleasure is the thought of his youngest son in the practice of law—miraculous, somehow, that a child of his understands the law, could steer himself through whatever complicated legal maze.

When my father's voice winds down, they speak of other things: crops in the Mississippi Delta, where my father lives now, the long dry spell, Olivia's latest letter, postmarked Borneo. (Olivia, married to an oilman, has spent the last six years living in strange places—South America, Holland, the West Indies. She will leave Borneo just in time, one of the few lucky enough to escape the Japanese and their POW camps.)

Then, "Son," my grandfather says, "how would you like another drink?"

"That would do fine." My father waits respectfully by the bed while my grandfather takes the ring of keys from the bedside table, locates the proper key. Then my father unlocks what used to be a linen closet, refills the two small glasses, relocks the closet, returns the key. They sit in the morning quiet, and this time my grandfather merely lifts his glass in a silent salute, and they drink once more. This is their daily routine for the week of my father's visit.

By afternoon, my grandfather has sedated himself against the pain which plagues him (although he never mentions pain of any sort), against the slow-moving hours. He may sleep. He thinks my father spends those hours in the courthouse fifty miles away, although while he rests, his two sons visit together—my father and Uncle Lawrence walking the small town streets, meeting in my grandfather's old office, at the clothing store, now Lawrence's office entirely. Sometimes they both walk back to the house and have tea with my grandmother, but on those days, their voices are whispers, they are all distracted by nerves. My grandmother keeps glancing at the ceiling as if it might tell her if they've been overheard.

The brandy is never mentioned and my father smiles to think of my grandfather's secret treatment, until the last day, when his mother stops him in the hall, mid-morning, on his way to the bathroom.

"Matthew," she says in her old scolding voice, "are you getting your father drunk again today? I'm ashamed of you."

"Why, Mama," he protests, "what on earth do you mean?"

"You know full well," she says in her best haughty voice, then walks off quickly with her arms full of fresh linen. She has done her duty, protested the use of liquor under her roof, and can now pretend the confrontation is successfully over.

"Son, could you do with another drink?" my grandfather asks before lunch-time.

After the ritual of the keys and before my grandfather lifts his glass, "Matthew," he says. "Look out for Lawrence, he spends too much money, he's headed for trouble."

"Lawrence is okay, Papa," my father says. "He's doing fine."

"Say you will," my grandfather urges quietly.

"Yes, I will."

"And Livvie. Watch out for her too. You're the youngest in years, but I depend on you, Son."

"Livvie too," my father says.

"I won't even mention your mother; no need to, I know."

"No sir, no need at all."

In the July sunshine that fills the room, my grandfather lifts his glass and my father raises his own glass high. They drink.

Then, "Tell me," my grandfather says, "have you had a chance to visit with your old friend, Legs?"

Their murmuring voices fill up the final day.

It is afternoon. My father has taken his mid-day medication. Pills to lull him, soothe him to rest. One yellow, one red, one blue.

"And you never knew him," he says to me now, his voice thickened, his eyelids lowering against his will. My grandfather died two weeks before my birth, November 1941.

"But I know him now," I say, "I remember all your stories."

No, my father shakes his head. I never saw him, how can I possibly know? He will try again tomorrow, anyway, spiralling back to show me what he thinks I still do not see.

"His life was as necessary as mine," he says impatiently, "as important as your own."

"Rest now," I say, and wait until he sleeps.

BODIES LIKE MOUTHS

JOHN J. CLAYTON

John Clayton teaches creative writing and modern literature at the University of Massachusetts, Amherst. He has
published in *American Review, The Massachusetts Review, Antioch Review, Best American Short Stories,* and
the PRIZE STORIES.

During the winter of 1955, Chris took courses at Columbia. He
came from Indianapolis; New York stunned him. Knowing nothing, he took a room in a railroad flat uptown near school: one
room, 11 x 7, bed with a defeated mattress. It was cheap, and he
could use the kitchen along with the three other roomers—after
the Dirksons had finished.

At night, when he got home from work, Dirkson used the kitchen first. He seemed to slow down his meal so he could feel his
power. After he and his wife were through, it was Mr. Dirkson
who cleaned up, sponging counter and linoleum wrathfully so
that no trace of their lives remained. The roomers listened, each
from a separate room, hearing the scraping and scrubbing as a language of hate—all *right*, you little bastards: I want to see it the
same way tomorrow morning.

Then he hollered, "Kitchen's free!"—and the roomers came in,
carrying each his own paper bag. Each to his own cupboard space,
own refrigerator half-shelf. At the end of their meals, each separate, everything disappeared; the kitchen belonged again to nobody.

Chris never stayed in the kitchen long. In Indianapolis, his
mother's kitchen had been the happiest room in the house. But
here: on the wall over the table with its green oil cloth, one
yellowing picture—*girls holding roses*—cut out of some magazine
years before and glued to cardboard. A single fluorescent light
hanging from the middle of the ceiling tore at Chris' stomach.

Copyright © 1977 by Ploughshares, Inc. Reprinted by permission.

The one window was black on the outside with soot sucked into the inner courtyard of the building—a kind of air space, like a large, dirty chimney with windows. The dirt seeped into the old towel left always between upper and lower sash to keep out drafts and dirt. And, inescapably, the rancid smell, smell of despair, clung to the old paint, the ceiling plaster. Years later, remembering—that bleak room was somehow redeemed by the strength of his memory, memory like an act of love.

Dirkson in underpants and an undershirt. Annie the next-door roomer laughs and jiggles a thumb—"Some beauty, huh?" She walks around in a ragged terry cloth bathrobe. Not much of a beauty herself. Chris longs for lean, blonde angels. Her breasts are small and her waist thick—not fat, but solid. She has long, fuzzy brown hair that would look beautiful fifteen years later but in 1955 looks messy. Her eyes are shrewd—he is afraid of what they might see. "Some beauty," she says again. Chris' smile doesn't commit him. "Oh, Jesus! Another great roomer," she says.

From behind their closed bedroom door and his own bedroom door, he can hear Mr. and Mrs. Dirkson, fighting. Dirkson's voice, murderous, is muted by his throat, muffled by the doors. Sarah's voice—whatever the words—sneers. Something thuds. A curse, repeated, in a tense monotone. Chris comes out into the hall and stares at the Dirksons' door: a blurred television screen.

A key turns in the front door lock. Jose tiptoes in behind a short, darkskinned kid—a kid not more than sixteen. Jose looks maybe sixteen himself, but he must be older—he's here on government scholarship from the Philippines. Jose raises a finger to his lips—Chris grins: rings on every finger—gold, brass, glass, semiprecious stones. They disappear across the hall into Jose's bedroom.

"YOU goddammed bitch!"—explodes through the Dirksons' door. Annie sticks her head out of her door and looks at Chris. Her eyebrows lift. She lifts a Schlitz in toast to one more brawl. They both withdraw into their rooms. From Jose's room Chris hears a fluent run in minor key on guitar. A flamenco strum and *ai-eeee!!* He can't hear Jose's song—only the repeated words, louder than the rest—Flores . . . flores . . . flores . . .

Alone in New York: outside the apartment it was no grim prison. Secrets bloomed like sea anemones, charged, tumescent. He walked a lot, carrying a burden of terror and love-feelings, nowhere to put them down. Walking: down Broadway, across Central Park South, down Lexington. Looking at women. Legs whispered to him so fervently—aaah, the swell of calves in nylon—he could hardly stand it. Painful, the curve of coat over hip, curve in his mind, curve rushing and singing like a roller coaster. In his *mind*, though not recognized as in his mind—intuitions of a sacred language that he could comprehend only in profane form. Hungry all the time—love with nothing he knew to love, love sniffing into every dark place. His heart was touched—as if the city were an old panhandler, old ticket-taker.

Love spilled out onto the facades of elegant town houses from the turn of the century, houses he couldn't hope to enter, moulded cornices, windows the shape of old ladies in dreams, huge windows full of green plants. Jazz clubs in cellars he wished he had the nerve to enter. Lebanese groceries, Italian groceries, bodegas. These he entered; he ate good bread for the first time, ripping off the chunks and chewing hard, as if chewing were a form of loving.

Sometimes he followed a girl in topcoat, creating her (oh, her elegant walk, her lean body, must be wearing a leotard—a dancer —hello, I'm Chris) followed her to the 116th Street subway kiosk (hello . . . my name is . . .) and leaned over the railing while she dissolved into the undulating subway dragon, yellow hair fading into the dark crowd.

Fearing and loving, in all-night Hayes-Bickford cafeterias, talking to gamblers about women. Home again at midnight, the piled-up cushions on his bed tumbled, under the streetlight, into odalisques in leotards.

The Five Spot. I am invisible. Hipsters passing funny cigarettes. Someone named Miles Davis. I don't understand the music but I bob my head.

Dirkson, in underpants and undershirt, cut onions and complained about the tax forms he had to work on. The taxes or the onions made his eyes tear, and he cursed and wiped them with the back of his hand. "That's right," he said to Chris but really to himself. "Leave it to the goddamned onion to finish the job. All day the goddamned garage door kept opening and closing you wear a coat you sweat so you take it off and freeze your ass off." Next to the tax forms were three sharpened pencils, a box full of papers, a bottle of Budweiser. "Painful," Dirkson said. "Fucking painful."

Dick is thumping some woman in the next room. The springs shriek like mice or guinea pigs, and the headboard slams the wall. Chris finds he's clenching his jaw, and he tries to relax: first thing in the morning! First thing in the morning—Christ! He gets up and sticks his head out the door—sees the bathroom door is shut: Dirkson up to go to work.

Chris puts water up to boil. Even from the kitchen he can hear Dick. The bastard. Two hours a day he swims, comes home with any of three different women, all really pretty; they groan and grapple till eleven and are doing it again at 6:30. Athlete's schedule. He should tell him something.

Sitting over coffee, he hears laughter, click of a door latch, and Dick comes into the kitchen with the woman. She looks flushed but her hair is neat and her white blouse is crisp and tucked inside her peasant skirt. Dick smiles good morning and that's all. Why doesn't he introduce us? Does he remember my name? She boils water. Curly black hair tumbles halfway down her back.

Chris is in love with her.

Then Dirkson comes out of the bathroom and stands, arms akimbo, and glowers at Dick. Chris figures on some yelling—even at the other end of the apartment they must have heard, and Dirkson hates noise.

Dirkson glowers; then he grins, you even see his teeth: "You make one hell of a racket, you know that?"

"I can imagine," Dick drawls.

"You're some guy. Yessir!" Dirkson laughs and shakes his head in pleasure and embarrassment.

"I do my best, Mr. Dirkson."

"I'll bet. Miss, does he do his best? I'll bet he does."

She just smiles. Chris would like to obliterate this smug son of a bitch: his lecherous eyes. Both of them. But also—he's fascinated at the change in Dirkson. And this woman, her presence, is for Chris like morphine he was given in a hospital once. He is suffused with love.

He sips his coffee while these two bastards congratulate each other for being men. And didn't she mind—she was the runner's track, vaulter's pole, lane for the swimmer? Is that what women really wanted? It was 1955. Everyone winked and said yes, that's what women really wanted: to be fucked into grateful obedience.

Dirkson goes back inside to dress. Chris remembers the *look*. He knows it from high school locker room, dances of Friday nights. That look—it made him nauseous, made him drop out of the field; let them run on, around and around the track, without him.

She looks at him, she smiles—"Want some more coffee?"

"We've got to get going," Dick says. "He can fix his own."

Chris wishes he could lift this bastard by his hair and clamp his neck to the wall. Instead, he smiles and takes the pot from Sylvia's hand.

Love flesh: he wanted to hold his life, shining, in his hands, and he didn't know where else to look, how else to sanctify it: breast flesh, leg flesh, curve of hip into thigh. He didn't know that flesh was metaphor, metaphor piled on metaphor, and that history made and remade the metaphors. He was poisoned by the metaphors but he didn't know that yet. It all seemed his private, single struggle, personal humiliation—at being a man, at not being a man. Outside, along Broadway, mothers pushed baby carriages and walked children in a protest march: their milk, their food were being poisoned by radiation. From his bedroom window he could hear them chanting. A few blocks away, at Columbia, he took *political science* and *history*. All that was outside. Then there was the private, the *inside*: sex and love and being a man and finding something to do with his life he could at least stomach. His own pain, his possession. Ultimately—everyone told him—Man is Alone.

"Een Manila, wan I was twelve year old, the soldiers, Japanese soldiers, took me, they rape me. Ees how eet all started."

"Jose, you couldn't have been raped by Japanese soldiers. They were gone, the war was over, by the time you were twelve."

"Okay, okay. American soldiers then. What's the deeference?"

He burst out laughing. Putting on an imaginary top hat, he danced on top of the bed, on top of the table.

"Be careful of the books, will you?"

"Oh, the books!" He bowed deeply.

Annie sliced up vegetables on the cutting board; she used her own iron skillet to saute them. While they simmered, she scrubbed off the board and opened a Schlitz with her Swiss Army knife. Chris ran the cold water a long time, until some of the poison and despair were out of the pipes. In her robe, Annie looked dilapidated and blousy, already a little like Sarah Dirkson.

Mr. Dirkson was in the john. Annie pointed with her thumb. "He spends a sweet little time in there, huh? You think he jerks off in there?"

He wanted to hush her—the Dirksons' room was two doors down. But he laughed.

"Oh. Oh, my. Was that some laugh!" Annie said. "God, what a place I'm living in."

"I'm sorry."

"He's sorry."

Vivaldi from Jose's record player. Suddenly the bathroom door jerked open. "Hey!—Will you keep that goddamned thing *down?*"

"You going to be living here for long?" Annie asked.

"I doubt it."

"Sure. You want to do a funny cigarette?"

"You hear me, Jose?" Dirkson bellowed. Jose opened his door a crack and Vivaldi splashed through the apartment.

"Ees poetry, Meester Dirkson."

"Shut it."

Jose sighed. His hands opened to the heavens and his rings—one, two, even three—on every finger, flashed. His poet brass knuckles.

Dirkson and Jose both closed themselves in again.

Annie took the pan from the stove—she ate off it, ignoring a plate.

"Why do you stay here?" Chris asked.

"Come *on*. It's cheap. But I'm splitting for a while, thank God. Listen—you didn't answer my question."

"I don't smoke."

"I don't mean tobacco."

"Thanks—really—but no. *No.*"

"Thank God I'm splitting for a while."

Dirkson came out of the bathroom. "It's free. Don't forget to clean up after yourself."

Chris sat in his room, reading Auden. His only decent course was in poetry, with Babette Deutsch. Such a delicate, crisp lady. She touched him with the power of the unspoken at the heart of the spoken. Auden's simple speech vibrated in his mind. He wished he could make such language. With his lips he formed empty whispers as if they were real words, real lines of poetry. He wished he could reach in and pull out the words.

The doorbell. Annie ran down the hall to get it. Chris opened his own door a crack. A big guy, very black, smiled and lifted her up by the waist and kissed her. She let herself slump against his shoulder. Then they were gone. Chris heard them laughing down the stairwell, heard the front door slam. He looked at Auden's words again but couldn't make sense. Looked out his window to see Annie and her friend, but they were nowhere in sight.

Sometimes at night he couldn't sleep. Even with three blankets he was cold, and had to pile his coat and jacket on the bed. The weight felt like some other body—he didn't try to think whose. Toilet paper stuffed in the crack around his window casement didn't help much. Too much steam heat all day, then cold all night. On his ceiling feet scuffled—the children upstairs, the Iraqui student, his family. He lay propped up on pillows and stared out at the brownstone across the street. A woman's silhouette behind a window shade, the light behind her. He wanted to see her, whoever she was, wanted to watch her making love. A long scream. A couple laughing in the street. An auto horn, furious. A bottle smashing against wall or pavement. He shut his eyes. It got late, he felt panicky—so much to do tomorrow—he needed sleep. Drowzed, drowzed: birds, a tunnel, solemn dialogue with a Teacher. Laughter: laughter from Jose's room. Then quiet in the apartment. In the cold wind he felt it creak as if this were a dark ship. A voice in Spanish—Jose was talking in his sleep again. The bodies, rocking, each in its own metabolic rhythms, its separate secret processes. The crew slept. Bodies crumpled, curled, as if folding around a dream stone, a stone in sleep. He heard no one but sensed them all: hungry bodies, hurting bodies, sexual bodies glowing in secret. Bodies like mouths. Sexual swimmers going deeper into longing.

"You get your goddamned bags packed, Jose. I want you out of here by tonight."

"Oh, please, Meester Dirkson." Jose got down on his knees. Skinny kid, he looked twelve years old. Dirkson like Zeus above him. Jose fluttered his eyelids: "Please, Meester Dirkson, Jose ees just a harmless fairy. You wouldn't be so cruel to Jose?" He clung to Dirkson's knees. "Where can I go? I am so weethout money."

Chris couldn't stand it. Jose was eating this up, loving the scene, overplaying it just this side of parody. If Dirkson had suspected he was being put on, he could have shoved Jose away. "Come on, come on, let *go*, Jose."

"The end of the week, Meester Dirkson?"

"Sure, okay," he said, pulling away and brushing off his cuff from something dirty. "The end of the week, Jose." When he was gone, Jose danced a tiny, delicate silly dance, a devil dancing on eggs, and he grinned—a little boy with big, crooked, yellowing teeth. He reached his arms up and clasped his fingers around Chris' neck while he kept up his delicate dance and hummed a little tune. Chris smiled but pulled back. "Oh, don' worry. I am not pheesically attracted to you. Eet ees sad." He sighed. "But not ultimately. 'All things fall and are built again . . .' Yeats, si! He *knows*. Ultimately, what ees sad? Nothing."

"Oh, bullshit."

"Sure, sure, evertheeng ees bullshit. Ees ees sad."

Chris waved him off and went into his own room and closed the door. But a minute later Jose knocked and slipped in like a cat or the wind. He sat crosslegged on the bed and rolled a cigarette.

"Een Manila during the war, I learn to roll cigarettes and drunks. At seven year old I make out okay."

"But you, you're a genius, didn't you tell me?"

"Laugh at me, I don' care, Chris. I *am* a genius. Like Goethe, like the holy Mozart, like Rilke and Yeats and Chaplin. Chaplin ees a very high saint, Chris." He held his fingertips together at his heart in devotion, then grinned wickedly. "I, however, am not a saint."

"You've read an awful lot. You're here on some scholarship?
The Philippine government?"

"I am as poor as the leetle cockroach in the keetchen."

"Annie tells me you spend all your money on boys and that you
live on hamburgers."

"Now you sound like Meester Dirkson." He sulked.

"Oh, Jose!"

"Where am I going to go?" he wailed in a tiny voice and buried
his head in the pillows. Real tears!

"Poor Jose. What about the Y? Listen, I'll help you look for a
room, okay?"

"Okay." A tiny, child's voice. One eye peeked up from the pillow. "You want to sleep with me?"

Sarah Dirkson sits in a bleached-out, flower-print housedress,
not reading the *Daily News, not* drinking from her quart of ale.
Her skin looks puffy, her eyes red; what seems strange to Chris is
that she sits back, relaxed, as if she were watching an invisible TV
and weeping over a soap opera. Chris fixes himself a cup of instant and sits down. "I'm sorry, Mrs. Dirkson."

"You're a good kid. It's nothing."

"Is it your husband?"

"He means well. Anyway, that's not the point, is it?"

He shrugs and shakes his head. "Sorry?"

"I *mean*, it's my *life*. My *life*," she says again as if it's a pun or
the punch line of a joke he isn't picking up. Defeated, she keeps
crying, her mouth slack, without definition; Chris finishes his
coffee in a hurry and goes back inside to study.

Later he smells bread baking. In this place! Mrs. Dirkson baking bread.

He studies French grammar and memorizes vocabulary. A sinking feeling that he will never need to know that *tache* meant a
stain; savant, skillful; nourrir, to feed, to nurse . . .

When he hears the knock, he realizes he expected it. He remembers his bed is cluttered with clothes. "Come in?"

"Here's bread. I baked plenty. My mother used to bake bread."

"Mine too. Thanks." He feels invaded. Maybe she's trying to
take him to bed, wants him to ease her life. Suddenly her blousy
body and fleshy face make him feel a little nauseous. How could
he make it with her? He never could. He retreats into a dead

smile. "Thank you." He takes the plate and sets it on his study table, a flowering plant among the 3 x 5's. They both regard it.
"*Try* some."
"Sure. Hey . . ." With what knife? He looks around for help.
"*Break* it."
"Sure." He feels he is violating the bread. He rips at it, catching dough under his nails. Smiling, smiling, he stuffs some in his mouth. "Wow. Wonderful."
"*Isn't* it good?" Her face is full of pleasure now. He can only nod. Stuffing and chewing, he nods. It's dry. Too big a piece. Why didn't she think of butter?
"I figured you never got any homemade stuff."
"That was really thoughtful," he mumbles through the gluten. He concentrates hard on his chewing, and his eyes close.
"You're some student, I just bet. Look at those books all over."
"I'm a slob. I'm not very neat. It's great bread." His mouth aches. The loaf lies broken apart and embarrasses him.
"You don't seem to have any friends."
"I've only been in New York a month."
"You've got to be careful of course, not to mix with the wrong people. I approve of that. Take someone like Jose. Christ, I don't want to talk about people behind their backs, but Jose was probably a sweet, innocent boy back in the Philippines. Well you look at him now—these kids he picks up, he ain't giving them candy in his room. Don't I know it—New York is a terrible place. But you can't live in your books all the time, can you?"
"You're right," he says, wanting her to leave.
"I'm not talking about a tramp like Annie. Do you realize she went off with that . . . colored man five days ago? Well, is she crazy?" She thought a moment. "Well. Who the hell am I to tell somebody else a *damned* thing? I'm some prize package if you know what I mean." She shrugs and walks out; stops, her hand rubbing the door jamb. "Anyway, if you need anything . . ."
"Thanks, Mrs. Dirkson."
"Sarah. Sarah." She leaves him alone, thank God, but the silence is powerful, it makes him ache; like a god it pursues him out of the room into the noisy side street, onto Broadway. Smell of fried rice and beans. A tinny record in Spanish from a music store. No silence here. Men in cheap clothes, leaning against cars, are in the know. Some *know* he doesn't possess. The young women pass-

ing who glance at him live at a level of sexuality so intense it would wipe him away. But under the jangle of Broadway his love starts to come back, like a muscle in spasm, loosening. His eyes ache as he looks too hard for someplace to put the love down. He sees three children, three children walking a cocker spaniel. Loving children: always easy; always a relief.

Annie was back.

In the kitchen she sat brooding over her coffee. Dick washed the dishes and hummed a blues her way as if she were supposed to catch the unspoken words. She ignored him. Chris took a can of pineapple juice from his refrigerator shelf and poured out a glass. "Annie—you want some?"

She shook her head.

"You sure?"

She turned a sour look on him. "I'm not in such a great mood."

Dick kept up his song, the humming increasingly suggestive; he seemed to be soaping her back instead of a plate. Suddenly she turned—"And *you*—" she snapped at Dick—"just fuck off. I don't need your crap one bit."

"What happened to your big boyfriend?"

She ignored him. "*This* one—" she told Chris—"tried to put his hands on me the first day I moved in. He's real sweet . . . Hey, you, why don't you go hum at the pigeons?"

Dick wiped his hands and kept humming, grin on his face, all the way to his room.

"What was he humming at you?"

"Oh. Just a blues. Because the guy I was with is black?"

"It turned out lousy?"

"Why don't you just go away? You want to suck energy out of my problems? Go away."

"I'm just sorry for you. Jesus!" He got up.

"You're good at being sorry for people. I know the type. You eat that shit up, don't you? You're such a sweet, sensitive fucker. You eat that shit up. I don't see you saying a goddamned thing to that prick, however." She turned off her eyes—a stranger.

A stranger. Foreigner. Some language I no talk so good.

Dirkson tried the door; it was bolted from the inside. With one thrust of his heavy shoe, he smashed it open. From his own doorway Chris looked past Dirkson, past Jose. A darkskinned kid with

a lot of curly hair was pulling up his pants, eyes like a trapped rabbit. Jose was still on his knees. He looked back over his shoulder
at Dirkson, Dirkson godlike above him. Probably that would have
been all except for some yelling. But then Jose grinned; he
grinned, he ran his tongue across his lips and wiped them with his
fingertips. As if to say, Too late, Meester Dirkson. Dirkson let out
a roar, like an animal, and smashed his heavy work shoe into
Jose's head; Jose went down, and Dirkson picked him up by the
hair and belt, picked him up and carried him to the front door.
There he held him under one arm—Jose didn't struggle, was probably not conscious—screamed over and over, "You fucking pig,
you fucking pig!" while he managed to open the front door locks
and toss him down the stairs.

Jose tumbled like a rag doll, offering no resistance, and crumpled, slack, on the landing. Dirkson slammed the door and turned
away, obviously scared, embarrassed. He yelled at Chris, "WHAT
kind of goddamned house does he think I run?"—and brushed
past him.

"I'm giving notice," Chris yelled after him. "And right now I'm
calling the police."

Annie went out into the hall.

"I don't give a shit *who* you call."

Sarah Dirkson had her hands on her husband's arms trying to
calm him—he shrugged her off and went back to their room.

"Oh, my God, my God in Heaven!" Sarah Dirkson knotted the
belt of her robe and went out with Chris to pick up Jose. But
Jose, somehow, had slipped away. Annie was standing there.
There was blood on the steps, blood on the bannister. They heard
the downstairs door slam.

"He's some tough kid," Sarah Dirkson said.

The teenager slipped past them and ran down the stairs.

"Hey, you—you stay the hell away from here!" she yelled after
him. Then, turning, she put her arms around Chris' shoulders and
leaned her head against his chest. Stiffly, tears thickening his eyes,
he held her, gave comfort, wondered now where the hell was he
going to live.

Annie went inside and left them standing there.

He got dressed and went out, forgetting his books. He had to
look for a place to live. But what he was really looking for was
Jose—he took the subway to the Village and hunted without a

hope. He had the feeling that this beautiful monster, New York, had swallowed him up.

What he was really looking for . . . but if it was Jose, why did he poke into Village bars? Jose never went to a bar. Chris stood in entrance ways. Afraid of the bartender's eyes. Of the one or two men sitting at the bar. He could imagine whole lives about them. Or no—not imagine the lives: imagine that there was something to imagine, something to feel for. So, on trust, he felt for it. He poured his own energy into half-lit rooms, then wondered at it as something foreign to him. Twelve years later, when Dylan was singing of Desolation Row, he always saw this image of men in the half light of a Village bar.

He wandered through coffee houses, looking and not looking, finally stopping for an espresso at Rienzi's. Soft Mozart chamber music reminded him of Jose. Then a boy flashed by outside on Macdougal Street. Jose? Chris swigged his espresso and hurried after. The boy was just turning a corner—a shock of black hair—or was that somebody different again from the boy he'd seen?

Where did the kid go? Chris was blocks away from Macdougal, down sidestreets folding into sidestreets. Now he was just walking. Looking for *vacancy* signs on the doorways of brownstones and graystones, looking for the mystery. A woman in a window—a black woman with a Siamese cat—grinned his way. He felt a glow of love for her, for the city, felt that, after all, it wasn't swallowing up Jose, but hiding, protecting him.

Somewhere there was a room. He walked until he came to Macdougal, pleased with himself that he could find it again. Over another cup of espresso he looked through ads in the *Village Voice*.

At the next table, a young man and two women were talking—incomprehensibly—about some article by Norman Mailer, about Fritz and Laura, about the Poujadists in France. A long speculation about the roots of fascism. The name Reich . . . Reich . . . Reich. Chris felt their excitement and concern and locked it into his heart as a model of something for himself. Then their talk submerged beneath Vivaldi and espresso. Walking over to a rack, he lifted a copy of *Le Monde* hanging on its wooden dowel and brought it back to his table. Struggling with the French, he tried to feel at home.

Three light taps at his door. He opened—Jose with a beret over a bandaged skull. A cut along his cheekbone had been dressed but not bandaged.

"You're okay?"

"I tol' you I take care of Jose."

"That was pretty stupid—" Chris mimicked Jose: tongue along the lips, fingertips wiping them dry. "You provoked him."

"Did I do that?" Jose asked in a tiny child's voice.

Chris laughed. "Well? You need some help, genius?"

"Eef you could store some boxes, I sneak back and got some boxes packed."

Chris looked around and laughed. "Store *where?*"

"Under the bed? I got a place, ees okay—just a couple days."

"I'm leaving. I gave notice."

"Ai-eeee! For me? Chris!" Jose smiled his most delicate smile and fluttered his eyelids.

"Jose, please cut that out."

Under the bed was already crowded, but they crammed things in. Jose hummed a song. "Thees ees from divine Mozart, the *Magic Flute*. Papageno, hees song, wan he ees gagged for hees lies."

"It sounds appropriate, Jose."

A tapping at the door. "It's me. *Annie.*"

She slipped in and sat with Chris on the bed. Jose reenacted the beating in mime.

"That bastard," Annie said. "I'd love to stomp on his balls."

Chris looked at her, dismayed.

"Mr. Sweetness here," she said.

Jose hummed Papageno's song. He sat on Annie's lap—Chris realized how very small he was. His bright eyes looked deep into Chris' and he recited, "Wan longing comes over you, seeng the great lovers. Ees Rilke," he sighed. " 'Those whom you almost envied, those forsaken, you found so far beyond the requited in loving.' "

"You see?" Annie said. "You see? Jose understands everything. Let's go down for a six pack."

"I swear to God, I don't know why I stick around here. So I can learn to paint? I'm no painter. I mean. So what am I hanging around? It's more alive than Cleveland, I guess—sadder, too. Sometimes I get so I want to scream. Billy told me to split a couple of days back. I mean. I was a real shit to him. But even if I were Miss Honey Pussy of 1955, it would have been the same. So I went out on the street, I stood on the corner of 8th Street and Sixth Avenue trying to peddle my ass. Well, first off, my ass practically froze. And then, nobody bought. You always figure, shit, what a lousy thing—to sell your ass? What you never imagine is, maybe nobody'll want to buy."

"Oh, Annie!" Jose kissed her ear and she brushed him off.

"I suppose if I got dolled up and went to the right place—"

From the Dirksons' bedroom they could hear his snarling, not the words.

"Poor woman." Chris felt a sweet melancholy here in this tiny room, with the one-bulb lamp on the wall over the bed, the three of them in a cabin in some floating city, a terrible ship slipping through the night, or city like a psychotic sleepwalker not know-ing where—and the three of them safe. Remembered as a child taking a sandwich to bed, secretly, propping up the covers with a toy gun, sitting in the cave of his bed with a flashlight, reading stories . . .

Dirkson's voice became a roar. ". . . Bastards! . . ." They looked at each other wondering who the word referred to, know-ing it made no difference.

"Goodbye, Chris, Annie—I geev you a kees." Suddenly, Jose slipped under the bed and took a paper bag from one of his boxes. A finger to his lips; like a sprite, he was gone.

A minute later the lights went out. They looked at each other. Annie said, "Shhh . . . Jose."

They waited.

The bedroom door, the Dirksons' door, banged open, and Dirk-son, barefoot, in underwear, clumped down the hall. Noise in the kitchen. Then "Sarah! Goddamnit, somebody's been tam-pering—"

Sarah's slippers. "Stop yelling—it's eleven o'clock." Chris imag-ined a malicious ariel tiptoeing down the stairs, out onto streets where he was no less at home than here. At home nowhere, any-where.

Then the lights went on.

"I bet the little bastard came back." Dirkson slammed the door of the fuse box.

Chris stood in the kitchen doorway. "Trouble, Mr. Dirkson?"

"You seen that little bastard? I bet you have." Then he noticed Annie. "She just coming out of your room? What's she doing in your room? You mind if I look in there?" He went in. No Jose. Dick came out of his room. Alone tonight, he wore his sweat suit and track shoes, but his eyes looked bleary. "What's going on?"

"That little faggot." Playing hide-and-seek, Dirkson pushed on through the apartment. Sarah took a beer from the frig, opened and swallowed deep. Chris saw her look at Dick a long, long look, then hand him the beer. Dick grinned at her and she laughed like a young girl. "Life is funny," she said to some invisible audience— the imaginaries who really understood and cared. "Ain't it, just ain't it?"

Then a roar from the bedroom. Dirkson with his shoes in his hands. "That little bastard—he filled these up with something." He took a spoon and dug, but it wouldn't give. Annie took a look. "Plaster of paris. Just forget it, Mr. Dirkson."

He threw one shoe, then the other, against the kitchen door. The first thudded and fell, the second left a long split in the wood. "How'd he get in there?" Then he realized and rushed back inside. "THAT FUCKING BASTARD!"—Chris knew now that he had never really heard Dirkson raise his voice before. Dirkson went for the phone. "He stole my pants, my wallet, my money, my papers, I don't know what else, the little fucking thief."

But the phone was dead.

"The wire's cut, Mr. Dirkson," Annie said.

"You mind your own business." He pushed past Sarah; they heard Dirkson at the bedroom window.

"These buildings all connect," Annie said. "He must have climbed up on the roof and down some other stairs."

"I had my *pay* in that wallet, five goddamned days of keeping cabs moving, busting my ass in that crappy place, you think it's funny?"

Chris saw in his mind's eye his own father, who worked in an insurance office and never cursed, never raised his voice—but his feelings weren't all that different. Chris felt sorry.

Sarah leaned against her husband's arm. "Oh, Fred, Fred, your money." She was crying. He only half pushed her off.

"Everybody can get the fuck out of here. I mean tomorrow, the next day. I mean *you*—" he rammed a finger into Chris' chest—

"and you, too, Annie. Not you, Dick, of course, but the rest of this trash."

Annie laughed and went to her room. Chris closed his door, put a chair against it, and undid a couple of Jose's boxes—now how could he get them back to him?

A crumpled felt hat with a parrot feather, a collection of Beethoven string quartets, an eyebrow pencil, a column of four poses of himself from a subway photo booth—grinning, malicious, terribly sad. A couple of soiled T shirts, a notebook of poems in Spanish, a packet of ragged letters, an American flag, an old newspaper photo of Franklin Delano Roosevelt, a pile of magazines with cover pictures of nearly naked athletes with oiled torsos, a torn pair of blue corduroy pants—a child's size.

He stuffed everything back, put the chair back by the table, got into bed and waited for sleep. Tomorrow he'd be out on the street. A new room somewhere. Jose's things would have to go with him.

Chris lay curled up, imagining Jose out on the street somewhere. Someday he'd pick up the wrong boy or steal from the wrong landlord and somebody would kill him. He remembered Jose tumbling down the stairs, saw the blood again, felt Dirkson's shoe thud against his skull, his own skull. He prayed, though he had stopped believing a long time ago, Dear God, please protect Jose, keep him safe.

A tap on the door, Annie came in, sat on the bed and lit up one of those funny cigarettes of hers. Chris felt trapped. A few years later he would have seen Annie and the funny cigarette as somewhere to run *to*; but this was 1955, and he was already enough of a family disaster for not finishing at Indiana University and entering an insurance business, a wholesale drug outfit, a used car dealership. It was 1955, and the smoke from Annie's funny cigarette might as well have worn horns and a tail; it took him years before, looking back, he kind of loved her for how scared and needful she must have really been that night. Remembered her with love. She sat on his bed, sat on the edge of his bed. He could see, in the streetlight, her flannel nightgown, her hair loose around her shoulders. She didn't look at him. She took a deep drag and passed over to him the funny cigarette, passed it over and he took it as if it were the commonest thing he'd ever done, though he figured—one drag and he was finished. And he said, Then I'll be finished, I want to be finished. He sucked deeply the way she did and held in the smoke. She took back the cigarette and it was like throwing himself away but he held in the smoke and Jesus he felt a hum and a buzz through his body and his head loosened. Then she was passing it back, and he did it again.

She didn't talk. Into her silence he poured the mysteries that would break his life apart. When the cigarette got too small to bother with, she swallowed the tiny dead butt and, pulling down the covers, got into bed with him. A couple of children at camp, he thought, not expecting to think that. But then he was shocked, when she touched his bare legs, at the terrific intensity of the touch or of the touch of his fingers to her nightgown, the curve of her thighs and ass. It made him gasp, and she put a finger to his lips; she shaped, with her hands, his back and shoulders. Oh my God. He pulled off his jockey shorts, he kissed her and almost got lost inside the kiss, his first marijuana kiss, his first kiss in hell. Then he was inside her body and his heart loosened and poured out, and he felt incredible gratitude and simple peace and this didn't seem much like hell. "Come on," she said, and made him move harder, so he did, almost angry. "Come *on*." He started to come, and laughed, she hushed him, but he started bucking and roaring and bellowed and came like hell; she moved hard then, and came—or pretended.

He was nearly asleep. She pushed him to one side of the bed. "You make too damn much noise. But I'm staying. If he barges in, to hell with him. I'm not sleeping by myself tonight."

When Chris woke it was just dawn. His head felt a little light; the buzz was gone. Annie was curled up at the other side of the bed, turned away. He wanted to run his hand along the soft, flannel curves of her, he wanted to make love again, but he was afraid to wake her, afraid to disturb things. He felt—knowing, sure, that this feeling was fragile, that it would collapse like a hardwood coal that kept its fire shape until you touched it—that the city pulsed in this room, that the center of the city was here, the two of them, this bed, and that in some sense, like a spider in the center of a web, he was in touch with the extremities.

Then he must have fallen back to sleep. "Well, Jesus Christ," he heard, and woke up. Annie was sitting up, looking into the little mirror on the wall. "Look what you did to my mouth."

"I'm sorry. Is it bleeding?"

"It's puffed up. I better be careful about you." She leaned over the bed and kissed him on the tip of his nose. "Thanks for last night. I would have felt lousy sleeping alone. I don't know why."

She slipped out; he heard the door to her bedroom open and close. And the feeling—that here was the center, that the city was inside this room—dissolved. The city was *out there* again—not in his room, not even in Annie's room—just somewhere *out there*.

Hungry to begin. He'd seen three ads for sharing an apartment —none of them were in when he'd called—and he found out from a waiter at Rienzi's about the notice boards at N.Y.U. Smiling, he remembered Jose's boxes: he'd have to take them along—and how could Jose find him? He saw himself lugging Jose's boxes from furnished room to furnished room for years and years.

To begin. Plenty of energy, even a kind of courage. Images of windows with green plants, jazz from record players in converted lofts, the smile of the black woman stroking her cat. A room somewhere—he was very hungry to go out into the city; city, body of himself, but it would be fifteen years before, laughing to himself, he really understood. Body of himself—hunger for what he didn't know was already in himself, himself not separate from the life that pulsed through him.

LADIES AND GENTLEMEN, THE ORIGINAL MUSIC OF THE HEBREW ALPHABET

CURT LEVIANT

Curt Leviant's short stories have appeared in *The Quarterly Review of Literature, The Literary Review,* and other magazines, and have been included in Martha Foley's *Best American Short Stories* and other anthologies. His first novel, *The Yemenite Girl,* published in 1977, was given the 1977 Edward Lewis Wallant Book Award, presented annually for the best work of fiction of Jewish significance. Mr. Leviant lives in the Greater New York area.

From the top of the stone steps I looked down into the large sunny courtyard where groups of people stood scattered. Men came and went under the archway that led to the street. Elderly women in kerchiefs sat on stone benches that faced the rear wall of the synagogue. Two lads in *yarmulkes* and *payes* stood talking, holding on to the iron wedding canopy filigreed with Hebrew letters, as though supporting it for some unseen couple.

From where I stood I saw a man behind a concrete pillar, his head covered with the black fedora religious Jews wear the world over.

"*Shalom.* If I am not mistaken, you are from Israel," he said in heavily accented English, pounding in Hungarian fashion the first syllable of each word.

"No."

"Forgive me for intruding but I heard you speaking with the rabbi in the dining room, and I thought I heard some Hebrew words, so I assumed you lived there. Excuse me."

"I assure you, no harm done." Then I added, "You speak an excellent English, sir."

Copyright © 1977 by B'nai B'rith. Reprinted by permission.

He brightened. "But if you speak Hebrew, I can also converse with you in the holy tongue. Or others not so holy."

"I don't speak Hebrew . . . Have you ever been to Israel?" I asked just to be polite.

"Regretfully, I have never been to Israel, even though it is one of my fondest wishes to go."

Neither of us moved. I stood at the top of the steps, he behind the concrete pillar. I had the sensation I was speaking to a disembodied head. The man had high, wide cheekbones, a boyish face and a luminous smile.

"What other languages do you speak?"

"Yiddish, German, French, Hungarian of course, Russian and Italian. Though I have never been to France, Russia, or Italy, though I completed my studies in Frankfurt. I also have never been to England or America. But I have traveled widely on the plains of Texas and in various places of the world. . . ."

Only now as I walked down the steps did the rest of his body float into view.

". . . without ever leaving the Budapest library."

He was short, crippled in both legs, I saw; his hands were bent.

"You are from America, correct? I can tell by your accent. Are you having a good time?"

"Yes. Budapest is a beautiful city."

"Veneer. But for a tourist excellent. To understand, walk the darker streets, see the grey houses . . . You are a physician?"

"No."

"Because in the restaurant Madame Dalno—we call her the Czar—called you Doctor."

"I am a Ph.D."

"It is honor to make acquaintance of a fellow intellectual. In what specialty is your doctorate, may I ask?"

"Musicology. And yours?"

His mouth fell open. A red flush came over his cheeks. His eyes shone, on the verge of tears.

"I am very fortunate. I am so happy . . . Oh,"—he clapped his hands together with a twist of one shoulder—"that I should have such good fortune, I did not know I am worthy of."

"Friedmann!" a voice shouted. We turned to the doorway. There stood Madame Dalno, hefty and double-chinned, with a round, officious face, hair wrapped in a white coif.

"Please Friedmann!" she shouted in English. "Perhaps you are disturbing the Herr Doctor. Enough. He is a very busy man."

Friedmann withdrew. He gestured—was he teasing her?—the by-your-leave hand motion one sees in seventeenth century French comedies.

I turned and said to Madame Dalno: "Mr. Friedmann honors me with his conversation." She closed the door.

Friedmann put his hand over his mouth and said softly, "The Czar is a very strong woman. Like biblical Joseph, provider of food."

As we spoke, several people in the courtyard drew near. One woman—wisps of black hair grew out of her chin and above her lip—tugged at my elbow. "Perhaps you can spare something for *tzedoke*," she said in Yiddish. Others, too, stood with outstretched hands. I reached into my pocket.

A clap of hands. I turned to the doorway. Madame Dalno again, dispersing the beggars.

"When the Czar claps," Friedmann muttered, "people move. Meals without cost are not easy to come by."

"Mr. Friedmann," I said.

"*Engineer* Friedmann," he said, "Ferdinand." I walked in step with his halting stride. "I cannot tell you how pleased I am that you are a musicologist, Herr Doctor."

"Please, my name is Isaac Gantz. I prefer not to be called Herr Doctor."

"If you please." He bowed. "At long last I have met someone in the field. And as a token of friendship I have something of interest which may excite curiosity."

"An old Hungarian folk instrument?"

"No. It has nothing to do with Hungary except that it has been here for a while. It concerns the Hebrew alphabet."

"Well, Engineer Friedmann, I'm not really a linguist. It's music that interests me."

"I am not a linguist either, even though I speak seven languages. It is music that interests me as well. Yes. As Da Vinci said: '*Le figurazione delle cosi invisibile.*' You look puzzled, Herr Doctor! Surely, you know the great Leonardo's classic definition of music—the shaping of the invisible."

I nodded hesitantly. "Your alphabet has notes?" I asked.

"Many things. Crucial. Old. Pristine. Seminal. It goes to the heart of the matter. To basics. To quote the old book of philosophy, it is so astounding that once you experience it, it is like the gallop of horses, horses of fire, horses of wrath, horses of darkness, horses of black night."

"The image alone gives me the creeps."

"A thousand pardons. I had no wish to frighten you. I merely wanted to give you feeling of what material I possess. You shall be delighted. Fascinated. This is my pledge."

"I'm fascinated already. Tell me what you're talking about."

"Of course. I have the knowledge of—that is to say, I am honored to be in possession of the original music of the Hebrew alphabet. With much supporting material."

"The what?"

"The original music of the Hebrew alphabet."

"I didn't even know there is such a thing."

"But there is. There is."

"Has it been published?"

"No, no. Not published."

"Not published? Incredible. Have you told anyone about this? Do they know?"

Friedmann put his hand over his mouth. "What do they know? What do they understand? If they see paper, they call it paper. Ink, they call it ink. But the mystery of ink on paper, quill on parchment, they do not understand. Some people, of course, I have told. Not major details. Not substance. Merely description. Outline. There is no one to talk to here."

"Well, you certainly can talk to me." I felt as though I had stumbled onto the Rosetta Stone. In the nineteenth century, Mendelssohn discovered Bach. Then Bizet's Symphony in C was found. Not too long ago, another hitherto unknown Mendelssohn Violin Concerto was brought to light. Perhaps now it was my turn. "If this is so, Engineer Friedmann, you may have one of the most valuable treasures in Jewish history, in the history of music. Possibly one of the astounding finds in the history of world culture."

Friedmann lowered his eyes. "I am a modest man."

"Where is this item? How did you find it?"

"How did I find it? It is a long story, Doctor Isaac. Now is not the time for it. What are you doing in Budapest, may I ask?"

"I was at the musicology congress in Vienna, and since Budapest is so close, I decided to visit. Perhaps we'll photograph it and publish the document. Maybe I can publicize it for you in the musical world."

"Everything is possible. If—" Friedmann stopped.

"If what?"

"If you fulfill my request: Please find my relatives."

I felt myself in a fairy tale world. The king shows me his daughter. I fall madly in love with her. Then the wizard imposes on me an impossible task to win her hand. I had already seen myself and my find on page one of the *New York Times*, with the headline: MUSICOLOGIST REPORTS MAJOR DISCOVERY: ORIGINAL MUSIC OF HEBREW ALPHABET.

"Where should I look for your relatives?"

"In America. That is, New York."

"But what has that to do with scholarly material? With our research?"

"It has everything to do with it. My relatives are important to me."

"I promise I shall do my best as soon as I return to the United States," I said. "I consider this a sacred mission."

Friedmann tilted his head, looked up at me. There was just a hint of a laugh at the edges of his almond-shaped eyes.

"If you will be so kind as to excuse me, I cannot help smiling to myself. I see many Jews here over the months. All are friendly. As anyone who takes the interest to visit the *kehilla* must be. But somehow something happens by the time they return to America. Many promises, none kept."

"I'll find them in the Manhattan phone book."

"It is kind of you. You understand my point of view."

"Of course. But, I'm disappointed. You sparked my interest. I don't know if I can come back. Travel is expensive. I'm only a teacher in a small college." I bent close to him and said softly, "I'll tell you confidentially, I must publish an important study in order to retain my job."

"You mean that in America, in free America, they will discharge you from your post if you do not publish something in a journal?"

"The system is called publish or perish."

"Oh, that is terrible. Here under the Germans the system was called Hungarian or perish. If you were not a Hungarian, you were shot by the river."

"You are mistaken, Engineer Friedmann."

"I am not. Not. Not." He bounced awkwardly on his toes. "I saw my parents, my sisters, my friends slain. In this city of beautiful veneer. Only I survived—the last of the Friedmann line. That I do not want to hear from an American who was not here."

"A thousand pardons . . . It's not capital punishment, God forbid, but perish in the sense that you lose your job. Jobs are scarce now. People with doctorates are driving taxis, working in the post office. That I won't do; I'd rather die."

Friedmann put out his hands, palms up. "Please. Life is foremost. That is my entire philosophy. No dying."

"Even if you don't show me the manuscript, at least describe its contents. Or give me sufficient background so I'll be able to write . . ."

"No, no writing. This belongs to me. Us."

"Us?"

"Us is my colleague and I. My partner. Ferenc Furer."

"You didn't tell me there are two people in this."

"My dear Doctor. There are many things I did not tell you. One cannot work alone. You said writing. Absolutely not. I refuse."

I drew a deep breath. "You don't understand. I won't publish it. But on a *stipendium* application, if I give an indication of its contents, I may be able to get money to return here. Otherwise, I won't be able to come back."

"You will. Don't worry, you will. You provide addresses of my relatives and then we get deeper into material."

He stretched out his hand. I shook it. I expected it to be moist, nervous, but it was warm and dry, surprisingly soft, hairless, babyish.

"When will you come?" he asked.

"Is tomorrow after lunch good for you?"

"Why not?" He hitched up one shoulder and with an awkward but evidently practiced movement went into his pocket and pressed into my hand a soft off-white card that had been in his wallet for years.

"My visit card. Note the address. Not too distant from this point. Excuse fourth floor . . . Now if you will be so kind, take

out pen and write down names of the people you will find for
me."

I jotted down names, relationships, places of birth and occupations. Then he said, "Adieu," turned swiftly and hobbled away.

I walk around Budapest, the city of someone else's dreams. I
marvel at the seven bridges, each with a history of its own. I peel
veneer, replace veneer. I cross and recross the Chain Bridge that
spans the calm Blue Danube. I love the silhouette of the elegant
grey buildings along the river, so old world European.

I pass where the ghetto wall was erected; here Hungarians who
had been neighbors with Jews for decades turned them over to the
Germans when they made their roundups; here Mrs. Basanyi said
sweetly, "*Herr Offizer*, Mrs. Schneider is still upstairs with a
sprained ankle," and then the Germans and their Hungarian
helpers took all the Jews of the courtyard and shot them by the
river, at the foot of the Chain Bridge.

Then I came to Friedmann's apartment—two poorly illumi-
nated rooms on the fourth floor of a walkup. I knocked on the
open door and, hearing no reply, entered. The small kitchen had a
wooden table, one chair, an electric hot plate and a cabinet on the
wall above the tiny, single-faucet sink. The streaked white walls
hadn't been painted in years. Cartons and paper-wrapped packages tied with string were scattered on the floor, as though Friedmann had just moved in or was preparing to move out.

Friedmann entered from another room, formally attired in fedora, Sabbath jacket, tie and ill-matching trousers. He stood there,
as if saying: This is what I possess. I wanted to ask Friedmann
about himself. Where he came from, where educated, why he
didn't work at his profession, what had happened to him during
the war. Was his infirmity from birth, or had the Germans or
Hungarians tortured and crippled him?

He pulled out the chair and asked me to sit. When I refused,
we both stood. He leaned on the chair.

"You have done me a great kindness in coming to visit me," he
said.

"Actually, Engineer Friedmann, yours is the kindness."

"No, it is a great honor for me." He smiled, his smooth face radiant. "Although I do not have too many visitors here in my
humble abode, I welcome each one to the best of my ability. Please

excuse my small English. I have not spoken so much English since my schooling. I hope I do not intrude upon, or offend, your developed sensibilities of style."

"On the contrary, Engineer Friedmann," I said.

Friedmann bowed. "Although I am still abiding by our agreement of yesterday, and hence shall not at this time reveal any more about our common matter of interest, to show you how much I am interested in your welfare I shall read you a sort of prolegomenon."

He cleared his throat, took a folded page from his jacket pocket; and with one hand behind his back, he began to chant, with the rocking motion of a man praying.

"The secret of the *aleph-beys* was handed over personally by the angel Raziel to Adam who gave it to Abel. His brother Cain was jealous and killed him for it. It was then taken from Cain. As soon as the mark was placed on his forehead he forgot the melody, which was held for some ten generations until it was given to Noah after the Flood, and then to the Patriarch Abraham, whose Hebrew name I have the honor of bearing. His son Ishmael was caught stealing the alphabet by Sarah, and for this Sarah chased Ishmael and his mother Hagar from the house. Abraham gave the music of the alphabet to Isaac, and Isaac intended to give it to Esau, in payment for the prepared meals that his hunter son served him. However, in a dream, an angel—I do not know if it was Raziel or not—told him to give it to Jacob. In a historic encounter, Jacob later wrestled with the angel Raziel who tried, a test it was, to take back the secret music of the alphabet, but Jacob prevailed. He had passed the test of strength and only suffered a wound in his thigh bone, which made him limp. Jacob, in turn, passed the music on to Joseph, who earned the enmity of his brothers; for Joseph, to tease his brothers, foolishly chanted parts of the alphabet, but never sang a complete letter to them.

"And so it went from generation to generation. David was inspired by the melodies to compose the Psalms. He too teased with the melody, playing—like Joseph—parts of it for Saul. This drove Saul to the verge of madness and once in frustration he even threw a spear at David.

"In the Hebrew *aleph-beys*, there are twenty-two letters—a fact attested to by philologists, and the medieval kabbalists and philos-

ophers who were expert at using the *aleph-beys* for their own purposes."

Friedmann drew a deep breath, almost a sigh, and continued
reading. "In our musical system of notation there are twelve
notes. On the piano, seven white keys, five black. On the violin,
no colors. In the Hebraic system of convergences and correspondences, there is balance, evenness, parallelism—the hallmark
of biblical poetry. And there are the ten *sefirot,* the fiery numbered characteristics of God, which as the *Zohar* teaches us are
the foundation of the entire work of creation. The twelve notes
which are heard but not seen, and the ten *sefirot* which are neither heard nor seen, but are of a sublime musical fire, make up the
number twenty-two, which corresponds meticulously to the sum
of Hebrew letters, and just as in Kabbala where there is union of
heavenly and earthly, and each chooses his partner in fusion, so
the twenty-two letters wed the note-*sefirot* combination of twenty-
two. Of the twenty-two letters, ten are imperfect because they are,
or can be, completed, or can change their sound and shape according to position and grammatical rules. Twelve are absolutes, firm,
immutable in sound. To these twelve the twelve notes go; the
weaker ten need the divine fire, the heavenly music of the *sefirot*
in order to become whole . . . Do you follow?"

"Yes," I said politely. My head was reeling. "I am trying to follow. May I take notes?"

"I have no notes to give you now."

"I meant note-taking. As in a notebook."

"No. Please do not take my notes. What I am saying you must
remember. It will get more complex, but you must be worthy—
note-worthy!" he laughed.

"There are so many correspondences here that you will jump
with delight at the perfection of the blending of all these items,
yes, their uncanny musical genius, their divine order."

I felt uncomfortable, for the introduction of the divine into
what was, or appeared to be, a scientific, scholarly matter made
me suspect that it might not be fully reliable.

I looked around for Friedmann's books. Perhaps he kept them
in his little bedroom or in the cabinet on the wall.

"Where are your books?"

"I have no books."

"What?"

He shook his head. "Not one. Not needed. What need have I
of books? I have too many possessions as is, and I am attempting
to cut them to the minimum. My collection of books, one of the
finest in the world, is in the library."

"Are you finished with your presentation?"

"Finished? Hardly have I begun." Then he held his head. "Oh
I am so apologetic. Here you are standing and I have not even
offered you anything. May I offer you a cup of tea?"

"No, thank you. I've just eaten."

"It is just as well. I have no sugar and I am out of tea. And my
electric ring is broken, too."

Finally, Friedmann, shaking his head, said, "That is all for
today."

"But what about the melody? The original music of the Hebrew alphabet," I raised my voice against my will. "Can't you give
me a hint? Like Joseph did his brothers? Or David to Saul?"

"Oh," he said, smiling coyly, his face luminescent as an angel's.
"I do not like to tease people. Remember our agreement, our
oath? . . . But let me assure you that you will return."

As I left him, Friedmann replaced his manuscript in his
jacket pocket and with much difficulty began unknotting his
tie.

A few minutes after customs at Kennedy, I ran to the nearest
phone booth, pulled out my passport folder and looked for Friedmann's list. A sour feeling went through me as I emptied the
folder, searched my pockets. I couldn't find the card on which I'd
written the addresses! I returned home and there made a thor-
ough search of my luggage. Zero. I knew I'd put Friedmann's list
in a safe place, among my important papers. Again and again I
searched the contents of my billfold; I went through all my shirts,
jackets, trousers—once I felt something in a jacket pocket: an old
photograph of myself: my image mocking me. I searched the
manuscripts and books I'd taken along. Nothing. I remembered
only Friedmann's name and the floor he lived on. In Budapest, I'd
find him. But returning to Budapest without finding his relatives
was senseless. It hurt me to imagine Friedmann laughing at me as
yet another in the long line of friendly but unreliable American
tourists.

Then I had an idea. In a Jewish yearbook, I looked up the

addresses of the communal offices, and wrote four letters: to Madame Dalno, to Friedmann c/o Dalno, to the rabbi I'd met and to a prominent communal leader, Dr. L. Geller.

Two months passed without a reply. Meanwhile, things were getting worse at the college. Directives came down that faculty was to be cut and that tenure was to be abolished. As a junior faculty member with relatively few publications and a speciality that wasn't readily marketable, I was vulnerable.

Then one day, with a suddenness that still surprises me, I opened my passport folder and came upon the list. It had been there all along, on the reverse side of a card filled with names of contacts in Vienna. I simply had not bothered to turn it over.

That same day—of course, Friedmann would contend kabbalistic convergence—a reply came from Dr. Geller, director of Budapest's Jewish Historical Institute, with Friedmann's address, and with a brief postscript: "Why do you want it?" In a note of thanks for his courtesy, I told Geller briefly: my interest in research in old music.

Next I got hold of the Manhattan directory and looked for an Albert Bok. Of the three Boks listed one was Hung Phen Bok, hardly a middle European; another was John Bok, rejected as out of clan; the third was Sarah Bok. She answered on the second ring.

"Hello, my name is Dr. Gantz. I met an Engineer Ferdinand Friedmann in Budapest, and he asked me to try to locate some relatives named Bok. Are you by any chance related to an Ignatz Friedmann who owned a chocolate factory in Vienna?"

"Yes," she said happily. "Ignatz was not *my* uncle, but the relative of my late husband, Albert. His mother was a Friedmann."

We chatted a few minutes and then she gave the number of her husband's cousin, Wolfgang Leopold Bok, in Atlantic City. I dialed, and a cultivated European voice answered.

"Hello, this is Dr. Gantz. I have regards from a long lost relative of yours in Budapest, Engineer Ferdinand Friedmann." I then read the entire list of relatives, where they'd lived and what they'd done. Bok recognized all the names—except Ferdinand Friedmann's.

I told him that I'd write Friedmann that night. I could have sworn I was happier than he.

I sent my letter to Friedmann registered, return receipt re-

quested. A month went by, then two months. I called Bok, and
he told me curtly that he'd written but had received no reply. I
sensed Bok reprimanding me—as if I were at fault both for having
brought up the Friedmann affair *and* for Friedmann not respond-
ing. To impress Bok, I kept accenting phrases such as, "So Friedmann said to me, 'Doctor Gantz, I'd be so happy if you could find
my relatives,'" and "In my capacity as an objective person, a doctor, I find that . . ."

"Well, why didn't he answer me?" Bok insisted.

"He might not have answered," I said lamely, "because he is
sick, or perhaps because he didn't get the letter. Did you send it
registered?"

"No."

"I sent mine registered. With return receipt."

"Who signed it? Friedmann?"

"No. Strangely enough, the receipt came back, but not with his
signature."

"The whole thing is puzzling. Neither I nor my wife remember
him."

"Yet he seems to know not only everyone in the family, but
their occupations and businesses as well. Maybe . . ."

But I stopped. I didn't say: Maybe he was rejected because he's
a cripple and nobody wants to have anything to do with him.

"Maybe what?"

"Maybe you'll still hear from him."

"Could be. Thank you."

Several more weeks passed. By spring, I was worrying if my annual contract would be renewed, and if I'd get a travel grant to
Budapest. Friedmann's silence disappointed me. I kept my word;
why didn't he have the courtesy to respond? I didn't want to dis-
cuss the find with professionals, lest my territorial rights be vio-
lated, and lest they laugh at me. I checked into articles, listings,
indexes but found nothing that remotely resembled Friedmann's
subject.

Then I received two letters. The first came from Friedmann.

Dear Doctor Gantz:

*I am glad to have the honoured opportunity of writing in re-
sponse to your kind letter. First, I want to apologize heartily at
why I have not replied, and for your kind deed of providing my*

relatives' addresses. The reason was not neglect, nor ingratitude, God forbid. It is because I was at hospital briefly, but thank God, I am much better now. I am sorry if I have given you worrisomeness. I am flattered that a person of your elevated distinction is interested in me, in my life and in my work.

I have always been the breadloser in my family, owing to my condition and to my predilection for thought and ideas rather than the more ignoble side of life.

I am honoured to engage in a correspondence with you, esteemed Herr Doctor, and only wish to inform you as of now that I was born in Budapest, and received my engineering education in Frankfurt, upon the completion of which I returned to Budapest where I have remained ever since, sharing the same fate of my fellow Jews during the bestial German occupation, but miraculously surviving. While writing to you, I have at this same time written to my relatives in New Jersey. Once again, I beg you to accept my gratitude for your kindness in helping me to locate members of my dear family.

Sincerely yours.
Ferdinand Friedmann, B.Sc.Eng.

Of the manuscript, not a word.
The second letter was from Professor Geller.

Dear Doctor Gantz:
Thank you for your letter.
Please be informed that Friedmann, God save us, is an unfortunate man who cannot be depended upon to consistently behave in a rational manner. The original music of the Hebrew alphabet has been his idée-fixe, his joint enterprise with his friend, partner and driving force, who unfortunately must also be placed in the same mental category. If you wish, I can offer some examples of the far-fetched projects they have pitifully attempted to propound:

1) Saving coffee grounds to do research on their possible conversion to practical use.
2) Printing money on vitamin-enriched edible paper, so that if there is not enough food to purchase for the money, one could, as a last resort, eat the money for food.
3) Harnessing the energy of moonlight.

The above absurd ideas are regularly presented as "scholarly papers" by the team of Furer and Friedmann, the two madmen of Budapest. But there is nothing more other-worldly and insane (perhaps even brilliantly insane) than this original music of the Hebrew alphabet. I urge you not to involve yourself; and should you be thinking of this in scholarly terms, as a possibly intriguing element of a long lost world, do not delude yourself with false hopes any longer, lest later disappointment be more severe than earlier.

Sincerely yours,
Dr. Laszlo Geller

P.S. I hope you will visit me in Budapest.

My first reaction to the letter was disbelief. One cannot dismiss a man as a madman just because he has something astounding to offer the world. I mulled over Dr. Geller's letter for a week; meanwhile, I had occasion to read some articles that gave me satisfaction.

Dear Dr. Geller:
Many thanks for your cordial letter. I appreciate your kindness in trying to do me a good turn, but I do not think that at this stage I should reject out of hand Friedmann's discovery. In the history of culture, new discoveries and inventions have always been labelled the products of madmen. To support the above contention I am enclosing a xerox copy of an article in last Saturday's New York Times which lists as a new patent by a team of industrial scientists from the Nescafe corporation an innovative method for inexpensively converting coffee grounds into usable paper.
I shall be honored to make your acquaintance if I am in Budapest this summer, as I hope to be.

Sincerely,
Isaac Gantz, Ph.D.
Instructor of Musicology
Frederick Cole College

Then I called Bok who had also received a letter. He was still puzzled. "The story is not much clearer," he said. "As I told you, we do not recall any Ferdinand Friedmann. There is another question here. Our family was in Vienna from 1929 to 1938. Friedmann knew we lived there; it is obvious from all the notes. Why then did he not attempt to contact us then? What does he want? And why did he wait so long before answering?"

"He was hospitalized," I said. "He explained that in his letter to me."

"Does he want any material help? He doesn't mention it in his letter."

"He specifically told me he doesn't want money. He begged me: 'Dr. Gantz, find my relatives.' I think, Mr. Bok, you should realize how hard it is for them in Europe, especially Hungary."

I felt that Bok suspected me of creating a relative; that I was involved in some sort of con game. What if some stranger had called me up and told me he'd met a relative of mine I'd never heard of in some godforsaken land? Wouldn't I be wary? The suspicion I sensed in his hesitant voice prompted the same in me—a sort of sympathetic vibration, fanned in part by Professor Geller's letter. Perhaps during the war Friedmann had met a man with a name like his, and from him he had learned the history of the Friedmann family and the names of relatives he remembered. And so Ferdinand Friedmann, lonely, forlorn, poor, ill, unfamilied, an orphan in every sense of the word, arrogated the other Friedmann's family as his own, considered himself the rightful heir to this family list, and made plans to contact members of his family. But why had Ferdinand waited so long?

I hesitated, and then told Bok that Ferdinand lived in very poor circumstances, and that he was deserving of help, that indeed I had helped him out with a gift of cash.

"Now, well, that I didn't know. He said nothing about that in his letter."

"I know. He doesn't *want* his new-found relationship with you to be built on a donor-taker basis."

I hesitated again, and then I told Bok that Ferdinand Friedmann was a cripple and that the poor man must climb four flights to his tiny apartment.

"Oh," Bok said. "That I didn't know either. He said nothing about that."

Too late. I had just destroyed my friend as a normal human being in the eyes of his unseen relatives, and reduced him to an object of pity.

"Friedmann doesn't want anyone to feel sorry for him. He's a brilliant man, with the sort of syncretic intellect one associates with the finest European minds."

"May I ask you, doctor, what you were doing in Budapest? It's not exactly the playground of Europe."

"Well, part vacation, part research."

"Of course, you are a doctor. What is your medical specialty?"

Now he had me. I had set the pattern with my little misleading use of title in order to gain greater credence for myself. I didn't want him to think of me as an irresponsible *artiste*, a musician who cannot be trusted. "I am not a *doctor* doctor. I have a doctorate in medieval and renaissance music."

"I was under the distinct impression with your repeated use of doctor that you were a physician. Now it turns out you're a musician."

"I do research in musicology. I'm not a mere performer." There was no need to tell a complete stranger about the embattled division in the field of music between those who only played, and those who analyzed, discovered and made sense and order out of the chaos of the creative tradition.

I sensed that since he'd discovered I wasn't a physician the scale had tipped; I no longer had the upper hand.

"Tell me, how does this Friedmann interest you?"

"Like any other human being would interest me," I said somewhat aggressively. "If a Jew comes up to me with tears in his eyes, especially behind the Iron Curtain, and presses a list of names into my hand and pleads, 'Find my relatives,' wouldn't you consider this a sacred obligation, a *mitzva* of the highest order?"

"I would, doctor. You are perfectly right."

"Excuse me," I lied, "my doorbell is ringing. Good talking to you."

"Goodbye, doctor, and thank you. We'll be in touch."

To my surprise and joy, I soon learned that my travel grant to Budapest was approved, and my contract at the college was renewed for another year. In June, I was in Budapest again, wandering past that outdoor iron marriage canopy into the secluded *kehilla* courtyard.

After lunch, I met Friedmann, hat on the back of his head, waiting by the concrete pillar. He greeted me as if he had ex-

pected me and took my hand with obvious pleasure. "Ah, Doctor
Gantz, I knew you'd be back. Come. I have much to tell you."

We walked to his house without saying a word. Friedmann
hadn't changed; neither had his apartment. One table, one chair,
and a cabinet on the wall. The cartons and packages—filled with
coffee grounds, paper money, moonlight?—were still scattered on
the floor.

"Please sit down. I am going to tell you a story.

"Some years ago, I do not remember how many, in peaceful
days before the war, I was walking in the fields near Debrecen. It
was a quiet, beautiful spring day. I felt as if I were in a nineteenth
century idyllic story. You know, something out of the early Hesse,
Grillparzer or Robert Musil.

"It was a perfect combination of mood, weather and countryside. I heard a bird. Then I *thought* I heard a bird, singing a melody I have never heard before, for a bird does not have such
melodic range. I cupped my hand to my ear. It was a man singing
to himself. An old peasant. I stopped and listened until he had
finished. Then I approached and asked him what he had been
singing. He was apparently somewhat deaf and did not hear me.
What sort of words were these?, thought I, as the melody went
through my mind. But when I extricated myself long enough from
the spell of the enchanting melody, I realized he had not been
singing any words, but was reciting. He had a thick white mustache curled up at the ends like a hussar and a sash around his
waist, as though he had just descended from his horse. You know
what this old hussar was singing?

"The Hebrew alphabet!

"'Do you know Hebrew?' I asked him. He laughed. 'No. I do
not know Hebrew.' 'Do you know you are singing the Hebrew alphabet?' 'That I do!' 'When did you learn it?' 'Oh, a long time
ago. Sixty years. I got the melody in exchange from a holy man.
Hasid rabbi. For a shepherd's song he heard me singing.' 'Can you
teach it to me? I too collect beautiful music.' 'No. I forgot it. Like
he said I would. He wanted it only for the holy prayers. Lost. Like
the notes that dribble out of the fife.'

"'And he gave you the melody of the alphabet?' I asked. 'Yes.
That he did. He told me he would give me a secret. Something
that had been passed from his grandfather's grandfather back to
the angel Raziel. But to me he gave it because he knew that I

knew no Jews. He said he had no sons and there were too many quarrels in his circle of churchgoers.'

" 'Do you know what you were singing?' 'Yes. It is the lost music of the original alphabet. And I, a Christian, know the secret!' 'Teach it to me.' 'No. I will lose this melody, too.' 'You will not. I am from the family of the holy angel Raziel. My name, too, is Raziel. Lend me the melody.' 'No. I will forget the melody.' 'I promise you will not lose it. Look. You light a match and give your fire to a friend who also smokes a pipe. Does your flame become smaller? No. Is it taken away? No. The melody you give is like a fire. You will not forget your songs.'

"But the peasant shook his head.

" 'Then I will sing the melody for you to prove that I belong to the Raziel family, but you only tell me if I have sung it correctly.' The peasant agreed and I sang several letters of the melody for him. 'Holy saints,' he said. 'A miracle!'

" 'No miracle,' I said, 'I listen once and absorb melody. If you blow a note on your fife even without my looking I can tell you what note it is.' But instead of admiring this ability of mine, the old peasant muttered: 'Witchcraft. Leave it to the Jews. First they make me forget my song and now they copy my alphabet music like a mirror. The priest is right, the devil is in the Jews.' And without another word, he walked away.

"And that, my dear friend Doctor Gantz, is the story of how I acquired the original music of the Hebrew alphabet."

The time had come to make my request. By telling me the story, Friedmann had shown his trust in me. Now I knew he would be ready to show me the music.

Friedmann opened up one of a dozen cartons and string-wrapped paper packages on the floor. With his back turned to me, he took out a sheet of paper and began to read.

"There is a mysterious link between the *aleph-beys* and the universe we live in. The basic elements of the universe are water, fire, earth—formed from the three basic letters: *mem, shin, aleph.* Moreover, the *aleph-beys* has seven doubled letters. These correspond to the seven planets of the ancients. So then, seven days of week, seven planets and seven orifices in the human body. Three plus seven is ten.

"Now there remain twelve plain letters with which the twelve constellations were created. The letters, then, are not only symbols, but the elements and building materials of God's creative word—the basic forms of everything that exists. Pay heed: twelve letters, twelve notes, twelve tribes, twelve months. Tribes, space; months, time. The magic number is, will always be, twenty-two. Twelve notes out of which all music grows, and then ten numbers out of which all numbers grow. Remember, too, the ten moral numbers, the commandments, out of which all common law grows, for we can have no nature, no reality, no culture, without law. The ten and twelve yield twenty-two letters out of which all words, knowledge, destiny, grow."

As Friedmann spoke of the alphabet he looked even younger— angelic, virginal, unsullied by this world.

"Engineer Friedmann, I'd like to ask you a personal question."

He looked up at me and spread his crooked hands, waiting.

"Have you ever been kissed by a woman?"

Friedmann looked down at his hands and legs, as if to display himself as his answer. Then he gazed up at me, his face shining.

"Your question is more to confirm a formed supposition. Nevertheless, I shall answer you. Since it is something I have not experienced, I consider myself a master in imagination. A perfect critic. The answer is no. But there is a certain beauty in *not* experiencing something. Once someone, to poke fun at me for keeping *kashrut*, said: 'Why don't you try bacon, just once? You don't know how delicious it is.' My reply was: 'You don't know how delicious it is *not*.'

"But I can imagine how powerful, how intense can be the kiss of a woman, like the kiss of God. Unbearable. One might not survive it. But now I know why I can bear the beauty, the intensity of the melody of the Hebrew alphabet. *Because* I have never been kissed, there is enough reserve physical strength in me to absorb this severe metaphysical shock. If I would have been another—and had the kiss of a woman, God, goddess—the melody for me would have been like standing squarely in the path of a bolt of lightning.

"And now, permit me to continue. Just as every Hebrew letter has a different shape, even a different feel, so each letter has its own melody . . . Do you have a favorite letter?"

"I haven't thought of it."

"*Ayin* is mine. Not in print. In script. The way it starts at one end and loops around itself and ends on the other side. Perfectly balanced. Standing on an egg, crossed arms up. There is a mag-

nificent rhythm in the written letters—even a structural leit-
motif, as if the *aleph-beys* were an artistically realized composi-
tion. The basic form of most letters is a semi-circle. A circle divided by a NW to SE line at a 45° angle. Here . . ." Friedmann
rushed to a cabinet otherwise empty: I saw make believe cups
dangling on nonexistent hooks—he took out pencil and paper. "I
shall draw it for you. Like this, see? This top part, there you have
it. This is the basic form of about half the *aleph-beys* . . . The *ayin*
does not have it. Maybe . . ." he put a finger to his cheek,
"maybe that is why I like it. It is shaped differently. Beautiful, not
so, Herr Doctor?"

I nodded.

"There is another reason why I like *ayin*. Because of its pun
meaning. *Ayin* means eye. Notion of seeing, of encompassing everything. And yet, spelled with an *aleph*, *ayin* means nothingness.
The word exists, yet it represents nothingness." Friedmann raised
a bent finger. "That is all for today, I am fatigued."

The following day I made an appointment to meet Dr. Laszlo
Geller of the Jewish Historical Institute, the only active Jewish
school behind the Iron Curtain. Geller is something of a hero, for
singlehandedly he maintains research in Jewish culture and history
in Hungary, and is the guardian of the famed Fensterwald Collection of 333 incunabula and rare manuscripts. After talking for a
while about his work, he began to speak of Friedmann:

"What you said in your letter is very interesting. But I still
maintain that the two of them are not quite all there: Furer is
sound of body, but mad; Friedmann, *nebekh*, is crippled *and* mad.
Have you ever met Furer?"

"No. I only heard of him from Friedmann."

"Come here." He beckoned me to the window. "Look down
below. See that short man with the Vandyke beard? He waits for
me every morning. From 7:30 to 10. Four weeks already . . ."
Geller nervously pressed his steel-rimmed glasses to his nose. "Because of him I have to come and go via rear entrance which fortunately he does not know exists . . . Tell me, have you heard the
music?"

"No. Not yet."

"Neither has anyone else."

"What do *you* think of it, Dr. Geller?"

"Friedmann and his best friend Furer are in league to perpetuate each other's fantasies. A society of the mad. My secretary told me that Furer was constantly phoning me on an urgent matter. He had found the original music of the Hebrew alphabet. But I had had enough of madness. Budapest is a convention of the mad: survivors of attics, cellars, forests, sewers, survivors of death camps, survivors of torture." He lowered his voice. "Survivors of fascism, nazism, communism. Budapest is the basket that catches them all. They congregate here from all the villages, hoping that Budapest, like England for the melancholy Dane Hamlet, will cure them. That is why I told my secretary to tell Furer I was not in. He stopped phoning. I thanked God. Too soon. Furer started waiting at the entrance. But enough of this. Come, let me show you some of the Jewish sites of Budapest."

We started the descent from the third floor. After one flight, Geller leaned over the railing and saw someone on the ground floor.

"Oh my God," he whispered. "Friedmann! Well, it's either him here, or Furer there. Let's go. The poor man must have walked an hour to get here."

"Ah, Professor Geller," Friedmann said, and then spotting me, exclaimed: "And you too, Doctor Gantz, what good fortune!"

"Good morning, Engineer Friedmann," Geller said. "To what do I owe this honor?"

"Please, Herr Professor. I have something to show you." Friedmann puffed, breathed heavily. His shirt, the hat band on his fedora, were wet with perspiration. He lifted a finger that told us to wait. "It is outside."

Friedmann hobbled out. Geller shrugged. I sat down on the steps. A minute later, the door opened and Furer ran in.

Furer began in Hungarian, but seeing me, he switched to English. Unlike Friedmann's clear baritone, Furer had a tremulous high-pitched voice.

"Aha! So there you are." He opened the door halfway and shouted, "Ferdinand! He's here!" Geller turned to the stairs as if to flee and then stopped.

Furer, a little taller than Friedmann, took a deep breath. He had a broad, high forehead and a little triangular chin-beard, which he combed and teased with his fingers. Lines etched deeply on either side of his thick lips gave his face a tragic cast. Furer

held the door open for Friedmann, who was beaming. Victory. He
had engineered the Furer-Geller meeting.

"Doctor Gantz," Friedmann said. "Please meet my colleague,
Ferenc Furer."

We shook hands.

Furer cleared his throat and began.

"Herr Professor, I have been waiting so long to see you. Why
did I call so many times and not find you in, not even once? Why
have I waited for you since early in the morning for four weeks to
great inconvenience to myself, having to rise before my usual hour
of rising, and you are never in your office because you are so busy
elsewhere? Because I have something very important for you."

"The original music of the *aleph-beys*," Geller said.

"Your secretary told you. A reliable woman."

"But Herr Furer, please . . ."

"*Doctor* Furer."

"Doctor Furer, excuse me. You have a doctorate?"

"Of course. The University of Vienna, Doctor of Jurisprudence.
But owing to the turn of history, I neglected that field and devoted myself, *ourselves*"—he threw a smile at Friedmann—"to
other affairs."

"Dr. Furer, please understand that I will be very happy for you,
for myself, for all of Israel, if you have indeed discovered what
you say you have discovered. But music is not one of my special-
ties. I can hardly sing the *kiddush* without drifting off key . . ."

Furer put his hand into his jacket pocket and withdrew a bulg-
ing soiled white envelope. In it was a handwritten manuscript.

"I shall read you only a part of it. Friedmann will sing, for I no
longer carry a melody well either. Have you ever heard Ferdinand
sing?"

"I confess I have not," Geller said.

"Neither have I had the pleasure," I added.

"Ferdinand has a voice like an angel."

"From the Raziel family," said Friedmann happily. "A matter
of genes."

Geller looked at his watch. "A thousand pardons, but I am not
the man for you. I must go now."

"But you are making a big mistake, professor. Wait! You cannot leave us now. In the history of culture there have always been
astounding discoveries. The Rosetta Stone was held to be a for-

gery. Grimm's law was rejected. The Mayan inscriptions were considered the work of charlatans, fools. I could go on . . ."

"I cannot abide it any longer," Geller burst out. "Coffee grounds! Energy from moonlight!"

"No. Moonlight is not our project," Furer shouted.

"Edible paper money," Geller continued. "Alphabet music. Please, please leave me alone. There are many people I have to take care of."

Furer and Friedmann looked at me.

"I wrote to you, Professor Geller," I finally blurted out. "In America, they discovered a new process for making paper from coffee grounds."

"Another one of our ideas stolen, Ferdinand," Furer said.

"Wait," I said. "Because of the energy crisis, the U. S. Space Agency is working on harnessing the energy of moonlight."

"I said moonlight is not our project," Furer shouted again.

Friedmann shook his head. "We do not keep moonlight in water barrels like the fools of Chelm."

"Look, gentlemen," Geller said. "I have an idea. I shall send you to Professor Imre Kertesz. If he says that it is worthwhile, I will gladly listen to your lecture."

"With Ferdinand singing?"

"Of course."

"Naturally," I added. "Wouldn't one expect Engineer Friedmann to sing it? After all, he heard it first during that famous walk in the fields near Debrecen."

"Oh no," Furer said gently. "So you told him that, Ferdinand? It didn't happen to him. It happened to *me*."

"No, it happened to *me*."

"Friedmann thinks it happened to him because he has heard it so often he assumes it is *his* story."

"Then why is it that *I* know the melody?" Friedmann asked.

"Because I taught it to you, then forgot it. Or because since we all heard it at Sinai, you know it, too."

"A very interesting argument, Ferenc, but for your information I *was* present. And it *is* my story. It was a day in May or June. I distinctly remember the weather in the outskirts of Debrecen."

"Ferdinand, my colleague and friend, I don't think we should argue. We agreed not to argue about this point."

"True, Ferenc, that is our agreement. And with the statement

that in the first place it *is* my story and in the second place that
you yourself, Furer, told me that the story did not happen to you
either but that you heard it from someone else, I consider our little dispute closed."

"Yes, indeed," Professor Geller said, with an ironic smile, "with
Friedmann singing. And if it is authentic I shall have it taught to
the synagogue choir. We shall record it."

"No," Furer said solemnly. "No recordings."

"I shall call Kertesz for an appointment. He'll write you. In two
weeks, come back to me."

Friedmann bowed; Furer nodded. Arm in arm, they walked out
the door.

"Who is Professor Kertesz?" I asked Geller.

"The greatest musicologist in Hungary. He is 83 or 84, and
hasn't published in fifteen or so years. He claims to be working on
something important, that sly old fox, but he will not answer a
question. A first-rate scholar, even though early in his career there
was some foolish rumor that a major article was actually written
by a young associate . . . By the way, do you compose or play an
instrument?"

"Neither." I tried not to answer stiffly. "I am solely devoted to
musicology."

"Ah yes. Like Kertesz."

"Is he Jewish?"

"Of course. A perfect Galitzianer. Brought here when he was 6."

"Then *he'll* take the idea."

"Don't be absurd. When there is zero there is nothing to take."

"But Friedmann promised . . . Excuse me . . ."

"Where are you going? What about our tour?"

"Pardon," I said over my shoulder. "Some other time. I must
find Friedmann before it's too late."

I raced past dingy buildings. But I couldn't find them. They
must have taken a taxi, I thought, as I myself entered one and
directed the driver to Friedmann's apartment. Up, gasping, to the
fourth floor. Locked. I ran to the communal kitchen, but dour
Madame Dalno did not know where Friedmann was.

A day later, I found Friedmann at his usual place.

"Engineer Friedmann," I said breathlessly. "Why did you go to
Kertesz? You promised this information to me."

"I did it for you. To give it greater respectability."

"Did you see him?"

"It is only correct to tell Professor Geller first, since he was instrumental in the arrangement. Come."

We walked to a store around the corner and phoned Dr. Geller, who told us to see him the following morning.

"I cannot imagine they have seen him," Geller said as we waited. "I did not even have a chance to call Kertesz."

"Friedmann was very excited. It seems they have already seen him," I said.

At last, the door opened and the two came in. Furer enthusiastically shook Geller's hand and mine.

"You saw Kertesz?" Geller asked, incredulous.

"Yes, yes," Furer said.

"Thank you, Dr. Geller, for arranging it," Friedmann added.

"But I did not even have a chance to call!" Geller said.

"I called," Furer said, "and told him you sent us. We wanted to waste no time."

"And he listened to you?"

"Yes," Friedmann nodded happily. "And he invited me to sing."

"And you gave him the melody?" I cried.

"And the old man listened patiently?" Geller asked.

"He was fascinated."

"He was quite . . . quite . . ." Furer hesitated.

"Courteous," Friedmann concluded for him. "You see, he believed in us. I sang for him. Twice. First time he did not hear me."

"Twice?" I shouted.

"Friedmann really did not want to sing it a second time."

"I have never sung it twice. It takes too much strength out of me. I am not a strong man . . . But since the professor of musicology requested it, I did him a favor."

"And . . . and what did Professor Kertesz say in conclusion about your research, about your discovery?" Dr. Geller asked.

"The professor of music," Friedmann grinned. His large liquid lips spread until his radiant smile covered most of his face. His eyes misted, glittered with joy.

"He said, I am . . ."

"*We* are . . ." Furer joined in.

"*Meshuge*," they both chanted.

"Totally *meshuge*," Furer sang triumphantly.

"*Mazeltov*," Geller said dryly. With a formal bow, he shook Furer's hand, then Friedmann's. I placed my hands behind my back. "I am delighted that Professor Kertesz and I are in perfect agreement."

Silence. Dead stock still. No clock ticked. A crack in the wall moving softly along the plaster was the only sound I heard.

A perfect paradox. If they were mad, then the original music of the Hebrew alphabet did not exist; and if they were not, then the music was no longer mine.

"Engineer Friedmann?" I asked, knocking on the open door. "Are you home? It's me."

"Yes," I heard from behind a door, "and no."

Friedmann emerged with a fedora on his head and a long-sleeved white nightshirt that hung just over his hipbones.

"Look," Friedmann began without any small talk. "See this note?"

He showed me a C on a sheet of music that he had drawn. "Sing it."

I did.

"Good. Now sing A and B."

Friedmann stood there, in his short nightshirt, giving me my first music lesson.

"All right. You have just sung A, B, C. You have begun the alphabet. You have described musically three letters. But since Hebrew is older, its melody is more complex. If an A can have a certain tone, surely it can apply to the Hebrew alphabet, the world's first alphabet, where letters are so closely bound to poetry and poetry to *trop* and music.

"The original melody of the Hebrew alphabet is too powerful, too unbearable. Like gazing directly at sunlight."

"You hinted once before, Engineer Friedmann, that because I've been kissed by women I won't be able to withstand the melody. But I *shall*. What the old peasant could stand, I can stand. If Kertesz could, I certainly can."

"If so, I shall now sing the original melody for each letter of the *aleph-beys*."

Friedmann began—I did not believe it was happening—then

stopped. Would the wizard in my envisioned fairy tale snatch away my princess once more?

"You are uncomfortable, doctor. You are perspiring. It is too hot here for a jacket, Doctor Gantz."

"I'm chilly, Engineer Friedmann."

"I cannot sing if I believe you to be uncomfortable. Here, let me have your jacket."

He tugged at my lapel with one hand, and at a sleeve with his other hand. I complied.

"Put it on the chair, please," I said.

"No. It may get soiled. I shall place it in my other room."

"Fine, then I'll just remove this packet of cigarettes."

"But I cannot abide smoke. If I undergo the strain of singing the alphabet I must be at ease. Smoke makes me cough."

"But I won't smoke."

"No matter. Even the appearance of a packet of cigarettes makes me ill. I am being polite. I shall place your jacket in the other room."

I sighed.

Eyes closed, Friedmann began to sing. He had a ringingly clear beautiful baritone. I had not realized that from a body like his such sounds could come. His face shone; he looked angelic. He sang the first five letters. Each letter had its own tune, yet the melody was related to the letter that followed. Not only was the melody lovely, modally pre-medieval, attesting to its ancientness, but in its formation, and in Friedmann's impeccable delivery, meticulous phrasing and modulation, it seemed to sculpt in the air the form of the letter. The sound of the *aleph*, for instance, *looked* like an *aleph*. It started at one high point, descended in descrescendo and then began, as it were, high on the opposite side again and continued with another downward glissando. The melody of the *bet* appeared lateral, then vertical, then lateral (the notes in reverse) once more, a miniature rondo. In general, the characteristics of the melody were a psalmodical recitative of a few tones (scarcely surpassing the trichord or tetrachord) with frequent symmetrical cadences and with a pure declamatoric rhythm, without any traces of that chromatic style which European consciousness knows nowadays as "Jewish" or "Eastern."

Suddenly, Friedmann stopped. He opened his eyes, seemed to

come down to earth, wiped some drops of perspiration from his forehead.

"*Nu?*" he said. "It gives you the creeps?"

"I can't explain it."

"It reminds you of horses of fire, horses of darkness, galloping horses of iron?"

"Horses of fire, horses of light," I said.

"But something is bothering you."

"Yes. I want to know what proof you have that this is indeed the authentic, pristine, original music of the Hebrew alphabet. Don't even consider it *my* question. Consider it a question I shall undoubtedly be asked."

"Proof!" Friedmann jumped. "Rpoof," he stuttered. "What rpoof do *you* have that *you* exist? Come, Herr Doktor! Give me a footnote!"

"Even two. My passport and my birth certificate."

"Naive American!" Friedmann limped to a packet on the floor, untied a string. "Look!" He waved an identity card with his picture. "Look! Aryan name. Ludwig Ignatz von Lockholz. Does this mean Lockholz exists? He was created to save me during the war. So don't tell me about documents, footnotes, proof. The existence of the song is the existence of the song. It exists because the melody lives. It has been passed on from father to son."

"Who will you pass it on to? Do you have any children?"

"I have never married . . . Even though I am old enough to be your father."

"At first, I thought you were a youth. But now I realize you must be 40 or 43, even though you don't look that old."

"More. Much more."

"Fifty?"

"I am 67." He smiled and that boyish radiance once again suffused his face. "It is the melody that keeps me young. It is like the elixir of life."

"Do you intend to pass the music on to anyone?" I felt my heart pounding.

"It depends. We shall see. I have a partner to consult, you understand."

"Please continue," I asked.

"No. I think that will be all. You want too much documen-

tation, Dr. Gantz. You have theory, interest, curiosity—but no
fire. A handshake but no faith. No *sefirot*, no melody."

"Please. I shall give you all the money I have."

"But I don't need money. I have too many possessions as is."

"This is what I've come for. An important foundation has given
me travel money to study, thus acknowledging the authenticity
of your possession. Engineer Friedmann, my livelihood, my career,
is at stake. Please! My very future. Sell me the complete melody."

"No. I will not sell it. Nor will I give it, because you wanted to
take it. Don't look so surprised. You think I am naive? You think
that because I close my eyes and transport myself to realms far removed, that I eat the stale fish that Madame Dalno occasionally
serves? That suddenly you come in with a packet of cigarettes
when I have never seen you smoking before? I may be mad, my
dear Dr. Gantz, but I am not stupid. You wanted to record the
melody secretly, without permission, on that little tape-recorder
which gives impression it is a packet of cigarettes."

"Only so I won't forget it. I apologize. I'm sorry I tried to fool
you."

"The melody must be remembered. It is unforgettable."

"I'll bring you to the United States."

Friedmann leaned forward and clenched his twisted arm into a
fist. "The human brain, as Beethoven said, cannot be bought and
sold like pounds of coffee or a round of cheese."

"How do I know you're not Lockholz? Suppose you took over
some Ferdinand Friedmann's identity, and thus acquired all his
relatives. Suppose you're not Friedmann."

"Does that make the melody false?"

"How do I know you're not looking for someone else's relatives?"

"Does that disqualify, or make less potent, the original music
of the Hebrew alphabet?"

"How do I know you're Jewish, in fact?"

Friedmann grew pale. He rolled up one sleeve. "See the tattooed numbers. Look carefully. And now this." And again he bur-
rowed into a package, not untying the strings, but opening the
edges, and emerged with another identity card issued by the Germans. "Check the numbers. Arms and card. Now you believe? As
for Jewish . . ."

He lifted up his white nightshirt.

"Forgive me." My head reeled. "It has been a long journey. Friends back home won't believe half of what I'll tell them, Engineer Friedmann."

"Engineer Friedmann? Who is that?"

"What?"

"I may even be you. Each man, present at Sinai, may have shifted person, persona, personality. All of us, at one time or another, are other people. Just as we are other people in addition to ourselves, so are we the sum total of our past and future experiences. Like the letter *bet*, first letter of the Torah, lateral and vertical. To express it another way, there is no man who is not at each moment what he has been and what he will be."

"Then my hunch was right, Engineer Friedmann. I *thought* you might not be Friedmann but someone else."

"You are right. I am not the Friedmann, for I cannot imagine that God would punish a poor man like me with being crippled and having to eat at others' tables and having a mind and education that cannot be put to practical purposes. He did not do it to me; He would not; He did it to Friedmann, poor Friedmann who is already dead, so he certainly would not mind being crippled. For after all, is not crippled preferable to dead? Would not one want to come back crippled, like Friedmann, come back from the dead, for life is always preferable to death, not so, Herr Doctor?"

"I agree. Forgive me for talking to you like this. I'm sorry. Thanks for everything." I shook his hand quickly and backed toward the door.

"Wait! I want to present you with a copy of the manuscript. To look through me and see I am not really Friedmann, only a man with an imagination could accomplish. It is too bad you are not a composer. You might have done well. I shall notate for you the music of the alphabet and send it to you."

"What about Kertesz?"

"I shall write you about him when I mail you the notations."

All this took place in June; I spent July and August doing research in various European libraries. On the plane back to New York, like the girl in the fable, I was counting my chicks. I would have everything. Manuscript, music, the works. With such a find, I could keep my job and would make a stir in musical circles. Perhaps offers from other institutions. Page one of *The New York Times*.

When I got home I went through the accumulated mail. There was a special delivery letter from Friedmann, and the latest issue of *The Musical Quarterly*, which I opened first, anxious to see if my review of the new edition of Adalbert Ignatius's *Early Renaissance Music in the Court of Spain* had appeared. There it was, with my name on the bottom of the cover. I imagined that perhaps in the Winter or Spring issue, my lead article would appear, titled, "The Original Music of the Hebrew Alphabet." I imagined it so powerfully, I created the letters, letters which as Friedmann said, have their own melody, their own form, into the title swimming on the cover of *The Musical Quarterly*. My eyes unfocused; the letters blurred—I tried to recreate the melody of the *aleph*. Then a pit opened beneath me, into which my soul, my entire being that could be loosened from the corporeal, fell. I saw: "The Original Music of the Hebrew Alphabet" by Professor Imre Kertesz.

I opened Friedmann's letter:

Dear Dr. Isaac Gantz:

You probably found out by now the sad news that Kertesz deceived us. He called us meshuge, *and Dr. Geller agreed, but meantime he took our work seriously. Kertesz tricked us, that nasty old Galitzianer.*

But I have better news for you. You will remember that I sang the alphabet twice for Kertesz, though it is very difficult for me to do. But when I sang the second time, I did not sing correct melody, for I suspected he asked me to repeat the complicated set of melodies for the purposement of recording. And because of this experience I was able to discern that you too had recording equipment. So instead of singing the correct melody, I sang some variations of Polish folksongs that my grandmother of blessed memory taught to me when I have been a child. So you may write to the magazine and thereby fulfill your publish or perish assignment and tell them the real melody which is on the manuscript that under separate cover will is on its way. Without doubt a clever musicologist-folklorist will identify the Polish tunes.

Your friend and colleague,
Ferdinand Friedmann, B. Sci. Eng.

Friedmann's odd combination of present and future in the next-to-last sentence puzzled me. But I felt better. I began reading Kertesz's article which, happily, was full of misinterpretations and misunderstood points. Reading it, I formulated my own article in rebuttal, while hearing Friedmann's voice and the ambiance of sanctity he created as he sang the first five letters of the Hebrew alphabet for me. For hundreds of generations the melody had not been publicly known, but passed down from father to son, from family to family. I had heard the melody that Abraham had sung, that King David chanted. Perhaps, then, I thought, this song should *not* be known, but maintain its silence, its anonymity, as it had during the past five thousand years of the alphabet's existence. It had been in my power to make it known to the public, but I had a greater power in my possession: *not* to make it known. The romantic in me urged silence. Something indeed would be broken if the secret music of the Hebrew alphabet would be revealed, and hence, against my professional judgment, I wished that I had not learned it. Nevertheless, isn't there an element of destiny here? For we are what we are and what we will be, like the sides of the letter *bet*, lateral and vertical, present and future, will and is, *will is*. But then I thought about transmission. Should it stop with Friedmann? Or me? Friedmann's Hebrew name is Abraham. Mine, Isaac. On the other hand, perhaps just as Friedmann was not Friedmann, perhaps I was not Isaac, but Ishmael, caught stealing the original music of the Hebrew alphabet, for which I'd be banished and have the music taken away. If, as Friedmann said, everyone at the same time may be both himself and someone else, perhaps he was Friedmann, Lockholz, and the nameless Jew he really was, and I was Isaac and Ishmael, both blessed by and punished for the original music of the Hebrew alphabet, and perhaps I was Friedmann, too. And even if the cycle would begin again, and I *were* the Isaac to his Abraham, how could I pass on a melody I had not heard completely and knew imperfectly? And which fairy tale prince would *I* tease and play the wizard to before I'd consent to give him the original music of the Hebrew alphabet, which I'd heard one lovely day while walking the fields near Debrecen? But if Friedmann was not Friedmann, then perhaps the melody was not real either, and just as Friedmann had sung Polish folktunes to Kertesz, perhaps he had sung other false songs to me, too. But even though my intuition, my soul—the soul I do not deny, even though I am a doctor, a Ph.D.—tells me that I had had the privilege of listening to an ancient, unheard set of melodies—melodies the like of which are not to be found today—still there surfaces in me that nasty rpoof-seeking demon, insinuating his way through me, nibbling at my memory, enveloping like a merciless amoeba the few notes I still possess and cling to, and mice-sharp teeth gnawing at the letters of the *aleph-beys* until all the varying tunes of the original music sound like one, and all the letters look alike, a perfect circle divided by a NW to SE line at a 45° angle, o in Latin, *samekh* in the Hebrew alphabet, *samekh* also standing for Satan, the perfect circle severed, much like the perfect, partial melodies of the Hebrew alphabet that David sang before Saul were severed by the spear the king cast in frustration at the fairy tale king-to-be.

VERONA:
A YOUNG WOMAN SPEAKS

HAROLD BRODKEY

Harold Brodkey won first prize two years in a row, in the
1975 and 1976 PRIZE STORIES volumes. He was born in
Staunton, Illinois, and now lives in New York City. His
stories have appeared in *The New Yorker* and *Esquire*.
He is the author of *First Love and Other Sorrows*. A
novel, *Party of Animals*, will be published by Farrar,
Straus & Giroux in 1978.

I know a lot! I know about happiness! I don't mean the love of
God, either: I mean I know the human happiness with the crimes
in it.

Even the happiness of childhood.

I think of it now as a cruel, middle-class happiness.

Let me describe one time—one day, one night.

I was quite young, and my parents and I—there were just the
three of us—were traveling from Rome to Salzburg, journeying
across a quarter of Europe to be in Salzburg for Christmas, for
the music and the snow. We went by train because planes were
erratic, and my father wanted us to stop in half a dozen Italian
towns and see paintings and buy things. It was absurd, but we
were all three drunk with this; it was very strange: we woke every
morning in a strange hotel, in a strange city. I would be the first
one to wake; and I would go to the window and see some tower or
palace; and then I would wake my mother and be justified in my
sense of wildness and belief and adventure by the way she acted,
her sense of romance at being in a city as strange as I had thought
it was when I had looked out the window and seen the palace or
the tower.

We had to change trains in Verona, a darkish, smallish city at

First published in *Esquire* Magazine. Copyright © 1977 by Esquire Magazine,
Inc. Reprinted by permission.

the edge of the Alps. By the time we got there, we'd bought and bought our way up the Italian peninsula: I was dizzy with shopping and new possessions: I hardly knew who I was, I owned so many new things: my reflection in any mirror or shopwindow was resplendently fresh and new, disguised even, glittering, I thought. I was seven or eight years old. It seemed to me we were almost in a movie or in the pages of a book: only the simplest and most light-filled words and images can suggest what I thought we were then. We went around shiningly: we shone everywhere. *Those clothes.* It's easy to buy a child. I had a new dress, knitted, blue and red, expensive as hell, I think; leggings, also red; a red lodencloth coat with a hood and a knitted cap for under the hood; marvelous lined gloves; fur-lined boots and a fur purse or carry-all, and a tartan skirt—and shirts and a scarf, and there was even more: a watch, a bracelet: more and more.

On the trains we had private rooms, and Momma carried games in her purse and things to eat, and Daddy sang carols off-key to me; and sometimes I became so intent on my happiness I would suddenly be in real danger of wetting myself; and Momma, who understood such emergencies, would catch the urgency in my voice and see my twisted face; and she—a large, good-looking woman—would whisk me to a toilet with amazing competence and unstoppability, murmuring to me, "Just hold on for a while," and she would hold my hand while I did it.

So we came to Verona, where it was snowing, and the people had stern, sad faces, beautiful, unlaughing faces. But if they looked at me, those serious faces would lighten, they would smile at me in my splendor. Strangers offered me candy, sometimes with the most excruciating sadness, kneeling or stooping to look directly into my face, into my eyes; and Momma or Papa would judge them, the people, and say in Italian we were late, we had to hurry, or pause, and let the stranger touch me, talk to me, look into my face for a while. I would see myself in the eyes of some strange man or woman; sometimes they stared so gently I would want to touch their eyelashes, stroke those strange, large, glistening eyes. I knew I decorated life. I took my duties with great seriousness. An Italian count in Siena said I had the manners of an English princess—at times—and then he laughed because it was true I would be quite lurid: I ran shouting in his *galleria*, a long room, hung with pictures, and with a frescoed ceiling: and I

sat on his lap and wriggled: I was a wicked child, and I liked myself very much; and almost everywhere, almost every day, there
was someone new to love me, briefly, while we traveled.

I understood I was special. I understood it *then*.

I knew that what we were doing, everything we did, involved
money. I did not know if it involved mind or not, or style. But I
knew about money somehow, checks and traveler's checks and the
clink of coins. Daddy was a fountain of money: he said it was a
spree; he meant for us to be amazed; he had saved money—we
weren't really rich but we were to be for this trip. I remember a
conservatory in a large house outside Florence and orange trees in
tubs; and I ran there too. A servant, a man dressed in black, a very
old man, mean-faced—he did not like being a servant anymore
after the days of servants were over—and he scowled but he
smiled at me, and at my mother, and even once at my father: we
were clearly so separate from the griefs and wearinesses and cruel-
ties of the world. We were at play, we were at our joys, and
Momma was glad, with a terrible and naïve inner gladness, and
she relied on Daddy to make it work: oh, she worked too, but she
didn't know the secret of such—unreality: is that what I want to
say? Of such a game, of such an extraordinary game.

There was a picture in Verona Daddy wanted to see; a painting;
I remember the painter because the name Pisanello reminded me
I had to go to the bathroom when we were in the museum, which
was an old castle, Guelf or Ghibelline, I don't remember which;
and I also remember the painting because it showed the hind end
of the horse, and I thought that was not nice and rather funny,
but Daddy was admiring; and so I said nothing.

He held my hand and told me a story so I wouldn't be bored as
we walked from room to room in the museum/castle, and then we
went outside into the snow, into the soft light when it snows,
light coming through snow; and I was dressed in red and had on
boots, and my parents were young and pretty and had on boots
too; and we could stay out in the snow if we wanted; and we did.
We went to a square, a piazza—the Scaligera, I think; I don't
remember—and just as we got there, the snowing began to bellow
and then subside, to fall heavily and then sparsely, and then it
stopped: and it was very cold, and there were pigeons everywhere
in the piazza, on every cornice and roof, and all over the snow on

the ground, leaving little tracks as they walked, while the air trembled in its just-after-snow and just-before-snow weight and thickness and grey seriousness of purpose. I had never seen so many pigeons or such a private and haunted place as that piazza, me in my new coat at the far rim of the world, the far rim of who knew what story, the rim of foreign beauty and Daddy's games, the edge, the white border of a season.

I was half mad with pleasure, anyway, and now Daddy brought five or six cones made of newspaper, wrapped, twisted; and they held grains of something like corn, yellow and white kernels of something; and he poured some on my hand and told me to hold my hand out; and then he backed away.

At first there was nothing, but I trusted him and I waited; and then the pigeons came. On heavy wings. Clumsy pigeony bodies. And red, unreal bird's feet. They flew at me, slowing at the last minute; they lit on my arm and fed from my hand. I wanted to flinch, but I didn't. I closed my eyes and held my arm stiffly; and felt them peck and eat—from my hand, these free creatures, these flying things. I liked that moment. I liked my happiness. If I were mistaken about life and pigeons and my own nature, it didn't matter *then*.

The piazza was very silent, with snow; and Daddy poured grains on both my hands and then on the sleeves of my coat and on the shoulders of the coat, and I was entranced with yet more stillness, with this idea of his. The pigeons fluttered heavily in the heavy air, more and more of them, and sat on my arms and on my shoulders; and I looked at Momma and then at my father and then at the birds on me.

Oh, I'm sick of everything as I talk. There is happiness. It always makes me slightly ill. I lose my balance because of it.

The heavy birds, and the strange buildings, and Momma near, and Daddy too: Momma is pleased that I am happy and she is a little jealous; she is jealous of everything Daddy does; she is a woman of enormous spirit; life is hardly big enough for her; she is drenched in wastefulness and prettiness. She knows things. She gets inflexible, though, and foolish at times, and temperamental; but she is a somebody, and she gets away with a lot, and if she is near, you can feel her, you can't escape her, she's that important, that echoing, her spirit is that powerful in the space around her.

If she weren't restrained by Daddy, if she weren't in love with him, there is no knowing what she might do: she does not know. But she manages almost to be gentle because of him; he is incredibly watchful and changeable and he gets tired; he talks and charms people; sometimes, then, Momma and I stand nearby, like moons; we brighten and wane; and after a while, he comes to us, to the moons, the big one, and the little one, and we welcome him, and he is always, to my surprise, he is always surprised, as if he didn't deserve to be loved, as if it were time he was found out.

Daddy is very tall, and Momma is watching us, and Daddy anoints me again and again with the grain. I cannot bear it much longer. I feel joy or amusement or I don't know what; it is all through me, like a nausea—I am ready to scream and laugh, that laughter that comes out like magical, drunken, awful and yet pure spit or vomit or God knows what, that makes me a child mad with laughter. I become brilliant, gleaming, soft: an angel, a great bird-child of laughter.

I am ready to be like that, but I hold myself back.

There are more and more birds near me. They march around my feet and peck at falling and fallen grains. One is on my head. Of those on my arms, some move their wings, fluff those frail, feather-loaded wings, stretch them. I cannot bear it, they are so frail, and I am, at the moment, the kindness of the world that feeds them in the snow.

All at once, I let out a splurt of laughter: I can't stop myself and the birds fly away but not far; they circle around me, above me; some wheel high in the air and drop as they return; they all returned, some in clouds and clusters driftingly, some alone and angry, pecking at others; some with a blind, animal-strutting abruptness. They gripped my coat and fed themselves. It started to snow again.

I was there in my kindness, in that piazza, within reach of my mother and father.

Oh, how will the world continue? Daddy suddenly understood I'd had enough, I was at the end of my strength—Christ, he was alert—and he picked me up, and I went limp, my arm around his neck, and the snow fell. Momma came near and pulled the hood lower and said there were snowflakes in my eyelashes. She knew he had understood, and she wasn't sure she had; she wasn't sure he ever watched her so carefully. She became slightly unhappy, and so she walked like a clumsy boy beside us, but she was so pretty: she had powers, anyway.

We went to a restaurant, and I behaved very well, but I couldn't eat, and then we went to the train and people looked at us, but I couldn't smile; I was too dignified, too sated; some leftover—pleasure, let's call it—made my dignity very deep. I could not stop remembering the pigeons, or that Daddy loved me in a way he did not love Momma; and Daddy was alert, watching the luggage, watching strangers for assassination attempts or whatever; he was on duty; and Momma was pretty and alone and *happy*, defiant in that way.

And then, you see, what she did was wake me in the middle of the night when the train was chugging up a very steep mountainside; and outside the window, visible because our compartment was dark and the sky was clear and there was a full moon, were mountains, a landscape of mountains everywhere, big mountains, huge ones, impossible, all slanted and pointed and white with snow, and absurd, sticking up into an ink-blue sky and down into blue, blue shadows, miraculously deep. I don't know how to say what it was like: they were not like anything I knew: they were high things: and we were up high in the train and we were climbing higher, and it was not at all true, but it was, you see. I put my hands on the window and stared at the wild, slanting, unlikely marvels, whiteness and dizziness and moonlight and shadows cast by moonlight, not real, not familiar, not pigeons, but a clean world.

We sat a long time, Momma and I, and stared, and then Daddy woke up and came and looked too. "It's pretty," he said, but he didn't really understand. Only Momma and I did. She said to him, "When I was a child, I was bored all the time, my love—I thought nothing would ever happen to me—and now these things are happening—and you have happened." I think he was flabbergasted by her love in the middle of the night; he smiled at her, oh, so swiftly that I was jealous, but I stayed quiet; and after a while, in his silence and amazement at her, at us, he began to seem different from us, from Momma and me; and then he fell asleep again; Momma and I didn't; we sat at the window and watched all night, watched the mountains and the moon, the clean world. We watched together.

Momma was the winner.

We were silent, and in silence we spoke of how we loved men and how dangerous men were and how they stole everything from you no matter how much you gave—but we didn't say it aloud.

We looked at mountains until dawn, and then when dawn came, it was too pretty for me—there was pink and blue and gold, in the sky, and on icy places, brilliant pink and gold flashes, and the snow was colored too, and I said, "Oh," and sighed; and each moment was more beautiful than the one before; and I said, "I love you, Momma." Then I fell asleep in her arms.

That was happiness then.

A HERO
IN THE HIGHWAY

James Schevill's books of poems include *Private Dooms
and Public Destinations: Poems 1945–1962, The Stalin-
grad Elegies, Violence and Glory: Poems 1962–1968, The
Buddhist Car and Other Characters,* and the forthcoming
The Mayan Poems, 1978. His plays have been produced
throughout the United States, Canada, England, and
Europe. His new novel, *The Arena of Ants,* has just been
published (August 1977). In 1975 he was given the Gov-
ernor's Award in the Arts in Rhode Island. During the
1960s he was the director of the Poetry Center in San
Francisco. Currently he lives in Providence, Rhode Island,
where he is a professor of English at Brown University.

1

Leaving Mexico City on the new highway north, I can't believe
my eyes. The road turns incredibly sharply, proudly around the
steep mountainside, a path to destiny like all Mexican roads
rather than a mere highway. Accustomed to Mexican driving after
many months I am tuned to surprises. Anything human or animal
may turn up around the next corner. Still I gape and can't believe
what I've seen. As a journalist I'm used to reporting crazy news
even if it doesn't get published. Maybe there's a story here if I
turn back.

2

An Indian is living in the middle of the highway. Impossible.
There isn't any room. Cars and trucks smoke by him on both
sides of the road. There he is on a narrow island of rocks. Somehow when they bulldozed the cliff for that curve they must have

Copyright © 1977 by The Curators of the University of Missouri. Reprinted
by permission.

come upon one of those tiny, steep, impossible farms that Indians cling to. Perhaps part of the "slash and burn farm" slid into the roadway. More likely the crazy Indian slipped into a patch of land the road crew was working on and then he simply refused to leave. Why didn't they throw him out? Call the police if necessary. Maybe there is a story in this, even television—a last Indian living in the midst of a modern highway.

3

When I approach the Indian he throws rocks at me. A crazy man! "I am your friend!" I cry in Spanish, "*Amigo!*" He throws more rocks. Probably he doesn't even understand Spanish. After all there are a lot of illiterates in this country. I have an idea. I pretend to be hit by a rock and fall down as if badly injured. After a long wait he approaches me cautiously. As he kneels over me I grab his hand. "*Amigo!*" I cry. That much Spanish he can understand. Frightened he pulls away and tries to hide in his little hovel with a thatched roof. But he doesn't throw any more stones. When I enter the hovel he turns his back on me. Suddenly I decide the only way to win his confidence is to sleep there, to assure him of my companionship and my desire to understand his situation. We lie back to back, without speaking, like two motionless logs for the entire night. The sense of his tension makes me afraid to sleep. From such ordeals comes the beginning of understanding.

4

In the morning I begin to study the nature of this strange island in the highway. I get no help from the Indian. When I try to talk to him in the simplest Spanish or in the clearest international sign language, he grimaces at me with contempt. He won't even share his food with me, although he seems to eat hardly anything. According to what I've read about Mexican Indians it's unheard of that they don't share their food. To refuse a guest food gets your family into trouble with the gods. When I point to my mouth, pleading my hunger, he gestures toward the garbage and tin cans littering both sides of his highway island. As cars and trucks speed by the drivers often shout obscenities and throw their waste at us. If I stay here long I'll have to learn how to eat garbage. Is it worth it?

5

I've found a way to stay for a few days without eating garbage. As the cars speed by I kneel as if I'm praying before a rock shrine. Sympathetic passengers throw me food, fruit, even soft drinks. As I sit eating the Indian looks at me directly for the first time. Even if it's a wary look he doesn't turn away now. I think he has a new respect for me. But he won't eat any of my food when I offer him some.

6

I'm determined not to give up. Even though the Indian can't or won't talk about this crazy highway island, I've begun to appreciate his incredible achievement. It's not just that he's sitting here undisturbed on a chunk of federal highway property. It's what he's made of the barren property. He's built a hut on it even if it's only a crude, open Indian hut with a thatched roof. He's dug a deep well for brackish water that I stay away from. To protect the highway island from the pounding traffic he's even built stone walls and decorated them with a peculiar zig-zag design like an Aztec ornament. An anthropologist once told me that this kind of design had to do with fire and lightning. Fire and lightning . . . There are a lot of storms up here in the mountains. None seems to hit us. Maybe this Indian does have some kind of magic. Still that's ridiculous . . . This morning we had a real thunderstorm and I found myself crouching next to the Indian by the zig-zag wall. The Indian had one hand placed tight on the zig-zag, so I put my hand on it too. We sat there as the storm crashed about us but never against us.

7

I've filed my first story. It seems to be changing things around for us. The Indian can't understand what's happened. The cars and trucks don't throw garbage at us any more. Now, besides food, beer, Coca-Cola, they throw us candy and god knows what. I almost got hit by a flashlight last night. I'm sleeping in a sleeping bag that a passing camper hurled over the zig-zag wall. The Indian still wraps himself up to sleep in a blanket, even though I offered him my sleeping bag and tried to tell him it's easy enough to get another. Today I actually heard cheers from cars going by

in low gear. The Indian seemed scared. He's beginning to sulk
and sit in his hut all day. I've got an idea to cheer him up,
brighten this rocky highway island. Flags! I make a sign and hold
it up. Soon we're swamped with flags. Mostly Mexican and American, but that's all right. I fly them side by side around our island.
We're a real international frontier. We glitter with color. Somehow the Indian doesn't like the flags. I catch him tearing them
down. *Why?* You have to respect flags. I'm teaching him the
Spanish word for country, "Patria." He keeps repeating it over
and over again. Maybe he's beginning to understand a little what
it means to be a national hero.

8

Today I found it necessary to go into Mexico City to the Federal Department of Highways to try and get some background on
the story. Maybe the engineers know something about the Indian,
at least what tribe he's from. Since the Indian won't talk the
story's going to die unless I can build up the facts. It's a real bu-
reaucracy in the Highway Department. I see one official after another. "Sorry, Señor, I know nothing about an Indian." "You say
there's an Indian in the highway. But it's impossible. That is one
of our newest and best highways." Finally, in late afternoon, I
get to the top official. At least he looks like the top official because
he wears the most expensive clothes and white suede shoes. He
apologizes profusely for the delay. Never mind. On his desk is a
file. "Yes, Señor, we have a report here about an Indian in the
highway. A minor affair. No problem. The engineers decided to
leave him there. After all he is an Indian. The land belongs to the
Indians. You have heard of 'Ejido' land?"

"You mean the new highway was built on land that belonged
to the Indians?"

He doesn't bite. "All of our land, Señor, belongs to the Indians.
It is a gift of our great heritage, the Mexican Revolution. If we
need land for highways or housing we reimburse the Indians. We
do not steal the land from them." He's looking at me sharply, critically now, Mexican to American, and I don't want to argue the
point.

"Do you know what tribe the Indian belongs to?"

The official examines the report while I squirm. "No, Señor, the
Indian evidently does not talk Spanish."

"Is there any indication why he wanted to stay there in that impossibly dangerous, barren place?"

"No. However, there is something interesting here. One engineer suggests that it may have to do with death."

"With *death*?"

"While bulldozing the cliff for the road the engineers evidently uncovered a grave. That brought the Indian to the site. After that he would never leave."

"Is there any indication what kind of grave? Was it a sacred ancestral grave of his tribe?"

"Who knows, Señor. The engineers brought in an anthropologist, but he couldn't decide. There weren't enough bones and no ornaments."

"Is there anything more in the file?"

"No, Señor. On the highways, if you know Mexico, it is best to leave Indians alone."

I try to get a closer look into the file, but he keeps sliding it away from me. It's a thick file too. If there were only some safe way to lift it for a while and photo-copy the contents. I bet there's a lot more important stuff in it than he tells me.

9

On the way back to the highway island I think about what to do. The story is getting clearer. The Indian is there to prevent the desecration of an ancient burial site. If I can only find more evidence of the burial site. . . . That might be dangerous if the Indian objects to my digging around. If I can only gain his confidence, get him to eat some of the free food he disdains, make him realize that he's becoming a national hero. Teach him the Spanish word for hero, *Héroe*, maybe it'll get to him like *Patria*. With any luck it might be close to the word for hero in his ancient Indian language. The trouble is he's so silent he doesn't even seem to speak an Indian language. Still it's worth trying. Only a few words and he might begin to comprehend.

When he sees me, though, there's trouble. He starts to throw rocks again. I can't believe it. It's getting to be repetitious. Not that I expect him to welcome me back with a big embrace, but we were beginning to get along. "*Patria*," I cry at him. "*Héroe!*" But he keeps throwing rocks, not small ones either. Luckily the rocks are so big he gets tired after a while. He goes into the hut to lie down. I go over and offer him some food and a soft drink to show him there's no hard feelings about the rock-throwing. Damn it, I've got to start again to win him over. He lies there rigidly, his back turned to me.

10

In the middle of the night I hear him stirring. Probably he has to go out and take a piss. He's always pissing on the road, never on the highway island come to think of it. Maybe that means something even though a family newspaper wouldn't be interested in it. I turn over in my sleeping bag and try to relax. Suddenly his short, thin figure is above me. What the hell? He's got a knife in his hand. It glitters in the moonlight shining through the open doorway. Desperately, quickly with my old army training, I grab his arm and hang on. Thank god I'm twice as big as he is, otherwise . . . It's still a real struggle because I'm on the defensive. Although I keep in good shape and exercise a lot it's like fighting a wildcat who's pounced on you. At last, sweating, I get into position to chop at his arm and the knife drops to the floor. The Indian flees outside and hurls himself down on the ground, rolling around in the agony of defeat. I pick up the knife. It's heavy hard stone covered with beautiful green jade. The handle is shaped in the head of a snake. Quetzalcoatl. By god, it's an ancient Aztec sacrificial knife. He was trying to cut my heart out. I can't believe it. Why else would he come at me with an old green stone knife like this? I've got to admit it's a beautiful knife. Did he get it from an old grave around here? Are there other treasures? Better keep the knife. It's safer. What a souvenir it'll make at home. Better stay awake tonight even though he'll probably never dare to attack me again.

11

Despite my frantic efforts to stay awake, I doze off in the early hours of the morning. I wake up with a start. A strange, eerie silence. No cars, no pounding of trucks, only birds singing outside of the hut. What's happened to the traffic? I grope my way outside wondering if the Indian has gone. A long line of silent cars and trucks clogs the highway. Has there been a terrible accident on the road? Why are they all staring at the highway island? Rows of people, businessmen in dark suits, tourists in sport shirts, truck drivers in heavy boots, all standing silently, solemnly staring at the one almost leafless tree in the corner of the highway island. As I approach I see the Indian hanging there, his body dangling from a noose. He's dressed in jeans, boots, white shirt, sombrero like one of those Judas dummies dressed like hacienda owners you see hanging from church doorways in Indian villages during Easter weekend ceremonies. The crazy fool! Maybe there's still time to save him. I rush up and cut him down. Useless. Too late. As I bend over him I draw back. Over his face is a white mask.

12

A year later I drive back to the highway island. It's a National Shrine now, celebrating The Unknown Indian. Everything has been polished up. The crude hut where we slept is a miniature museum full of Indian artifacts from the area. My contribution is the sacrificial knife which shines with its glowing green jade in a special case. I gave them the case too with an American lock so the knife would be more difficult to steal. Anyway peasants here are probably too superstitious to steal a sacred knife like this. My name isn't mentioned anywhere. That's what might be expected. I asked for the Mexican and American flags to be displayed together, but there's only a Mexican flag. Nothing much remains of the Indian. He hated being photographed, afraid like other Indians that the camera would steal his soul. Only his threadbare blanket is preserved in plastic in the hut. His grave is in the center of the highway island. The inscription says only: HERE LIES THE UNKNOWN INDIAN. The grave is topped with an enormous statue of a naked Indian warrior attacking an armored Spanish soldier in the Conquest. A famous Mexican sculptor was commissioned to create it. You can see it for miles down the highway. There's even a small parking lot next to the Shrine, although they had to narrow the road and curve it more to build the lot.

When I think about the Indian I'm glad that I helped to tell his story. It was a shame that I was only just beginning to communicate with him. I dream of his white mask sometimes. Did he think that he'd failed his people, that he was a Judas? No, that's ridiculous. It must have been the pressure of his poverty, his loneliness, the traffic that got to him and caused his breakdown. How could even an Indian survive for long in these barren rocks amidst

all the pollution of these cars and trucks? Anyway he taught me a
lot about courage and determination, even if he did blow his
mind and attack me with that damn sacrificial knife. The one
thing I regret is that I was never really able to get all the facts.
Still I was lucky enough to deduce the major elements of the Indian's story even though he couldn't talk. In the end it was a real
adventure. My stories about the Indian and how he came to be a
hero are often reprinted in journalism anthologies. It's not every
journalist who gets to create a Hero in the Highway.

HANGING FIRE

EDITH PEARLMAN

Edith Pearlman's stories have appeared in *Seventeen,
Redbook, Ingenue,* the *Carleton Miscellany,* and *The
Massachusetts Review.* A new story will be published in
the *Ascent* of Winter 1978. She lives in Brookline, Massachusetts, with her husband and children. She is presently
at work on a novel for teen-agers and (with a collabo-
rator) on a mystery novel.

Nancy at Cynthia's wedding had made a kind of hit. That is, one
of Cynthia's uncles fell in love with her.

"My dear Miss . . . Hanks?"

"Hasken."

"That's what I said. Sweet girl graduate. Lovely green stalk.
How old are you, Hanks—twenty?"

"Twenty-one," Nancy had admitted. A pair of dancers hung
above their table. Nancy shook her beaded bag over her plate. As
her eyeglasses landed she grabbed for them. The dancers, revealed
as Cynthia and her new husband, floated away.

"Glasses, and that filmy green dress—you remind me of a studi-
ous naiad," said the uncle. When his hand crept between goblets
towards the girl's elbow, his wife at last claimed him. "I am *not*
an old fool," he protested as he was led away.

Thus the wedding. The next afternoon Nancy, in dungarees
and tee shirt, slumped against the window of a Greyhound. The
bus was rumbling northwards along a New Hampshire highway.
Her duffelbag lay in the overhead rack. Nancy drew a compact
from her back pocket and opened it. That uncle might be no fool,
but he had a poor eye for similarities. She was not a nymph.
What she did resemble, though, was a tutor—a tutor of German
literature, say: the sort of fellow who used to hire out to young

Reprinted from *The Massachusetts Review.* Copyright © 1977 by The Massachusetts Review, Inc. Reprinted by permission.

gentlemen hiking in the Dolomites. He'd quote Goethe while his charges frolicked with barmaids. Nancy had seen pictures of such scholars in biographies—limp hair just covering the ears, and long chins, and gold-rimmed glasses. The likeness was remarkable. She ran a comb through her bangs, and wondered where the Dolomites were.

The trees along the highway were taller now, and greener: Maine. Nancy shifted in her seat and took out her worry beads. When in doubt, tell your assets. A bachelor's degree, *cum laude*; a boyfriend, Carl; a skill at certain languages; a good forehand. Yes, and she was an expert skier. She was discreet, too; for more than a year she had borne a hopeless passion for an itinerant tennis coach, and not a soul suspected. She'd do. Ahead waited her family, such as it remained—three kinswomen, *couchant*. She'd be fine.

At six the bus pulled into the Jacobstown depot. Nancy debarked, compact, comb, and beads in the back pocket, duffelbag over the shoulder. She walked quickly away from town. Sidewalks narrowed, then withered altogether. The road climbed a hill. At the top, a board on a pole marked the entrance to the Jacobstown Country Club. The girl sat down beneath the sign.

A few days ago at around this time her relatives, driving back from her Commencement, would have reached this spot—weary ladies with champagne headaches. Nancy could imagine their approach. Aunt Laurette would have been at the wheel of the jeep, her heavy lips folded like arms. Nancy's mother would have been beside her, as thin as asparagus. Old Cousin Phoebe nodded in back. They chugged uphill, raising dust, awakening a vagabond on the grass . . . and, sitting up, Nancy saw that what had stopped today was a Renault, not the family jeep. Two golden eyes glowed at her. "Miss Hasken?"

" . . . yes."

"It's Leopold Pappas," he said, telling her what she could herself see, presenting her with a situation which she had herself invented, and many times: that on this hill, at this hour, he would appear, sweaty from the game just won, and invite her to ride with him, to leap, to soar . . . "Hey. Can I give you a lift?"

"I'll level with you. I walk on purpose."

"Oh. Good for the digestion."

" . . . I suppose."

"See you at the Club this season?"

She nodded.

He rolled away.

Blank-mindedness, for five or ten minutes. Then Nancy lumbered to her feet, hoisted the duffelbag, and tramped on. Soon she had reached her mother's property. The pines and firs were dense. She left the road, walked along a path, and reached a clearing. Still under cover of trees, she gazed at her home.

It was a low, white house, silvery now in the summer evening. An ample porch encircled the first floor. Upstairs, dormers and turrets. The house was comfortable. Plays could be written here, or revolutions planned. At present, on the porch, three St. Petersburg countesses were enjoying high tea. Their posture seemed a shade too arrogant—one had to squint to be certain—yes; arrogant. Nancy sighed. She drew something from her pocket, raised it, took aim . . .

"Is that you, Nancy?"

"Yes, Mom." She walked across the lawn and swung a leg over the porch rail. Cousin Phoebe leaned forward and tapped her knee.

"What were you doing out there? Something silver flashed."

"Steel," corrected the girl. "A steel comb."

"Oh. I imagined it a pistol."

Nancy handed her the comb, and swung the other leg over.

"Welcome," said the nasal voice of Aunt Laurette.

"Welcome," said Mrs. Hasken gently.

"Welcome," said Phoebe.

They were drinking gin out of teacups. Mrs. Hasken was placid. Aunt Laurette grinned under her globe of orange hair. Phoebe was currying her skirt with Nancy's comb. They were not aristocracy after all—only stand-ins.

"Tut," said Phoebe. "Tut, tut, tut, tut, tut, my girl; it's not so bad to have come home."

Nor was it. Often during the semester just past, Nancy had furiously contemplated her future, coming up always with a single agreeable vocation: governess. But these days, who required a governess? Genteel spinsters took up other trades now, Nancy figured. Veiled, they turned up in Washington as prostitutes or lobbyists. As for her friends, some were settling into New York apartments. Some were hitching West. One had gone to live on a houseboat.

But such enterprises were out for Nan. She had her family to consider . . .

They were at this moment considering her, regarding her coolly over their gin like the aunts they all more or less were, for Phoebe seemed closer than a cousin, Mrs. Hasken more remote than a parent. But whether aunts or ancestors, lineal or collateral, these dotty ladies were Nan's by blood. In consanguinity lay their claim —consanguinity, and affection.

She slipped from the rail and settled on the glider. Phoebe handed her a gin-and-mint. Her mother smiled. Laurette began to whistle.

"Hello, Nancy," said a housemaid at the window.

"Hello, Inez." Inez vanished.

"Did you dance a lot at that wedding?" asked Mrs. Hasken.

"Some, with Cynthia's uncles."

"Men are creeperoos," said Laurette. Each winter she flew to the Caribbean for two disappointing weeks. "Do I really resemble Simone Signoret?"

"Like sisters," said Cousin Phoebe.

"How's Carl?" Mrs. Hasken inquired.

"Since yesterday," added Phoebe.

". . . fine."

"You don't love him." Mrs. Hasken's grey eyes were spoked and rimmed with black, like a mourner's rosette. She had been a widow for ten years.

"No, I don't," said Nancy.

"He loves you," remarked Phoebe.

"The way of the world," said Laurette briskly. "Usually the shoe's on the other foot. Anyway, what's love? Duping, derangement. I like Carl."

"I say, take him," said Phoebe. "Or else, don't."

"Maxima Gluck is dead," said Mrs. Hasken.

"The old schoolteacher? Too bad."

"Also Mr. Sargent." Mrs. Hasken fastened her gaze on an inch of wicker. Cousin Phoebe massaged a veiny calf. Aunt Laurette calculated the price of the scenery.

Phoebe said, "We are thinking of adopting a twelve-year-old boy."

"Any particular one?"

"No. We might settle for a second TV."

"Your mother has taken up weaving," said Laurette.

Mrs. Hasken said, "We are otherwise unchanged."

"Since yesterday," said Laurette.

The porch glider hadn't much in the way of springs, and her partner the duffelbag was dead to the world, but Nancy tried to pump anyway. Glider scraped floorboard, halted. "I'll unpack," murmured Nancy, and fled.

Upstairs in her room clothes flew around; finally a framed Carl emerged from a sweater. His face was as thin as hers. He was bespectacled also, and they had the same Julienne hair. At college other students had often mistaken them for relatives—brothers, Nancy supposed. She left him on the desk and walked out onto a small wooden balcony. There she adopted a *rentier*'s stance—arms spread, hands on the rail. She would track down an interesting job, she vowed. She would study Hesse and Mann. She would refuse to make a nightly fourth at bridge, and to pay calls on local drips. This austerity would clear her decks for action. Still she wondered: did the present deliver up the future, or must you chase your destiny like a harpoonist? Presently she heard her mother calling her for dinner. She ran inside and pulled off her clothes and put on a long black skirt and a blouse with conical sleeves, wearing which she felt like a schoolmaster, in drag. Piously she ate her meal. The evening passed.

Thus Nancy's first day home. The next few were inconclusive, but by the end of the second week she had wedded herself to the porch glider. In its embrace she was studying Laurette's collection of detective novels. She slept late each morning, and whenever she awoke found breakfast waiting, prepared by a joyous Inez. Inez had a lover, Nancy's mother reported from the far side of the table. Nancy inspected the ads. In town, Laurette, who managed a dress shop, was pushing her summer merchandise. Cousin Phoebe, under a tree, worked on her memoirs.

Dinners began with cocktails on the porch, ended with beer in the living room.

"Are you planning to get a job?" Mrs. Hasken occasionally inquired.

"Yes."

"Of course she is," said Phoebe.

"Soon," promised Laurette. "Let's go to the movies."

Every third evening the jeep bounced into town. Laurette at its wheel. On the way home it was Nancy who drove, slowly probing a leafy darkness. In the front seat she and Laurette were as silent as lovers. The other two drowsed in back.

She felt pampered: an adored young nephew. She observed no routine except to turn up three afternoons a week for her tennis lesson. On the court she was all energy . . .

"No slashing!" shouted Leo. "The racquet is not a sabre."

A July Monday, a turquoise sky. Nancy, at net, frowned. Leo lobbed a high one. Nancy held her racquet stiff above her head, like a protest sign. The ball struck its face and ran down its neck.

Leo joined her at net. During the winter a mild paunch had developed above his belt. His right knee bore a familiar scar.

"Not bad. Work on the angle," he said.

"Okay," she said. "See you Wednesday."

That night at dinner, Phoebe said, "I hear he's loose."

"What do you mean, loose?" snapped Laurette. "Débauché or incontinent?"

"Unbuttoned," answered Phoebe. "Last year he kept to himself. This year he's been seen with every bit of fluff in town. Are you aware that he used to teach Art History? And then loafed in Europe for several years? And is at last attending medical school? He's thirty."

"Thirty-one," said Nancy. "He's relaxed, is all."

"His eyes are like lozenges," panted Laurette.

Nancy began to arrive early for her lessons. Her costume didn't change, though—baggy seersucker shorts and a tee shirt. Brown hook-on lenses covered her everyday specs. She carried the newspaper. It became their custom to take a break half way through the session, sitting side by side on a whitened bench. Leo, who'd grown fond of certain localities during his six months abroad, talked about his favorites. At a certain London hotel, where the tapestries are faded and the linen a wreck, you can feel heir to all that is gentle. Courtyards in Delphi are chalk by day, flame and cinnamon in the twilight. One hesitates to visit the Palais Royale, yet behind that cold colonnade can be found an ice cream parlor and a Rumanian upholsterer.

"You love to travel," Nancy accused.

"Sure."

"People should stay put."

"Should they? You too might like to explore new places."

"Maybe the Dolomites," she mumbled.

Leo wore a battered felt hat, the hat of a peddler's pony. His amber eye reminded her of decongestant. She yearned to paint his throat.

"Let's go to the movies!" Laurette kept suggesting.

"Let's!" Nancy swooned the moment she sat down, watched the flick laxly, was always convinced that from this syncope she would emerge altered. Next to movies she liked best to be reading on the porch. By August she had abandoned detective fiction in favor of the fat, lazy novel.

Sometimes she biked into town and moped at the library. Long windows opened onto sprinkled grass. One day at about five-thirty she looked up from her book and saw Leo on the far side of the lawn. Beside him stood a young woman lavishly dressed. In the street was his Renault. Leo examined a parking meter, his thumb over the coin slot, his chin on his chest—the meter had contracted something serious. His companion sucked in her stomach. Presently they walked on. Nancy left the library and pedalled towards home. As usual, she paused at a large rock just off the road, near the Country Club. This boulder overlooked Leo's home for the season, a one-room cabin that Nancy had mentally furnished with cot, braided rug, and, on a hook, the nag's hat . . . Nancy stood watch for a while, then mounted her bike and churned home.

"I miss you," wrote Cynthia. "What are your plans now?"

Nancy lay on the glider like a corpse. A straw hat, a boater, rested on her brow. *Sir Charles Grandison* guarded her crotch. Flies buzzed on the ceiling. It was eleven o'clock on a Monday, the first morning of Laurette's vacation. Laurette stalked onto the porch, wearing a housecoat and a headdress of rollers.

"Nan, I'm going to New York in a couple of weeks. Come along. We'll stay in a nice hotel."

"Okay."

Laurette sat down near the rail and presented her face to the sun. "We'll have a ball," she declared. "We'll get you an autumn outfit—a velvet pants suit, maybe. Wherever did you pick up that hat?"

"In a charity ward. Will you badger the salespeople?"

"Yep." Laurette closed her eyes. "Though comedy is my true thing. My ex-husband chose me because I was droll."

Nancy remembered him, a chemist with an off-center mouth.

He had married again, fathered four sons. "Why did you give him the gate?" she asked.

"Thought I could do better." The woman raised her head and blinked. Sunlight illumined her orange hair. "Do I really . . . ?"

"Like sisters," Nancy assured her.

When Laurette had gone Nancy peeked again at her other letter. "I love you," it still said. "I consider that it's time we . . ." She stared at the flies for some minutes, during which Mrs. Hasken drifted onto the porch and sat down.

"Would you like the glider, Mother?"

"I don't think so." Her face was beautiful despite its extreme thinness. At fifty she had not yet turned grey. She was a woman who had worn hats, hummed tunes, laughed at radio wags. She had endured the illness and decay of the man she loved, and his dying. Alone, she'd attended ballet recitals in drafty barns, clapped at graduations, and waited up for Nancy, lying sideways on a couch whose brocade carved a cruel pattern into her cheek.

"Remember 'Glow Worm'?" asked Nancy.

"I don't think so. That *pas de deux?*"

"Irma Fellowes pushed me across the stage like a broom."

"Chubby Irma. She's married now."

"How are you feeling?"

"Fine!" Fingers flew to cheek. "Don't I look fine?"

No. But Nancy had already spoken with their physician, a belly with a beard.

"High blood pressure," he'd said. "Under control."

"Shouldn't she be on a special diet?"

"No. How's life treating you?"

"So-so."

"Ha-ha. Lots of chaps blushing you up?"

"Too few."

"Tsk. Get married, girl."

The message was coming through. Marry, said Laurette's hot eyes—or prepare to wisecrack your way down the years. Marry, warned Phoebe. Or you too may play the fool at someone else's court. "Marry!" Cynthia had wailed, her train a bandage around her arm. "Hey, Nan, get married yourself. Everyone wants to dance with you!" Marry, sighed Mrs. Hasken. Before I withdraw. "Marriage," said Carl's letter, "would benefit us both."

Why not? She was not the sort to set men on fire. She was

lanky and ungifted. She was lucky that Carl wanted her. She thought hard about that decent young man, so hard that he appeared before her, scholar, don. To a bunch of small rowdies he might some day be The Head. He smiled, nearly destroying her— he had a darling smile. She set him on the rail. Next she conjured up the man she wanted, and after checking him for details—the scar on the knee, the paunch—placed him beside his rival.

Nancy was sure the three of them could find contentment. Wearing knickers and caps they'd hide out in a cave. Late on a January night they'd spy wolves sliding across the ice. When Spring came they'd drift down-river in a home-made raft . . . She twisted on the glider as if in pain. Young women of twenty-one did not play Huck Finn. They got married, sensibly, or made themselves otherwise useful.

What was up, anyway? Truths ducked their heads whenever she drew near. Also she had begun to suffer from sinusitis. The next morning she rose at five and took a walk in the woods, and the day afterwards, also. By the third day of tramping out at dawn she was reliably clear-headed in the morning, enraged by afternoon. She abandoned the sport.

That evening, using some grimy yellow paper, Nancy wrote: "Dear Carl, I can't. I'm sorry." Merciful, she stopped there. "Fondly, Nan." And mailed the thing.

"You don't look pleased," said Leo the next afternoon. No sun, but the fog was scorching. They sat on their bench, Leo wearing his pony's hat, Nancy her straw one.

"Dysphoria," mumbled the girl, uncomfortable under his medical gaze. Her chest was abnormally flat, he'd notice; her shoulders too high; the long chin had been designed as a bookmark . . .

"Hey!"

She roused herself. "Hot," she explained.

"Too hot for tennis."

"Much."

Leo said idly, "Come down to my cabin for a glass of beer." Whereupon Nancy, in a panic, stammered, "I'm expected at home."

"Oh."

". . . half a glass. Would be okay. Do you own a half-glass?"

"I'll halve one," he promised.

A path dived between the trees. Leo led the way. Nancy studied his humble nape. Soon they were approaching the cabin. She took the last steep run like a novice, arms outstretched, palms prepared to meet a wall. Leo, still ahead of her, opened the door, and she flew past him into the room. She flopped onto the cot and threw her straw hat on a table. Leo squatted before a refrigerator. Nancy unhooked her Polaroid cheaters. He handed her a mug. She removed her glasses altogether. A blur seated itself in a chair.

"My uncorrected eyesight is twenty four-hundred," opened Nan. "The Army would never admit me, except as chaplain. The Foreign Legion requires reasonable vision also."

"Oh."

"Many important people have been myopic. It correlates with inventiveness and anxiety." She plucked at the table, found her glasses. Sighted again, she smiled at Leo as if she had outwitted him. "Do you play squash in addition to tennis?" she inquired.

"No. Ping-pong's my other sport."

"Bridge is mine."

"I prefer poker."

"Oh yes."

"Yes."

Outside, the fog abruptly lifted. Sunlight flashed into the cabin. A yellow diamond fell upon the central oval in the braided rug. Nancy examined the intersection of quadrilateral and ellipse, and reviewed the method for calculating its area. From this exercise she went on to consider certain authors. Oscar Wilde. Thomas Hardy. Shakespeare; *Much Ado*; Beatrice and Benedick and their raillery. Profitable to avoid such nonsense. "We're alone in your cabin," she told Leo's scar. "I'd like to take advantage of the opportunity."

"Oh?"

"I'm in love with you."

"Oh. Nancy, I'm old enough to be your . . ."

"Grandfather. I'll overlook it. Will you marry me?"

". . . no."

". . . I didn't catch that."

"No."

"Unacceptable," she croaked. "You're the one I want."

"Only at the moment," said Leo soberly.

"I'm not at all impoverished," persisted Nan.

"Nancy. Do cut this out."

"All right," said Nancy, fast, "then let's just dwell together. I'll be your slavey sister. Mend, darn, dish up the stew, rinse out the undies of your paramours . . ."

"No."

"No?"

"No."

Nancy soared. She felt detached, exalted. To be defeated, she realized, is also to be disburdened. One travels the lighter. Nevertheless . . . Leo's coughdrop eyes shone. His enormous sneakers were like ocean liners. She longed to embrace his midsection and plunge her nose into his belly. She recalled the arid nights on Carl's pallet. There might be commerce between men and women that she was as yet ineligible for.

She remained on the cot, in an aggrieved slouch. Stretching one arm she managed to pick up her hat and place it aslant on her head. Then she rammed her fists into the pockets of her shorts. "Care to reconsider?"

"No, puss."

The *boulevardier* shrugged. "Then that's that."

Leo leaned forward. "Hey. Listen. Listening? Fortune favors the brave, Nan. Life won't find you here. Go somewhere else for a bit. Fifty million Frenchmen can't be wrong . . . Hey, sweetheart, don't cry."

". . . rarely cry. Not crying now."

He crouched before her, his hands soothing her shoulders. "See the world, girl."

"Can't. Have an obligation."

"Sure. To yourself. *Femme* up a little. Try Paris."

"*Le haute couture?*" she asked, curious.

"*La vie.* Look at the swans in Zurich. Study the healthy life in Amsterdam. Learn love from Italians, in Rome."

"I'd hoped to pick up some pointers from you. In Jacobstown," said Nancy crustily. Leo, laughing, kissed her twice: hard, cousinly busses. Since a rejected suitor could expect no more, they had to suffice.

At five Nancy biked up to the porch. The women smiled as she swung one leg over the rail. Having decided against rooming with Carl, the girl thought, and having failed with Leo, content yourself with riotous reunions like this one. You may recollect that you have an obligation. Every so often you can chase crazily after the impossible. Diverting! Still astraddle, she endured a vision of herself in the seasons ahead—a dandy's jacket, a ruffled shirt; praised, indulged; androgynous beyond repair. She blinked the rascal away.

Early the next morning a spare person trousered in denim and stoled in duffel slid out of the Hasken house. On the porch stood three solemn but uncrushed figures. Eyeglasses glinting, Nancy walked steadily. At the bus depot she leaned against the storage boxes. Istanbul? Too thievish. And Zurich was too square. In Amsterdam one could be run down by a bike. She crossed to the counter, bought her ticket, and gazed for a while at the coffee machine. She would make up her mind at Cook's. Briefly Nan wished she'd enjoyed a more bracing adolescence; wished she'd put to sea before. Then, supporting her duffelbag, she climbed onto the southbound bus.

THE SCHREUDERSPITZE

MARK HELPRIN

Mark Helprin is the author of *A Dove of the East and
Other Stories* and *Refiner's Fire: The Life and Adventures of Marshall Pearl, A Foundling*. He is a frequent
contributor to *The New Yorker* and other magazines. He
has served in the British Merchant Navy, the Israeli in-
fantry, and the Israeli Air Force. Since writing *The
Schreuderspitze* he has become proficient in Alpine moun-
taineering.

In Munich are many men who look like weasels. Whether by ge-
netic accident, meticulous crossbreeding, an early and puzzling
migration, coincidence, or a reason that we do not know, they
exist in great numbers. Remarkably, they accentuate this unfortunate tendency by wearing mustaches, Alpine hats, and tweed. A
man who resembles a rodent should never wear tweed.

One of these men, a commercial photographer named Franzen,
had cause to be exceedingly happy. "Herr Wallich has disappeared," he said to Huebner, his supplier of paper and chemicals.
"You needn't bother to send him bills. Just send them to the
police. The police, you realize, were here on two separate occasions!"

"If the two occasions on which the police have been here had
not been separate, Herr Franzen, they would have been here only
once."

"What do you mean? Don't toy with me. I have no time for
semantics. In view of the fact that I knew Wallich at school, and
professionally, they sought my opinion on his disappearance. They
wrote down everything I said, but I do not think that they will
find him. He left his studio on the Neuhausstrasse just as it was
when he was working, and the landlord has put a lien on the

Copyright © 1977 by The New Yorker Magazine, Inc. First appeared in *The
New Yorker*.

equipment. Let me tell you that he had some fine equipment—very fine. But he was not such a great photographer. He didn't have that killer's instinct. He was clearly not a hunter. His canine teeth were poorly developed; not like these," said Franzen, baring his canine teeth in a smile which made him look like an idiot with a mouth of miniature castle towers.

"But I am curious about Wallich."

"So is everyone. So is everyone. This is my theory. Wallich was never any good at school. At best, he did only middling well. And it was not because he had hidden passions, or a special genius for some field outside the curriculum. He tried hard but found it difficult to grasp several subjects; for him mathematics and physics were pure torture.

"As you know, he was not wealthy, and although he was a nice-looking fellow, he was terribly short. That inflicted upon him great scars—his confidence, I mean, because he had none. He could do things only gently. If he had to fight, he would fail. He was weak.

"For example, I will use the time when he and I were competing for the Heller account. This job meant a lot of money, and I was not about to lose. I went to the library and read all I could about turbine engines. What a bore! I took photographs of turbine blades and such things, and seeded them throughout my portfolio to make Herr Heller think that I had always been interested in turbines. Of course, I had not even known what they were. I thought that they were an Oriental hat. And now that I know them, I detest them.

"Naturally, I won. But do you know how Wallich approached the competition? He had some foolish ideas about mother-of-pearl nautiluses and other seashells. He wanted to show how shapes of things mechanical were echoes of shapes in nature. All very fine, but Herr Heller pointed out that if the public were to see photographs of mother-of-pearl shells contrasted with photographs of his engines, his engines would come out the worse. Wallich's photographs were very beautiful—the tones of white and silver were exceptional—but they were his undoing. In the end, he said, 'Perhaps, Herr Heller, you are right,' and lost the contract just like that.

"The thing that saved him was the prize for that picture he took in the Black Forest. You couldn't pick up a magazine in Germany and not see it. He obtained so many accounts that he began to do very well. But he was just not commercially-minded. He told me himself that he took only those assignments which pleased him. Mind you, his business volume was only about two-thirds of mine.

"My theory is that he could not take the competition, and the demands of his various clients. After his wife and son were killed in the motorcar crash, he dropped assignments one after another. I suppose he thought that as a bachelor he could live like a bohemian, on very little money, and therefore did not have to work more than half the time. I'm not saying that this was wrong. (Those accounts came to me.) But it was another instance of his weakness and lassitude.

"My theory is that he has probably gone to South America, or thrown himself off a bridge—because he saw that there was no future for him if he were always to take pictures of shells and things. And he was weak. The weak can never face themselves, and so cannot see the practical side of the world, how things are laid out, and what sacrifices are required to survive and prosper. It is only in fairy tales that they rise to triumph."

Wallich could not afford to get to South America. He certainly would not have thrown himself off a bridge. He was excessively neat and orderly, and the prospect of some poor fireman handling a swollen bloated body resounding with flies deterred him forever from such nonsense.

Perhaps if he had been a Gypsy he would have taken to the road. But he was no Gypsy, and had not the talent, skill, or taste for life outside Bavaria. Only once had he been away, to Paris. It was their honeymoon, when he and his wife did not need Paris or any city. They went by train and stayed for a week at a hotel by the Quai Voltaire. They walked in the gardens all day long, and in the May evenings they went to concerts where they heard the perfect music of their own country. Though they were away for just a week, and read the German papers, and went to a corner of the Luxembourg Gardens where there were pines and wildflowers like those in the greenbelt around Munich, this music made them sick for home. They returned two days early and never left again except for July and August, which each year they spent in the Black Forest, at a cabin inherited from her parents.

He dared not go back to that cabin. It was set like a trap. Were he to enter he would be enfiladed by the sight of their son's pictures and toys, his little boots and miniature fishing rod, and by her comb lying at the exact angle she had left it when she had last brushed her hair, and by the sweet smell of her clothing. No, someday he would have to burn the cabin. He dared not sell, for strangers then would handle roughly all those things which meant so much to him that he could not even gaze upon them. He left the little cabin to stand empty, perhaps the object of an occasional hiker's curiosity, or recipient of cheerful postcards from friends travelling or at the beach for the summer—friends who had not heard.

He sought instead a town far enough from Munich so that he would not encounter anything familiar, a place where he would be unrecognized and yet a place not entirely strange, where he would have to undergo no savage adjustments, where he could buy a Munich paper.

A search of the map brought his flying eye always southward to the borderlands, to Alpine country remarkable for the steepness of the brown contours, the depth of the valleys, and the paucity of settled places. Those few depicted towns appeared to be clean and well placed on high overlooks. Unlike the cities to the north—circles which clustered together on the flatlands or along rivers, like colonies of bacteria—the cities of the Alps stood alone, *in extremis*, near the border. Though he dared not cross the border, he thought perhaps to venture near its edge, to see what he would see. These isolated towns in the Alps promised shining clear air and deep-green trees. Perhaps they were above the tree line. In a number of cases it looked that way—and the circles were far from resembling clusters of bacteria. They seemed like untethered balloons.

He chose a town for its ridiculous name, reasoning that few of his friends would desire to travel to such a place. The world bypasses badly named towns as easily as it abandons ungainly children. It was called Garmisch-Partenkirchen. At the station in Munich, they did not even inscribe the full name on his ticket, writing merely "Garmisch-P."

"Do you live there?" the railroad agent had asked.

"No," answered Wallich.

"Are you visiting relatives, or going on business, or going to ski?"

"No."

"Then perhaps you are making a mistake. To go in October is not wise, if you do not ski. As unbelievable as it may seem, they have had much snow. Why go now?"

"I am a mountain climber," answered Wallich.

"In winter?" The railway agent was used to flushing out lies, and when little fat Austrian boys just old enough for adult tickets would bend their knees at his window as if at confession and say in squeaky voices, "Half fare to Salzburg!," he pounced upon them as if he were a leopard and they juicy ptarmigan or baby roebuck.

"Yes, in the winter," Wallich said. "Good mountain climbers thrive in difficult conditions. The more ice, the more storm, the greater the accomplishment. I am accumulating various winter records. In January, I go to America, where I will ascend their highest mountain, Mt. Independence, four thousand metres." He blushed so hard that the railway agent followed suit. Then Wallich backed away, insensibly mortified.

A mountain climber! He would close his eyes in fear when looking through Swiss calendars. He had not the stamina to rush up the stairs to his studio. He had failed miserably at sports. He was not a mountain climber, and had never even dreamed of being one.

Yet when his train pulled out of the vault of lacy ironwork and late-afternoon shadow, its steam exhalations were like those of a man puffing up a high meadow, speeding to reach the rock and ice, and Wallich felt as if he were embarking upon an ordeal of the type men experience on the precipitous rock walls of great cloud-swirled peaks. Why was he going to Garmisch-Partenkirchen anyway, if not for an ordeal through which to right himself? He was pulled so far over on one side by the death of his family, he was so bent and crippled by the pain of it, that he was going to Garmisch-Partenkirchen to suffer a parallel ordeal through which he would balance what had befallen him.

How wrong his parents and friends had been when they had offered help as his business faltered. A sensible, graceful man will have symmetry. He remembered the time at youth camp when a stream had changed course away from a once gushing sluice and the younger boys had had to carry buckets of water up a small hill, to fill a cistern. The skinny little boys had struggled up the hill. Their counsellor, sitting comfortably in the shade, would not let them go two to a bucket. At first they had tried to carry the pails in front of them, but this was nearly impossible. Then they surreptitiously spilled half the water on the way up, until the counsellor took up position at the cistern and inspected each cargo. It had been torture to carry the heavy bucket in one aching hand. Wallich finally decided to take two buckets. Though it was agony, it was a better agony than the one he had had, because he had retrieved his balance, could look ahead, and, by carrying a double burden, had strengthened himself and made the job that much shorter. Soon, all the boys carried two buckets. The cistern was filled in no time, and they had a victory over their surprised counsellor.

So, he thought as the train shuttled through chill half-harvested fields, I will be a hermit in Garmisch-Partenkirchen. I will know no one. I will be alone. I may even begin to climb mountains. Perhaps I will lose fingers and toes, and on the way gather a set of wounds which will allow me some peace.

He sensed the change of landscape before he actually came upon it. Then they began to climb, and the engine sweated steam from steel to carry the lumbering cars up terrifying grades on either side of which blue pines stood angled against the mountainside. They reached a level stretch which made the train curve like a dragon and led it through deep tunnels, and they sped along as if on a summer excursion, with views of valleys so distant that in them whole forests sat upon their meadows like birthmarks, and streams were little more than the grain in leather.

Wallich opened his window and leaned out, watching ahead for tunnels. The air was thick and cold. It was full of sunshine and greenery, and it flowed past as if it were a mountain river. When he pulled back, his cheeks were red and his face pounded from the frigid air. He was alone in the compartment. By the time the lights came on he had decided upon the course of an ideal. He was to become a mountain climber, after all—and in a singularly difficult, dangerous, and satisfying way.

A porter said in passing the compartment, "The dining car is open, sir." Service to the Alps was famed. Even though his journey was no more than two hours, he had arranged to eat on the train, and had paid for and ordered a meal to which he looked forward in pleasant anticipation, especially because he had selected

French strawberries in cream for dessert. But then he saw his body in the gently lit half mirror. He was soft from a lifetime of near-happiness. The sight of his face in the blond light of the mirror made him decide to begin preparing for the mountains that very evening. The porter ate the strawberries.

Of the many ways to attempt an ordeal perhaps the most graceful and attractive is the Alpine. It is far more satisfying than Oriental starvation and abnegation precisely because the European ideal is to commit difficult acts amid richness and overflowing beauty. For that reason, the Alpine is as well the most demanding. It is hard to deny oneself, to pare oneself down, at the heart and base of a civilization so full.

Wallich rode to Garmisch-Partenkirchen in a thunder of proud Alps. The trees were tall and lively, the air crystalline, and radiating beams spoke through the train window from one glowing range to another. A world of high ice laughed. And yet ranks of competing images assaulted him. He had gasped at the sight of Bremen, a port stuffed with iron ships gushing wheat steam from their whistles as they prepared to sail. In the mountain dryness, he remembered humid ports from which these massive ships crossed a colorful world, bringing back on laden decks a catalogue of stuffs and curiosities.

Golden images of the north plains struck from the left. The salt-white plains nearly floated above the sea. All this was in Germany, though Germany was just a small part of the world, removed almost entirely from the deep source of things—from the high lakes where explorers touched the silvers which caught the world's images, from the Sahara where they found the fine glass which bent the light.

Arriving at Garmisch-Partenkirchen in the dark, he could hear bells chiming and water rushing. Cool currents of air flowed from the direction of this white tumbling sound. It was winter. He hailed a horse-drawn sledge and piled his baggage in the back. "Hotel Aufburg," he said authoritatively.

"Hotel Aufburg?" asked the driver.

"Yes, Hotel Aufburg. There is such a place, isn't there? It hasn't closed, has it?"

"No, sir, it hasn't closed." The driver touched his horse with the whip. The horse walked twenty feet and was reined to a stop.

"Here we are," the driver said. "I trust you've had a pleasant journey. Time passes quickly up here in the mountains."

The sign for the hotel was so large and well lit that the street in front of it shone as in daylight. The driver was guffawing to himself; the little guffaws rumbled about in him like subterranean thunder. He could not wait to tell the other drivers.

Wallich did nothing properly in Garmisch-Partenkirchen. But it was a piece of luck that he felt too awkward and ill at ease to sit alone in restaurants while, nearby, families and lovers had self-centered raucous meals, sometimes even bursting into song. Winter took over the town and covered it in stiff white ice. The unresilient cold, the troikas jingling through the streets, the frequent snowfalls encouraged winter fat. But because Wallich ate cold food in his room or stopped occasionally at a counter for a steaming bowl of soup, he became a shadow.

The starvation was pleasant. It made him sleepy and its constant physical presence gave him companionship. He sat for hours watching the snow, feeling as if he were part of it, as if the diminution of his body were great progress, as if such lightening would lessen his sorrow and bring him to the high rim of things he had not seen before, things which would help him and show him what to do and make him proud just for coming upon them.

He began to exercise. Several times a day the hotel manager knocked like a woodpecker at Wallich's door. The angrier the manager, the faster the knocks. If he were really angry he spoke so rapidly that he sounded like a speeded-up record: "Herr Wallich, I must ask you on behalf of the other guests to stop immediately all the thumping and vibration! This is a quiet hotel, in a quiet town, in a quiet tourist region. Please!" Then the manager would bow and quickly withdraw.

Eventually they threw Wallich out, but not before he had spent October and November in concentrated maniacal pursuit of physical strength. He had started with five each, every waking hour, of pushups, pull-ups, sit-ups, toe-touches, and leg-raises. The pull-ups were deadly—he did one every twelve minutes. The thumping and bumping came from five minutes of running in place. At the end of the first day, the pain in his chest was so intense that he was certain he was not long for the world. The second day was worse. And so it went, until after ten days there was no pain at all. The weight he abandoned helped a great deal to expand his physical prowess. He was, after all, in his middle twenties, and had never eaten to excess. Nor did he smoke or drink, except for champagne at weddings and municipal celebrations. In fact, he had always had rather ascetic tendencies, and had thought it fitting to have spent his life in Munich—"Home of Monks."

By his fifteenth day in Garmisch-Partenkirchen he had increased his schedule to fifteen apiece of the exercises each hour, which meant, for example, that he did a pull-up every four minutes whenever he was awake. Late at night he ran aimlessly about the deserted streets for an hour or more, even though it sometimes snowed. Two policemen who huddled over a brazier in their tiny booth simply looked at one another and pointed to their heads, twirling their fingers and rolling their eyes every time he passed by. On the last day of November, he moved up the valley to a little village called Altenburg-St. Peter.

There it was worse in some ways and better in others. Altenburg-St. Peter was so tiny that no stranger could enter unobserved, and so still that no one could do anything without the knowledge of the entire community. Children stared at Wallich on the street. This made him walk on the little lanes and approach his few destinations from the rear, which led housewives to speculate that he was a burglar. There were few merchants, and, because they were cousins, they could with little effort determine exactly what Wallich ate. When one week they were positive that he had consumed only four bowls of soup, a pound of cheese, a pound of smoked meat, a quart of yogurt, and two loaves of bread, they were incredulous. They themselves ate this much in a day. They wondered how Wallich survived on so little. Finally they came up with an answer. He received packages from Munich several times a week and in these packages was food, they thought—and probably very great delicacies. Then as the winter got harder and the snows covered everything they stopped wondering about him. They did not see him as he ran out of his lodgings at midnight, and the snow muffled his tread. He ran up the road toward the Schreuderspitze, first for a kilometre, then two, then five, then ten, then twenty—when finally he had to stop because he had begun slipping in just before the farmers arose and would have seen him.

By the end of February the packages had ceased arriving, and he was a changed man. No one would have mistaken him for what he had been. In five months he had become lean and strong. He did two hundred and fifty sequential pushups at least four times a day. For the sheer pleasure of it, he would do a hundred and fifty pushups on his fingertips. Every day he did a hundred pull-ups in a row. His midnight run, sometimes in snow which had accumulated up to his knees, was four hours long.

The packages had contained only books on climbing, and equipment. At first the books had been terribly discouraging. Every elementary text had bold warnings in red or green ink: "It is extremely dangerous to attempt genuine ascents without proper training. This volume should be used in conjunction with a certified course on climbing, or with the advice of a registered guide. A book itself will not do!"

One manual had in bright-red ink, on the very last page: "Go back, you fool! Certain death awaits you!" Wallich imagined that, as the books said, there were many things he could not learn except by human example, and many mistakes he might make in interpreting the manuals, which would go uncorrected save for the critique of living practitioners. But it didn't matter. He was determined to learn for himself and accomplish his task alone. Besides, since the accident he had become a recluse, and could hardly speak. The thought of enrolling in a climbing school full of young people from all parts of the country paralyzed him. How could he reconcile his task with their enthusiasm? For them it was recreation, perhaps something aesthetic or spiritual, a way to meet new friends. For him it was one tight channel through which he would either burst on to a new life, or in which he would die.

Studying carefully, he soon worked his way to advanced treatises for those who had spent years in the Alps. He understood these well enough, having quickly learned the terminologies and the humor and the faults of those who write about the mountains. He was even convinced that he knew the spirit in which the treatises had been written, for though he had never climbed, he had only to look out his window to see high white mountains about which blue sky swirled like a banner. He felt that in seeing them he was one of them, and was greatly encouraged when he read in a French mountaineer's memoirs: "After years in the mountains, I learned to look upon a given range and feel as if I were the last peak in the line. Thus I felt the music of the empty spaces enwrapping me, and I became not an intruder on the cliffs, dangling only to drop away, but an equal in transit. I seldom looked at my own body but only at the mountains, and my eyes felt like the eyes of the mountains."

He lavished nearly all his dwindling money on fine equipment. He calculated that after his purchases he would have enough to live on through September. Then he would have nothing. He had expended large sums on the best tools, and he spent the intervals between his hours of reading and exercise holding and studying the shiny carabiners, pitons, slings, chocks, hammers, ice pitons, axes, étriers, crampons, ropes, and specialized hardware that he had either ordered or constructed himself from plans in the advanced books.

It was insane, he knew, to funnel all his preparation into a few months of agony and then without any experience whatever throw himself alone onto a Class VI ascent—the seldom climbed *Westgebirgsausläufer* of the Schreuderspitze. Not having driven one piton, he was going to attempt a five-day climb up the nearly sheer western counterfort. Even in late June, he would spend a third of his time on ice. But the sight of the ice in March, shining like a faraway sword over the cold and absolute distance, drove him on. He had long passed censure. Had anyone known what he was doing and tried to dissuade him, he would have told him to go to hell, and resumed preparations with the confidence of someone taken up by a new religion.

For he had always believed in great deeds, in fairy tales, in echoing trumpet lands, in wonders and wondrous accomplishments. But even as a boy he had never considered that such things would fall to him. As a good city child he had known that these adventures were not necessary. But suddenly he was alone and the things which occurred to him were great warlike deeds. His energy and discipline were boundless, as full and overflowing as a lake in the mountains. Like the heroes of his youth, he would try to approach the high cord of ruby light and bend it to his will, until he could feel rolling thunder. The small things, the gentle things, the good things he loved, and the flow of love itself were dead for him and would always be, unless he could liberate them in a crucible of high drama.

It took him many months to think these things, and though they might not seem consistent, they were so for him, and he often spent hours alone on a sunny snow-covered meadow, his

elbows on his knees, imagining great deeds in the mountains, as
he stared at the massive needle of the Schreuderspitze, at the hint
of rich lands beyond, and at the tiny village where he had taken
up position opposite the mountain.

Toward the end of May he had been walking through Altenburg-St. Peter and seen his reflection in a store window—a storm
had arisen suddenly and made the glass as silver-black as the
clouds. He had not liked what he had seen. His face had become
too hard and too lean. There was not enough gentleness. He
feared immediately for the success of his venture if only because
he knew well that unmitigated extremes are a great cause of failure. And he was tired of his painful regimen.

He bought a large Telefunken radio, in one fell swoop wiping
out his funds for August and September. He felt as if he were paying for the privilege of music with portions of his life and body.
But it was well worth it. When the storekeeper offered to deliver
the heavy console, Wallich declined politely, picked up the cabinet himself, hoisted it on his back, and walked out of the store
bent under it as in classic illustrations for physics textbooks
throughout the industrialized world. He did not put it down once.
The storekeeper summoned his associates and they bet and coun-
terbet on whether Wallich "would" or "would not," as he moved
slowly up the steep hill, up the steps, around the white switch-
backs, onto a grassy slope, and then finally up the precipitous
stairs to the balcony outside his room. "How can he have done
that?" they asked. "He is a small man, and the radio must weigh
at least thirty kilos." The storekeeper trotted out with a catalogue.
"It weighs fifty-five kilograms!" he said. "Fifty-five kilograms!,"
and they wondered what had made Wallich so strong.

Once, Wallich had taken his little son (a tiny, skeptical, silent
child who had a riotous giggle which could last for an hour) to
see the inflation of a great gas dirigible. It had been a disappointment, for a dirigible is rigid and maintains always the same
shape. He had expected to see the silver of its sides expand into
ribbed cliffs which would float over them on the green field and
amaze his son. Now that silver rising, the sail-like expansion, the
great crescendo of a glimmering weightless mass, finally reached
him alone in his room, too late but well received, when Berlin station played the Beethoven Violin Concerto, its first five timpanic

D's like grace before a feast. After those notes, the music lifted him, and he riveted his gaze on the dark shapes of the mountains, where a lightning storm raged. The radio crackled after each near or distant flash, but it was as if the music had been designed for it. Wallich looked at the yellow light within a softly glowing numbered panel. It flickered gently, and he could hear cracks and flashes in the music as he saw them delineated across darkness. They looked and sounded like the bent riverine limbs of dead trees hanging majestically over rocky outcrops, destined to fall, but enjoying their grand suspension nonetheless. The music travelled effortlessly on anarchic beams, passed high over the plains, passed high the forests, seeding them plentifully, and came upon the Alps like waves which finally strike the shore after thousands of miles in open sea. It charged upward, mating with the electric storm, separating, and delivering.

To Wallich—alone in the mountains, surviving amid the dark massifs and clear air—came the closeted, nasal, cosmopolitan voice of the radio commentator. It was good to know that there was something other than the purity and magnificence of his mountains, that far to the north the balance reverted to less than moral catastrophe and death, and much stock was set in things of extraordinary inconsequence. Wallich could not help laughing when he thought of the formally dressed audience at the symphony, how they squirmed in their seats and heated the bottoms of their trousers and capes, how relieved and delighted they would be to step out into the cool evening and go to a restaurant. In the morning they would arise and take pleasure from the sweep of the drapes as sun danced by, from the gold rim around a white china cup. For them it was always too hot or too cold. But they certainly had their delights, about which sometimes he would think. How often he still dreamed, asleep or awake, of the smooth color plates opulating under his hands in tanks of developer and of the fresh film which smelled like bread and then was entombed in black cylinders to develop. How he longed sometimes for the precise machinery of his cameras. The very word *"Kamera"* was as dark and hollow as this night in the mountains when, reviewing the pleasures of faraway Berlin, he sat in perfect health and equanimity upon a wicker-weave seat in a bare white room. The only light was from the yellow dial, the sudden lightning flashes, and the faint blue of the sky beyond the hills. And all was quiet but for the music and the thunder and the static curling about the music like weak and lost memories which arise to harry even indomitable perfections.

A month before the ascent, he awaited arrival of a good climbing rope. He needed from a rope not strength to hold a fall but lightness and length for abseiling. His strategy was to climb with a short self-belay. No one would follow to retrieve his hardware and because it would not always be practical for him to do so himself, in what one of his books called "rhythmic recapitulation," he planned to carry a great deal of metal. If the metal and he reached the summit relatively intact, he could make short work of the descent, abandoning pitons as he abseiled downward.

He would descend in half a day that which had taken five days to climb. He pictured the abseiling, literally a flight down the mountain on the doubled cord of his long rope, and he thought that those hours speeding down the cliffs would be the finest of his life. If the weather were good he would come away from the Schreuderspitze having flown like an eagle.

On the day the rope was due, he went to the railroad station to meet the mail. It was a clear, perfect day. The light was so fine and rich that in its bath everyone felt wise, strong, and content. Wallich sat on the wooden boards of the wide platform, scanning the green meadows and fields for smoke and a coal engine, but the countryside was silent and the valley unmarred by the black woolly chain he sought. In the distance, toward France and Switzerland, a few cream-and-rose-colored clouds rode the horizon, immobile and high. On far mountainsides innumerable flowers showed in this long view as a slash, or as a patch of color not unlike one flower alone.

He had arrived early, for he had no watch. After some minutes a car drove up and from it emerged a young family. They rushed as if the train were waiting to depart, when down the long trough-like valley it was not even visible. There were two little girls, as beautiful as he had ever seen. The mother, too, was extraordinarily fine. The father was in his early thirties, and he wore gold-rimmed glasses. They seemed like a university family—people who knew how to live sensibly, taking pleasure from proper and beautiful things.

The littler girl was no more than three. Sunburned and rosy, she wore a dress that was shaped like a bell. She dashed about the platform so lightly and tentatively that it was as if Wallich were watching a tiny fish gravityless in a lighted aquarium. Her older sister stood quietly by the mother, who was illumined with consideration and pride for her children. It was apparent that she was overjoyed with the grace of her family. She seemed detached and preoccupied, but in just the right way. The littler girl said in a voice like a child's party horn, "Mummy, I want some peanuts!"

It was so ridiculous that this child should share the appetite of elephants that the mother smiled. "Peanuts will make you thirsty, Gretl. Wait until we get to Garmisch-Partenkirchen. Then we'll have lunch in the buffet."

"When will we get to Garmisch-Partenkirchen?"

"At two."

"Two?"

"Yes, at two."

"At two?"

"Gretl!"

The father looked alternately at the mountains and at his wife and children. He seemed confident and steadfast. In the distance black smoke appeared in thick billows. The father pointed at it. "There's our train," he said.

"Where?" asked Gretl, looking in the wrong direction. The father picked her up and turned her head with his hand, aiming her gaze down the shimmering valley. When she saw the train she started, and her eyes opened wide in pleasure.

"Ah . . . there it is," said the father. As the train pulled into the station the young girls were filled with excitement. Amid the noise they entered a compartment and were swallowed up in the steam. The train pulled out.

Wallich stood on the empty platform, unwrapping his rope. It was a rope, quite a nice rope, but it did not make him as happy as he had expected it would.

Little can match the silhouette of mountains by night. The great mass becomes far more mysterious when its face is darkened, when its sweeping lines roll steeply into valleys and peaks and long impossible ridges, when behind the void a concoction of rare silver leaps up to trace the hills—the pressure of collected starlight. That night, in conjunction with the long draughts of music he had become used to taking, he began to dream his dreams. They did not frighten him—he was beyond fear, too strong for fear, too played out. They did not even puzzle him, for they unfolded like the chapters in a brilliant nineteenth-century history. The rich explanations filled him for days afterward. He was amazed, and did not understand why these perfect dreams suddenly came to him. Surely they did not arise from within. He had never had the world so beautifully portrayed, had never seen as clearly and in such sure, gentle steps, had never risen so high and so smoothly in unfolding enlightenment, and he had seldom felt so well looked after. And yet, there was no visible presence. But it was as if the mountains and valleys were filled with loving families of which he was part.

Upon his return from the railroad platform, a storm had come suddenly from beyond the southern ridge. Though it had been warm and clear that day, he had seen from the sunny meadow before his house that a white storm billowed in higher and higher curves, pushing itself over the summits, finally to fall like an air avalanche on the valley. It snowed on the heights. The sun continued to strike the opaque frost and high clouds. It did not snow in the valley. The shock troops of the storm remained at the highest elevations, and only worn gray veterans came below— misty clouds and rain on cold wet air. Ragged clouds moved across the mountainsides and meadows, watering the trees and sometimes catching in low places. Even so, the air in the meadow was still horn-clear.

In his room that night Wallich rocked back and forth on the wicker chair (it was not a rocker and he knew that using it as such was to number its days). That night's crackling infusion from Berlin, rising warmly from the faintly lit dial, was Beethoven's Eighth. The familiar commentator, nicknamed by Wallich Mälzels Metronom because of his even monotone, discoursed upon the background of the work.

"For many years," he said, "no one except Beethoven liked this symphony. Beethoven's opinions, however—even regarding his own creations—are equal at least to the collective pronouncements of all the musicologists and critics alive in the West during any hundred-year period. Conscious of the merits of the F-Major Symphony, he resolutely determined to redeem and . . . ah

. . . the conductor has arrived. He steps to the podium. We begin."

Wallich retired that night in perfect tranquillity but awoke at five in the morning soaked in his own sweat, his fists clenched, a terrible pain in his chest, and breathing heavily as if he had been running. In the dim unattended light of the early-morning storm, he lay with eyes wide open. His pulse subsided, but he was like an animal in a cave, like a creature who has just escaped an organized hunt. It was as if the whole village had come armed and in search of him, had by some miracle decided that he was not in, and had left to comb the wet woods. He had been dreaming, and he saw his dream in its exact form. It was, first, an emerald. Cut into an octagon with two long sides, it was shaped rather like the plaque at the bottom of a painting. Events within this emerald were circular and never-ending.

They were in Munich. Air and sun were refined as on the station platform in the mountains. He was standing at a streetcar stop with his wife and his two daughters, though he knew perfectly well in the dream that these two daughters were meant to be his son. A streetcar arrived in complete silence. Clouds of people began to embark. They were dressed and muffled in heavy clothing of dull blue and gray. To his surprise, his wife moved toward the door of the streetcar and started to board, the daughters trailing after her. He could not see her feet, and she moved in a glide. Though at first paralyzed, as in the instant before a crash, he did manage to bound after her. As she stepped onto the first step and was about to grasp a chrome pole within the doorway, he made for her arm and caught it.

He pulled her back and spun her around, all very gently. Her presence before him was so intense that it was as if he were trapped under the weight of a fallen beam. She, too, wore a winter coat, but it was slim and perfectly tailored. He remembered the perfect geometry of the lapels. Not on earth had such angles ever been seen. The coat was a most intense liquid emerald color, a living light-infused green. She had always looked best in green, for her hair was like shining gold. He stood before her. He felt her delicacy. Her expression was neutral. "Where are you going?" he asked incredulously.

"I must go," she said.

He put his arms around her. She returned his embrace, and he said, "How can you leave me?"

"I have to," she answered.

And then she stepped onto the first step of the streetcar, and onto the second step, and she was enfolded into darkness.

He awoke, feeling like an invalid. His strength served for naught. He just stared at the clouds lifting higher and higher as the storm cleared. By nightfall the sky was black and gentle, though very cold. He kept thinking back to the emerald. It meant everything to him, for it was the first time he realized that they were really dead. Silence followed. Time passed thickly. He could not have imagined the sequence of dreams to follow, and what they would do to him.

He began to fear sleep, thinking that he would again be subjected to the lucidity of the emerald. But he had run that course and would never do so again except by perfect conscious recollection. The night after he had the dream of the emerald he fell asleep like someone letting go of a cliff edge after many minutes alone without help or hope. He slid into sleep, heart beating wildly. To his surprise, he found himself far indeed from the trolley tracks in Munich.

Instead, he was alone in the center of a sunlit snowfield, walking on the glacier in late June, bound for the summit of the Schreuderspitze. The mass of his equipment sat lightly upon him. He was well drilled in its use and positioning, in the subtleties of placement and rigging. The things he carried seemed part of him, as if he had quickly evolved into a new kind of animal suited for breathtaking travel in the steep heights.

His stride was light and long, like that of a man on the moon. He nearly floated, ever so slightly airborne, over the dazzling glacier. He leaped crevasses, sailing in slow motion against intense white and blue. He passed apple-fresh streams and opalescent melt pools of blue-green water as he progressed toward the Schreuderspitze. Its rocky horn was covered by nearly blue ice from which the wind blew a white corona in sines and cusps twirling about the sky.

Passing the bergschrund, he arrived at the first mass of rock. He turned to look back. There he saw the snowfield and the sun turning above it like a pinwheel, casting out a fog of golden light. He stood alone. The world had been reduced to the beauty of physics and the mystery of light. It had been rendered into a frozen state, a liquid state, a solid state, a gaseous state, mixtures, temperatures, and more varieties of light than fell on the speckled floor of a great cathedral. It was simple, and yet infinitely complex. The sun was warm. There was silence.

For several hours he climbed over great boulders and up a range of rocky escarpments. It grew more and more difficult, and he often had to lay in protection, driving a piton into a crack of the firm granite. His first piton was a surprise. It slowed halfway, and the ringing sound as he hammered grew higher in pitch. Finally, it would go in no farther. He had spent so much time in driving it that he thought it would be as steady as the Bank of England. But when he gave a gentle tug to test its hold, it came right out. This he thought extremely funny. He then remembered that he had either to drive it in all the way, to the eye, or to attach a sling along its shaft as near as possible to the rock. It was a question of avoiding leverage.

He bent carefully to his equipment sling, replaced the used piton, and took up a shorter one. The shorter piton went to its eye in five hammer strokes and he could do nothing to dislodge it. He clipped in and ascended a steep pitch, at the top of which he drove in two pitons, tied in to them, abseiled down to retrieve the first, and ascended quite easily to where he had left off. He made rapid progress over frightening pitches, places no one would dare go without assurance of a bolt in the rock and a line to the bolt— even if the bolt was just a small piece of metal driven in by dint of precariously balanced strength, arm, and Alpine hammer.

Within the sphere of utter concentration easily achieved during difficult ascents, his simple climbing evolved naturally into graceful technique, by which he went up completely vertical rock faces, suspended only by pitons and étriers. The different placements of which he had read and thought repeatedly were employed skillfully and with a proper sense of variety, though it was tempting to stay with one familiar pattern. Pounding metal into rock and hanging from his taut and colorful wires, he breathed hard, he concentrated, and he went up sheer walls.

At one point he came to the end of a subtle hairline crack in an otherwise smooth wall. The rock above was completely solid for a hundred feet. If he went down to the base of the crack he would be nowhere. The only thing to do was to make a swing traverse to a wall more amenable to climbing.

Anchoring two pitons into the rock as solidly as he could, he clipped an oval carabiner on the bottom piton, put a safety line on the top one, and lowered himself about sixty feet down the two ropes. Hanging perpendicular to the wall, he began to walk back and forth across the rock. He moved to and fro, faster and faster, until he was running. Finally he touched only in places and was swinging wildly like a pendulum. He feared that the piton to which he was anchored would not take the strain, and would pull out. But he kept swinging faster, until he gave one final push and, with a pathetic cry, went sailing over a drop which would have made a mountain goat swallow its heart. He caught an outcropping of rock on the other side, and pulled himself to it desperately. He hammered in, retrieved the ropes, glanced at the impassable wall, and began again to ascend.

As he approached great barricades of ice, he looked back. It gave him great pride and satisfaction to see the thousands of feet over which he had struggled. Much of the west counterfort was purely vertical. He could see now just how the glacier was riverine. He could see deep within the Tyrol and over the border to the Swiss lakes. Garmisch-Partenkirchen looked from here like a town on the board of a toy railroad or (if considered only two-dimensionally) like the cross-section of a kidney. Altenburg-St. Peter looked like a ladybug. The sun sent streamers of tan light through the valley, already three-quarters conquered by shadow, and the ice above took fire. Where the ice began, he came to a wide ledge and he stared upward at a sparkling ridge which looked like a great crystal spine. Inside, it was blue and cold.

He awoke, convinced that he had in fact climbed the counterfort. It was a strong feeling, as strong as the reality of the emerald. Sometimes dreams could be so real that they competed with the world, riding at even balance and calling for a decision. Sometimes, he imagined, when they are so real and so important, they easily tip the scale and the world buckles and dreams become real. Crossing the fragile barricades, one enters his dreams, thinking of his life as imagined.

He rejoiced at his bravery in climbing. It had been as real as anything he had ever experienced. He felt the pain, the exhaustion, and the reward, as well as the danger. But he could not wait to return to the mountain and the ice. He longed for evening and the enveloping darkness, believing that he belonged resting under great folds of ice on the wall of the Schreuderspitze. He had no patience with his wicker chair, the bent wood of the windowsill, the clear glass in the window, the green-sided hills he saw curving through it, or his brightly colored equipment hanging from pegs on the white wall.

Two weeks before, on one of the eastward roads from Altenburg-St. Peter—no more than a dirt track—he had seen a child turn and take a well-worn path toward a wood, a meadow, and a stream by which stood a house and a barn. The child walked slowly upward into the forest, disappearing into the dark close, as if he had been taken up by vapor. Wallich had been too far away to hear footsteps, and the last thing he saw was the back of the boy's bright blue-and-white sweater. Returning at dusk, Wallich had expected to see warmly lit windows, and smoke issuing efficiently from the straight chimney. But there were no lights, and there was no smoke. He made his way through the trees and past the meadow only to come upon a small farmhouse with boarded windows and no-trespassing signs tacked on the doors.

It was unsettling when he saw the same child making his way across the upper meadow, a flash of blue and white in the near darkness. Wallich screamed out to him, but he did not hear, and kept walking as if he were deaf or in another world, and he went over the crest of the hill. Wallich ran up the hill. When he reached the top he saw only a wide empty field and not a trace of the boy.

Then in the darkness and purity of the meadows he began to feel that the world had many secrets, that they were shattering even to glimpse or sense, and that they were not necessarily unpleasant. In certain states of light he could see, he could begin to sense, things most miraculous indeed. Although it seemed self-serving, he concluded nonetheless, after a lifetime of adhering to the diffuse principles of a science he did not know, that there was life after death, that the dead rose into a mischievous world of pure light, that something most mysterious lay beyond the enfolding darkness, something wonderful.

This idea had taken hold, and he refined it. For example, listening to the Beethoven symphonies broadcast from Berlin, he began to think that they were like a ladder of mountains, that they surpassed themselves and rose higher and higher until at certain points they seemed to break the warp itself and cross into a heaven of light and the dead. There were signs everywhere of temporal diffusion and mystery. It was as if continents existed, new worlds lying just off the coast, invisible and redolent, waiting for the grasp of one man suddenly to substantiate and light them, changing everything. Perhaps great mountains hundreds of times higher than the Alps would arise in the sea or on the flatlands. They might be purple or gold and shining in many states of refraction and reflection, transparent in places as vast as countries. Someday someone would come back from this place, or someone would by accident discover and illumine its remarkable physics.

He believed that the boy he had seen nearly glowing in the half-darkness of the high meadow had been his son, and that the child had been teasing his father in a way only he could know, that the child had been asking him to follow. Possibly he had come upon great secrets on the other side, and knew that his father would join him soon enough and that then they would laugh about the world.

When he next fell asleep in the silence of a clear windless night in the valley, Wallich was like a man disappearing into the warp of darkness. He wanted to go there, to be taken as far as he could be taken. He was not unlike a sailor who sets sail in the teeth of a great storm, delighted by his own abandon.

Throwing off the last wraps of impure light, he found himself again in the ice world. The word was all-encompassing—*Eiswelt*. There above him the blue spire rocketed upward as far as the eye could see. He touched it with his hand. It was indeed as cold as ice. It was dense and hard, like glass ten feet thick. He had doubted its strength, but its solidity told that it would not flake away and allow him to drop endlessly, far from it.

On ice he found firm holds both with his feet and with his hands, and hardly needed the ice pitons and étriers. For he had crampons tied firmly to his boots, and could spike his toe points into the ice and stand comfortably on a vertical. He proceeded with a surety of footing he had never had on the streets of Munich. Each step bolted him down to the surface. And in each hand he carried an ice hammer with which he made swinging cutting arcs that engaged the shining stainless-steel pick with the mirror-like wall.

All the snow had blown away or had melted. There were no traps, no pitfalls, no ambiguities. He progressed toward the summit rapidly, climbing steep ice walls as if he had been going up a ladder. The air became purer and the light more direct. Looking out to right or left, or glancing sometimes over his shoulders, he saw that he was now truly in the world of mountains.

Above the few clouds he could see only equal peaks of ice, and the Schreuderspitze dropping away from him. It was not the world of rock. No longer could he make out individual features in the valley. Green had become a hazy dark blue appropriate to an ocean floor. Whole countries came into view. The landscape was a mass of winding glaciers and great mountains. At that height, all was separated and refined. Soft things vanished, and there remained only the white and the silver.

He did not reach the summit until dark. He did not see the stars because icy clouds covered the Schreuderspitze in a crystalline fog which flowed past, crackling and hissing. He was heartbroken to have come all the way to the summit and then be blinded by masses of clouds. Since he could not descend until light, he decided to stay firmly stationed until he could see clearly. Meanwhile, he lost patience and began to address a presence in the air—casually, not thinking it strange to do so, not thinking twice about talking to the void.

He awoke in his room in early morning, saying, "All these blinding clouds. Why all these blinding clouds?"

Though the air of the valley was as fresh as a flower, he detested it. He pulled the covers over his head and strove for unconsciousness, but he grew too hot and finally gave up, staring at the remnants of dawn light soaking about his room. The day brightened in the way that stage lights come up, suddenly brilliant upon a beam-washed platform. It was early June. He had lost track of the exact date, but he knew that sometime before he had crossed into June. He had lost them in early June. Two years had passed.

He packed his things. Though he had lived like a monk, much had accumulated, and this he put into suitcases, boxes, and bags. He packed his pens, paper, books, a chess set on which he sometimes played against an imaginary opponent named Herr Claub, the beautiful Swiss calendars upon which he had at one time been almost afraid to gaze, cooking equipment no more complex than a soldier's mess kit, his clothing, even the beautifully wrought climbing equipment, for, after all, he had another set, up there in the *Eiswelt*. Only his bedding remained unpacked. It was on the floor in the center of the room, where he slept. He put some banknotes in an envelope—the June rent—and tacked it to the doorpost. The room was empty, white, and it would have echoed had it been slightly larger. He would say something and then listen intently, his eyes flaring like those of a lunatic. He had not eaten in days, and was not disappointed that even the waking world began to seem like a dream.

He went to the pump. He had accustomed himself to bathing in streams so cold that they were too frightened to freeze. Clean and cleanly shaven, he returned to his room. He smelled the sweet pine scent he had brought back on his clothing after hundreds of trips through the woods and forests girdling the greater mountains. Even the bedding was snowy white. He opened the closet and caught a glimpse of himself in the mirror. He was dark from sun and wind; his hair shone; his face had thinned; his eyebrows were now gold and white. For several days he had had only cold pure water. Like soldiers who come from training toughened and healthy, he had about him the air of a small child. He noticed a certain wildness in the eye, and he lay on the hard floor, as was his habit, in perfect comfort. He thought nothing. He felt nothing. He wished nothing.

Time passed as if he could compress and cancel it. Early-evening darkness began to make the white walls blue. He heard a crackling fire in the kitchen of the rooms next door, and imagined the shadows dancing there. Then he slept, departing.

On the mountain it was dreadfully cold. He huddled into himself against the wet silver clouds, and yet he smiled, happy to be once again on the summit. He thought of making an igloo, but remembered that he hadn't an ice saw. The wind began to build. If the storm continued, he would die. It would whittle him into a brittle wire, and then he would snap. The best he could do was to dig a trench with his ice hammers. He lay in the trench and closed his sleeves and hooded parka, drawing the shrouds tight. The wind came at him more and more fiercely. One gust was so powerful that it nearly lifted him out of the trench. He put in an ice piton, and attached his harness. Still the wind rose. It was difficult to breathe and nearly impossible to see. Any irregular surface whistled. The eye of the ice piton became a great siren. The zippers on his parka, the harness, the slings and equipment, all gave off musical tones, so that it was as if he were in a place with hundreds of tormented spirits.

The gray air fled past with breathtaking speed. Looking away from the wind, he had the impression of being propelled upward at unimaginable speed. Walls of gray sped by so fast that they glowed. He knew that if he were to look at the wind he would have the sense of hurtling forward in gravityless space.

And so he stared at the wind and its slowly pulsing gray glow. He did not know for how many hours he held that position. The rape of vision caused a host of delusions. He felt great momentum. He travelled until, eardrums throbbing with the sharpness of cold and wind, he was nearly dead, white as a candle, hardly able to breathe.

Then the acceleration ceased and the wind slowed. When, released from the great pressure, he fell back off the edge of the trench, he realized for the first time that he had been stretched tight on his line. He had never been so cold. But the wind was dying and the clouds were no longer a great corridor through which he was propelled. They were, rather, a gentle mist which did not know quite what to do with itself. How would it dissipate? Would it rise to the stars, or would it fall in compression down into the valley below?

It fell; it fell all around him, downward like a lowering curtain. It fell in lines and stripes, always downward as if on signal, by command, in league with a directive force.

At first he saw just a star or two straight on high. But as the mist departed a flood of stars burst through. Roads of them led into infinity. Starry wheels sat in fiery white coronas. Near the horizon were the few separate gentle stars, shining out and turning clearly, as wide and round as planets. The air grew mild and warm. He bathed in it. He trembled. As the air became all clear and the mist drained away completely, he saw something which stunned him.

The Schreuderspitze was far higher than he had thought. It was hundreds of times higher than the mountains represented on the map he had seen in Munich. The Alps were to it not even foothills, not even rills. Below him was the purple earth, and all the great cities lit by sparkling lamps in their millions. It was a clear summer dawn and the weather was excellent, certainly June.

He did not know enough about other cities to make them out from the shapes they cast in light, but his eye seized quite easily upon Munich. He arose from his trench and unbuckled the harness, stepping a few paces higher on the rounded summit. There was Munich, shining and pulsing like a living thing, strung with lines of amber light—light which reverberated as if in crystals, light which played in many dimensions and moved about the course of the city, which was defined by darkness at its edge. He had come above time, above the world. The city of Munich existed before him with all its time compressed. As he watched, its history played out in repeating cycles. Nothing, not one movement, was lost from the crystal. The light of things danced and multiplied, again and again, and yet again. It was all there for him to claim. It was alive, and ever would be.

He knelt on one knee as in paintings he had seen of explorers claiming a coast of the New World. He dared close his eyes in the face of that miracle. He began to concentrate, to fashion according to will with the force of stilled time a vision of those he had loved. In all their bright colors, they began to appear before him.

He awoke as if shot out of a cannon. He went from lying on his back to a completely upright position in an instant, a flash, during which he slammed the floorboards energetically with a clenched fist and cursed the fact that he had returned from such a world. But by the time he stood straight, he was delighted to be doing so. He quickly dressed, packed his bedding, and began to shuttle down to the station and back. In three trips, his luggage was stacked on the platform.

He bought a ticket for Munich, where he had not been in many many long months. He hungered for it, for the city, for the boats on the river, the goods in the shops, newspapers, the pigeons on the square, trees, traffic, even arguments, even Herr Franzen. So much rushed into his mind that he hardly saw his train pull in.

He helped the conductor load his luggage into the baggage car, and he asked, "Will we change at Garmisch-Partenkirchen?"

"No. We go right through, direct to Munich," said the conductor.

"Do me a great favor. Let me ride in the baggage car."

"I can't. It's a violation."

"Please. I've been months in the mountains. I would like to ride alone, for the last time."

The conductor relented, and Wallich sat atop a pile of boxes, looking at the landscape through a Dutch door, the top of which was open. Trees and meadows, sunny and lush in June, sped by. As they descended, the vegetation thickened until he saw along the cinder bed slow-running black rivers, skeins and skeins of thorns darted with the red of early raspberries, and flowers which had sprung up on the paths. The air was warm and caressing—thick and full, like a swaying green sea at the end of August.

They closed on Munich, and the Alps appeared in a sweeping line of white cloud-touched peaks. As they pulled into the great station, as sooty as it had ever been, he remembered that he had climbed the Schreuderspitze, by its most difficult route. He had found freedom from grief in the great and heart-swelling sight he had seen from the summit. He felt its workings and he realized that soon enough he would come once more into the world of light. Soon enough he would be with his wife and son. But until then (and he knew that time would spark ahead), he would open himself to life in the city, return to his former profession, and struggle at his craft.

THE EXACT NATURE OF PLOT

SUSAN FROMBERG SCHAEFFER

Susan Fromberg Schaeffer was born in Brooklyn in 1941. She was educated in New York City public schools and at the University of Chicago, from which she received her Ph.D. in 1966. She is a full professor of English at Brooklyn College. In addition to two novels, *Falling*, and *Anya* —winner of the Edward Lewis Wallant Award and the Friends of Literature Award—she has written three previously published collections of poetry. Her last, *Granite Lady*, was nominated for a National Book Award. Her new novel, *Time in Its Flight*, will be published in 1978.

I remember exactly how it began. It was November 16 in our small town, a cold, brilliant night, the clear, glassy wind hurrying strangers home. My husband was at college, teaching. I had just woken up from a nap. A friend called, and I told her as soon as the program I always watched was over at seven-thirty, I was going to begin the novel. At seven-thirty, I turned off the television and sat on the couch contemplating the number of patterns in the living room. There was one for the pillows, one for the curtains; the living room rug was Persian, another pattern, the couch's upholstery fabric; then half way through, I could not remember if I had counted the tapestry on the wall, the pattern of the crocheted afghan, the crocheted pillows. It was like adding up a long column of figures and losing your place somewhere in the middle; some streak of stubbornness prevented me from making a list, marking down the subtotal, then standing securely on the plateau of the straight horizontal black line. Suddenly, the room twisted slightly, as if seen by an insect's mosaic eye. This was the reward of avoiding work, I told myself, and sat down at the typewriter, and as I had promised, began work on the novel.

The novel went unusually well, flourishing like a weed in a hot-

Copyright © 1976 by The Little Magazine. Reprinted by permission.

house, then, as the process became more advanced, sprouting thick, fat leaves, fleshy, like the leaves of African violets. There seemed to be no stopping it. Every night, at eight o'clock, I would read the last line I had written, and by eleven o'clock, another twenty pages would have joined the others, lying loosely, like leaves, in the manila folder. When it was all done, I would take the marble statue of the Chinese dog and place it carefully in the center of the pile, weighing down the pages; for some reason I could not quite understand, I had been reluctant to number them, and did not relish the idea of the cat spattering them erratically over the rug in the study, a patterned Spanish rug, of blue and black. At this time, I began to have a sense of when the novel would be finished; I knew, too, that it would be exactly four hundred and twenty five pages. When asked about its progress, I would invariably answer that it would be complete by December 27, and when anyone looked surprised, would mutter that it was just a matter of typing. No one asked further questions.

But it was about this time that I began to notice that my memory was not as good as it used to be. In the past, friends had resented my ability to recite, verbatim, conversations we had had over twenty years ago; they seemed to consider this tenacity of the brain cells a fault in my character, and indeed, I had often wished for a less accurate version of the past. But near the beginning of December, I would find myself forgetting perfectly routine things: Had I made my husband's dinner? I would go into the kitchen and look at the sink; yes, there were two dirty supper plates, one still streaked with ketchup and hot sauce, two glasses, two cups and saucers, a thick black sludge at the bottom of each cup like Egyptian silt. But still I was not sure. Were these dishes from last night, or had they just been placed in the sink, carefully placed in the sink, for they were my grandmother's dishes, a few hours before? I would find myself leaving the typewriter and travelling back and forth to the sink, eager for clues. There were the peelings from the carrots. Had they begun to wither and brown? They appeared fresh. Then it was almost certain I had made dinner. It was certain I had. I would go back to the typewriter, but as I wrote, it occurred to me I could not remember *what* I had made— if indeed I had made anything at all. I told myself this confusion came because I was new as a writer; I was simply suffering from the celebrated abstraction of artists; it proved I was the genuine thing. At the end of each session, the twenty pages had completed themselves, adding themselves to the fattening pile. Then, for days, I could remember everything about every meal I had cooked: every detail; how many times I had ground the pepper mill over the chicken livers, and the sound of typing, like sly teeth in the cabinets, an incessant clicking, somewhere inside the walls, was something I could easily ignore: so it was a passing thing after all.

It bothered me more, when, in the middle of a chapter the baby began to cry; it wasn't that I had any doubts about whether or not she had been fed; I simply couldn't remember her name. But this was the sort of lapse I was accustomed to; at parties, I would forget the name of someone I had known for thirty years, and I would try to pretend it was a joke while the old friend completed the introduction himself. Still, it was embarrassing. From previous experience, I knew the thing to do was stop thinking about the blank space; suddenly, the name would swim into focus, a fish into the net. Perhaps, I thought as I went to get the baby, it had something to do with my age. I couldn't remember when my birthday was, or how old I was; I would have to look at my wrist, I thought, when I tested the milk to make sure it wasn't too hot; perhaps this wasn't my baby at all, but my daughter's. I would have to look at my wrist and see if it were flecked with little age spots, the brown spots, the toad flesh. But I had a premonition I would not do this; I did not know whether it was a fat wrist, or a thin wrist; whether it was arthritic, or supple and strong. After I fed the baby, I wondered where I had gotten the bottle, and when someone was coming to take her back; it seemed more and more of these details remained unaccounted for, and it seemed that this sketchiness, this erasing of my mental blackboard, this chalk dust fogging my eyes, had something to do with the typewriter, the endless clicking of keys. It would stop when I stopped.

My husband, now: his was a name I could remember. Adam, the first. Of course, he had not been the first, but it was something about the courses he taught that had interested me first; later that night, he came home. I always made a point of being finished when he came back to the house from his night class. "How did it go, dear?" That was the question I would always ask, invariable. Tonight, he made a face to signify that it had not gone well. I wanted to ask him what had not gone well; I could always tell him it was the nature of the subject, and not his fault at all, but then it occurred to me I didn't know what subject it was he was teaching. "Have you eaten?" I asked him instead. "Not since dinner," he said, thus making it unnecessary for me to ask him about dinner. But December 27 was getting closer; I was getting closer to the day of my liberation; this would soon be over. "I'm going to school now," my husband said, putting something in his briefcase, and I started to protest that he had just gotten back. I stopped myself, because I was not really sure. Instead, I went into the kitchen, and, as was becoming my custom, looked at the plates in the sink and the squares on the calendar, each day looking more and more like unfurnished rooms, never more than two objects a piece.

I really did not have very far to go. It was almost nine. "So that's how you see it?" he asked, his voice threatening. "Will you stop reading over my shoulder?" I demanded, "you know how nervous it makes me." "I never was very polite," he said grumpily, taking a seat across the room from me. "Don't stare at me while I write!" I demanded nervously, "besides, I didn't know you were coming tonight," I complained, in a voice unusually querulous. "I decided it was necessary," he said, crossing his legs, staring at me. "I asked you to stop!" I burst out at him, "you're thinner than ever, you know," I went on crossly, "I can practically see the wood grain of that chair through your arm." "You always had a sharp eye," he said, staring at me. That remark made me terribly nervous. "Can't you do something else until I'm finished?" I demanded; he seemed amused by my discomfort. "Disgusting, to be so thin!" I muttered under my breath. "Not until I show you something," he said. "For God's sake, what is it, get it over with," I shrieked, beside myself with impatience. "It's not important," he said, as if that explained the constant nature of his interruptions. I was silent with rage. "Well, here it is," he said, beginning to take something out of his pocket; in spite of myself, my eyes were riveted on his hand. "No," he said, changing his mind, and putting it back, "there's something else I want to show you first," and he got up, coming toward me. "Look at my arm," he said, "when I get up a layer of wood grain sticks to it; that's why you think you can see through me," he explained. "Do you mind?" I demanded, getting out a clean sheet of paper, "leave that chair alone, it took me long enough to get it repaired." He was sitting down again, smiling. "So? What is it?" I couldn't concentrate on anything at all. "Just this," he said, reaching into his pocket, and taking it out again; it crackled like crepe-paper, and I noted he kept his hand over most of it. "Get on with it!" I insisted, shrill. He opened his hand, and the paper unfolded; it was a crepe-paper dog, like a Halloween ornament, but a dog instead of a cat. "Very good," I said, indignant, "I don't know what's the matter with you." "I thought you wanted to see it," he said wounded, and then I heard its snarl. It was the largest dog I had ever seen. It had two gigantic fang teeth in its lower jaw, and its lower jaw was misformed so the lower bone jutted out past the upper one, the lower teeth pushing in front of the upper ones; I had never seen such an ugly dog. "He's very smart, too," he went on, "attack-trained." I sat still, saying nothing. "Get her!" he commanded in a low voice; the dog sprang at me, slavering; he was going to rip out my throat; his fur was mottled and patched, like the worn skin of an old coat. When I tried to get up, I found I was rooted to the seat, a page in a book no one would open or turn. "Well, that's the way it is," he said, folding the paper dog up and putting him back in his pocket. "I just thought you'd like to see it," he said, getting up and leaving. Later, I could not remember whether he had put on his coat, or had gone out the front door or the back. "Pest!" I thought to myself viciously. When was my husband coming home? I didn't for a minute believe the rumors he had died, the hints, the implications that came out of the margins of thin air.

The next night, he was back in the same chair. "Don't start with that dog," I warned him, "I won't stand for it." "Dog?" he asked absently, falling asleep, his cheek propped on his fist. He shook himself awake, just like a dog himself. God, he was thin! "I knew I had something to tell you," he said groggily, gesturing vaguely with his transparent hand, "she wanted to talk to you about something," he mumbled, dropping off. He seemed to have aged greatly overnight. "I can't talk to anyone right now," I said. "This is the only time I ever get to work; it's simple enough, 8 to 11, people ought to be able to remember." "Well, you can't always have your own way," she said in that puritanical voice, irritating beyond belief. "It doesn't seem like I'm asking for much," I answered automatically. "You said we always used to fight on Mondays," she said, "over the grocery money. You know, that wasn't true. I got my allowance on Fridays, and none of you were even up when your father left." "I don't see why you're always rehashing ancient history," I said, trying to ignore her. "But it wasn't that way at all; I had complete control over the money." "Actually, little fish," ("Don't call me that," I shouted, "you know I can't stand it!") "it had nothing to do with money," she said, getting up and starting toward me; he was asleep in his chair. "I don't want to see it!" I said, terrified; I could see she had something in her hand. "Actually, little fish," she went on, "it had to do with this;" she came and stood in back of me, and held her hand over my shoulder; in her palm was one perfectly formed breast. "And you said I was very young. Actually, I was quite a bit older; you can see that from the veins; see the way they stand out? And the nipple? Look at it carefully, now, you can see it's been nursed at." "What on earth are you talking about?" I demanded, trying to look to the right, but all I could see was where he was, his thin legs crossed in his chair, the grain showing through the skin. "You said we met at school," she went on, "but really, we met at a dance. I was wearing a black dress; you know, in those days, no one wore bras, the dresses were tight and slippery; we were doing the charleston, and out flopped this breast; there it was, white as marble, with its blue veins, and its nipple standing up like a flower. Your father practically dropped dead of embarrassment." "What did you do?" I asked in a hoarse whisper. "Put it back, of course," she said, putting the breast back in her pocketbook where it turned into a lace-trimmed handkerchief. "And the next thing," she said, "was when we went to the movies, and my girdle was too tight and I took out one of the stays and started playing with it, and it flew out of my hand and hit a man way up front. I still remember," she went on meditatively, but beginning to grin, "he had such a bald head, the picture on the screen was reflected in it, the burning of Atlanta." "Your father didn't mind at all when he found out about my two little children." "Two little children!" I repeated incredulously, "you don't know what you're talking about!" "You said you wanted the truth," she said, pouting. "Look," I said, "before you turn into the lace coverlet, or whatever it is you do, would you mind asking Bessie to iron my linen napkins; I don't have the time; I have to get this finished." "I don't understand," she said, shaking her head, "you were always so neat." "I was a slob," I shouted at the top of

my lungs, "all writers are slobs." "And we always thought you'd
get married; your father couldn't wait to be a grandfather."
"Mother, for godsake," (was she senile, or what?), "you know all
about the grandchildren." But she wouldn't answer me, just sat in
the other chair, staring at me, and occasionally dabbing at her
eyes with the lace-trimmed handkerchief. "It serves her right," a
third voice said, male and deep, and hard, like a hard novel. Now,
who, in god's name, was that? "What is this, Grand Central Station?" I demanded out loud, "how am I going to get anything
done?" "We'll take care of it all," the new voice said, but by now,
it was ten-thirty, and I had only written fifteen pages, and I was in
a great hurry, and ignored them all.

The next night was the twenty-sixth. Usually, by this time the
bills for the next month would have begun to come in, but I
could not remember having been to the mailbox, or if I had been
there, finding any bills. "These details must be attended to," I
told myself, didactic, getting out a new sheaf of paper. But it was
safe to put things off, because in the morning I would be free of
restrictions. Thinking about that made me wonder what the
weather would be like in the morning. I turned the radio on, hoping for a report. There was nothing but static. "I should have
changed the batteries," I mumbled to myself, turning on the Ze-
nith on the desk. I was surprised at the vividness of the dial, its
exact markings, the fluorescent green of the needle indicating the
station, while the desk itself seemed awkward, ungainly, as if it
had been drawn on construction paper by a child with a broken
crayon. The radio's dial glowed in the dark like a cat's eye, but
there was no sound, just an occasional crackle, like a sheet of
crumpled paper, unfolding.

I sat down at the typewriter; freedom was hanging over it like a
great, hanging lamp. The typewriter switched on immediately, its
electric purr soothing as a cat. There they were, three of them
now; he was sitting in a chair, the wood showing through his arm,
but more wide awake, and my mother, sitting straight up, as if at
a graduation, her handkerchief tucked into the throat of her
dress. "You said she had black hair," a deep voice to the left of
her protested, "but it was blonde, the most beautiful blonde I
ever saw. No wonder I was afraid to let her out of my sight." To
mark his words, he reached into his pocket, and took out a long
braid of blonde hair. "Here," he said pointing to the end where it

tapered into silver, "this is what happened when she got older; it turned silvery white, like that song she was always singing, 'shine on silvery moon.'" "Harvest moon," my mother corrected him. "But he's right," she said to me, "she was blonde; the other children were so jealous, they used to pull her hair." "What nonsense!" I exclaimed, feeling like pulling out clumps of my own. "And she never really got to know her father; you thought she was her father's favorite child, but her father took her sailing, and a storm came up, and he was struck by lightning right in front of her." "I can't stand any more of this," I said, pressing my fingers against the keys so hard the ten tips turned white as moons; I had the sensation their print lines were disappearing, beginning to erase, *"you are all insane,"* I said it as slowly and as positively as I could. "You're the one who can see through people," the thin legs said, uncrossing themselves. "You just don't want to believe it," my mother went on, "it doesn't fit in with your idea of what she was like, but he's right; that's how it happened, in a boat, whether you like it or not." "Right out of the Perils of Pearl Pureheart," I sneered, "how can you expect me to be such an idiot?" "Well, we never expected it, exactly," my mother said. "We've just learned to live with it," he said, fingering the braid. "Please, will you put that thing away, I'm almost finished, I have to get done." I was startled at the sound of my voice, thin and reedy, pleading, the muted soprano of fear. "And how do you think we liked it, when you said all those things?" he demanded. My mother nodded, miserably. "What difference did it make to you?" I demanded, "you just went on as usual, I didn't change anything." "You didn't know what you were doing," he said in his deep voice, "you should have thought about it more." "All right, I'll think about it later," I said, typing a few more words. "You'll think about it now," my mother said, advancing on me menacingly; behind the curtain, I could hear a snarl. All three were starting to move toward me at once. Suddenly, one of them started to giggle, as if he had been poked in the side, ticklish. "You see, the thing is," my mother said, laughing, "there just weren't enough chairs." She suddenly seemed to have gotten very young. "Not enough chairs at all," he said. But he was thin! "You don't have to worry about the dog," he said, "it's only the chair we want." "Well, you can't have it," I said, definite, "you have to learn how to behave when you're a guest." "Well," my mother said gently, "that's not exactly right,

I mean about our being the guests." Then they started scrambling about the chairs; there were three of them and only two chairs. Musical chairs! "Mother, cut it out!" I ordered her, annoyed to distraction, "your bad hip, you'll be in a wheelchair in the morning!" "Her chair!" he shrieked, taking out the braid and running over to me; he began tickling me with it on the cheek, on the arm. "Musical tables, turning the tables!" my mother giggled like a girl. "Get away from me!" I demanded, "You know I'm ticklish; I've got to get done." "Ticklish, she was always ticklish," the first one said triumphant. Finally, I jumped out of my chair. I was going to throw them all out. But *he* was sitting in my chair with his wood-grained arms, and he was starting to type! "Now this *is* too much," I exploded, tilting the chair forward, so he fell out, sliding down onto the floor. But immediately, my mother had slid in, and she was typing, line after line after line. "Out, out!" I shrieked, tipping the chair again, but she just laughed and pointed at one of the empty chairs on the other side of the room. Suddenly, I was desperate to get to it. I ran across the room, but he got there first. "This braid is a pretty good pendulum!" he said happily, swinging it back and forth in front of me. I saw the chair next to him was empty, and scrambled for it, but he got into it first. Then I ran to the one by the typewriter, but the dog was in it, snarling his snarl. "Musical chairs!" my mother laughed happily. Suddenly they were all running faster and faster, and there was always one chair empty, and that was the one I had to sit in, always. That is all I remember, all I have ever remembered, where I sit in my room, its four walls like four book jackets, shut in between hard covers, that mechanical voice, mechanical laughter, the mechanical tapping of keys. Days, I argue silently to myself about the probable color of my hair, nights about the names of my children, but they are on the last page, or the page before the last page, and they say I am the crepe-paper dog, or hinged like the crepe-paper dog, or bound like the crepe-paper dog, I can't get it right, it has all been taken care of, the last line has been written, this is the right shelf, and nothing at all can be done.

MAGAZINES CONSULTED

Antaeus
    Ecco Press—1 West 30th Street, New York, N.Y. 10001

Antioch Review
    P. O. Box 148, Yellow Springs, Ohio 45387

Apalachee Quarterly
    P. O. Box 20106, Tallahassee, Fl. 32304

Aphra
    Box 3551, Springtown, Pa. 18081

Ararat
    Armenian General Benevolent Union of America, 628 Second Avenue, New York, N.Y. 10016

Arizona Quarterly
    University of Arizona, Tucson, Ariz. 85721

Ark River Review
    c/o Anthony Sobin, English Department, Wichita State University, Wichita, Kan. 67208

Ascent
    English Department, University of Illinois, Urbana, Ill. 61801

Atlantic Monthly
    8 Arlington Street, Boston, Mass. 02116

Boston University Journal
    775 Commonwealth Avenue, Boston, Mass. 02215

California Quarterly
    100 Sproul Hall, University of California, Davis, Calif. 95616

Canadian Fiction Magazine
    P. O. Box 46422, Station G, Vancouver, B.C., Canada V6R 4G7

Canto
    11 Bartlett Street, Andover, Mass. 01810

Carleton Miscellany
    Carleton College, Northfield, Minn. 55057

Carolina Quarterly
  Box 1117, Chapel Hill, N.C. 27515
The Chariton Review
  Division of Language & Literature, Northeast Missouri State
  University, Kirksville, Mo. 63501
Christopher Street
  60 West 13th Street, New York, N.Y. 10011
College Contemporaries
  4747 Fountain Avenue, Los Angeles, Calif. 90029
Colorado Quarterly
  Hellums 118, University of Colorado, Boulder, Colo. 80304
The Colorado State Review
  360 Liberal Arts, Colorado State University, Fort Collins,
  Colo. 80521
Confrontation
  English Department, Brooklyn Center of Long Island Uni-
  versity, Brooklyn, N.Y. 11201
Cosmopolitan
  224 West 57th Street, New York, N.Y. 10019
Crucible
  Atlantic Christian College, Wilson, N.C. 27893
Cutbank
  c/o English Dept., University of Montana, Missoula, Mont.
  59801
Dark Horse
  262 Kent Street, Brookline, Mass. 02146
December
  P. O. Box 274, Western Springs, Ill. 60558
The Denver Quarterly
  Dept. of English, University of Denver, Denver, Colo. 80210
Descant
  Dept. of English, TCU Station, Fort Worth, Tex. 76129
Epoch
  159 Goldwyn Smith Hall, Cornell University, Ithaca, N.Y.
  14850
Esquire
  488 Madison Avenue, New York, N.Y. 10022

Eureka Review
   P. O. Box 366, Willows, Calif. 95988

Fantasy and Science Fiction
   Box 56, Cornwall, Conn. 06753

Fiction
   c/o Dept. of English, The City College of New York, N.Y. 10031

Fiction International
   Dept. of English, St. Lawrence University, Canton, N.Y. 13617

The Fiddlehead
   Dept. of English, University of New Brunswick, Fredericton, N.B., Canada

Forum
   Ball State University, Muncie, Ind. 47306

Four Quarters
   La Salle College, Philadelphia, Pa. 19141

GPU News
   c/o The Farwell Center, 1568 N. Farwell, Milwaukee, Wis. 53202

Georgia Review
   University of Georgia, Athens, Ga. 30601

The Great Lakes Review
   Northeastern Illinois University, Chicago, Ill. 60625

Green River Review
   Box 56, University Center, Mich. 48710

The Greensboro Review
   University of North Carolina, Greensboro, N.C. 27412

Harper's Magazine
   2 Park Avenue, New York, N.Y. 10016

Hawaii Review
   Hemenway Hall, University of Hawaii, Honolulu, Haw. 96822

Hudson Review
   65 East 55th Street, New York, N.Y. 10022

Iowa Review
   EPB 453, University of Iowa, Iowa City, Iowa 52240

Kansas Quarterly
  Dept. of English, Kansas State University, Manhattan, Kan.
  66502
Ladies' Home Journal
  641 Lexington Avenue, New York, N.Y. 10022
The Literary Review
  Fairleigh Dickinson University, Teaneck, N.J. 07666
The Little Magazine
  P. O. Box 207, Cathedral Station, New York, N.Y. 10025
Lotus
  Department of English, Ohio University, Athens, Ohio 45701
Mademoiselle
  350 Madison Avenue, New York, N.Y. 10017
Maine
  P. O. Box 494, Ellsworth, Me. 04605
Malahat Review
  University of Victoria, Victoria, B.C., Canada
The Massachusetts Review
  University of Massachusetts, Amherst, Mass. 01003
McCall's
  230 Park Avenue, New York, N.Y. 10017
The Mediterranean Review
  Orient, N.Y. 11957
Michigan Quarterly Review
  3032 Rackham Bldg., The University of Michigan, Ann
  Arbor, Mich. 48104
Midstream
  515 Park Avenue, New York, N.Y. 10022
Moment
  55 Chapel Street, Newton, Mass. 02160
Mother Jones
  607 Market Street, San Francisco, Calif. 94105
The Mysterious Barricades
  The Rainbow Press, 1332 Riverside Drive, #51, New York,
  N.Y. 10033
The National Jewish Monthly
  1640 Rhode Island Avenue, N.W., Washington, D.C. 20036

New Directions
333 Sixth Avenue, New York, N.Y. 10014
New Letters
University of Missouri–Kansas City, Kansas City, Mo. 64110
The New Renaissance
9 Heath Road, Arlington, Mass. 02174
New York Arts Journal
560 Riverside Drive, New York, N.Y. 10027
The New Yorker
25 West 43rd Street, New York, N.Y. 10036
The North American Review
University of Northern Iowa, 1222 West 27th Street, Cedar Falls, Iowa 50613
Northwest Review
129 French Hall, University of Oregon, Eugene, Ore. 97403
The Ohio Journal
164 West 17th Avenue, Columbus, Ohio 43210
Ohio Review
Ellis Hall, Ohio University, Athens, Ohio 45701
The Ontario Review
6000 Riverside Drive East, Windsor, Ont., Canada N8S 1B6
Paranthèse
59 East 73rd Street, New York, N.Y. 10021
The Paris Review
45-39–171st Place, Flushing, N.Y. 11358
Partisan Review
Rutgers University, New Brunswick, N.J. 08903
Perspective
Washington University, St. Louis, Mo. 63130
Phylon
223 Chestnut Street, S.W., Atlanta, Ga. 30314
Playboy
919 North Michigan Avenue, Chicago, Ill. 60611
Ploughshares
Box 529, Cambridge, Mass. 02139
Prairie Schooner
Andrews Hall, University of Nebraska, Lincoln, Nebr. 68508

Prism International
Dept. of Creative Writing, University of British Columbia, Vancouver 8, B.C., Canada

Quarterly Review of Literature
26 Haslet Avenue, Princeton, N.J. 08540

Quarterly West
141 Olpin Union, University of Utah, Salt Lake City, Utah 84112

Quartet
1119 Neal Pickett Drive, College Station, Tex. 77840

Quest/77
300 West Green Street, Pasadena, Calif. 91129

Redbook
230 Park Avenue, New York, N.Y. 10017

Reed
English Department, San Jose State University, San Jose, Calif. 95192

The Remington Review
505 Westfield Avenue, Elizabeth, N.J. 07208

Revista/Review Interamericana
305 Cesar Romon (altos), Hato Rey, Puerto Rico 00919

Rolling Stone
625 Third Street, San Francisco, Calif. 94107

Seneca Review
Box 115, Hobart & William Smith Colleges, Geneva, N.Y. 14456

Sequoia
Storke Student Publications Bldg., Stanford, Calif. 94305

The Sewanee Review
University of the South, Sewanee, Tenn. 37375

Shenandoah
Box 722, Lexington, Va. 24450

Silver Vain
P. O. Box 2366, Park City, Utah 84060

The Smith
5 Beekman Street, New York, N.Y. 10038

The South Carolina Review
Dept. of English, Clemson University, Clemson, S.C. 29631

The South Dakota Review
Box 111, University Exchange, Vermillion, S.D. 57069
Southern Humanities Review
Auburn University, Auburn, Ala. 36820
Southern Review
Drawer D, University Station, Baton Rouge, La. 70803
Southwest Review
Southern Methodist University Press, Dallas, Tex. 75222
Story Quarterly
720 Central Avenue, Highland Park, Ill. 60035
The Tamarack Review
Box 159, Postal Station K, Toronto, Ont., Canada M4P 2G5
Transatlantic Review (ceased publication in 1977)
Box 3348, Grand Central P.O., New York, N.Y. 10017
Transfer
San Francisco State University, San Francisco, Calif. 94132
Tri-Quarterly
University Hall 101, Northwestern University, Evanston, Ill. 60201
Twigs
Pikeville College, Pikeville, Ky. 41501
University of Windsor Review
Dept. of English, University of Windsor, Windsor, Ontario, Canada N9B 3P4
U. S. Catholic
221 West Madison Street, Chicago, Ill. 60606
Vagabond
P. O. Box 879, Ellensburg, Wash. 98926
The Virginia Quarterly Review
University of Virginia, 1 West Range, Charlottesville, Va. 22903
Vogue
350 Madison Avenue, New York, N.Y. 10017
Washington Review of the Arts
404 Tenth Street, S.E., Washington, D.C. 20003
West Coast Review
Simon Fraser University, Vancouver, B.C., Canada

Western Humanities Review
    Bldg. 41, University of Utah, Salt Lake City, Utah 84112
Wind
    RFD Route 1, Box 810, Pikeville, Ky. 41501
Works
    A.M.S., 56 East 13th Street, New York, N.Y. 10003
Yale Review
    250 Church Street, New Haven, Conn. 06520
Yankee
    Dublin, N.H. 03444